BRAVE *love*

A. M. KUSI

This book is a work of fiction. Names, places, characters, organizations, events, and incidents are either products of the authors' imaginations or are used fictitiously. Any resemblance to actual persons, living or dead, or to businesses, companies, events, institutions, or locales is completely coincidental. Any trademarks, product names, service marks, and named features are assumed to be the property of their respective owners and are only used for references.

Published by A. M. Kusi 2021

amkusinovels@gmail.com

Visit our website at www.amkusi.com

Editor: Anna Bishop of CREATING ink

Sensitivity Edit: Renita McKinney of A Book A Day

Proofreader: Judy's Proofreading

Cover Design: Regina Wamba of ReginaWamba.com

ISBN: 978-1949781212

OTHER BOOKS BY A. M. KUSI

A Fallen Star (eBook FREE on all retailers)

(Book 1 in The Shattered Cove Series)

Glass Secrets

(Book 2 in The Shattered Cove Series)

Defying Gravity

(Book 3 in The Shattered Cove Series)

The Lighthouse Inn

(Book 4 in The Shattered Cove series)

His True North

(Book 5 in The Shattered Cove series)

In The Grey

(Book 6 in The Shattered Cove series)

The Orchard Inn (eBook FREE on all retailers)

(Book 1 in The Orchard Inn Romance Series)

Conflict of Interest

(Book 2 in The Orchard Inn Romance Series)

Her Perfect Storm

(Book 3 in The Orchard Inn Romance Series)

<u>**_One Holiday Kiss (eBook FREE on all retailers)_**</u>

(A Shattered Cove Short Story)

For a complete list of all our books, visit:

<u>**WWW.AMKUSI.COM/BOOKS**</u>

This book is dedicated to everyone out there choosing to be brave and fighting for the love you deserve.

"Now, every time I witness a strong person, I want to know: What dark did you conquer in your story? Mountains do not rise without earthquakes."
— Katherine Mackenett

“We are all broken . . . that's how the light gets in.”
– Hemingway

GET A FREE SHORT NOVEL

Join our newsletter to get a FREE short novel that's not available on any retailer. Plus updates about new releases, giveaways, pre-orders, sneak peeks, and more.

Visit the website below to join now.

WWW.AMKUSI.COM/NEWSLETTER

1

PIPPA

Pippa pushed one of her cotton-candy-colored braids out of her face as she focused on the computer screen in front of her. Moving her mouse, she clicked the order button. She didn't *really* need more books, but it couldn't hurt to have a few extra copies of the latest romance release. The paperbacks seemed to be flying off the shelves of her store these days—enough so that she could finally hire some more help.

A snort came from her side where Lady, her golden retriever and service dog, looked up at her with her brown puppy eyes.

"Oh, don't look at me like that. More books means more treats."

Lady's ears perked up. Pippa chuckled and got to her feet, grabbing a few books from the desk that needed to be re-shelved.

"Come on. I'll get you one from the office."

Pippa locked the door and walked through the shop, checking to make sure everyone was gone before she closed for the day. Her stomach grumbled. *When was the last time I ate? Oh, right—the protein bar for lunch.*

The clicks of Lady's paws padded behind her. She passed the large sculpture she'd made of a woman reading a novel, her expression one of fascination as her hand reached out as if to turn the page. The entire sculpture was made from pages of books that she'd gotten from Goodwill. Taking stories that gave so many joy and escape and recycling them into something beautiful was a hobby of hers. Several of her smaller sculptures were scattered around the store. Some were more realistic, like the beehives on the counter, while others were more fantastical, like the mermaid perched in the folds of an open book with one page textured to look like waves.

Pippa's wide hips knocked the shelf to her right, causing a book to fall sideways. She straightened it and made her way to the aisle marked by a white sign with black letters depicting a quote by Lloyd Alexander: "Fantasy is hardly an escape from reality. It's a way of understanding it."

She smiled to herself. The Oyster Bookstore was her own oasis. Here, her imagination could run wild. There was greenery in every corner, plants that kept the air clean, and the colors on the walls were vibrant. Each row had a separate quote—some by famous authors and some featuring famous concepts. Instead of a boring self-help sign, she had, "In life, nobody will help you until you're willing to help yourself." Instead of parenting, she had, "Children learn more from what you are than what you teach. - W.E.B. Dubois."

One of her favorite sections was up the front to the right where you first walked in—a section dedicated to all things Puerto Rico, from authors and artists to cooks, photography, and of course their queer culture. It was a piece of her history she was proud to share.

Pippa placed the two paperbacks on the shelf and inhaled.

The smell of books never got old. If someone could infuse it in a candle, they'd make a fortune off of just her.

She walked into the bathroom. All the stalls were open—except for one at the far end. *Oops.* "Anyone in here?"

"Me," came a small voice and then a sniffle. *Was it the little girl I saw earlier?*

"I was just closing up. Do you need anything?" Pippa asked.

More sniffles came from behind the wooden door.

"Are you okay?" Pippa asked, concern growing in the pit of her stomach.

"I . . . I, um . . . I'm bleeding."

Pippa's eyes widened. "Do you need a doctor? Can I come in and help?"

The latch unlocked and a young girl, surely no more than twelve or thirteen, stared up at her. Tears stained her freckled face, her strawberry-blond hair falling loose around it. She crossed her arms as if she were hugging herself.

Pippa scanned her body, checking her over for signs of injury. "Where are you hurt?"

She shook her head. "I'm not. It's . . . I think I got my . . . you know."

Realization flooded Pippa and her shoulders relaxed. "You mean you got your period?"

The girl nodded. Her eyes slid to the floor, suddenly taking interest in the scuff marks.

"Is this your first one?"

She nodded again, her eyes taking on a sad sheen.

Pippa's heart squeezed at the lost expression on the girl's face.

"This is something to celebrate!"

The girl flinched and looked up at her with an incredulous expression.

Maybe I'm coming on a little too strong. "You've become a woman today. That is something so sacred and special, and I am honored it happened in my bookstore."

"I bled on my pants," she said shyly.

"It happens to all of us." Pippa waved her hand in front of her face. "Nothing to be embarrassed about."

"I don't . . . I don't know what to do," the girl admitted.

"Well, it's a good thing I have a lot of experience in this department." Pippa walked to the cupboard by the sink and pulled out the box of pads and tampons she kept under there just in case someone needed one. *Empty.*

"Crap. Well, I don't have any pads or tampons because I use a cup."

"A cup?" The girl's eyebrows rose in question.

"A menstrual cup. It's a reusable silicone cup that you . . ."

The young woman's panicked eyes frantically moved around the room.

"Hey. It's okay. This happens to everyone with a uterus at some point. I'm gonna help you out so you can feel prepared. I'm Pippa, by the way. What's your name?"

"Aspen." She sniffled and then her cheeks bloomed red. "I don't want to tell my dad. This is the most embarrassing day of my life." Her tears started again.

Pippa pulled her into a hug, holding her while she cried. "The first time I got my period, I was in class, and everyone laughed at the huge blood stain on my pants. No one told me. Not one person stopped to let me know. I went to three classes before a teacher noticed and told me to go to the nurse's office."

Aspen pulled away. "Oh my God."

Pippa nodded. "Then I had to call my dad and tell him why I needed him to come get me, and then he had no idea what I needed and came home with these giant pads. I was mortified."

"Where was your mom?" Aspen asked.

Pippa took a deep breath. The pain had faded with time, but it was still there, a hollow ache inside. "My mom died when I was a kid."

"Mine died when I was a toddler. I don't even remember her," Aspen admitted.

"That sucks."

"Especially right now." Aspen's voice was a whisper.

"I'm gonna help you so you don't have to go through all the embarrassment I did. But there is no shame in having your period. This is something that is normal and natural, and it happens to more than half the earth's population." Pippa smiled, hoping to help alleviate some of Aspen's concern.

"Will you tell my dad for me?" The young girl tucked a piece of her reddish-blond hair behind her ear, her blue eyes pleading.

"Where is he?"

"At the Stardust Café across the street."

Pippa smiled. "I'll do better than that. You go sit at the front desk and use the sweater I have draped against the seat to wrap around your waist. I'll go get him. What's his name?"

"Mason Wright."

"Okay. I'll be right back."

Pippa led Aspen to the front desk. She took a quick turn around the store, checking that no one else was inside before she left. She locked the door behind her and then crossed the street, holding on to Lady's leash.

Opening the door to the bakery, she had one thing on her mind: helping a young girl out and saving her some of the pain and embarrassment she'd endured growing up. It was so hard being without a mother in times like that. Pippa ached for little Aspen. If only she could do—

She slammed into something hard and warm. Hot liquid burst from a cup. Pippa jumped back. Coffee drenched the mountain of a man in front of her. Lady barked sharply.

"Fuck!" he yelled. His deep voice sent a shiver through her.

Pippa looked up into the deepest sapphire-blue eyes she'd ever seen. His full lips turned down only half of his face. Thick, pink scars marred the other side of his profile, twisting his flesh. Her head tipped upwards—this man towered over her five-foot-one frame. He must have been more than six feet. The scars continued down his thick neck, disappearing under his plaid shirt. Her gaze wandered down his bulky chest to the massive arms with defined lines of muscle. She swallowed, her lady parts waking up, alert and hungry. Her eyes flicked back to his.

Anger radiated from him. "Take a picture. It'll last longer." He turned to the counter, his voice softening just a bit, "Remy, I need a mop."

Remy, the woman Pippa had come to know from her frequent stops into the specialty gluten-free bakery and café, appeared behind the counter. "Sure thing."

"I'm sorry. I wasn't looking where I was going. Can I buy you a replacement?" Pippa asked.

The man kept his back to her. "No."

She should have slowed down, but still, he didn't need to be an asshole about it. Pippa sighed and led Lady to the front counter as Remy walked out with the mop.

The man reached over and took it from her. "I got it."

"Thanks." Remy's eyes flashed to hers as the grumpy asshole started cleaning the mess. "Hey, Pippa. What can I get you?"

"Uh, well, actually, I wondered if you could tell me which one of your patrons is Mason Wright?"

Remy smiled, her gaze focusing over Pippa's shoulder. *Please no. It couldn't be. Could it?*

"He's the one you just ran into." Remy smiled.

Pippa's gut knotted as she closed her eyes. "Oh, fuck."

2

PIPPA

Pippa swallowed nervously. Lady, so attuned to her owner, licked her hand as if to comfort her.

"His bark is worse than his bite," Remy whispered across the counter.

Pippa gave her a curt nod and straightened her back. That sweet little girl hiding in her shop was relying on her. She stepped towards the giant angry man as he finished cleaning the mess she'd made.

"Uh, Mr. Wright?"

He walked past her and around the corner to hand the mop to Remy, seemingly ignoring her.

Pippa cleared her throat and tried a little louder. "Mr. Wright?"

His blue eyes flashed as he turned back to her, annoyance written across his face.

"Are you Aspen's dad?"

His expression softened for a moment before concerned lines appeared between his eyebrows. His gaze darted across the street. "Yeah. Why?"

"Aspen asked me to come over and find you—"

"What's wrong? Did she get hurt?" He didn't wait for her reply before he was barreling out the door. Pippa ran after him as he darted out into the middle of the road. He jerked his hand up to stop traffic as if he wouldn't let anything get in his way. A sedan stopped abruptly to let them pass, a horn honking as they crossed.

"She's fine!" Pippa called after him, waving and mouthing, *I'm sorry*, to the driver.

Mason pulled on the door to her shop but it didn't budge. "It's locked."

"I know. I thought it was safer to leave her locked in."

His shoulders straightened as he swerved around and walked up to her. Mason loomed above her, anger once again written in his twisted snarl. She backed up until her shoulders hit the glass window of her store. Lady growled near her side.

"Why did you lock my daughter inside your fucking store?" His voice was deep and dangerous, sending a chill spiraling through her.

Her eyes widened. "Oh, no! I—she asked me to come and tell you something, and she couldn't leave the store because she's, uh . . ."

"She's what?" he demanded.

She winced. "She has her period."

He blinked as if not understanding what Pippa had said.

"Your daughter became a woman today . . . yay . . ." Her voice was pitiful with false enthusiasm. He seemed volatile. Was Aspen safe with him? How could such a sweet little girl come from . . . him?

Mason backed away, finally giving her some room to breathe. "She started her period?"

"Yes. And she, um, well, it got on her pants, and she was embarrassed to come tell you and asked that I did."

Panic flashed in his eyes. "I don't . . . fuck! I thought we had more time."

"I was about her age when I started . . ." *Good job, sharing your menstrual cycle history with a complete stranger. This is why I'm still single.* "I don't have anything here in the shop for her. But if you wanted, I could meet you in the pharmacy and show you what to get for her? Unless you have it covered?"

He ran a hand over his face. "I need to see my daughter."

"Oh! Right, of course, um, right. Keys." She pulled the ring from her pocket and moved to put the key in the door. As soon as the lock turned, his arm shot out to the handle. She jumped back. Lady's eyes darted between her and Mason. His face was open—dare she say, even kind.

He was just trying to be polite. Not trying to hurt her. *Phew.*

Regret flashed in his expression as he opened the door for her, motioning for her to go in first. Pippa ducked her head and went in, moving to the front desk where Aspen sat, red-faced, her eyes darting to the floor. "Daddy?"

"Hey, sweet pea." Mason got on his knees to wrap his arms around his daughter. Some of the unease in Pippa's gut unfurled at the sight of this intimidating giant softening into a puddle at his daughter's feet. *He'd only been worried for her safety.* And Pippa knew better than most just how far a father was willing to go for a daughter he loved.

"Did Pippa tell you?" Aspen asked.

Mason brushed his thumb over her freckled cheek. "Yeah. She said you, uh, got your period."

Aspen nodded, a fresh blush spreading down her neck. "Please don't get me giant pads to wear to school."

Mason's gaze cut to Pippa and then back to his daughter. "Well, actually, Pippa has offered to help us figure out what you need. If that's okay with you?"

Aspen's eyes widened, her shoulders lowering as she exhaled. "Yes. Definitely yes."

Pippa smiled, hoping to set them both at ease. "Great, I'll lock up behind you and meet you over there."

Mason stood, wrapping his arm around his daughter. Aspen got to her feet, with Pippa's sweatshirt clumsily wrapped around her waist. It was too much fabric for such a little girl, but it was all Pippa had.

She locked up behind them and cut down the side of the building along an alley, with Lady by her side. She didn't need to hold her leash, but kept the harness on over the service dog vest with the patches instructing people to not pet her.

She showed up to the pharmacy a few minutes later. Mason leaned against his blue truck, Aspen by his side.

"Did you walk?" he asked.

She nodded. She didn't have a choice. Driving was not an option for her. "Ready?"

Aspen grasped her hand. "Can't my dad go in and I wait in the car?"

Pippa crouched down, her colorful braids slipping over her shoulder. "There is nothing to be ashamed of or embarrassed about. In fact, in some cultures, they believed when a woman had her period, she became a goddess."

Aspen's eyes grew wide. "Really?"

"Really. Before colonizers came and changed the rhetoric, that time of the month for women was seen as the most sacred. In fact, some cultures thought women were so powerful during this time, they believed that a man's *mana*—or soul—would get sucked out because they couldn't handle such sacred power."

"Wow." Aspen looked up to her dad. "You better give me some space, Dad. Wouldn't want to suck your soul." She giggled.

One side of Mason's mouth quirked into a smile and damn if it didn't stir up something inside her. "I'll take my chances."

"Well, let's get this over with," Aspen said, giving Pippa's hand a squeeze.

Pippa led her inside and down the long rows to the back corner near the pharmacy counter until they were at the feminine products section. Mason's gaze scanned the row of pink and floral boxes, his big frame at odds with the delicate packages, as he scratched the back of his neck as if lost.

"If you want to go swimming, you'll need some tampons." Pippa held up the correct container.

Aspen's eyes grew wide as she studied the box and Mason paled.

"It's better to have them and not need them than to need them and not have them. These ones are smaller for lighter days and great for beginners."

Mason took the box from her.

"You'll probably be more comfortable with pads to start." She met Mason's gaze. "Always get the ones with the wings."

"What about the cup?" Aspen asked, brushing a strand of hair behind her ear shyly.

Pippa searched the shelves. "Looks like they carry a Diva Cup here. There are others, and sometimes you have to experiment before you find the right one for you, but this is a little advanced. If I were you, I'd start with the pads and eventually the tampons. Get the hang of things before you go to the cup."

"Okay." Aspen nodded, seeming more at ease than before.

"Is that it?" Mason asked.

"Not quite. You may want a heating pad and some ibuprofen if you don't have it." Pippa pointed to another aisle towards another part of the store.

"I'll go grab those," he said, grabbing an extra package of pads.

"Sometimes her body will crave chocolate around her period because of the magnesium in it. Are you okay if we go get some salty and sweet snacks? My treat," Pippa said.

His sapphire orbs flicked between Aspen and her before he nodded. "I'll be right up."

She led Aspen to a section near the front, and they picked out a packet of chips. "Which chocolate is your favorite?"

"I like Twixes."

"Mmm. Caramel and chocolate. Wise choice. I'm a Reese's girl myself." Pippa leaned down to pet Lady's head.

"What's her name?" Aspen asked as she followed Pippa to the end of the aisle.

"Lady."

"Are you going to get in trouble for having her in the store?" Aspen peeked over her shoulder.

Pippa glanced towards the front, studying the cashier as a man with a hoodie approached the counter, hands in his pocket. "No, Lady is a—"

"Put the money in the bag or I'll blow a fucking hole in your head." The man in the hoodie spoke just loud enough for Pippa to hear.

Chills skated over her skin. Her heart raced in panic. Lady whined and barked once. The robber spun to face them.

Pippa grabbed Aspen's hand and shoved her behind her, hiding her beyond the endcap—out of view of the front of the store.

The gun swerved her way. "You better keep that bitch on her leash."

Pippa's other hand tightened on Lady's harness as she nodded and got down to her knees. The thief turned back to the cashier, switching between watching her and the scared man behind the register.

"Hurry up!" he ordered.

Pippa's body trembled. Lady started barking and alerting. "Shhhhh." She petted her. "It's okay, girl. Sit."

The thief ripped the bag away from the cashier and walked towards Pippa, gun once again aimed her way. "You deaf, bitch? I told you to keep that mutt quiet."

Pippa's chest heaved. If he came any closer, he'd see Aspen. She pressed her hand against the trembling little girl beside her, trying to push her farther away from danger.

"N-no. My dog's just scared." She risked a glance at his blue eyes. His pupils were the size of pinpoints.

The thief's arm lifted. The metal glinted in the florescent lights. "Maybe I should give her something to be scared about."

"No!" Pippa screamed as terror gripped her chest in its icy fingers.

3
───────

MASON

Mason balanced the packages of feminine products in one hand while he picked up a heating pad with the other. *How can my little girl be a woman already?* Just yesterday she was a tiny little baby who'd fit in the palm of his hand. Now, here he was, so far out of his element.

His own mother had taken off before he was fifteen. His wife had always been so private about that time of the month. He had no experience in this department. *I thought I had more time.*

Well, he didn't. And if it wasn't for the curvy beauty, he'd be even more lost. *And what did I do to repay her?*

Her fear had been evident as he'd crowded her against her shop. He'd been worried for his daughter's safety, and nothing —and no one—came before Aspen.

A dog barked at the front of the store, snapping him out of his pity party. Mason grabbed a bottle of ibuprofen—didn't hurt to have an extra at home just in case.

More barking came from the front.

"Hurry up!" an angry voice commanded.

Adrenaline coursed through his veins. His heart rate spiked. All his senses jumped on alert. Mason headed towards the front, his stomach knotting with a gut feeling.

"You deaf, bitch? I told you to keep that mutt quiet."

Red-hot anger burst in his chest. *Aspen and Pippa.* Mason set the packages onto the floor and crept down the aisle, his eyes flicking to the circular mirror at the side of the wall. His heart leapt into his throat.

"N-no. My dog's just scared." Pippa's voice trembled as the man with a mask and a gun leveled on her walked closer.

Aspen's strawberry-blond head shook from around the end of the aisle just out of sight of the perp. Pippa pressed against Aspen, as if trying to get her farther away from danger. *She's protecting her.*

"Maybe I should give her something to be scared about." The cocky asshole aimed the gun towards the dog.

It was now or never.

"No!" Pippa screamed.

Mason charged towards the man with the gun, running into danger instead of away—the way he'd been trained. No hesitation.

His shoulder connected with the man's gut. Mason gripped the enemy's arm, pushing the gun down. He tackled him to the ground.

"Oomph!"

Mason pinned him to the floor. The man grunted and struggled, but Mason quickly twisted the weapon from him, tossing it away before he pulled the man into a headlock, clamping his legs around his waist.

Dirty fingernails scraped against his arms as the blue eyes in the mask rolled upwards. Mason's body thrummed with energy and pulsed with fury. How dare this asshole put his daughter in danger?

"Mason." Pippa's wide eyes met his. "He's out."

Mason's gaze cut to the limp body in his hands. He was tempted to hang on just a little longer so this man could never harm anyone ever again.

"Daddy?" Aspen's terrified voice cut through his angry haze.

Mason released the criminal and picked up the weapon, tucking it into the back of his jeans.

Aspen stepped towards him, but he held his hand out to stop her. "He's gonna wake up in about five seconds. Stay back."

Mason twisted his arms behind the thief's back and pinned his body down. He was gonna wake with one hell of a headache and be one pissed-off motherfucker.

Mason cast a quick glance at his daughter. Everything in him wanted to wrap her up into his arms and soothe her fears. Pippa did that for him, hugging Aspen close, and tucking her into her side so that the bookstore owner still was closer to danger than his little girl.

"Over there, Officer," the cashier at the front said, drawing his attention to Bently, the sheriff and one of his friends, coming into the pharmacy, gun drawn.

"He's down," Mason said.

"Where's the weapon?" Bently demanded.

"Back of my waist," Mason informed him.

Bently peered over him, presumably searching for the gun, before his shoulders relaxed. He tucked his own gun back into the holster and exchanged it for handcuffs.

The guy on the ground groaned and tried to thrash, but Mason held him steady while Bently locked the cuffs on him. Mason handed over the weapon the thief had used after he stood, and kicked the open bag of money towards Bently. "This was his."

Deputy Vargas wasn't far behind. She ran down the aisle, her eyes focused and alert.

Vargas accepted the gun, checking it over. "Not loaded."

Mason shook his head. Asshole must have got off on making Pippa scared.

"Don't worry. Attempted robbery with a weapon is gonna put him away for a long time." Bently pulled the mask off the criminal's face as the man groaned, and swore.

Mason took a step toward his daughter. Aspen ran into his waiting arms, her sobs coming harder as he held her. He smoothed his hand over the back of her head. "Shhhh. It's okay, sweetheart. You're safe now." His gaze rose to meet Pippa's. "Thanks to you."

Her eyes widened as if in surprise before they skated to the man being hauled out of the store, kicking and screaming. She'd seen just a fraction of what Mason was no doubt capable of. She trembled. A part of him wanted to wrap his arms around her and pull her into his embrace too. Let her know that he wouldn't let anyone hurt her. Make sure his girls were good.

His girls? That was crazy. She was virtually a stranger—a kind one who'd protected his daughter with her life, but still, a stranger.

Lady yipped, pressing her snout into Pippa's chest.

"Why don't you head out front? I'll have to get a statement from you, but it can wait if you need some time." Bently returned and motioned to Aspen, whose sobs had subsided.

Mason nodded and patted his daughter's back, still trying to comfort her. "Let's go, sweet pea."

Aspen reached out and grasped Pippa's hand. Bently cut

Mason a questioning glance, which Mason ignored. Mason led them out of the store to his truck.

Aspen hugged Pippa tight. "I was so scared."

Pippa reached over to rub the sweaty hair from Aspen's forehead. "Me too." Pippa's brown eyes met Mason's. "Thank you for . . . what you did back there."

He nodded. He did what he'd had to. He didn't deserve praise, but she had taken care of his child at the potential expense of her own life. She had protected his baby girl. For that, she'd have his undying gratitude.

Pippa swiped her braid over her shoulder. Her tan cheeks glowed in the summer sun. He let his gaze wander, taking her in for the first time close up. She was wearing some sort of V-neck short-sleeve crop top, showing off the curve of her ample breasts, and a sliver of her thick waist. A pair of high-waisted jean shorts accentuated her wide hips, leading down to her brown thick thighs and toned calves. Pink-painted toes peeked out from a pair of flip-flops. A golden toe ring on her middle toe glinted in the sunlight.

"I'm gonna go back inside for our supplies. Can you two wait here?" Mason asked. Normally he wouldn't leave his daughter with a stranger, but Pippa had shown her true colors under pressure. She was pure sunshine.

"Sure," Pippa agreed, taking Aspen's hand.

Mason kissed his daughter's forehead and ran into the store for the items she needed. When he returned, Pippa's dog had jumped up with her paws on Pippa, barking, and pressing her snout into the woman's waist.

"What's up there, Pippa? What are you looking at?" Aspen asked.

Mason's gaze snapped to Pippa's face. Her eyes rolled back. Her cheek twitched. *Is she having a seizure?*

Pippa fell. He dropped the bag of his purchases and

caught her. Her body jerked as he laid her carefully on the ground. *Definitely a seizure.*

"Daddy? What's wrong?" Aspen's panicked voice rose.

"It's okay, sweetheart." Mason's medical training kicked in. He cradled her head carefully as Pippa's body thrashed, and he checked his watch to time the episode. He turned her to her side as she grunted. Pippa's gold medical bracelet glinted in the sunlight.

The golden retriever laid her head and front paws across Pippa's chest. Pippa's body arched

"Daddy!" Aspen screamed.

"It's okay, A. She's having a seizure. I know it looks scary, but she'll be okay." *I hope.*

"Should I get Bently?" Aspen asked.

"Not yet. Let's just give her a few minutes. If it lasts longer, we'll call an ambulance."

"Should we try to hold her tighter?" Aspen asked, reaching out for Pippa's clenched hand.

"No. We can hurt her if we try to stop the movements or get hurt ourselves. Just go in the truck and wait for me."

"But, Dad—"

"Please listen to me."

Aspen blinked, fear-stricken. He wanted to comfort her, but Pippa needed him right now. The door shut to the passenger side of his truck as his daughter's wide eyes watched on. She had obviously grown attached to this woman in a short time.

"It's okay. I got you. You're safe." Mason spoke the words, hoping he could comfort Pippa.

A small crowd had gathered around them.

"Her lips are turning blue!" a man across from him said.

"Someone call an ambulance!" A woman gasped.

"Just wait," Mason instructed.

A few seconds later, the trembles subsided. Her body still twitched from time to time, and there was a pool of urine on the asphalt between her legs. He pulled off his flannel shirt and wrapped it around her.

What sounded like snoring came from her. Her muscles still twitched. He kept his hands under her head, even though the hot asphalt bit into his skin. A few minutes later, her breathing evened out and the blue faded from her now pink lips. He breathed a sigh of relief. The most dangerous part was over.

"Pippa?"

"Mmmgghh," she answered, her eyes closed.

He wiped the drool from the side of her mouth and focused on the small crowd that had gathered. "It's over, folks. She'll be alright. Go back to your day." He was sure the last thing Pippa would want was an audience when she came out of it. He waited a few minutes and tried again as her eyes flickered open.

"Can you tell me your name?" he asked.

"Uuughma."

It wasn't over yet.

He waited a few more minutes as her drowsy eyes stayed open. "Hey, you okay?"

Pippa blinked as if confused, her gaze darting around. "Mmm."

"What's your name?" Mason repeated.

"Piwa." She struggled to sit up. "Off." Pippa pointed to the empty space by her side. The dog listened immediately.

"Cheeh . . . me," Pippa said before the dog sniffed her and then sat obediently by her side. "Good girl."

Mason helped guide Pippa to a sitting position.

"You?" she asked. She seemed to be struggling to focus on him.

He opened his mouth and then closed it. She didn't remember him? "I'm Mason Wright."

Her lids remained half closed as if she were about to fall asleep.

"Do you want me to get you to the hospital?" he asked.

"No." She shook her head vehemently and winced. Her hand grasped the back of her neck. "Home. Sleep."

Her head lolled to the side as her eyes fluttered closed.

"Shit. Okay. Hold on." Mason slipped his hand under her arms and another beneath her knees before lifting her. "Aspen, open the door."

His daughter listened, climbing out of his way. Mason slid Pippa into his passenger seat and buckled her in. "Climb in the back, A."

Aspen did as he said, her worried gaze locked on Pippa.

He motioned for the dog to climb in. "Come on, girl."

The dog jumped up, curling next to her human's feet and laying her head on Pippa's lap. Mason shut the door and pulled out his cell phone, dialing the one woman who might know what to do.

Charli picked up on the second ring. "Hey, Mase."

"Hey, Charli. I need your help."

"What's up?" she asked as her baby giggled in the background.

"I saw you with a woman in the bar a while back. She works at the bookstore. She's got colorful braids, about five feet one—"

"Oh, that's Pippa."

"Yeah. Does she have any family nearby?" he asked.

"Nope. She's alone here. I think she has a sister in Boston."

Damn. He couldn't leave her by herself even if he knew where she lived. So what was he supposed to do?

"Well, could you maybe meet me at my house as soon as possible? I'll explain when you get there."

"Everything okay?" Charli asked worriedly.

"Hope so."

"I'll be right over," she promised.

Mason hung up the phone and climbed in the driver's side. He started the car, turning to check on Pippa. She was asleep, her full pink lips parted as a few tiny hairs at the edge of her hairline blew in the breeze from the open window. This woman had kept his daughter protected and now it was his turn to return the favor.

I'll keep you safe.

4

PIPPA

Pippa's eyes fluttered open. The fan on the ceiling came into focus. Her brows drew together. She didn't own a fan. *Where am I?*

Lady's collar tinkled as her head rose from the bed before she licked Pippa's cheek. Pippa reached out to stroke her fur. "Where are we, girl?"

She sat slowly, every muscle aching and the pounding in her head increasing. Her eyes darted to the cup of water near the bed on a small table by the plain lamp lighting the dim room. She wasn't in the habit of drinking from strange places. She pushed off the soft blanket as she slipped her feet onto the carpeted floor.

What's the last thing I remember? The bookstore and the phone call with Troy, her new hire, who was starting next week. Then ordering some extra stock . . . and that was it. Blank.

Her gaze snagged on the grey sweatpants she wore. The word *NAVY* ran down the side of one leg. They were most definitely not hers.

Fear dug its claws into her chest. Who had dressed her? Or, more importantly, who had *undressed* her?

She stood on her trembling bare feet, her head swimming. Reaching out for the side table, she waited until the dizziness passed. Her stomach churned, nauseous. *Must have been a big one this time.*

Pippa reached out and twisted the doorknob, breathing a sigh of relief when it was unlocked. *So I'm not being held prisoner.* Lady snorted next to her as if she could read her thoughts. "Okay, maybe I've read a few too many dark romances."

Lady followed beside her through the hallway towards the set of stairs. Carefully, she made her way down, discovering new aches and pains with every step.

A familiar face looked up from the bottom step, setting Pippa's nerves at ease.

"Hey, I was just heading up to check on you," Charli, the co-owner of The Shipwreck bar and one of her best customers, said.

"Where am I?" Pippa's voice was scratchy and dry.

"My friend Mason and his daughter, Aspen's house. They were with you when you had a seizure. You didn't want to go to the hospital so he brought you home for you to rest."

Pippa's gaze darted around the open foyer where Charli waited. A door that she assumed led to the front of the house sat to her right. Built-in coat racks with large sweatshirts and bright smaller ones hung behind her.

"He didn't want you to be afraid when you woke up, so he called me," Charli offered.

That was . . . thoughtful.

"Did you change me?"

Charli nodded. "Yeah, your clothes are in the dryer."

I must have wet myself. No matter how many times it happened, the embarrassment didn't lessen.

"Come on, let's get you something to drink and put Aspen's mind at ease. They've been worried about you."

They had been? Pippa nodded and followed Charli to a bright spacious kitchen where two people sat. A little girl she recognized from regular bookstore visits sat on a high stool at the pine-top counter next to a hulk of a man with his back to her.

"Sleeping Beauty is awake," Charli announced before walking to the fridge and opening it.

Aspen turned around, her smile wide and beaming. "Pippa!" She slipped off her stool and ran up to her, the impact jarring Pippa's body. She winced as Aspen wrapped her arms around Pippa's waist.

"Aspen, what did I tell you?" The man's voice was gruff.

Pippa's gaze flashed to his. Blue eyes swirling with a mixture of emotions stared back at her. He seemed familiar somehow. His nose was a little crooked, like he'd broken it at some point. Half his face swirled with pink scars starting on one of his high cheekbones and disappearing into the dirty-blond neatly trimmed beard that made him look like a lumberjack.

Aspen recoiled, fear flashing in her eyes. "I'm sorry I forgot. Did I hurt you?"

Pippa's attention focused back onto the little girl, and she offered her a smile. "I'm okay."

Aspen grinned, seemingly relieved.

"Here you go. I'll go check on your clothes." Charli handed her a bottle of water.

Pippa unscrewed the cap and took a drink before she asked the man, "What happened?"

"You don't remember?" Aspen asked.

A familiar frustration rose. She hated losing time like this. Not knowing chunks of her life was just one thing her generalized epilepsy stole from her. "The last thing I remember is taking a call in the bookstore. How did I get here?"

The man stood, reaching out his hand as if to shake hers. "I'm Mason Wright. We met before, but last time you woke up you didn't remember me."

She took his hand, electricity thrumming up her arm, sending warm tingles racing through her body.

She gasped, pulling her palm back. Was that another seizure coming on?

"You came into the café to get me because Aspen here had, uh, become a woman in your bookstore." Mason rubbed the back of his head self-consciously.

"I did?"

He nodded. "You offered to help us get her the supplies she needed at the pharmacy, and while we were there, someone tried to rob the store."

Pippa gasped, her eyebrows shooting up her forehead. "*Dios mio.*" No wonder she'd had an episode. That was a lot of stress.

"After, when we were outside, you had a seizure. I didn't know what to do, so I brought you home and called Charli," Mason finished.

"Wow."

"I can take the dog out if you want to wait here for Charli; she should be down with your clothes soon. Unless you want to?" Mason asked.

She nodded and handed over the leash. "I would appreciate it."

Lady went with him, turning back to look at Pippa once before she wagged her tail. Who knew how long she'd been asleep? Poor girl probably needed to do her business.

"Are you really okay?" Aspen's timid voice asked.

Pippa turned to her and took a seat by her side. "Yeah. I have epilepsy and sometimes I get seizures."

"That was really scary."

Pippa nodded. "They can be."

"Does it happen a lot?"

"Often enough, but usually I don't get tonic-clonics. Sometimes when I'm under a lot of stress, this happens," Pippa explained.

Aspen's head tipped to the side. "Tonic what?"

"Tonic-clonics are the bigger seizures."

"All set," Charli interrupted, holding out Pippa's folded shorts.

"Thank you." She slid off the stool and grabbed the clothing.

"There is a bathroom down the hall to the right." Charli pointed.

Pippa hurried to the door and closed herself inside. There was only a sink with a mirror over it and a toilet in the room. She stripped the pants off and folded them. Next, she grabbed her shorts. Her panties had been tucked inside. Heat bloomed in her cheeks. She was grateful Charli had taken care of this instead of Mason.

She got dressed and brought out the folded sweat-pants. One of the pictures on the wall caught her atten-tion. A smiling Mason without scars had his arm wrapped around a thin redheaded woman who looked like an older version of Aspen. Was that Mason's wife? *Of course the first man who makes me want to look twice in forever would be taken.*

The front door opened and Mason came in with her dog right behind him. Lady came over to her, sniffing her and then sitting next to her.

"Thank you for taking care of Lady and me. I don't know

how I managed to walk up those stairs, but I'm sure it wasn't without a lot of help," Pippa said.

"You didn't walk. You were passed out before I got you to my truck. Of course I called Charli to make sure she'd be here first. I would have never taken you otherwise," Mason said matter-of-factly as he took the pants from her.

He'd lifted her? "You carried me? That couldn't have been easy." She was no petite woman.

"It was fine." Mason's eyes slipped over her body, his jaw tensing.

Is he disgusted by me?

To say he was fit would be an understatement. He was huge, but if the bulging muscles from his short-sleeved shirt were any indication, the man was all muscle.

"Thank you for, uh, taking care of me today."

"You saved my daughter. I'd say I'm still in your debt." His deep voice sent a shiver through her.

He's married. Her body needed to get the memo he was off-limits.

Not to mention he probably saw me wet myself and then had to carry my fat ass. If the look in his eyes was any indication, the attraction was one way. Not that it mattered. She was perfectly happy by herself . . . most days.

"Finn just called and Jamison is getting fussy, so I should get going," Charli said, breaking her thoughts. "Do you want me to drop you off at home in my car, Pippa?"

Pippa turned to the woman she'd gotten to know over the last several months. "I would appreciate that. Thank you. I just need my shoes."

Mason pointed to the neatly stacked row of footwear on the floor underneath the sweatshirts. She slipped her feet into her flip-flops.

Charli nodded to Mason. "Have a good night at work."

"Will do," Mason said, focusing on Charli.

Aspen came running over, a familiar sweatshirt in her hand. "Here's your shirt you let me borrow."

Pippa took the clothing from her. "Thanks."

"Will you be okay at home alone?" Aspen asked, worriedly.

Pippa smiled, touched that this little girl seemed to care for her. "Absolutely. I have Lady here to keep watch over me."

Aspen's eyes darted to the dog. "Can I pet her?"

"Normally, I would have to say no, but I think after everything we've been through together, it's okay if you say goodbye."

"Does she bite?" Aspen asked, shying away.

"Nope, but when people pet her or try to talk to her, she gets distracted. She's not like a regular pet; she's a working dog. Her job is to watch me and alert me when I'm going to have a seizure. So, if she's distracted, she can miss something and then I could end up getting hurt."

"Oh. It's okay. I don't need to pet her, then." Aspen dropped her hands.

"I'm okay right now. You can give her a scratch behind the ears. She loves that."

The young girl reached out to pet the dog as Lady sniffed her. "She's so soft."

"She is. It was nice to see you today."

"I'll be in next week to get the new copy of *Selfie*." Aspen smiled and backed up.

"Oh, yes, that seems to be a popular comic lately."

"It's my favorite." Aspen beamed.

"Mine too." Pippa winked and gave her a small wave goodbye.

Mason held the door open and Charli headed out. Pippa walked by him, a clean masculine scent wrapping around her as she looked up. Like fresh rain and mountain mist. "I know I said it already, but thanks again for everything."

Mason nodded curtly. He was probably glad to be rid of her. She didn't know why that bothered her so much. He was just a stranger. *A stranger who saw me pee myself and then had to lift all two hundred fifty pounds of me.*

On the bright side, she'd lived in Shattered Cove for over two years and had never run into him before.

She'd probably never have to see him again.

5

PIPPA

Pippa turned the page on the novel she was reading as her newest hire, Troy, set a stack of books in front of her.

"I think I found all the ones you requested." Troy handed her the handwritten note.

Pippa stood, accepting the list before tossing it in the trash. "Did you get a chance to watch those videos I sent you?"

Troy nodded. "Yeah. If you have a seizure, I'm grateful to know the basics on how to help. Does it happen often?"

"Often enough to have to tell all my employees about it, but for the most part, I get absence seizures."

"Those are the ones where you might look like you're staring off into space, right?" he clarified.

"Sometimes. And over here on the desk is a quick list of dos and don'ts." Pippa pointed to the printout on the wall to the side of the desk.

"I'll try my best to help you out if you have one," Troy promised.

She scanned the stack of children's books he'd grabbed.

"These are perfect. Did you get a chance to meet Miss Marsha Divine? She comes in weekly for drag queen story hour. She'll be reading some of these, and I'd like to have them set up over here for any parents who want a copy for themselves."

"I did. She seems lovely." Troy picked the first book and read the title. "*It Feels Good To Be Yourself: A Book About Gender Identity.*" He nodded and pushed some of the longer tufts of his brown hair from his face. His brown eyes crinkled at the edges when he smiled. "Sounds interesting. I wish they had books like this when I was growing up. It's really cool that you put this on here."

She beamed as a swirl of happiness flitted through her. "Just doing what I can to help spread kindness and acceptance to fight ignorance."

His gaze locked with hers before it dropped to her mouth. "My kinda woman."

Heat rose to her cheeks. Was he flirting with her? "Well, I'd better go check on things before they start the reading, since you have the front covered. If you need me, just holler."

Pippa got to her feet, Lady by her side as she made her way through the store. She scanned the shop, making sure none of her current customers wanted help as she made her way along one of the rows. An older woman sat in the corner window seat hunched over an Agatha Christie novel Pippa had specially ordered for her.

The book shop was bustling with customers and parents from all over town, packing their kids like sardines into the space surrounding the fabulous Miss Marsha Divine.

"I hope we aren't late," Remy said, holding her son, Phoenix's hand as her daughter skipped ahead towards the giant circular rainbow rug. There, other kids watched in awe as the drag queen shone in her sequined silver dress with a red feather boa.

"Nope. We're just about to begin."

Remy smiled and tucked her braided hair behind her back. "I guess I'll go find a seat. Oh, I see Jasmine is here already."

The door opened again as another woman walked in holding a little boy. *"¡Llegamos!" We're here.*

Pippa's mouth split into a smile at the familiar tongue. *"Bienvenidos."* She welcomed her.

"Hablas español?" the woman asked.

"Sí."

"Where is your accent from?"

"I'm Boricua. My mother was from the western side of the island." Pippa grinned, proud of her heritage. "And you?"

"I'm Mia, from Montemorelos, and you're my new best friend." The woman smiled.

"You haven't met Pippa yet?" Remy asked the newcomer.

"I'll admit I've only been using my e-reader for books. I know, please don't hate me." Mia bit her bottom lip.

Pippa laughed. "Oh, never mind about that." She switched to a whisper. "I, too, own an e-reader."

Mia grinned.

Pippa eyed the little boy in her arms. "Are you here for the story hour?"

"Sí. Aren't we, *mijo?"* Mia jiggled her son.

He laid his dark curly head against her chest, as if shy.

"So precious. We're about to start, so you might want to grab a seat."

Remy and Mia walked away, their little boys in tow. Another gust of wind danced over her skin as the door opened and Aaron, the owner of Hope Facility and the one who'd put her in touch with Miss Marsha Divine, came in.

"Hey, nice to see you again," Pippa greeted him.

Aaron towered above her as his gaze flicked over his shoulder and then back to her. "Nice to see you too. Did you know there happens to be a preacher out there passing out pamphlets to anyone who will listen on their way in about 'sins of the flesh'?"

Pippa's stomach sank as she turned her attention to the two men outside dressed in suits. *Not again.* "No, I didn't. Thanks for letting me know."

She peeked over her shoulder. Troy was busy scanning a customer's books into the register, and Miss Marsha was answering questions from eager little kids about her pronouns.

"I'm going to go talk to them." Pippa walked towards the door.

"Do you want me to come?" Aaron asked.

"Actually, yes." Pippa motioned to Lady. "Walk left." The dog slipped to her left side as Pippa opened the door into the warm summer air, a definite difference from her air-conditioned shop.

"Good afternoon. Would you be interested in hearing about the love of God today?" the pastor asked.

A young man stood beside him wearing a button-up shirt and brown khaki pants, each hand holding a different pamphlet.

"Pastor Calvin, I thought you agreed to do this somewhere else?" Pippa asked as politely as she could as she ground her teeth.

"But this sidewalk is public property, and even the least of these people deserve to hear about the love God has for them. They just have to turn from their sin and they will see the glory of God," Calvin answered, his smile never faltering.

"We both know why you chose this time to be in front of my store."

He leaned in, glancing at Aaron before returning to her. "I don't know what you mean. I just want to spread the love of God and save these sinners from eternal damnation."

Pippa sighed. She respected a person's choice to believe in whatever god they wanted, but pushing that belief on another or using it for shame was a different story.

"Leviticus 18:22 says, 'Thou shall not lie with mankind as with womankind: it is an abomination.' Homosexuality is not natural and it is a sin," Pastor Calvin said.

"Leviticus also says that eating lobster is a sin. That wearing clothing of more than one fabric is a sin." She motioned to his suit jacket. "That getting a tattoo is a sin. Planting more than one seed in the same field is a sin. That a man trimming his beard is a sin." She pointed to his clean-shaven face. "It would stand to reason that if those are all okay, then 'lying with mankind' should be too. Which was changed in nineteen forty-six, by the way. The original translation meant pedophilia, and it was an abomination." She took a deep breath. "Don't you believe Jesus died, making the old laws obsolete?"

The young man looked on with wide eyes as the preacher smiled. "You know your verses."

She gave him a curt smile. "I would really appreciate it if you guys did this somewhere else than in front of my store."

"We can do that. You two have a lovely day. Come on, Peter. Let's head to Green Park," Calvin said, nodding to the young man beside him.

Peter followed him, turning back to glance at her and Aaron before he scrambled to catch up to the fast-moving preacher.

Aaron chuckled next to her. "Damn, girl. You know your scripture."

"You can thank my very Catholic mother for that."

Pippa's smile wavered as memories of her mother flashed in her mind.

"I'm sure Marsha has already started. We should get back." Pippa led the way into the shop.

Aaron headed straight for the back where Miss Marsha had begun reading. Giggles came from the circular table in the back corner. She peeked around the corner as three familiar faces came into view. Aspen and her friends were huddled over the newest release of *Selfie*.

"I wish I could have superpowers," one of the girls commented.

"Which one would you want, Rachel?" Aspen asked.

"Probably the ability to be invisible," Rachel answered.

"What about you, Aspen?" the boy asked.

Aspen didn't hesitate. "To fly."

"David?" a woman's voice called from the front of the store.

"Over here, Mom." The boy stood. "I'll see you guys later."

"Bye," they called after him as a woman Pippa recognized from the diner, Brynn, cast her worried gaze over her son. Her shoulders relaxed as she pulled him into a hug. Relief painted Brynn's face. It was the same every time she came in here looking for him, as if she were afraid he would just disappear one day.

Lady nudged her hand and licked it. Pippa bent down and petted her when a sneering voice caught her attention.

"What are you, like, a dyke now?"

Hot anger lit Pippa's skin like liquid fire. She darted around the corner. Three girls surrounded Aspen and Rachel, their backs to Pippa.

"Just leave us alone," Aspen said firmly as Rachel shrunk

into herself as if she wanted to disappear. Aspen reached out and wrapped her arm around her friend.

"You're so gross. What's wrong, Aspen? Because you don't have a mom, you became a lezbo?" The same girl said this, and the two girls by her side giggled as if it were the funniest thing in the world.

"What's going on here?" Pippa snapped. *What does she mean Aspen doesn't have a mom?*

The group of girls jumped and spun around, eyes wide with guilty looks.

Their leader's face quickly formed into an innocent expression. "Nothing, just joking around with my friends."

Pippa tamped her anger and bit back the urge to call this bully a little bitch. *She's just a child.*

Pippa took a deep breath. Children were often a reflection of what they were exposed to, after all. "Can I let you in on a little secret?" Pippa asked.

The leader turned to her friends before she nodded to Pippa.

"What's your name?"

"Cara."

"Cara, other women are not your enemy. You girls are gonna have so much going against you in this world, trying to beat you down into submission. You will be criticized for your looks, your thoughts, who you love, who you don't love, what you wear, and your weight. The last thing you need to do is be unkind to another girl. We are all sisters."

The two sidekicks looked to the floor before turning back to Cara.

Cara rolled her eyes and snickered. "Well, Aspen here likes her sisters a little too much. Ewww, does that make it incest?"

Pippa leaned in so she was level with the young girl. "I'm

sorry you feel so bad about yourself that you have to put others down to feel better."

Cara's eyes grew wide before they lit with anger. "You're a fat bitch."

Pippa shrugged like the comment rolled off her and didn't bother her a bit. She'd had plenty of practice with girls like Cara. "I'm okay being a bitch if it means I stand up for what's right. You're a bully. You can choose to be kinder and you will have to if you three ever want to step foot in my store again. The Oyster Bookstore is a safe and inclusive place for everyone. If you can't be nice, you can consider yourself officially banned from the premises."

"You have got to be kidding me!" Cara whined.

"You can walk yourself out or I can call your parents."

"Let's go." One of the sidekicks grabbed Cara's arm.

"Shut up, Christie," Cara snapped.

"S-sorry, ma'am," the other girl said to Pippa before hurrying out the door with Christie at her heels.

"I'm telling my dad. You're going to regret treating me like this!" Cara screamed and stomped out of the store.

Pippa turned back to Aspen and Rachel. "You girls okay?"

Rachel nodded timidly before standing and gathering her things. "I better go too. My mom is probably done at the gym."

"That was awesome. I wish I had it on video." Aspen beamed at Pippa as Rachel gave them a quick wave and disappeared out of the store.

"Well, I want you to know you're safe here, especially since you and your father did the same for me last week," Pippa assured her.

"I want to be you when I grow up." Aspen sighed.

Pippa's belly fluttered. She'd done what she wished someone had done for her just once. Growing up with a plus-size body and a disability had made her the target of many bullies. People like Cara had preyed on any weakness they found. Add on to that the fact that she, too, had lost her mom, and that her dad had been in prison for a while, and Pippa had been outcast *numero uno*.

"Did you like the new episode?" Pippa motioned to the comic on the table.

Aspen's eyes lit up as she hugged it to her chest. "Definitely. I'm already halfway through."

"It's a pretty cool comic. What do you love about it so much?"

Aspen gushed about the heroine and her abilities to see other people's true self. "I wish we could all see people for who they were. I don't understand why people can be so terrible."

Like Cara? "Me too."

Aspen swiped a strand of hair behind her ear. Pippa's gaze snagged on the red scratch marks on her forearm she hadn't seen earlier. She reached out and grasped her wrist, turning the girl's arm to get a better look. "What are these from?"

Aspen tugged her arm away, hiding it behind her back and shrugging. "The 3Cs strike again." Aspen's earlier cheer was gone from her voice.

"The 3Cs?"

"Cara, Christie, and Crystal. They're on my soccer team, and when we had a scrimmage the other day, well, I don't know. It happened, but I still got the ball and scored."

Worry cinched Pippa's gut. Aspen was a sweetheart, and she didn't deserve this. Did Mason know? "Did you tell your dad about them?"

Aspen rolled her eyes. "You're almost as protective as he is. Is that your boyfriend?" She pointed to Troy at the front desk.

Boyfriend? "Troy? No. He's my new employee."

Aspen smiled mischievously. "So, you don't have a boyfriend?"

Pippa shook her head and laughed.

"You should totally come to my house again sometime and see the cool tree house my dad and Finn built for me. It has a built-in bookshelf and everything."

"That sounds amazing. I know I would have loved one of those when I was your age."

"Your dad didn't build you one?" Aspen asked.

Pippa shook her head. They'd never lived anywhere with room for a structure. "Nope. So I built my own." She opened her arms and spread them out towards the bookstore.

"That's awesome." Aspen's eyes lit up. "What are you doing tomorrow?"

"Tomorrow is my first Saturday off in so long. I plan on spending it at the beach." Pippa would splurge and order an Uber to take her. She needed to get out and feel the sand between her toes.

"Which one?"

"Shattered Cove Beach is the closest. Probably that one."

Aspen grinned. "Maybe I'll see you there."

That was an odd thing to say. *What are you up to, Aspen?*

A couple hours later, all was quiet. The parents and children had left and Troy was nearing the end of his shift.

"You did great today. Think you're ready to take tomorrow all by yourself?" Pippa asked, opening a new box of comics.

"Yes. And if I need anything, I have your number." Troy winked.

He was definitely flirting.

"You—"

"Are you the owner?" an angry voice demanded. A man marched up to them, his fists clenched, his face red as his gaze lasered on Troy.

Troy stood straighter. He had a couple inches on the other man.

"I am," Pippa said. "How can I help you?"

The other man's beady eyes darted to her before his lip turned up with disgust. He stepped closer, his shoulder brushing against Troy's chest. "You're the bitch that kicked my daughter out earlier?"

Lady growled beside her.

"You better watch the way you speak to her," Troy interjected.

The men stared each other down. The last thing she needed was a fight to break out in the middle of her bookstore and for her new employee to be assaulted. *Why was all this shit happening today? Was it Friday the thirteenth? A full moon?*

Pippa stepped between the two men, trying to calm things down. "Cara was insulting another patron and I kindly asked her to be nicer. When she continued to be belligerent, I asked her to leave and not come back until she could change her attitude. I have that right as a business owner. And I'm going to have to ask you to do the same."

"And what if I don't?" Cara's dad leaned over the desk as if to intimidate her.

"Then I'll call the police and have you escorted out." She picked up the phone and dialed the local sheriff's department, but paused before she hit call.

"This isn't over. No one disrespects me and mine!" The angry man snarled and swiped his hand over the counter, knocking the books and business cards onto the floor.

Pippa flinched.

Troy walked towards him. "Feel like a real man now?"

"Troy," Pippa said. His gaze met hers and she shook her head. Cara's dad stormed out of the shop, slamming the door behind him.

"Does that happen often?" Troy asked, bending over to pick up the mess.

She walked around to help him pick up. "It's never happened before. I'm sorry you had to deal with that." Pippa restocked the books on the counter.

Troy reached over to touch her arm. "Are you okay?"

She sighed and nodded, forcing a smile. "Absolutely. You can head out if you want. I'll be here at nine to open the store and make sure you're good to go before I leave for the day."

He hesitated, studying her a little longer before conceding. "Okay. I'll see you tomorrow, then." He grabbed his water bottle from the desk, gave her a salute, and walked out the door.

She checked the clock. Usually, she wasn't in a rush to close the store. But today had been one thing after the other. She needed some rest, good food, and to curl up with a book to escape the drama of the last twenty-four hours. She sighed and tipped her neck to the side, stretching it. Her hand moved to massage some of the tension from her shoulder. At least tomorrow she'd be off work.

Aspen's mischievous smile flashed in her mind. *Hopefully there will be no more surprises.*

6

MASON

Mason lugged the second board from the back of his truck. "Aspen, grab the paddles and the life jackets."

His daughter kept her back to him, peering towards the beach.

"Aspen?"

"Huh?" She flicked her gaze to him quickly before focusing back on the sand.

"The quicker you help me out, the faster we can get over there."

Aspen climbed into the back of the truck, saving his older knees from the extra strain. She grabbed the oars and life jackets.

"Why'd you grab three life jackets from the garage?" he questioned.

Aspen's cheeks flushed pink. "Oh, uh. Just in case, I guess."

"I'll bring this one and be back for the other board. Follow me with the accessories." She was thirteen, but he still didn't like the idea of leaving her without supervision. He'd seen firsthand the depravity of the world.

He tossed her a hat. "You got sunscreen on?"

"Yes." She rolled her eyes.

Damn, when had that started?

"Don't want to arrive with my beautiful daughter and leave with a cranky lobster," he teased, flicking the bill of her cap.

She looked away as if to hide her smile and deadpanned, "Really, Dad?"

He hefted the board over his head and led the way to the sand. There was a rock wall to the right of the beach which was usually covered halfway when the tide was in. Beyond that was more sandy beach and then the woods which led up to Black Cliffs, where some of the teenagers went to jump into the deep sea below—something his daughter would never do if he had anything to say about it.

Mason set the board on the sand and Aspen dropped the paddles and the life jackets.

"You grabbed an adult jacket. Don't you think it's gonna be too big on you?"

Aspen was scanning the beach again. "No, I'll be fine."

He didn't worry about it too much. She was a strong swimmer, and he'd be by her side. "Come with me back to the truck to get the other board."

"Dad, I'll be fine. You can see me the whole time and I won't move," Aspen argued.

He scanned the area around them. Families with young kids digging in the sand littered the beach. A few older teens tossed a Frisbee farther down the shoreline.

"Fine." He jogged back to the truck and retrieved the last paddleboard, checking on her as he returned.

As soon as he set it down, Aspen took off, waving. His gaze

snapped to where she was headed—toward a woman with the most heavenly curvy body. And boy was she showing a lot of it. Gone were the cotton-candy braids. Her hair was twisted into a dark bun on the top of her head, exposing her sun-kissed neck. She had a white swimsuit top with beaded straps tied around her neck. They were so thin, with one pull of the flimsy strands her large breasts would be freed. Her white see-through cover-up danced in the salty sea breeze.

A few inches of her tan tummy were exposed before the high-waisted emerald-green bottoms started. Thick, juicy thighs jiggled with her movements and his cock jerked in his board shorts. It was good to know the thing still worked. It had been so long since he'd been with a woman. But the last thing he needed to do was get a hard-on right now. He averted his gaze back to her face.

Her eyes widened in surprise as Aspen bounded up to her. He couldn't hear what she was saying from so far away, but Aspen pointed animatedly towards him before she grasped Pippa's hand. Aspen's eyes lit up and her smile widened. He hadn't seen her this excited in . . . a long time.

"Dad! Look who I found," Aspen said, practically dragging Pippa behind her.

Pippa's gaze met his before she turned back to his daughter, the golden retriever at her side.

"Hello." Pippa's voice was shy, but she held her head high with confidence.

It took every last bit of his self-control to not let his eyes drop down her figure and drink in every inch of her luscious curves. He gritted his teeth and nodded.

"Have you ever been paddleboarding?" Aspen asked her.

Pippa's amber gaze flicked to their equipment and then back to his daughter. "Nope, but I've always thought it looked fun."

"You should go now." Aspen offered her the life jacket as his suspicions kicked up a notch. Did Aspen know Pippa would be here? Impossible.

Pippa held up her hand. "Oh, no. I couldn't. I'm not supposed to do things like that."

Aspen quirked her eyebrow. "Why not?"

Pippa swallowed and flicked a nervous glance his way. "My epilepsy can make things like swimming dangerous."

"That sucks. Even if you have someone with you?" Aspen asked.

"Well, it's definitely safer if I have someone. I usually wait until my sister comes up for a visit, and then we go into the waves together."

His chest squeezed. It must be hard living life with so many limits.

Aspen turned to her dad, giving him a pleading look. "My dad was a Navy SEAL. He's an *okay* swimmer, but I'm sure he could keep you safe."

He chuckled at his daughter's tease.

Pippa's eyes widened and shot to his. "Oh no, that's okay. You guys enjoy your time. I'm just going to dip my feet in and sunbathe. I brought a book too." She motioned to her bag.

"I also have some medical training if it makes you feel any better. I'd be happy to take you out on the water." The words were out of his mouth before he could stop them. He didn't like the idea of her missing a chance to do something when he could give it to her. He owed her, after all —didn't he?

"I don't want to intrude." Pippa eyed the waves longingly.

"No intrusion at all. We were going out. You can come with us. Your dog can ride, too, if you want," Mason assured her.

Hope danced in her eyes as a smile split her lips, and it

stole some of the breath from his lungs. She was a beautiful woman, but when she smiled, she embodied pure sunshine.

"Okay. If you're sure it's not too much of an inconvenience."

He jerked his attention towards the waves. Mason needed the ice-cold New England sea to calm his raging libido.

"I'm gonna go hang out with David. He's under the green umbrella with his mom," Aspen announced.

"You're not coming?" Pippa asked before he could.

Mason scanned the beach, locating Brynn, with a white long-sleeved shirt and tan capris on. She must have been sweltering in this ninety-degree weather.

"I want to hang out with David. Can I, Dad? I'll go boarding later," Aspen promised. She'd been bothering him all morning about getting to the beach to go out on the water, and now she had blown him off for her friend. He supposed it was bound to happen sometime. She was officially a teenager now.

"Alright. But stay with Brynn and David," he gave in.

Aspen jumped excitedly. "Bye, Pippa!" She waved and was off.

"Ready?" he asked, keeping an eye on Aspen as she jogged towards the green umbrella and her friend.

"I guess."

"Put that life jacket on." He pointed to the one Aspen had left behind.

Pippa set down her bag and grabbed the floatation device.

"Is there anything valuable in there? You can put your stuff in my truck if you want?" Mason pointed to her things.

"Actually, would you mind?" She handed him her bag.

Pippa slipped her arms in the jacket, and struggled with the zipper.

"Here." He dropped the bag, gripped the edges of the life

jacket and cinched it, squeezing her tits together in the process. His gaze flicked over the swells of her breasts and then back to the zipper. *Stop ogling her.*

He zipped it as far as it would go. This vest wasn't made for someone so voluptuous.

"It'll have to do." His voice was rough, as if he'd swallowed a mouthful of sand.

She flinched.

"Is it too tight?"

She looked away. "It's fine."

Was she disgusted by him being so close? Some people were uncomfortable with his injury. He picked up her bag. "I'll run this to the truck and be right back."

After he returned, Mason picked up the board and walked into the water. "Let's get Lady on first."

Pippa followed his directions as they got her and the animal situated on the first board. She sat, one leg over each side. Nerves were evident on her face in the tight set of her mouth. But she didn't hesitate as he walked her through instructions on how to get up to kneel and paddle. When she was more comfortable, she paddled out to the smoother waters and he got on his own board, paddling to catch up to her. Cool ocean water dripped down his legs from his board shorts. The splash of the paddle melded with the watery sounds of the waves rocking the paddleboard. His skin was sticky with a mixture of saltwater and sweat. The hot sun beat down on them, and there wasn't a cloud in sight—just beautiful blue sky that went on for what seemed like forever. A few seagulls flew overhead before diving into the icy water for their meals.

It was so peaceful out here, away from the noise of the fellow beachgoers. A few fishing boats could be seen out in the distance, as well as the lighthouse.

Mason drew in a deep breath tainted with saltwater brine. It was one of his favorite things about living on the seacoast. Something about it just settled him.

He took his time coming to Pippa's side and stopped on the left, so she'd be on the good side of his face. "You're not too shabby at this."

She smiled and bit her lip self-consciously. "Is now a bad time to admit I'm terrified of seaweed, dark water, and sharks?"

He chuckled. "I never would have guessed."

She shrugged and then widened her arms as if to catch her balance. "It's my killer poker face."

He turned his head away so she wouldn't see his damaged smile.

"If you're so scared, then, why do it?" he asked.

She blew out a breath, her eyes scanning the glittering water. "I try not to let fear hold me back from living."

He stayed silent, digesting her words.

"Can I stand up now?"

He paddled closer. "Take it slow. Balance your weight."

Lady's nose rose as she kept a watchful eye on Pippa, her tongue wagging in the warm breeze.

Pippa bit her lip as she carefully stood. The board tipped but she righted herself. She giggled. Something he hadn't experienced in a long time drummed in his chest. His body heated as his gaze wandered over her. Fuck, he wanted to bite that juicy ass. His cock pressed against his shorts.

Pippa turned towards him, catching his gaze. He grimaced. *Fuck.* Pippa had to be in her early twenties and that meant he was most likely a decade older than her.

"You like owning a bookstore?" he asked, needing to get his mind into safer territory.

"Yes, I love it." Her eyes lit up. "What is it that you do? Are you still in the Navy?"

"No. I work security." He cleared his throat, trying to get a hold of himself. Maybe he should dive in for a quick swim to cool off.

"Are they going to jump from there?" Pippa asked, eyes focused on the Black Cliffs as a few small dots of people lined up at the edge.

"Yup."

"Doesn't anyone get hurt?" Worry was evident in her voice.

"Nothing serious. The water is really deep even when the tide is out and there aren't any rocks."

She shivered. "Have you ever done that?"

He shook his head. If he jumped and something went wrong, Aspen would be left without any parent. He couldn't take a risk like that. "Nope."

After a few more minutes of comfortable silence, Mason kept her in the corner of his vision, but he turned to get a better look and check on her. A few seagulls cawed above as they passed. The blue-green water rippled and crashed against the distant shore.

"Aspen seems like a great kid."

A swell of pride filled his chest. "She is."

"She adores you." Pippa switched sides she was paddling on.

He'd do right by his daughter. That was the promise he'd made after his wife passed. He owed her that much.

"We should probably head back." He glanced towards the beach, not able to make out Aspen from this distance.

"Okay." Pippa paddled, maneuvering her board towards the beach as he followed beside her. "This was fun. Easier than I thought."

Lady barked.

"Is she—"

Before he could finish his question, a big wave lurched in front of them. Pippa's board flipped upside down and she and the dog disappeared into the green murky depths. Mason dove into the water without hesitation. His arms raced around Pippa's body. He pulled her towards the surface, her life jacket pressed between them. He broke through the water a second before the dog swam their way.

"You okay?" Mason asked. Her back was to him, so he couldn't see her face.

"Yeah."

Mason flipped the paddleboard over and used his other hand to push the dog on top to safety before grabbing the oars and placing them on as well. Pippa started shaking in his arms. *Oh no!* He spun her around, worriedly checking her over.

She was laughing. Saltwater spilt down her face, her white teeth peeking out from her pink lips.

"I guess I spoke too soon about this being easy." She giggled, holding tighter to his shoulders. The extra contact stoked a fire inside him, chasing the chill of the cold water from his body.

Something snapped in his chest. He smiled and laughed with her, relief pouring over him. "Aren't you scared of man-eating sharks?"

Her smile faded as her eyebrows drew together. Golden-brown orbs locked on to his, lighting with arousal. "I guess not with you here."

Something akin to pride welled in his chest.

"You should do that more." Her pink shiny lips glistened in the sun. He wanted to taste the saltwater on her kiss.

"Do what?" he grated, his face only inches from hers.

"Laugh. Smile." Her gaze dipped to his mouth that he hadn't realized was still turned up.

Electricity buzzed along his arms where he held her against him.

He leaned in. Seawater dripped from the tips of his wet hair onto his forehead, doing nothing to cool the burn that raged in his body. Her hot breath tickled his lips, her wide amber eyes meeting his.

The dog barked and he jerked away.

What the fuck was I thinking?

As he packed up the boards in the truck, Aspen happily chatting beside him, he resolved to push Pippa from his mind. There was no way that beautiful *young* Pippa wanted him. And the last thing he needed was a distraction. He only had room for one girl in his life—Aspen. She would always come first, and no woman wanted to play second fiddle. Besides, the last time he'd had two women in his life, he'd screwed up and a killer had taken his wife from him.

Pippa needed to stay far away from him—for both their sakes.

7

PIPPA

Pippa finished washing the sand off her body before carefully getting out of the shower. Lady stood on guard next to her, her ever-faithful sidekick. Lady was one of the reasons Pippa could live on her own. It was possible without her, but she set not only Pippa's mind at ease, but her family's.

Pippa wrapped a towel around herself and inspected her dark hair. She ran a hand through the thick, wavy locks. Maybe she'd do some braids with blue this time.

A water droplet dripped down her neck, disappearing into the towel. She pulled it open, turning sideways and then to her front again, inspecting her naked self. Her skin jiggled with her movements. She pressed a hand to her soft stomach. She'd come to accept her figure and all her curves after spending so much time hating every inch, wishing she'd just wake up thin one morning. At some point, she'd embraced her cellulite and stretch marks. This was her body. There were plenty of plus-size women who were gorgeous, so why not her? Almost all her past boyfriends had loved her shape. So why was she feeling so self-conscious these days? Hadn't she dealt with this?

Mason's grimace flashed in her mind. *Right.* It figured the first man she'd found attractive in a long time would look at her as if it hurt him physically.

I thought there had been a moment. She'd been sure he was going to kiss her. But then he'd reared back so fast, she'd thought a shark had grabbed him.

Pippa shivered and went into her bedroom. She grabbed a comfy floral yellow sundress that cinched under her breasts and flowed out. She slipped it over her head as her phone buzzed.

Sophia's name flashed on the cell. Pippa clicked on the FaceTime button and waited for it to connect. Her sister's warm brown eyes lit up on the screen, followed by her sweet smile.

"Hey, Pip. How's it going?"

"Pretty good. I actually got in the ocean today."

Her sister's grin faded. Her brows drew together in concern. "Alone?"

Pippa shook her head. Guilt crashed over her. She'd been so excited to share her good news that she forgot for one second how worried her sister would be. *I hate this.* "No, no. You know I'm careful. A . . . friend was with me. I had a life vest on, and Lady was with me too. He took me paddle-boarding."

"He?" Sophia's smile was back.

Pippa giggled. "Yes, *he.*"

"*Nena,* spill it! I don't have all day."

"He's the dad of one of my customers. I happened upon them at the beach and one thing led to another. He took me out, and it was so cool."

"Is he married?" Sophia asked.

Pippa shook her head. "I don't believe she's in the picture."

Sophia smirked. "So, he's single?"

Single and in no way interested, if the disgust that had flashed in his eyes was any indication. A pang of hurt streaked through her chest. "Don't get your hopes up."

"Awww, why not?" her sister whined.

"I'm ninety-nine percent sure he's not into me."

"But there's still a chance? How do you know?"

Pippa adjusted the phone on her vanity as she grabbed her brush. She needed to get the tangles out before her hair dried. As she worked, she changed the subject. "How are you and Vivian doing?"

Sophia pointed her finger at the camera. "I see what you're doing. We're coming back to this."

Pippa chuckled and set her brush down before grabbing one of the spray bottles of product by the mirror. "Well, how is everything?"

Sophia sighed dreamily. "That's actually why I was calling." She cleared her throat, rubbing her nose with her hand as something glinted off her finger.

Pippa sucked in a breath and set down her product. "You got engaged!"

Sophia beamed. "It was so perfect, Pip. She surprised me with a scavenger hunt featuring all the special places we'd visited. Then, she popped the question where we had our first date."

Pippa's heart soared for her sister. "Show me that rock again."

Sophia focused the camera on her hand once more. A giant square-cut diamond filled the screen.

"It's beautiful, Soph. I'm so happy for you." Pippa's chest

grew full of emotion waiting to bubble out. Her vision turned blurry.

"Thank you! I really just can't even believe I'm engaged."

"You deserve all the happiness in the world, sis."

Sophia's gaze met Pippa's. "So do you."

Pippa shrugged. "I know." She partially lied. It wasn't that she didn't believe she was worthy of love; it was just that loving her came with a lot of burden.

"Babe? You ready?" Vivian's voice filtered in the background.

Sophia turned her head and called out, "I'll be right there." Her sister refocused on Pippa. "I gotta go. We're going to tell her parents. Oh, speaking of, you should call Dad. He's been asking about you."

Pippa made sure her smile didn't slip. "Sure. You have a good night."

"You too." Sophia blew her a kiss and then disconnected.

Pippa stared at her phone a moment longer before bringing her attention back to her hair. She'd call her dad tomorrow.

As she twisted her hair into a bun, she digested everything Sophia had said. Pippa was so happy for her big sister. She'd finally found someone who truly loved and cared for her, after Pippa had messed up Sophia's first relationship. Pippa closed her eyes and sighed. They were better off if she stayed away. She'd caused her family enough trouble.

Her father's face flashed in her mind. He'd paid the biggest price of all, sacrificing everything in hopes of giving Pippa a better life. *And look where it got him.*

She stood from her desk. Lady's head rose, her eyes looking questioningly towards Pippa. Reaching down, Pippa scratched behind her ears. "Let's go out for dinner tonight. I don't feel like eating by myself in the apartment. Besides, I happen to have a copy of the book Charli ordered. And maybe she can tell me a little more about the grumpy Navy man. Let's kill two birds with one stone and try out The Shipwreck's new menu. What do you say, girl?"

Lady got to her feet.

"It's settled, then."

Twenty minutes later, Pippa crossed the street and headed towards the entrance of The Shipwreck, her bag crisscrossed over her shoulder. A familiar figure leaned against the wood siding by the door, his arms crossed and expression serious.

What is he doing here? Her stomach summersaulted with anxious butterflies. *Oh, God. This is where he works security? That must be how he knows Charli.*

Mason's brows drew together and his blue eyes narrowed as they tracked her movements. Pippa's skin burned from his intense gaze. She offered him a smile and an awkward wave.

"Hey."

He just stared at her.

"Thanks again for today. I had a lot of fun."

His head tipped as if he'd started to nod and then thought better of it. What had happened to the guy she'd been on the paddleboard with? He'd at least spoken to her. Laughed with her. *I thought he was going to kiss me too.* Boy had she read him wrong.

"Do you need to check my ID?" she asked, reaching for her purse.

"No. Go ahead."

Three words. That was all she got. *Okay, then.* "Have a good night."

She walked by him, catching him tense out of the corner of her eye before she pushed open the door and entered what could only be described as the belly of a ship that had been sunk to the bottom of the sea. She'd been here once before, also to deliver books. Blue lights cast a watery hue over the room. Round fish tanks decorated the walls on either side of the dance floor where couples moved together to a heady, pulsing beat. Pippa pulled Lady's leash closer as she weaved past a couple of patrons towards the bar.

Finn, Charli's husband, was behind the counter fixing drinks. Pippa found an empty seat at the far end and pulled out the book for her friend.

"Hey, Pippa. Haven't seen you in a while. Can I get you something to drink or eat? We've got some new finger foods we're trying out on the menu," Finn offered.

"I'd love a virgin piña colada. And maybe a sampler plate?"

He nodded and grabbed a glass, filling it with ice. "Coming right up."

"Oh, I brought a book your wife ordered. Is she working tonight?" Pippa held up the novel.

He shook his head. "No, tonight's her night with Jamison at home. But I can give it to her. Do I owe you anything for it?" He accepted the book.

"Nope, she's all paid up."

He disappeared to the kitchen they'd added on since the first time she was here. Pippa's gaze caught on a familiar blue set of eyes by the door. She sucked in a breath. Mason looked away, scanning the rest of the room, on guard. His rebuff shouldn't hurt so much, but it did. Why was he so cold to her?

Maybe he resents me for disrupting his afternoon with Aspen and making him babysit my grown ass.

Finn returned with her drink and food. She dug in, draining her drink in no time. She ordered a second. She was out for the first time in a long time. She wasn't going to let that lumberjack of a man ruin her evening.

A burst of cologne wrapped around her. Whoever her new neighbor was, he smelled good.

"Eating alone?" A deep voice pulled her attention to her right.

Dark eyes stared back at her. A friendly smile turned up the corner of Pippa's mouth. "Not if you count my dog, Lady."

His eyes darted to her golden retriever, lying on the floor beside her. "She's beautiful."

"I think so too."

He reached out his olive-toned hand as if to shake hers. "I'm Ricardo Emerson, but everyone calls me Ricky."

She slipped her hand into his, but he pulled it to his mouth, kissing her knuckles.

"Very smooth move."

He grinned playfully. "You like it enough to give me your name?"

She chuckled. "Pippa."

"Well, Pippa, seeing how I'm here alone, and you're sitting by your lonesome, you feel like sharing a drink with me?"

She smiled. "Are you buying?"

"Of course."

"Then I'd say, absolutely."

Two hours later, Pippa clutched her stomach. It ached from laughing so hard. Ricky was hilarious. She'd learned he was a beekeeper along with his brother, Roman. He was one of four children and loved dogs. But what had her laughing so hard were the stories of his exes. He was a flirt, there was no doubt about it, but she could see them becoming good friends.

"Should we dance? Work off some of these piña coladas?" Ricky asked, after draining his last glass. He'd opted to have what she was drinking, even though it didn't contain any alcohol. It was a sweet gesture.

Pippa's eyes darted to the dance floor, anxiously. "I'm not actually that great of a dancer."

He held out his hand as he got to his feet. "Me either. Let's look horrible out there together."

She giggled and slipped her palm into his. "Care if we make this a threesome?" She pulled Lady's leash.

He smirked and led her to the corner near the edge of the room. "Just what every man wants to hear."

She laughed again and placed one hand around his neck. This was nice—enjoyable even. The lights flashed and she resisted the urge to glance at the door. Ricky was everything she needed to forget about her day. Still, she didn't want him to get the wrong idea. "I had a lot of fun tonight. Thank you for hanging out with me—as a friend."

"It was my pleasure." He spun her around and back, guiding her through the steps of the dance.

After a few moments, she laughed. "You liar."

"I don't know what you mean," he said coyly.

"You can too dance."

His smile widened, his eyes glittering with humor. "I may have undersold my abilities. But it got you out here, didn't it?"

She smiled and they danced another two songs before she yawned. "I think I should head home. It's getting late."

"Did you drive?" Ricky asked.

She shook her head. "I'll call a cab."

"I can give you a lift if you want?" Ricky offered.

She tugged her bottom lip into her mouth. "You don't mind?"

"Not at all."

She hesitated.

"If you need someone to vouch for my integrity, you can ask Finn," he offered.

She trusted her intuition when it came to men. Nothing about Ricky screamed danger. "I'd love a ride."

"Great. Let me run to the bathroom, and I'll meet you out front." He disappeared towards the restrooms and Pippa led Lady outside. She breathed in a burst of fresh air and jumped as a dark shadow moved out of the corner of her eye.

"Oh!" Pippa's hand flew to her chest.

Lady barked once.

Mason moved into the lights mounted on the side of the building. His scowl seemed more menacing in the shadow of night. "I hope you aren't planning to drive after all those drinks."

She tried to get her thudding heartbeat under control. He'd been watching her? He'd counted her drinks, but would barely say two words to her except to accuse her of being irresponsible?

Anger flared within her. "I can't drive, and I can't drink alcohol. I have epilepsy, remember? Those were virgin coladas —not that it's any of your business."

His gaze dropped to the road and then flicked back to her. "It *is* my business to make sure drunk drivers don't get into cars and drive off and kill people." His voice was harsh, making her flinch. Some of the wind was let out of her sails. *Well, damn.* It was his job, wasn't it?

"I'm sorry. You're right." She took a few steps towards the parking lot.

"Are you walking home?" His voiced tipped almost as if he were concerned.

She turned towards him. "No, Ricky is going to drive me. He also had virgin coladas, if you need to know."

Mason's jaw flexed, his sapphire eyes cooling before he left her without another word and disappeared into the bar.

"Okay, then. Nice to see you too," Pippa said aloud, sarcasm dripping in every syllable.

Another minute later, Ricky appeared, ushering her to his truck. "Ready to go?"

"Yes."

"You sure it's okay if I give you a ride? Don't want to step on anyone's toes." Ricky chuckled.

Pippa turned to him. "Whose toes would you be stepping on?"

"Mason seemed pretty upset you were leaving with me." His eyes lit with amusement as the corner of his mouth turned up.

Pippa rolled her eyes. "I don't know what his problem is. I literally met the man twice. Is he always that . . ." *Gruff? Cold? Unstable?*

"Protective?" Ricky supplied.

Mason was protective of her? She snorted in disbelief.

"He likes you." Ricky opened the passenger door for her.

She climbed in. "Could have fooled me," she mumbled. Lady hopped up and settled by her feet. There was just enough room.

If a man liked her, he'd need to actually show that. She wasn't subscribing to the toxic masculinity bullshit that said if a boy liked you, he picked on you or ignored you. Nope. That was crazy.

There was no way Mason Wright liked her. And even if he did, if that was how he showed it, she didn't want any part of his affections.

8

MASON

Mason checked his watch for the fifth time before his gaze flicked back to the door to the bookstore. *Where is she?* Aspen was supposed to be here ten minutes ago. That was the deal—he gave her space in the bookstore if she kept to their timeline. He'd been in here a few times to make sure this was a safe space for Aspen to be in alone. He'd never run into Pippa though; there had always been another woman here before, Tammy. She was probably done now that she was due to give birth any day.

He was trying to balance giving Aspen space for her blossoming need for more independence and still managing to keep her safe while he sat across the street in the café nursing a coffee and catching up on news and projects he worked on the side as a private security contractor.

He'd give her five more minutes and then he was going in after her.

The door across the street opened and his daughter's strawberry-blond hair blew in the breeze as she smiled, her mouth going a mile a minute. Pippa came out behind her.

Mason's chest tightened. She was wearing a pair of white shorts and a blue flowy shirt that rippled in the summer breeze. Her hair was down, waves of natural curls falling just past her shoulders.

Had she gone home with Ricky? Green jealousy swirled in his gut—and he had no right to it.

Aspen stepped into the crosswalk without looking either way. His heart lurched to his throat. Pippa's hand shot out across his daughter's chest, holding her back as a car drove past. Her dog waited patiently by her side.

Some of the tension left his body in a relieved exhale. *Guess I need to talk to my thirteen-year-old about how to cross a road again.*

Once it was clear, Pippa led Aspen across, nodding and smiling at whatever his bubbly daughter was going on about. He sat back at his table in the café closest to the register, drinking his coffee as they entered. Aspen's attention flicked to him before she gave him a quick smile. Pippa's gaze stayed on the chalkboard menu as both ladies walked to the cash register to order.

"I'll take a large latte with a shot of coconut. And we'll take two cookies. I'll have a chocolate chip mermaid, and what kind do you want, Aspen?"

His daughter shrugged. "No cookie for me, thanks."

Mason's brows drew together. Since when did his daughter turn down sweets?

Pippa turned towards her. "Does this have anything to do with the 3 Cs?"

What the fuck is a 3C?

Aspen's head dropped and her shoulders sagged.

Pippa bent to get on Aspen's level and tipped her chin up. "You are perfect just the way you are. This body is capable of amazing things, and it's all yours. Don't let anyone make you feel less for how you look. You. Are. Beautiful."

Whatever defense Mason had patched together to keep this woman out just crumbled until nothing was left but debris.

"So, which cookie?" Pippa asked, gently.

"A mermaid one." Aspen beamed up at Pippa as if she hung the moon.

"You heard the woman. Two mermaid cookies, please," Pippa said to Remy.

"Here you ladies go. Enjoy." Remy slid the goodies over.

Pippa sipped her coffee and pushed the bag over to Aspen. His daughter opened it and grabbed her treat out before handing it back to Pippa. They turned around, and Aspen walked over to him.

"Dad. Guess what?"

Pippa's eyes caught on his, widening for a moment as surprise flickered in them.

"Pippa let me use the register while someone paid today at the bookstore. Isn't that cool?" Aspen asked quickly before biting the head off her mermaid.

He nodded. "That's awesome."

"I want to own a bookstore when I get older." Aspen beamed up at her as if Pippa was her own personal superheroine.

"I better get back. Have a good afternoon." Pippa offered him a tight smile before Aspen wrapped her arms around the woman.

Pippa's grin softened, her neon-yellow nails contrasting with his daughter's red hair as she hugged her back.

"Bye, Pippa," Aspen said, releasing her.

"*Nos vemos.*" Pippa left without a backwards glance, leading her dog across the street and disappearing into the bookstore.

"Ready to go to Grandpa's?" Mason asked, getting to his feet.

"Yes. Did you grab my bag?"

"It's in the truck." He guided his daughter to where he'd parked and helped her in before going to his side.

After he pulled onto Main Street, he turned the country music down and asked, "What's a 3C?"

Aspen shrugged. When had his baby girl started pulled away and keeping things from him?

"Come on, sweet pea. You know you can tell me anything." *Why does Pippa know and I don't?*

"It's Cara, Christie, and Crystal from school. They're just mean to me sometimes."

His grip tightened on the steering wheel until his knuckles turned white. "What do you mean they're mean to you?"

"They call me names or say stuff to hurt my feelings. It's not a big deal, Dad. Pippa kicked them out of the bookstore the other day. You should have seen their faces." Aspen laughed.

"Aren't they on your soccer team?"

"Yeah."

He'd be having a conversation with their parents at the next game. Nobody messed with his little girl.

"Did you know Pippa makes the art sculptures in the bookstore? She showed me her workroom in the back. It's so cool. She even has little mice and fairy doors hidden in the shop. Some are in between the books on the shelves. It's so magical." Aspen went on about Pippa.

"You really like her," Mason pointed out.

"She is pretty cool for an adult."

He chuckled. "Am I not cool?"

She rolled her eyes as she bit back a smile. "You're alright too, Dad."

"Just *alright?* Sort of like my swimming skills?"

She laughed. He lived for these moments—where everything was okay in his world, his daughter was happy and carefree. They'd come further and were fewer between lately. He'd chalked it up to her becoming a teenager, but maybe something bigger was going on.

It seemed the bookstore owner had brought more joy to his daughter's life in a single afternoon than he'd witnessed all month. Maybe it was time he had a conversation with Pippa —if only talking to her didn't stir such wild emotions within him.

9

MASON

Mason chucked the empty coffee cup into the bin on the street as he looked both ways in preparation to cross. A familiar figure caught his eye. The skinny man leaned against the hardware store window, a lit cigarette sticking out of his mouth as he scowled at the scratch-off in his hand. Lester Marby wasn't who he wanted to see today, but he had a bone to pick with him about his daughter, Cara.

Mason approached, stopping a few feet in front of him, blocking the rays of the low sun from Lester's face. "Lester?"

Lester looked up with a scowl, tossing the ticket to the ground before wrapping his fingers around the cigarette. He inhaled, his thin lips puckering around the white stick before blowing a puff of smoke in Mason's face. "What the fuck do you want?"

Mason waved a hand in front of him, trying to get rid of the smoke. "Your daughter is bullying mine."

Lester's scoffing turned into a fit of coughing. "So? Maybe your kid should toughen up."

Mason gritted his teeth and counted to ten before answering. "You need to put a stop to it before I take matters in my own hands."

Lester's eyes narrowed as he stood to his full height, still much shorter than Mason. He threw the cigarette butt onto the ground as his voice rose. "Are you threatening my daughter?"

Mason shook his head. "No, I'm warning you to speak with her before I take this to the school and do everything in my power to have her expelled."

"Go ahead and try! You ugly asshole. Think you can tell me what to do. Who the fuck do you think you are?" Lester screamed, spittle flying out of his mouth as his angry eyes bulged.

A couple of women crossed the street to walk on the other side of the road, eyeing them warily. A father, who'd been window shopping nearby, picked up his child and walked in the opposite direction. A few others stopped and stared.

Mason's back stiffened. He took a step forward, and Lester flinched backwards. *Fucking spineless rat bastard.* "Speak to her, because if anyone hurts my little girl again, there will be problems."

Mason turned and walked away, ignoring Lester's curses. He crossed the road and headed for the bookstore. One confrontation down, one to go.

He pushed open the door to The Oyster Bookstore. Immediately, the smell of books hit his nose, melded with fresh, sweet greenery. His eyes scanned the large sculpture in the center of the room made from hundreds or maybe thousands of pages.

Mason headed straight for the front desk where a man in his mid-twenties sat, focused on the computer screen.

The man glanced up and offered him a friendly smile that wilted as Mason got closer and then returned a tad bigger, as if he needed to overcompensate for his split-second reaction. He was used to those kinds of responses with his injury on display.

"Good afternoon, I'm Troy. Can I help you?"

Mason scanned the area. "Is Pippa in?"

"No, she worked earlier. She's gone home for the day, but I can help."

Mason nodded and headed outside. Thanks to Aspen going on and on about Pippa, he knew just where to go.

He turned left and headed up the stairway to the apartment above the bookstore. Knocking, he took a deep breath, trying to prepare himself to see her again. But it was useless. There was no preparing for the way his body fired awake as her smile greeted him, even if it did drop a few degrees when her eyes widened in surprise.

"Oh. Hello, Mason." She tugged one of her full lips between her teeth.

His hand fisted at his side so he didn't do something stupid like use his thumb to tug it away. "Hey. I wondered if you had a minute to talk?"

She blinked as if that was the last thing she'd expected him to say. "Sure. Come on in." Pippa turned and walked inside. He followed and closed the door. His eyes dropped to Pippa's ass as it swayed, her hips moving side to side.

Something rich and savory filled his nose. "Smells good in here."

He scanned the small kitchen. The cupboards were painted a bright cheery yellow. The walls were white and covered in bright art of all kinds. There was a tiny moveable island with a basket of fruit in the center. A small table with a mason jar filled with wildflowers sat against one of the large bay windows overlooking Main Street with bright, see-through yellow curtains.

Behind him was a small living room with an elegantly styled bookshelf. It was decorated with a few glass globes filled with mini lights, and mice curled up with tiny books by the fire, or on an equally small chair with a cup of tea. A small coffee table was situated by her sofa. Beyond that were French doors leading to another room with the corner of a bed sticking out from where he stood.

Pippa walked over to the stove, using a wooden spoon to stir a pot of yellowish rice. "I'm making arroz con gandules with tostones."

There was enough there to feed an army. "I'm sorry. If you're expecting company, I can come back." *Was it for Ricky?*

She chuckled and shook her head. "No, it's just me. My mom always said that food was better shared. I was never taught how to make a smaller portion, so I still cook with what I know. I usually bring the extra down for my employee."

She feeds Troy?

"Would you like to eat with me?" Pippa reached into a cupboard on her tiptoes to grab a bowl. A sliver of skin showed where her shirt lifted and his cock jerked. Maybe it was time he went out and got laid if an inch of her back was giving him a hard-on.

"Mason?"

"Hmm?"

"Would you like to join me? As long as you don't snap at me again." Her eyebrow rose.

"Right. I'm sorry about that, by the way. But I'll probably grab something from the diner before I head into work."

She grabbed another bowl. "I've made more than enough. Lady's decent company but it would be nice to have another human join me."

Was that loneliness he detected in her voice?

"If you're sure it isn't any trouble." His stomach grumbled as she set the bowls and spoons on the small square table by the window. Apparently, he was hungrier than he'd thought.

She picked a dog dish full of food off the counter and set it on the ground. Lady walked over and started feasting.

"No trouble at all." She took the first seat and motioned across from her.

Mason sat. The savory smells wrapped around him. How long had it been since he'd had a home-cooked meal that he didn't prepare besides on holidays at friends' houses?

"I should have asked if you wanted a drink?" Pippa offered.

"Water would be good. I can get it." He stood.

"The cups are in the cupboard by the fridge."

He opened the first one and saw several prescription pill bottles lined in a row.

"Other one," Pippa directed.

Mason grabbed two glasses. He filled them with tap water and returned to the table, setting Pippa's in front of her.

"Thank you."

He settled back in his seat, digging in and taking the first bite. He groaned as his taste buds exploded. The rich spices in the hearty rice-and-bean mix were warming and comforting.

Pippa grinned. "Good?"

"So good." He took another bite.

"Have you ever had Puerto Rican food before?"

He shook his head. "No. I was in South America once for an op and had some similar dishes, but this is delicious."

"My mother was from Puerto Rico. She'd make this for my sister, Papi, and me every week. Sometimes she'd fry up some yucca with it." Her eyes glittered with the memory but it was tinged in sadness.

"When did your parents move here?" he asked.

"My grandparents immigrated here during the Great Migration from Puerto Rico in the late fifties because of the economy when my mom was only a toddler. My mother learned English in school but spoke to my sister and me only in Spanish. My grandparents died before I was born, but my mother was a proud Boricua." Pippa spoke fondly of her heritage.

"That's neat. I wish we learned more about other parts of our history in school. Aspen asked me about it, and I explained that Puerto Rico is a territory of the United States, but not a state."

Pippa nodded. "Second-class citizens. We can't vote in presidential elections unless we move from the island to the States and reside there. And we don't have any representation in the U.S. congress."

"I hadn't realized that was the case," Mason mused.

Pippa shook her head. "It's unfortunate but true. Anyways, what did you come here to talk about?"

Mason scraped the last bit of the rice from his bowl. He'd devoured it in no time.

"Do you want more? There's plenty."

"No, I'm good." He took a sip of water. He didn't want to eat her out of house and home. He was a big man with a big appetite.

His gaze snagged on the low-cut top she wore, her nipples pressing against the thin fabric. Clearly, she wasn't wearing a bra. Was she turned on?

Pippa's arms crossed over her chest. "Mason?"

Shit, he'd been caught staring. "I'm sorry, what?"

"What did you want to talk to me about?"

"Oh, uh, Aspen."

Pippa nodded. Her brown eyes softened at his daughter's

name. The corners of her mouth quirked up. "She's a special young woman. She mentioned it was just the two of you."

"Yeah." His voice was gruff. Pippa's smile dropped. *Shit.* "Is she . . . intruding on your time?"

Pippa leaned back in her chair, watching him intently. "Not at all. We have a lot in common, actually. My mother passed when I was twelve. And it was just my dad and me for a long time. My sister is ten years older than me, so she was already out of the house."

Mason's chest tightened at the pain in Pippa's eyes as she recounted losing her mother. Maybe that was why she could relate so well with Aspen.

"Your daughter is smart and creative, with a good head on her shoulders and a lot of empathy in her heart. I enjoy our time together . . . Does our friendship bother you?" The corners of her eyes creased in concern.

Mason shook his head. "No. Not at all. I just wanted to make sure she wasn't bothering you. I know you're a lot closer to her age than I am. How old are you, anyways?"

Pippa's eyes narrowed as she sat up a little straighter. "I'm not that young. I'm twenty-six."

Mason was thirty-four. Eight years her senior. She probably viewed him as an old man.

"Aspen seems to feel comfortable talking to you about things. I just wanted to know if I could count on you to let me know if she tells you something that could lead to her getting hurt or being put in danger?"

She tapped one neon-yellow nail onto the table twice. "Aspen adores you. I'm sure she would tell you herself."

"I didn't know who the 3Cs were until I overheard her mention them to you in the café," he admitted.

Her eyes dropped to her near empty bowl, and she nodded before meeting his gaze again. "I'll be sure to tell you if she shares anything that you would need to intervene on, but I won't betray Aspen's trust unless she's in danger."

"It's more the bullies I'm worried about. She told me there was an altercation between those girls and you in the store?"

Pippa sighed and stirred her food. "Yeah. I overheard the main one, Cara, calling Pippa and her friend some derogatory terms for lesbians. When I intervened, they turned that venom on me, and I promptly kicked them out."

His fists clenched. Cara was probably repeating what her father, Lester Marby, had been saying at home. The man was a bigot and had had to be hauled out of The Shipwreck on more than one occasion, drunk and ready for a fight.

Pippa's eyes widened as she leaned back from him as if he were about to blow up at her. That small flash of fear in her gaze was enough to snap him out of the angry red haze. "I'm sorry. I just hate to hear that my little girl had to deal with that."

Her shoulders relaxed as she took another sip of water. "It's okay. I get it. I was also the target of many bullies growing up."

"You were bullied?"

"I was the mixed, plus-size girl with seizures. Couldn't have found an easier target."

His gaze skated down her curves. She was gorgeous— every inch. Those bastards had probably been jealous. "I'm sorry."

She shrugged like it wasn't a big deal. "It's in the past. I know what and who I am."

You're beautiful. He held her gaze. The last thing she needed was an older man telling her that. It would probably make her uncomfortable.

She licked her lips, drawing his attention down. Fuck, he wanted to lean across this table and kiss her.

No.

Mason shot to his feet. "I better get going. Thanks for dinner." He picked up his bowl and silverware.

Pippa's hand touched his. Fire scorched his arm from the connection. She sucked in a sharp breath and pulled the dish from his hand. Did she feel this too? "I've got it. You have a good night at work."

He nodded and headed for the door. Mason opened it and turned back. She was behind him by a few steps.

"Thank you again for everything. You've done a lot for my little girl, and I won't forget it."

Pippa smiled. "It's no more than any other decent person would do."

"I'd say my debt to you is growing."

"Having to not eat dinner alone was nice. Not that I'm keeping track, but I'd say we're even."

Was she that simple to please? Would that be true for her in the bedroom too?

Fuck, I'm too old.

Pippa was something else.

Too bad she was off-limits.

10

PIPPA

Pippa looked past the stack of books on the front desk as a woman entered her shop.

"Good morning. I'm Pippa. Can I help you find something?" Pippa pushed her blue reading glasses farther up her nose.

"Actually yes. I'm wondering if you have this book?" The woman held up a sticky note with a name and author scribbled on it.

"Let me see." Pippa tapped a few keys, searching for the Cannabis-growing title the customer needed. "Looks like I can get it here in the next week. Does that work?"

The woman nodded. "Yeah, that should be fine."

"What's your name?"

"Nova Emerson," she answered.

Pippa's gaze whipped up to her again. "Are you Ricky's sister?"

Nova tipped her head to the side as if studying her more closely. "Yeah."

"Oh, I met him last weekend at The Shipwreck, and he

told me all about the cool stuff you and your family do. Sorry —didn't mean to put you on the spot."

Nova chuckled. "I thought maybe you were one of his crazy hookups."

Pippa shook her head. "Nope. He saved me from drinking alone and I pestered him with questions about working with bees. But the icing on the cake was finding out you got your medical marijuana-growing permit and became a pot farmer. I think that is so cool. I've always wondered . . ."

Nova leaned in. "Yeah?"

"I've heard there are some benefits to using marijuana to control seizures."

Nova smiled. "Absolutely. A few of my clients use it for that. They've had great success. Talk to your doctor and they can get you a card. Here's my contact for when you're ready." Nova handed over a black business card with a pot leaf on one side with her information next to it.

"I think I'll do that." After she'd taken the payment for Nova's book, she waved goodbye.

Aspen came rushing into the store a few minutes later, a huge smile on her face. "Guess what?"

"What?" Pippa asked, joining in on her glee.

"The town youth commission is putting on a midsummer's dance!" Aspen's voice rose a couple octaves.

Lady snorted and stood, sniffing Pippa before licking her hand and sitting back down. Pippa petted her and slipped her a treat. "Good girl." She turned back to Aspen. "That sounds so fun."

Aspen clapped her hands together excitedly. "Dad says I can buy a new dress for it, and I want you to come help me pick it out."

"Me?"

Mason entered the store, his unsure gaze catching Pippa's

as he walked closer. Half his mouth quirked up in greeting. It was cute. It was clear from their conversation the other day that Mason thought of her as a young girl—though the way he'd stared at her double Ds made her doubt he was blind and grumpy. And thirty-four was hardly too old for a twenty-six-year-old. Did he find her attractive too?

"Of course, you. Pleeeeease?" Aspen begged.

Mason put his hand on his daughter's shoulder. "Sweet pea, I said you could ask, not beg. Pippa might have other things to do." He mouthed *sorry* to her.

Pippa stood from behind the desk, tucking her loose curls behind her ear. "When do you need to go shopping?"

"Saturday," Aspen answered.

"Or Sunday. We really don't want to intrude, but I told Aspen she could ask." Mason cleared his throat as if nervous.

"It sounds like fun. I think I can do it—on one condition." She held out her finger.

"Anything!" Aspen rushed.

"You get your dad to buy us lunch." She winked.

"I think I can handle that." Mason's mouth twisted into what she would deem a smirk.

"Saturday it is, then," she agreed.

"Thank you. Thank you. Thank you! I have to go tell David. Can I run over to the High Tide Diner, Dad?"

"Look both ways before you cross the street," he reminded Aspen as she flew out of the shop.

Pippa laughed.

"She's a little excited." Mason chuckled before shaking his head.

"Just a little," she teased.

His aquamarine eyes swirled with some unnamed emotion as his gaze locked on hers. "Thank you for doing this."

She waved her hand. "It's no problem. Sounds like fun,

actually." The alternative was walking to the park with Lady like she did almost every day. Not that it wasn't nice, but she'd love some company and conversation for once.

"Can I get your number? I'll let you know when I'm on my way to pick you up." Mason pulled out his phone.

Heat rose to her cheeks as her belly flipped. Sure, he'd been grumpy, but the dinner they'd shared the other night had been super nice. *I wish he was asking for my number for other reasons.* But it was a start.

She rattled off her number, and a moment later, her phone pinged with an incoming text message.

"Now you have mine." He licked his lips.

God, how good would that beard feel on her thighs? Was it soft or rough?

"I'll pick you up Saturday at one if that works?" Mason asked, interrupting her thoughts.

"Sure," she squeaked, her eyes dragging down his short-sleeved flannel shirt to the black cargo shorts he wore. Was his cock proportionate to his ginormous size?

"Have a good evening," Mason said.

She flicked her gaze back to his, fire scorching her face from her lascivious thoughts. His blue eyes darkened. Was it just her, or was that desire sparking in those cerulean spheres?

11

PIPPA

"Wait here." Mason's deep voice sent a shiver through Pippa. The cab of his truck smelled like him, intoxicating her with a clean, masculine scent. He walked around the front of the truck towards her side.

Aspen sighed in the back seat.

Lady's brown eyes settled on her as the dog laid her head on Pippa's knees. Unease swirled in her belly. *Not here. Not today.*

Pippa reached out and offered Lady her hand. "Check me."

Her door opened. Mason held out a hand to help her down as Lady sniffed her and then licked her, signaling there was no threat of an oncoming seizure.

"Good girl." Pippa scratched behind her ear and slipped her other palm into Mason's. Energy crackled, zipping up her arm. *Is this an aura? Am I going to have a seizure after all?*

She stepped out of the truck, careful to watch her step. Mason kept her steady as she made it to the ground. Lady exited and sat beside her while Mason opened the back door for his daughter.

Aspen shot out of the car, a little blue purse crisscrossing her body. She rolled her eyes. "Do you have to do that every time, Dad? We are perfectly capable of opening our own doors. I am a woman now, you know."

Pippa bit back a smile and flicked her gaze to Mason as he slung his arm over Aspen's shoulders.

"I know that, sweet pea, and that's why I do it—so you know how you should be treated by a future partner."

Damn. If Pippa hadn't been taken with the big warrior before, there was no chance for her now.

They walked towards the mall entrance as Aspen asked, "What if I'm the one who wants to open the doors?"

Pippa giggled. Mason's gaze shot to hers, a flash of humor reflecting back as if to say, *I might be in over my head with this, but I'm doing my best here.*

"When the time comes, you can do that. For now, I got it. Let me enjoy the few years I have left of spoiling you." Mason reached his hand to Aspen's head, bringing her closer so he could kiss her temple. She playfully pushed him away before he opened the main doors for them to walk through. Who said chivalry was dead?

Aspen ran inside and opened the second set of doors, smirking at her father. He just shook his head and walked in after Pippa. It was something to behold, witnessing a giant man's man like Mason being wrapped around such a small girl's finger.

"You two are hilarious," Pippa mused as they headed towards a department store.

Mason's hand brushed against her arm as they entered the outlet, and a shiver cascaded through her. Pippa's brows pulled together as she drew in a sharp breath. Mason's gaze cut to hers before he looked away.

"So, what are we looking for? A specific style or color?" Pippa asked, walking over to a rack of clothes by Aspen.

"Something magical." Aspen beamed.

"And something modest," Mason added.

Aspen rolled her eyes. "Modesty is a patriarchal concept created to keep women subservient to men."

Pippa stopped walking, studying the father-daughter duo as Mason shrugged like this was just any other day and conversation for them.

"True, but it's my job to protect you, and I know that certain clothing will attract unwanted attention." Mason grabbed a long-sleeved, floor-length dress and held it out to Aspen.

Aspen's eyes narrowed as she crossed her arms and shook her head. "That's victim blaming. Women can wear what we want, and no one has the right to touch us without consent." She grabbed a much shorter spaghetti-strapped dress from another rack.

Pippa's eyes volleyed back and forth between the two.

Mason sighed. "Fair enough. You're right. Unfortunately, the world hasn't caught up with those basic concepts of autonomy and consent, so put your dad out of his misery and wear something that doesn't give me a heart attack, or I'll be chaperoning that dance."

Aspen let out a huff of frustration. Pippa remembered being that age when she craved more independence. She could see where Mason was coming from too. They both had valid points, so how could they compromise?

"Well, that's what I'm here for, right? Let's see what we can find that fits all of your criteria," Pippa suggested, taking Lady's leash in one hand and Aspen's hand in the other. She weaved through the store, searching for the elusive perfect dress.

"Is there a theme?"

"Summer Solstice." Aspen picked up a shiny, sequined white dress and then put it back.

"Can I help you?" Mason's voice was no longer light and easygoing, but curt like it had been the first time she'd run into him in the café.

She turned as a thin woman with a name tag shook her head and glanced over to Pippa.

"No need to follow her. We'll let you know if we need anything," Mason said, his message of *get away* clear as day.

His gaze followed the retreating store clerk and then snapped to her. *Was he protecting me?*

She was used to being followed around in stores so much so that sometimes, she avoided going altogether. Having Mason stand up for her made butterflies tumble in her belly and her chest fill with warmth. He nodded to her, not breaking the stare.

"What about this one?" Aspen held up a red mini dress with a cheeky smile as Mason growled. This little girl knew how to press her dad's buttons.

"You know what would look amazing?" Pippa asked, her eye catching on just the one.

"What?" Aspen followed her to a row of green dresses.

Pippa pulled out an emerald-colored velvet dress with lace three-quarter-length sleeves and a V-neck. "This will really make your eyes pop and go fantastically with your hair color."

Aspen smiled and plucked it from her hands. "Can I try it on?"

Pippa pointed towards the changing room signs and followed her, along with Mason. Aspen disappeared into the changing area alone while Pippa took a seat on a bench.

Mason settled beside her, his thigh pressed against hers. Heat bloomed from his touch. Liquid fire spread over her skin. *Get it together.*

"Thank you for coming today," Mason said, his arm stretching out on the bench behind her.

Arousal skittered across her skin like electric lust, gathering in her center. She blew out a breath, trying to calm her raging libido. *He's just a man. He's a single dad. He's not interested.*

Maybe it was time she downloaded a dating app. She needed something, or someone, to help take this edge off.

"I was happy to come . . . She seems very educated."

He smirked, and damn, it did things to her body that not even her vibrator had achieved lately. "I've always encouraged a healthy debate with her. I bought her a bunch of books, hoping to make up for the lack of female influence in her life. She took a strong liking to Gloria Steinem, Malala Yousafzai, Angela Davis, and that other one that gave that TED Talk about how we should all be feminists."

"Chimamanda Ngozi Adichie?"

He nodded. "Yeah. Of course, I wanted to read those books before handing them over so we could discuss them. It's something we seem to do together a couple times a month— or whenever I try to take her shopping." He chuckled.

Pippa joined in. His eyes caught on hers, darkening.

"I think you've done a great job with her," Pippa complimented, tucking a stray lock of hair behind her ear. "I know I said it before, but I mean it. My dad tried, but he wasn't able to really be there for a lot of my formative years." Guilt flashed in her mind, heavy and potent. She didn't want to ruin this beautiful afternoon, so she shoved it aside. It would be there later—it always was.

"That means a lot." Mason's voice softened. His gaze pierced through her as if trying to read her soul.

She blinked away and turned towards the changing room where Aspen was staring at them. The green dress fit to her body, not too tight, and flared out at her waist, stopping just above her knee.

"You look gorgeous!" Pippa grinned.

Mason didn't say anything for a second, so she elbowed him in the ribs.

"Wow. You look beautiful, sweet pea," Mason grated.

Pippa glanced at him. Were those tears in his eyes?

He cleared his throat and stood. "Is this the one?"

Aspen's nervous smile widened as she spun around. "It's perfect. Thank you, Pippa."

Pippa shrugged. "I'm just glad we found one that you both liked."

Aspen disappeared back in the changing room as Mason asked, "So what's next?"

"Now, she probably needs shoes."

"Okay. Then how about we go to Atlantis for dinner?" Mason's gaze burned the side of her face.

Dinner? She'd heard of Atlantis, but she'd never been. It seemed a little fancy. She looked down at the white peasant shirt and the pink shorts she had on. As she pinched the fabric of her top, her eyebrows drew together. She was a little under-dressed, wasn't she?

"What you're wearing is perfect." Mason's voice cut through her inner anxiety, as if he'd read her mind. "I mean, we could always run you home to change if you'd be more comfortable, but it's a casual atmosphere there."

She nodded. "Okay."

"Okay," he parroted, sticking both hands in his front pockets almost as if he were nervous. But that couldn't be true. This was a casual dinner between friends. It wasn't like it was a date. Aspen would be there, and Pippa had joked that they'd have to feed her for her to come shopping, although she'd meant more like mall cafeteria food.

Aspen reemerged from the changing room, handing over her dress to her dad. "Now what?"

Mason nodded to the other side of the store. "Now, we find you some shoes that you won't break your neck in, and then we're taking Pippa to Atlantis as a thank-you for claiming her Saturday."

Aspen's eyes lit up. "I love Atlantis. Have you ever been, Pippa?"

She shook her head. "Nope, but it sounds wonderful."

And so did spending more time with this little family.

Of course, it was just temporary. Mason had enough on his plate, raising a teen girl by himself. He didn't need any more burden. Regardless of the fact that the man had set her body on fire with just a brush of his hand, this would have to stay platonic.

It didn't mean he wouldn't play a starring role in her fantasies tonight.

MASON

Mason picked up his iced tea, wished it were something stronger, and took a swig. He needed a stiff drink to calm his nerves, but he was driving Aspen and Pippa home after this dinner. He couldn't stop staring at the beauty across from him.

Aspen was going on about a comic she was obsessed with, and Pippa gave his daughter her undivided attention. He couldn't complain; it gave him the freedom to study her, memorizing the curves of her face, the slope of her neck and bare shoulders. Her skin glowed in the low lighting of the restaurant. The flicker of a candle in a mason jar in the center of the table made her eyes sparkle.

He took another sip, capturing a piece of ice to chew on this time. He needed something to cool him down. The woman stirred awake parts of him that had been in hibernation for over a decade and inspired the discovery of a few more. *Bet she tastes as good as she smells—like sweet cherry pie.*

"Hey, Mase." Jasmine's voice interrupted his lustful thoughts.

He turned and took in the very pregnant co-owner of Atlantis.

Her boyfriend and the chef of the restaurant, Atlas, wrapped his arm around her waist and offered Mason a smile. "Hey, guys."

"How's it going?" Mason asked.

"Pretty good. Are you all enjoying the meal?" Atlas asked.

"It's so good," Aspen supplied as Mason nodded.

"Well, I'll have your server bring out a new dessert we're trying. Think you guys could give me some feedback in exchange for some free treats?" Atlas smiled.

"I think we could sacrifice a little more room, as long as you send out a few slices of that famous chocolate peanut butter cheesecake too." Ever since he'd overheard Aspen mention how much Pippa loved Reese's, he'd wanted to bring her some of this dessert.

Atlas chuckled. "Alright. It's a deal."

Jasmine turned to Pippa. "Is drag queen story hour happening this week? Zoey's been asking when we can go again. She loves Marsha Divine."

Pippa smiled, her eyes lighting up. "Yes. Friday at two."

"We'll be there. You guys enjoy the rest of your meal," Jasmine said before she and Atlas waved goodbye.

Pippa petted Lady's head by her side.

"So, what made you want to open your own bookstore?" Mason asked.

Aspen listened in with interest. Her attention hadn't gone far from Pippa since they'd picked her up that afternoon.

Pippa wiped her hands on a napkin and cleared her throat. "Well, when I was a little girl, I was stuck in hospitals for a very long time."

"Because of your epilepsy?" Aspen asked.

"Sort of. Epilepsy is more a symptom. I had a tumor on

my brain that they discovered when I was seven. I had surgery to remove it." Pippa touched the top of her head. "And for a little while, it worked."

Mason's chest squeezed tight. He couldn't imagine Aspen going through something like that. Brain surgery at seven? Pippa's parents must have been beside themselves.

"But?" Aspen prodded.

"The scar tissue caused some more problems and it got worse for a while." Pippa's gaze clouded over as she looked towards the other patrons in the restaurant.

"That sounds scary," Aspen added.

Pippa gave her a forced smile and nodded. "It was. But eventually I got on some medications that help control it as much as possible. And I have Lady here to watch out for me."

That's all? If Pippa were his, he wouldn't let her out of his sight.

But she's not mine.

So why did he feel this need to protect her?

"Anyways, my whole world was spent between the pages of books. Sometimes reading set off seizures, so I switched to audio books. But literature has always been a source of escape and calm for me." She straightened, passion entering her tone. "I wanted to spend my time doing something that made me happy. Books change lives. They educate and they help people connect in ways they might not otherwise have. I decided I wanted to run a shop that spread love and acceptance regardless of age, race, sexual orientation, gender identity, religion, ability, or what have you." Pippa's smile was blinding, yet he couldn't look away.

She shrugged, the clouds back in her gaze. "I know I might not be able to change the world, but maybe I can alter a few minds. I've carved out my own little corner where I can do something useful."

"Sounds pretty amazing to me." Mason's voice came out raspy.

Pippa searched his eyes as if seeking something.

"Do you have to be careful of flashing lights? I saw that in a movie once," Aspen said.

Pippa shook her head. "No, I'm not photosensitive. Only about three percent of people with epilepsy are. I have different triggers."

"Like what?" Aspen prodded.

"Aspen," Mason warned.

Pippa offered him a reassuring smile. "It's okay. I don't mind talking about it."

He nodded and finished his lobster.

"Stress is a big trigger for me, which is probably why I had a tonic-clonic seizure after the pharmacy."

"That's the big one, right?" Aspen confirmed.

Pippa nodded. "Hormones can trigger them, especially around my period if I don't get good sleep or forget to take my medications on time."

"But your medicine helps?" Aspen asked, concern evident in her voice. She'd gotten so attached to Pippa in such a short period of time.

Pippa placed her hand over his daughter's as if to comfort her. "It sure does. And Lady here lets me know when one is coming on, so I can usually get into as safe a position as possible."

It was the *usually* that twisted Mason's stomach into knots. So much could happen to her, especially living all alone.

"So, what about you? Navy SEALs and now security?" Pippa turned the conversation onto him.

He sat back in his chair. "Joined out of high school. Served in the Navy for four years and then served as a SEAL for just a couple years until . . ." *Until my wife was murdered.*

"Well, after it was just Aspen and me, I finished my contract and got out. I work at the bar mainly, but I do some private jobs on the side too."

"Like as a bodyguard?" Pippa asked, her eyes lighting up.

"Sometimes."

"Anyone famous?" She leaned forward, seeming keenly interested.

He smirked. "Maybe."

"So secretive. I bet he told you." She nudged Aspen, including her in the conversation, and it did something to his chest.

Aspen giggled. "Not even me."

Both ladies' eyes were on his again as their server returned with a tray of desserts.

Mason shrugged. "I signed an NDA, and I take my commitments seriously."

That was another reason he'd avoided relationships. He couldn't talk about his work sometimes. His wife had understood as a former Army veteran, but secrecy was hard to be patient about. His numerous divorced military buddies were living proof.

"Are you ready for dessert?" the server asked them, clearing their empty plates and setting them on her tray.

"Yes, thank you." Pippa lifted her dinner plate towards the woman's outstretched hand. Mason nodded.

The server replaced them with three dishes with peanut butter chocolate cheesecake along with fried disks of dough sprinkled with powdered sugar.

The server motioned to the latter. "Atlas told me to tell you these are hotteoks, a sweet Korean pancake filled with some brown sugar and a mixture of seeds and nuts."

"Thanks," Mason said. The server nodded and disappeared.

They each took one of the pancakes. Aspen studied hers, turning it in her hands and inspecting it like she was a food critic before giving it the smallest lick. Pippa's white teeth took the smallest bite of the dessert before she chewed. Mason's eyes locked on to her mouth. A small dusting of powdered sugar crested her upper lip. She swiped her pink tongue over it. Damn if he didn't want to taste it off her himself.

"I taste cinnamon," she said before taking another bite.

Aspen finally tasted it. Her eyes widened. "This is really good."

Two sets of eyes stared back at him. He opened his mouth wide and took a big bite. The dough was savory with a dash of salt, balancing out the nutty, sweet center.

"Ten out of ten for me." Pippa put the other half back on the plate.

"Not going to finish it?" Mason asked.

She shook her head. "Saving room for this cheesecake." She grabbed a fork and cut a bite-sized piece before slipping it between her lips. Her eyes rolled up, and for a moment, panic gripped his chest. But the moan of appreciation rumbling from her chest had his cock jerking to life once again.

"That good?" His voice came out strained.

Pippa grinned. "This is my favorite. Hands down. Nothing is better than peanut butter and chocolate, except peanut butter chocolate cheesecake. You might have created a monster, bringing me here. Now I'll be craving this all the time."

"Guess we'll just have to do this again, then." The words slipped from his mouth, exploding like an IED between them.

Tension thickened, making it hard to draw in a full breath.

She swallowed and locked her amber orbs on his, blinking twice. "That would be fun."

He shouldn't want her. She was a lot younger. He came

with a ton of baggage, and a kid, but his body didn't get that memo, if the steel rod in his shorts were any indication. He fought the urge to say more.

On the drive to her home, it took all his self-control to not reach over and take her hand in his as Aspen talked their ears off.

"Can you help me with my hair for the dance?" Aspen asked.

Pippa turned to Mason as if asking his permission, her eyes wide. "Oh, I wouldn't want to intrude on your special night."

"Please? Tell her it's okay, Dad," Aspen pressed.

Mason focused on the road ahead of him. "It's fine with me. Saves me from attempting another YouTube tutorial on how to do a chignon."

Pippa tipped her head to the side as if looking at him in a new angle, like he'd surprised her.

"So, what's your answer?" Aspen asked, her voice giddy with hopeful excitement.

"I think that would be fun."

"Yay! I'm gonna see if Rachel and David want to come over and get ready too."

"We could have some snacks," Pippa offered.

"It would be like a mini party before the dance. Oh my God, it's gonna be so fun!" Aspen squealed.

What have I signed up for now? How had one invite turned into a party? Tweens and their moms at his house getting ready for a dance, sounded like pure torture.

Mason flicked his attention to the beauty beside him. Maybe that made him a masochist, because he was looking forward to spending more time with Pippa—in any capacity.

Mason pulled up to the curb in front of the bookstore, then got out and walked around to open her door for her. Pippa said goodbye to Aspen, and gave Mason one last lingering glance before she climbed out.

He ground his teeth hard when she slipped from the car, her dog right behind her. Cherry fragrance permeated every breath he managed to suck in as she brushed against him and thanked him for dinner. His hands fisted at his sides, itching to touch her just one more time. But if he gave in, he'd cross a line neither of them should.

Instead, he got back in the driver's side of his truck, his gaze following the most perfect ass he'd ever seen until she disappeared into her apartment.

He drove home where a cold shower, his hand, and fantasies of a sexy bookstore owner who tasted like cherry pie would consume him.

If only that would be enough.

13

PIPPA

Pippa hefted her cosmetics bag from the back of Mason's truck.

"I didn't realize getting ready for a dance required so much . . . stuff." Mason's deep voice came up behind her as he grabbed the other two canvas bags.

Maybe I overdid it? When Aspen had asked if Pippa would help her get ready, Pippa might have gone a little overboard on a Pinterest search for ideas. It was going to be a mini party alright. She wanted to make this night special for Aspen. She wanted to give that young girl the world.

"I'm sorry." Her stomach clenched in embarrassment. *Here I go again, inserting myself where I don't belong.*

Mason turned to her, his hands full of makeup and hair supplies in sealed packages, and cartons of food she'd brought. "No, it's fine. I just didn't expect you to get this for my kid and her friends. Let me pay you back."

She waved her hand and followed him inside his house. "It's really not a big deal." She wouldn't tell him the appetizers were all homemade.

He led her into the kitchen and set down the bags. Lady's nails clicked across the wood floor as she followed them. Mason grabbed a bowl from his cupboard and filled it with tap water before setting it on the ground for her dog. It was a sweet gesture.

"Thank you."

His gaze dragged from her to the counter. "So, what do you need me to do?"

"Dad?" Aspen's voice called from the front of the house.

"In here," Mason answered.

Aspen ran in with her friend David. She wrapped her arms around Pippa and squeezed. "Pippa! I'm so excited for the dance."

"I can see that." Pippa grinned. The young girl's enthusiasm was infectious.

David's mom walked in, staying farther back. She met Pippa's gaze and turned her hand in a muted wave.

"Brynn, this is Pippa. She owns the bookstore. She's offered to do Aspen's hair and makeup for the dance," Mason introduced them.

Pippa offered her hand to the woman. "Nice to meet you officially. You work at the diner, right?"

"Yes." Brynn's voice was sweet and subdued.

"I'm going to show David my dress." Aspen grabbed her friend's hand and pulled him upstairs.

Brynn's gaze flicked to the bags on the counter. "Do you need any help?"

Ding-dong.

"That's probably Rachel and her mom," Mason said, before disappearing out of the kitchen.

"I'd love some help. Can you help me find a pitcher? We can mix the orange juice and Sprite, like virgin mimosas. I thought it would be fun for the kids," Pippa instructed.

Brynn hesitated, seemingly unsure. She tucked her short brown hair behind her ear, keeping her eyes directed at the floor. Every time Pippa saw the woman, it was as if she tried to fade into the background like a little scared mouse.

"Actually, how about you start uncovering the appetizers in the bags?" Pippa asked. Perhaps a smaller task would make her feel more comfortable.

Brynn nodded and went to work while Pippa opened three cupboards before she found what she was looking for. She pulled out the plastic pitcher and filled it up, adding the drink mix.

Mason returned, his eyes darting to the spread on the counter. She'd made a simple cheese and cracker board, one with veggies and dip, and a little something from her own culture: pionono.

"Wow, something smells delicious," the woman beside him said, setting down a platter of cookies with M&M's next to her spread. "You've really put a lot into this little party." She pressed her hand to Mason's back.

The act seemed so intimate. Pippa's body flushed with jealousy. Were Rachel's mom and Mason seeing each other? Her gaze flicked to the woman's bare left hand. Pippa shouldn't care, but the sick twist in her gut was impossible to control.

"Pippa did all this." Mason's gaze was blank.

Is he pissed? "Brynn helped." Pippa forced a smile.

"Pippa, this is Sandra, Rachel's mom," Mason introduced them.

"Nice to meet you." Pippa nodded with what she hoped was a friendly smile.

"What are these? Quiche?" Sandra asked, pointing to the savory appetizer Pippa had spent all morning on.

"Pionono. It's fried plantain stuffed with ground beef,

veggies, and some spices, and topped with scrambled egg. It's sweet and savory with a little kick from the cayenne," Pippa explained. They were one of her favorite appetizers.

Sandra made a sour face. "Oh, dear, can't have those. Trying to watch my figure. Sounds like a lot of carbs." She pressed her body closer to Mason, her elbow rubbing against his.

Was this the type of woman Mason went for? She did resemble his wife from the picture in the hallway. Both women were tall and willowy—and Pippa wasn't.

She swallowed the jealousy burning the back of her throat. "Well, I better head up and start Aspen's hair." Pippa grabbed the two bags that were left. "Come on, Lady."

Brynn silently followed her and the dog upstairs. Pippa tried not to think about Mason and Sandra alone. He wasn't Pippa's, and the sooner she accepted that fact, the better.

"Is David as excited about this dance as Aspen?" Pippa asked.

Brynn's lips quirked up at the edges. "Almost."

She followed the giggles to an open bedroom door with Aspen's name hanging on it in wooden turquoise letters.

"What do you think?" Aspen asked as the women entered. She spun, her dress flaring as she turned. The white sandals they'd picked matched perfectly.

"You look gorgeous." Pippa smiled.

David's gaze lingered on Aspen's dress almost longingly, as if he, too, wanted to wear it.

Brynn walked over and straightened his pink tie before running her hand through his shaggy dirty-blond hair.

"My mom took me to the salon this morning to get my hair done," Rachel announced, pressing one of the gems threaded into her hair. "They used so much hair spray, I think it's permanent."

"Pippa is going to do mine." Aspen smiled. "Ready?"

"Absolutely." Pippa got to work, setting up a little hair-styling station.

"I want gold nails. What do you think?" Aspen asked, holding up a bottle of nail polish from Pippa's stash.

"Definitely," David agreed.

"Do you want some pink to match your tie?" Aspen asked him.

His gaze cut to his mom's. Brynn offered him a reassuring smile.

"Sh-sure." David's cheeks blushed pink as he smiled shyly.

Rachel's nails had also been done at the salon, so she helped David and Aspen with theirs. Soon, all three kids were giggling and chatting about friends and the upcoming dance.

"Would you mind helping me?" Pippa asked, trying to draw Brynn into conversation. There was something so lonely in the woman's eyes.

Brynn walked over. "What do you need?"

Pippa walked her through the process. They curled Aspen's hair, pulling her reddish-blond locks into a fancy crown braid with a few ringlets left in front.

Pippa glanced at the woman from time to time. Brynn was about the same height as Pippa, but thin, as if a strong wind might blow her over. And there was a whole host of fractured pain in her gaze—like the woman had lived through hell and survived to tell about it.

When they'd finished, Brynn's gaze met hers, and Pippa smiled. "Thanks for your help."

Brynn's lips turned up at the edges before she sat cross-legged on the rug, leaning against Aspen's dresser.

Pippa joined her while the teens got busy finishing up their nails.

Brynn turned to her, her green eyes shining with gratitude.

"I wanted to thank you for everything you do at the bookstore. It's nice for David to have a spot where he feels accepted and safe."

"Oh?" Pippa turned to gaze at the young man as Aspen brushed some light eye shadow on his eyelids. "I'm glad he finds comfort in my bookstore. Is he interested in drag or just experimenting with his style?"

"I think he's still figuring it out. I'm glad that there are some people here who make him feel welcome." A flash of pain streaked through Brynn's gaze.

"How long have you lived in Shattered Cove?" Pippa asked.

"A couple years."

"Me too. So far, it seems as a whole, the town is very accepting. Of course, nowhere is perfect. But I can see myself settling down here for good. That's one of the reasons I bought my bookstore in Shattered Cove." Pippa waved her hand to the side.

Brynn nodded as Aspen approached them. "All done."

Pippa stood, pulled the box from her things on the bed, and handed it over to Aspen.

"What's this?" Aspen opened the box and gasped. The gold crown was decorated with clear stones that sparkled in the light of the room.

"It's so perfect!" Aspen wrapped her arms around Pippa's neck and squeezed.

"This is from my *quinceañera*. I thought maybe you'd like to use it tonight?" Pippa explained.

"What's a *quinceañera*?" Aspen asked.

"It's sort of like a huge birthday party that celebrates a girl's passage into womanhood. It was just sitting in my closet, so I figured I'd bring it along in case you wanted to wear it.

Make some good memories with such a beautiful crown that never got its celebration." Pippa hugged her back. "Shall I?"

Aspen handed her the accessory, and Pippa placed it on her head and adjusted her hair. Pippa held up a small mirror.

Aspen's eyes widened, and her mouth split into the biggest smile. "I feel like a queen."

"You are a queen." Pippa winked.

"How about some makeup?" Aspen smirked.

"Alright. Sit back down."

"Can you give me some colorful braids like yours someday?" Aspen asked as Pippa brushed some blush on her cheeks.

"Sure. We can use the colored weave or even yarn." Pippa added some light mascara and a gold shimmer of eye shadow. "All done."

Aspen got up and walked to the mirror hanging on her closet door. "I can't believe that's me."

"You look amazing," David commented.

"So beautiful, sweetheart," Brynn agreed.

"I love that dress." Rachel pinched the fabric between her fingers. Her stomach growled, and the kids laughed. "I'm starving, and my mom wouldn't let us stop for food."

"There are some snacks downstairs." Pippa started picking up her tools and makeup.

Brynn followed Rachel and David downstairs, leaving Aspen and Pippa alone.

Aspen pulled out a small velvet jewelry box from her desk drawer and handed it over to Pippa. "I got you something for all your help."

Pippa accepted it. "That's so sweet of you. You really didn't have to."

Aspen shrugged. "My uncle Sebastian always said it's

important to let the people we care about know how much they mean to us. I'm really glad you're my friend, Pippa."

Pippa's eyes grew blurry before she blinked away tears. Unable to speak, she opened the box revealing a gold necklace with half of a heart with the word *Best* inscribed on it.

"Oh my goddess." She pressed her hand to her chest.

Aspen pulled out a second necklace, the other half with *Friends* inscribed on it. "Would you help me put mine on?"

"Absolutely, sweetheart. I can't tell you how special this is. Thank you *so* much." Pippa gave her another hug before putting the necklace on each of them.

"Can we get a picture together?" Aspen asked, holding up a Polaroid camera.

"Definitely." Pippa held it out, and snapped their selfie. "Now a silly face."

Pippa stuck her tongue out and Aspen growled. They both laughed as Pippa set the photos on her desk to develop.

"Ready to go show your dad?" Pippa asked.

"Yes. But if he says it's too much makeup, you gotta back me up because us women need to stand together, okay?" Aspen held out her hand for Pippa's.

Pippa chuckled and slipped her palm into the young woman's. "Don't ever change, Aspen."

14

MASON

Mason took a bite of the appetizer Pippa had made to buy himself some time to respond to Sandra's question. He groaned. The food was so good. Flavors burst in his mouth. Pippa could *cook*.

"Does Saturday morning work for you?" Sandra asked.

The woman hadn't stopped talking about her ex-husband or her fitness regimen. She'd been hinting at a date for months.

"Not really."

"Oh, well maybe—"

"Mom, I'm hungry," Rachel blessedly interrupted them.

Sandra motioned to the food on the kitchen island. David and Brynn were right behind her. The kids dug into the snacks like there was no tomorrow.

"I'm gonna see if Aspen needs anything," Mason excused himself and headed toward the stairs.

Giggles filtered down to him. He wasn't used to so many people being in his home. But Aspen had begged to make this an event. And when she'd asked if Pippa could join in, he'd gotten excited about the prospect of her in his house again. When Pippa was around, it was like someone breathed life into a long-forgotten part of him. He'd been struck dumb when he walked into the kitchen at the image of such a gorgeous woman making herself at home in his house. But why would a young, beautiful woman like her settle for a damaged man like him?

"Daddy?"

Mason jerked his attention to the top of the stairs and halted his steps. Shock and awe beat his chest like a battering ram. Aspen stood at the top, her emerald-green dress flowing around her knees and making her look so sophisticated and grown up. Her hair seemed even more red, accented by the color of the dress, and was twisted into some sort of fancy braid with a crown sparkling on her head. She seemed so elegant, and much older than thirteen. When did his baby girl become this . . . stunning young woman?

"I think he likes it," Pippa teased from behind his daughter.

Mason swiped at the tears in his eyes before they could fall and cleared his throat. "You look beautiful, sweet pea. Breath-taking." He grinned. "In fact, maybe you should stay home." He walked the rest of the way upstairs.

"Daaaaad," Aspen whined.

He chuckled. "Give me a hug." His eyes caught on the gold necklace he'd purchased. She'd wanted to get a cheap version, but once Aspen had shared it was for her and Pippa, he'd forked over the cash for the real deal.

Aspen walked into his embrace. He leaned down and kissed her forehead before brushing his thumb over the sparkly crown. When had she gotten that?

"Pippa loaned it to me."

"I need a picture." He pulled out his phone.

"I want one with you." Aspen's big blue eyes looked up at him. He hated being in photos. But he'd do anything for her.

Pippa opened her palm. "Would you like me to take it?"

He handed the camera over and wrapped his arm around his daughter. He smiled, knowing it would come out as more of a grimace with only half his mouth turning up.

"Got it." Pippa handed it back.

"Now one with all three of us," Aspen said, pulling Pippa's hand towards Mason. Her gaze quickly flicked up to him, and then she stood beside his daughter. Mason had no choice but to wrap his arm around her shoulders and hold the phone out to capture all three of their faces. Tingles raced up his limbs as her sweet, fruity scent filled his nose.

"Say cheese," Mason joked.

He snapped a couple of photos and straightened. He slipped the cell into his back pocket without even looking at the images.

"This is the best night ever!" Aspen exclaimed, hurrying down to meet her friends.

Sandra drove Rachel and Aspen to the dance and promised to return his daughter safe and sound. Brynn left at the same time with David to catch the bus. Mason was surprised she'd even come. Usually, the woman didn't come within ten feet of him.

When Pippa returned from walking Lady, he helped load her things into the truck and opened her door before getting in on his side. He pulled onto the road. So many thoughts were reeling through his mind—like lists of why he had to control this visceral urge to reach out and touch her.

After several minutes of silence, he cleared his throat and cracked the window, trying to get a hold of himself.

"I'm sorry if it was too much." Pippa's voice sounded small.

His gaze cut to hers and then back to the asphalt in front of him. "It was perfect. More than I ever expected."

"Sometimes I can get carried away with Pinterest." She gave a self-deprecating laugh.

"I just don't want to take advantage of your kindness." He parked in front of the store.

She smiled. Her pink lips glistened. "I had fun tonight. Thanks for including me."

He nodded, scrambling out of the car before he did something stupid like lean over and kiss her.

He opened her door and reached out his hand to help her. Pippa's warm palm slid into his, igniting a blaze of lust. She stumbled, lurching forward, and he caught her in his arms. Her body pressed against his as their eyes locked. Electricity flashed, potent and powerful in his veins. Lust and desire swirled into a boiling frenzy. She licked her lips, her hot breath against his mouth nothing but pure temptation. All the reasons kissing her was a bad idea flew out the window. Any thread of control he'd grasped broke the second Pippa's golden-brown orbs glowed with arousal as she tipped her head towards him.

His mouth crashed against hers, hungry and needy. He swallowed her sharp gasp as a growl rumbled in his chest. Something possessive and heady filled him as his hands gripped her face. She gripped his arm. An explosion of raw unfiltered need rippled through his chest. Her lips parted and he slipped his tongue inside, tasting her. Fucking sweet as cherry pie. Her teeth dragged against his bottom lip, making his cock jerk. He pressed his hips against her as she whimpered.

Barking filled his ears. Tearing himself away from Pippa,

his eyes widened in horror. Her hooded gaze studied him as she licked her kiss-swollen shiny lips.

Fuck. Have I nearly caused her to have a seizure? What had he done?

"I-I didn't mean to . . . Shit, I'm sorry."

Confusion morphed to hurt in her eyes before she grabbed her bag and Lady's leash. She brushed past him and power-walked up her steps.

Everything in his body screamed to go after her. But what good would that do? Aspen was his priority and he couldn't afford any distractions. What could he bring to her life but baggage?

She was friends with Aspen. If he started something with her, when Pippa realized Mason couldn't give her what she needed—that he wasn't enough—Aspen would be without the woman she'd come to idolize over the past month.

"Fuck!"

15

PIPPA

Pippa played with the gold necklace that Aspen had gifted her as she sat back in the window seat. She had books to stack, but she just couldn't find the energy. She was always fatigued the first couple days of her cycle.

Her gaze settled on her cell phone in her lap. It had been two weeks since Mason had kissed her and she hadn't seen him nor heard from him. Fresh hurt flashed in her chest. *Was I that bad of a kisser?* Because, damn, she'd never been so completely captured by a set of lips before. He'd lit her body on fire. *And then he apologized as if it were all a mistake.*

Disappointment wound heavily on her shoulders, drawing them down. "He has enough responsibilities. He doesn't need to add me too," she said to the empty room.

Ring. Ring.

Pippa jolted as *Papi* flashed on her screen. She pressed accept. "Papi?"

"Hey, baby girl. How are you doing?" Her father's voice filtered through the phone.

"Pretty good." She absently pet Lady's head. "How about you?"

"I'm alright. Can't complain."

"Where are you and the big rig now?" Pippa smiled, imagining him in his giant truck, driving down the highway.

"Arizona today. It's hot as hell here." He chuckled.

"You should splurge on a motel with a pool, then."

"I might do that. So, how's the shop going? Selling a lot of books?" Her father coughed in the background.

"Sure am."

"And how's your seizures?"

Pippa rolled her eyes and let out a breath of frustration. Their conversations always turned to her health. "I'm good. Just the normal amount."

"Absence or tonic?"

"Yes."

"Both? What about—"

"I'm fine, Papi. Really. I'm doing everything I'm supposed to, and Lady has alerted me every single time." She hated that her father still worried so much, even thousands of miles away. Her moving out had enabled him to start really living, and she wouldn't take that from him again—not after all he'd sacrificed for her.

An image of him in a suit and tie dancing with her mother in the kitchen before he went to work at the bank flashed in her mind. It was a bittersweet memory that reminded her of all her parents had had and then lost. He'd never work in a bank again with his felony conviction. *Thanks to me.*

"Alright. I was thinking of coming to visit you one of these days. Maybe next month. I've got some vacation time saved up. Perhaps me and your sister and Vivian could come together to visit." The sound of cars zooming by in the distance filtered through the phone.

"I look forward to it." She'd love to get an actual hug from her dad and see her sister and her fiancée to congratulate them in person.

"Okay, well, I'll let you know. Gotta get back on the road, *princessa*. Love you."

"Love you too." She ended the call as the book shop door opened and Aspen darted inside.

Pippa might not have seen any trace of Mason, but Aspen had become a regular. Twice a week, she'd drop in with her friends and they'd huddle over the newest episode of the comic they loved. Today, Aspen was alone, her shoulders hunched as she grabbed a book from her bag and curled up in a sunny spot on a beanbag by the other window.

Pippa placed her phone in her pocket. She stood and walked over to the desk, picking a mini Twix from the pile of chocolate she hid behind it. She walked over to the young girl and handed her the candy.

Aspen glanced up and smiled, some of her invisible weight seeming to lift as she accepted the treat.

"Thought you looked like you could use something sweet." Pippa sat on the floor beside her and crossed her legs before leaning against a wall painted with a rainbow and a cheery quote.

Aspen closed the book and toyed with the chocolate wrapper, her eyes drawing down.

"What's up?" Pippa asked, concern twisting her belly in knots.

"Is it a lie if you just don't tell someone something?" Aspen tucked a strand of her reddish-blond hair behind her ear.

Pippa took a deep breath and exhaled before answering, "I believe that is considered a lie by omission. But it really depends on the situation."

Aspen bit her lip and looked at Pippa. "I think I lied to my dad, then."

Okay. This is a little awkward. "Oh?"

Aspen nodded. "I told him the dance was great. And it was until the 3Cs showed up."

Pippa leaned in, her brows drawn together. "Did they do something?"

"Rachel and I were dancing and having fun while David went to go get a drink. Cara, Christie, and Crystal came up and started saying mean things again. Rachel's kind of been avoiding me ever since." Aspen took a deep breath. "And today, she told me it's because she doesn't want anyone thinking she likes girls."

Pippa's heart broke for the young woman. She moved forward and wrapped her arms around Aspen, giving her a hug. "Now you listen to me. There is nothing wrong with someone attracted to the same sex. You can't help who you fall for. But I know you and Rachel are just friends. Those bullies have no right to target you like this." Pippa pulled back, cupping Aspen's face in her hands as she locked eyes with her. "There is nothing wrong with you. They are the ones with the issue. They must feel so insecure about themselves or angry about their lives and they are choosing to take it out on you. That's on them. You are perfect. You hear me?"

Aspen's eyes grew watery as she nodded.

"I have some experience dealing with these types of people. It's best to stand up to them. And to tell someone who can help that you trust, like your dad. I think you should share this with him."

Aspen rolled her eyes. "I told him about the soccer thing, and he made a scene in town. Cara's dad started yelling at him and everyone was staring. It's all they were talking about at school for two days. It just made it worse. Now when they see me, they bump into me on purpose or shove me."

Pippa sighed and dropped her hands to take Aspen's. "I wish there was a magic fix for this."

"I miss my friend." Aspen sniffed.

Pippa touched the half-heart necklace Aspen had given her. "You know, I've learned that the people who really love you will make an effort to stay in your life. If they don't, it's their loss. Because you are a special, smart, and talented young woman. I am honored to have met you."

Aspen smiled. "You mean that?"

"Every word . . . Can you make me a promise?"

Aspen swiped her tears away. "Sure."

"Promise me you'll tell your dad about what the 3Cs are doing. This abuse needs to stop, and he's in the best position to help you."

Aspen drew in a long breath and let it out before she nodded. "Alright."

"Good afternoon," Troy interrupted them with a grin.

"Hey." Pippa waved and offered him a smile. "There's a box of books that can be shelved behind the desk. Other than that, it's just the usual. I'll have my phone if you need me and I'll be back to lock up at six."

"Sounds good. Enjoy the rest of your afternoon." Troy gave Aspen a wave before he headed to the front desk as a few people entered the store.

Pippa turned back to Aspen. "You like that book?"

Aspen pressed her hand to the cover. "Yeah. It's—"

Lady barked.

"Aspen, you were supposed to meet me in the café twenty minutes ago." Mason's deep voice was short, making both Pippa and Aspen flinch.

Aspen scrambled to her feet and Pippa stood. The young

girl wasn't going to tell him anything if he used that tone. "It's my fault. We got caught up chatting," Pippa said.

Mason wouldn't even look at her. Instead, he focused on his daughter. "Let's go."

Don't I deserve some acknowledgement? He's the one who kissed me, damn it!

"Oh, what a cute dog. Hello, sweetie." A woman's voice drew Pippa's attention as the stranger reached out to pet Lady, who was wearing her vest that clearly stated *Do not pet or interact with me.*

Pippa held up her hand as a young man she recognized as Peter, from the church, stepped out from behind a stack of books. "No, please don't touch her."

"Oh, but she's so precious. Hey, girl." The woman's voice changed as if she were talking to a baby, and Lady's ears perked up, the dog's gaze on the woman.

Pippa reached for the leash. "I said—"

Ringing filled her ears as Mason stepped closer, making it seem like the walls were closing in. Everyone was too close.

He spoke. She couldn't make out the words; it sounded as if he were in a wind tunnel. Her face flushed, as if a hot towel had been wrapped around her head fresh from the dryer.

Oh no. Not again.

16

MASON

Mason's eyes darted to Pippa as she stopped talking mid-sentence. Her empty gaze stared ahead before her eyes rolled up. He gently pressed his hand to her shoulder. He'd seen these types of seizures before. If he wasn't gentle enough, she might become combative in this state.

Mason inserted himself between her and the woman, drawing her closer.

"Back the fuck off," Mason snapped at the woman who clearly hadn't listened to Pippa. The woman's eyes widened as she recoiled.

Lady's attention focused back on her owner. She whined and barked, pressing her nose into Pippa's thigh.

"I got her, girl." Mason kept a watchful gaze on Pippa. Her cheek twitched before she started walking forward. Mason kept his arm around her, ready to support her if she fell. His voice softened as he spoke to her. Pippa's sweet scent rocketed him back to the last time she'd been in his embrace. "I got you, baby. You're okay."

"What's wrong with Pippa?" Aspen asked.

"It's another seizure, sweetheart."

"But she's standing."

Pippa's eyes focused straight ahead once more. Mason led her over to a chair. "Aspen, ask Troy if he has a Gatorade for Pippa."

"She's got some here." Aspen disappeared around the corner as Mason returned his watchful gaze on Pippa.

He got her seated and asked, "You okay, Pippa?"

She blinked as if confused and nodded.

Aspen returned with a bottle of red liquid and the man from behind the front desk.

"Is she okay?" Troy asked, his face going a little pale.

Mason ignored him and asked Pippa, "What's your name?"

Pippa blinked and shook her head. "Why are you asking me that?"

"You had another seizure." Her gaze met his, confusion and something that looked a lot like annoyance flashed in her amber eyes.

"Follow my finger," he instructed as he moved it from side to side.

"I'm good," Pippa refused, her lips pursing as she focused on her lap.

Aspen set the drink in front of her.

"Thank you." Pippa twisted off the top and took a sip before standing.

Mason held her elbow. "You sure you don't want to rest a while longer?"

She shook her head. "Nope. I'm gonna take Lady out. She probably needs to do her business. Sorry for the spectacle." She glanced around to Troy, Aspen, the two patrons, and lastly, him. Hurt clouded her eyes.

"Let me help. I can take her out while you sit here and have a little more time to recover." Mason reached for the leash, but Pippa pulled away and shook her head. "No, it's fine. I wouldn't want to trouble you any more than I have. Seems like you were running late as it was." Pippa led the dog to the front door and disappeared around the corner.

Fuck. She was pissed and had every right to be. *I'm an idiot.*

"Is Pippa going to be okay?" Aspen's worried voice asked.

"Yeah, sweetie."

"Will I ever get seizures? Are they contagious?" Aspen tucked closer against him.

He smoothed one of his palms over her back, trying to comfort her as he led her outside. "No. They are not contagious. Remember, Pippa had a brain injury that causes her epilepsy. You don't have one, so you don't need to worry about it."

"Why didn't she fall and shake like she did last time?" Aspen asked as he opened the passenger-side door of his truck.

"There are different types of seizures. The first one you saw was one of the bigger ones. I don't remember what they're called, but most seizures don't look like that."

"Tonic-clonics," Aspen supplied.

"Right. Maybe it would help you if I showed you what to do if it happens to her and you're alone with her?"

"Yes," she agreed before he shut the door and walked around the truck.

He'd barely climbed in before she asked, "Do people die from seizures?"

His chest squeezed. He'd never taken to lying to his daughter. "Yes, but it's extremely rare."

"I don't want Pippa to die." Aspen looked up at him with her sad big blue eyes.

He enveloped her hand in his and squeezed. "She won't. Hers have to be relatively mild if she's able to live by herself." That wasn't actually true, but he couldn't stand the thought of his daughter worrying about Pippa.

"Shouldn't she have someone with her besides Lady?" Aspen's worry was spiraling.

"I'm sure she wouldn't be living alone if the doctors hadn't said it was safe. She has family, too, remember? They wouldn't leave her by herself if she was in any danger." *I hope.*

"But her family lives far away." A light entered her eyes. "Maybe we can be her family."

Aspen's innocent words were like a knife to his chest. She had the biggest heart.

He'd probably destroyed what little progress he and Pippa had made at getting to know each other after he'd kissed her and run. The woman had enough on her plate without having to deal with his issues too.

For two weeks, Pippa's moans and whimpers had haunted his dreams. Every single cold shower he'd had ended in him coming against the tiles, picturing Pippa's pink lips wrapped around him. She was a distraction. It had been torture trying to stay away.

If only he could get this crushing urge for Pippa under control.

17

PIPPA

Pippa blinked her eyes open. Blurry white filled her vision. *Where am I?* She tried to sit, but Lady's heavy weight kept her horizontal. Pippa pointed to the spot next to her. "Down, girl."

The dog obeyed, sniffing her and then licking the side of Pippa's face. Pippa winced as she sat, every muscle seeming to protest. The last thing she remembered was heating some leftovers. She slowly got to her feet, a landslide of exhaustion rolling over her. Her meal was still sitting in the microwave, untouched. She pulled on the handle and pressed her finger to the center. Her food was cold once again. *How long was I out this time?* Pippa pulled up her tracking app. *That makes sense now.* Her period was due soon. Every month, like clockwork, she'd get clusters of seizures around her cycle. Maybe she needed to get more help for the bookstore. Times were tight, but she could only do what she could do. And what if Troy was sick and she had a seizure? There'd be no one to keep the store open—and that store was a refuge for people. For girls like Aspen and boys like David. One more thing on her to-do list.

Pippa grabbed the glass of water on the counter and drained it before she headed to her bed. She just needed a little nap.

Her face hit the pillow and sleep enveloped her.

Pippa jolted upright. Lady's ears perked as her face turned towards the door. Pippa reached out and stroked the dog's fur.

Knock. Knock.

Pippa's forehead creased. Who could that be? A quick glance at her clock told her it couldn't be Troy; the bookstore was open for another two hours. Pippa got up and rubbed her eyes on her way to answer. She opened it and blinked in surprise.

"Hey, Brynn."

Brynn tucked a lock of brown hair behind her ear, her eyes darting to the ground nervously. "Hi. I, um, wondered if you, uh, if I could talk to you?"

Pippa widened the door and stepped aside. "Come on in."

Brynn stepped into the living room, keeping her arms pulled tight to her body as if she were afraid of taking up too much space.

"Would you like to sit?" Pippa motioned to the couch.

"Sure." Brynn took a seat.

"Can I offer you some water or juice? I also have tea?"

Brynn shook her head and sat. "No, thank you."

Pippa joined her, running a hand over her hair. God only knew what she looked like after rolling out of bed. "What can I do for you?"

"I just wondered if by chance you had any positions available at the bookstore? I'm looking for some extra hours in the afternoons after I get off my shift at the diner."

Pippa nodded. "Oh. I see. Well, actually, yes. I could use

some more help. Some of it might be last-minute coverage. Sometimes, afternoons can be hard for me . . . uh, for me to work. Would that suit you? I know you have David. He's welcome to hang out with you at the shop if you need."

Brynn's shoulders lowered as a small, relieved smile tilted her lips before it disappeared, and she looked at the ground again. "I, uh, don't suppose you might hire me under the table? I know it's a big ask, but I don't really have another choice. And I can't tell you why either." Brynn's hazel eyes met hers, her gaze making her seem so much older than her features presented.

Pippa took a deep breath. "That's a risk for me—one I'd be willing to take if you were in danger."

Brynn's gaze darted to the stain on the coffee table as her shoulders sunk and she nodded. "Yes."

Pippa slowly reached out her hand and placed it on Brynn's arm. "I can do that."

Brynn's expression softened as her eyes glistened with unshed tears. "Thank you. I can start this week, or whenever you need."

"How about you come in tomorrow after your shift and I'll walk you through the basics?" Pippa suggested.

"I'll be there." Brynn stood and Pippa walked her out. "Thank you again. I promise I'll be a hard worker."

"I have no doubt." Pippa smiled and waved as Brynn disappeared down the stairs. Pippa closed the door. *What was Brynn hiding from? Or maybe who?* Pippa headed towards the kitchen when another knock halted her steps.

Did Brynn forget something? Pippa opened the door and froze.

"Hey." Mason's deep voice sent a shiver through her. Anger welled inside her that he affected her so. He'd been so hot and cold with her. *Why is he here?*

"What do you need?" She straightened her spine, determined not to let him hurt her again.

"Uh." He scratched the back of his head. "Aspen was really worried about you."

So she sent her father? He could have texted. Pippa wasn't buying it. "You can tell her I'm fine." Guilt clawed at her. "I'm sorry if I scared her."

He stared at her a moment in silence, his jaw tense, his brow furrowed.

"Have a good day." Pippa tried to close the door and end the awkward stare-off, but Mason's hand whipped out and pressed it open.

Her eyes widened as he took a step closer.

"I was worried about you too," he said.

"I . . ." The air was thick with him so close. His rain-like masculine scent made breathing difficult. "I told you, I'm fine. Thanks for your concern, but I've been living with this for almost my whole life, and I can take care of myself."

"But I am concerned for you." His voice came out like gravel.

She swallowed.

His liquid gaze darkened and lowered to her mouth. "I'm not used to this."

"To epilepsy?" She scrunched her nose in confusion.

He shook his head. "To being so attracted to . . ." His eyes raked over her body. His jaw clenched. Was he disgusted?

Anger roiled in her belly. She stepped forward, jabbing her finger against his chest. "What? That you're attracted to a big girl? You think I didn't see the way you grimaced, looking at me in my bathing suit on the paddleboards? Or after you kissed me? I'm so sorry you're afflicted this way." Her voice dripped with sarcasm. "I don't know how such a sweet little girl like Aspen could come from such an asshole. You need to leave." She pushed the door to close it, but he pressed it harder, making it bang against the wall.

Lady barked as he stepped inside, anger flashing in his dark orbs. Pippa sucked in a surprised gasp.

"That's what you think I see when I look at you?"

She crossed her arms, straightening her spine. She wouldn't let him intimidate her. "Isn't it?"

"You couldn't be more fucking wrong." He growled.

"But you—"

"You're right about one thing. I hate how much I'm attracted to you."

She flinched. Fresh hurt flowed to the surface.

"But not for the reasons you assumed." His thumb brushed her lower lip. Tingles raced from his touch. "You are the most beautiful woman I've ever laid my eyes on."

What?

Calloused fingers traced her jaw. "When I look at you, I want to touch every inch and find out if you're as soft as I imagined. I want to map your body and worship between your thighs."

Holy hotness. Pippa's core clenched in response as her shorts grew damp.

"Why'd you stop kissing me the other night, then?" Her voice came out breathy.

"Because I have nothing to offer you. You're young and have your whole life ahead of you. I'm a single dad in my thirties. My daughter will always come first. And I can't afford any distractions." Regret flashed in his gaze as his hand trembled as if he were fighting a war—should he stay or should he go?

Fear that she would lose him, lose this connection that set her body alive, reared inside of her. The hesitation and anger she'd had towards him was gone, replaced with desire. "I'm not yours to worry about."

For a moment, they just stared into each other's eyes. Hers pled with him to give in to this. Even if it couldn't be for more than one afternoon, she'd give anything for a few hours in his arms. To feel so wanted by a man like him was heady and intoxicating.

"I can't . . . *We* can't. But that doesn't stop me from wanting to."

Disappointment settled in her gut.

"I should leave." His voice came out like sandpaper, blunt and rough. He didn't make a move, except for his calloused thumb stroking her cheek.

"Why aren't you?"

"I can't," he gritted.

Hope sparked in her belly as she leaned into his touch. "Why not?"

"Because I can't stop thinking about this mouth on mine." His other hand came up to cup her jaw, his thumb tracing the seam of her lips.

Emboldened, she flicked her tongue out, tasting him. Desire flared.

His gaze was nearly black as he leaned in, his breath hot against her mouth. "Tell me to go."

"I can't."

"Why?"

"Because I can't stop thinking about that kiss either."

Her front door slammed. His mouth crashed against hers. Pippa sucked in a sharp breath, her body igniting into a lust fire. His arms wound around her, pulling her as close as their clothing would allow. She gripped his thick, muscular shoulder as his tongue slipped inside her mouth, teasing hers with his musky clean taste. His touch scorched her. Arousal pooled in her body, gathering in her center, sliding into her soaked shorts. His hand gripped the back of her neck, holding her in place while his other moved down, fingers digging into the soft flesh of her ass possessively as he groaned.

Pippa whimpered, needing more. Her body was alight in a liquid fire of wanton need. She'd never been this turned on before and all from a kiss.

Mason pulled away, his chest heaving against hers. A needy sound left her at the loss of his mouth against hers.

"I can't . . . give you more than this . . ."

She swallowed the disappointment and nodded.

"But . . . "

"But?" She bit her lip, trying to tamp down her hope.

"But I'd really love to taste you." He cupped her sex, making it clear just what he was asking.

She moaned and clutched his defined chest for support as her legs turned weak, her knees trembling.

"Can I taste you, beautiful?" Mason's voice wavered like he was barely hanging on to his self-control.

Did he ever give up control? She nodded. "Yes."

His hands unfastened her shorts. Cool air rushed over her exposed skin as her shorts dropped to the floor.

Mason let out a growl. "No panties?"

She shook her head. "They're overrated."

He stood, pushing her against the door before he returned to his knees. His large, rough hands picked up one of her legs, hiking it over his shoulder.

A tinge of self-consciousness rippled through her with her pussy on display in front of his face.

"Fuck, you're perfect." Mason pushed her lower lips apart, dipping his nose to her sex and inhaling. Wetness seeped down her leg. His tongue lashed out, whipping pleasure through her like a bolt of lightning.

"Mason!" she yelped as he licked and sucked her into a frenzy. She gripped his hair, holding on as the one leg that remained on the ground gave out. Mason gripped her other thigh, placing it over his shoulder so that he held her up with her back against the door. She'd heard of this position, but never in a million years imagined someone her size would be able to do it. Mason stood, making her gasp.

He hummed against her clit as a keening cry left Pippa's mouth.

"Oh my God. OH. FUCK! Mason, I'm—"

He licked into her core before running his hot tongue over her clit and sucking. Pippa's orgasm ripped through her, pulling her apart and putting her back together all at once. She screamed until her voice was hoarse. Her chest heaved as his beard scratched against her sensitive flesh. She shivered. Her body floated, boneless and limp. *Have I ever come that hard before?*

Mason kissed her thighs before he unhooked her legs and slid her down to her feet. His arms were the only thing keeping her upright as she led him over to her bedroom.

The backs of her knees hit the mattress, and she collapsed onto the soft cushion. Mason pulled a comforter over her, leaned down, and kissed her again. Her taste melded with his, like she'd marked him. His beard scratched against her face.

He pulled back, his lips glistening, and his eyes half-lidded in lust. "I wish I had more to give you."

Couldn't he? "I'm okay with this." She smirked. "Honesty is all I ask, so I can adjust my expectations. You've given me that."

His brows drew together as if he wasn't sure whether he believed her or not.

"What about you?" She motioned to his cock.

His face flushed pink for the first time since she'd known

him. "I, uh, already came." His eyes darted away. "It's, uh, been a while."

Wow. Was she the first since his wife had passed? No, surely not. That was more than a decade. And he was way too good with his tongue to have been out of practice that long.

"Thank you for the orgasm."

His mouth turned up into a half smile. Her belly swirled with butterflies. *She'd been the one to illicit that response in him.*

"Trust me, it was my pleasure."

"Maybe I can return the favor sometime." She tried to sound nonchalant. He'd been clear he wasn't looking for a relationship.

"I meant what I said. This is all I can offer. Aspen is my priority."

"And I get that. We can be friends, can't we?" She understood his daughter came first. But that didn't mean they couldn't have some fun on the side, right? "Friends that sometimes enjoy certain benefits?"

"You'd be content with that?" His gaze narrowed.

She shrugged, acting like it wasn't a big deal. She'd had a few casual relationships before she moved to Shattered Cove. She'd always been the one to end them. Why would this be any different? "Absolutely."

He swallowed and turned as Lady jumped on the bed, whining.

Pippa laughed. "Oops. We gave her quite the show." *Oh God, the bookstore. I hope no one heard me.* Heat rose to her cheeks. She wasn't usually so loud during sex.

"Want me to take her out before I leave?" he offered.

"Would you? I'm not sure how long it will be until I can feel my legs again."

He smirked, his chest puffing out. "No problem. Come on, girl."

Lady looked at Pippa, asking permission. "Go on, Lady."

The dog jumped off the bed. "She has a leash by the door."

Pippa admired Mason's ass as he bent to clip the leash to her dog before he exited her apartment. Her chest twinged as he left. Mason was a complicated man. The way he cared for his daughter was just one more thing she loved about him.

Not that she loved *him*. No. She admired him. And hopefully, she'd get to see every inch of him and lick every delectable ab she remembered from the day at the beach.

That was all this was. Mutual lust and an arrangement to enjoy the benefits of being two consenting adults in a casual, sexually gratifying relationship.

So why did the niggle in the back of her head feel like a warning?

18

PIPPA

Pippa drained the last of her water before setting her cup and empty breakfast plate in the dishwasher.

Ding!

Pippa picked up her phone as she headed to the door. It was almost time to open the bookstore and get everything ready for their drag queen story hour later that day.

Sophia: *Has he stopped by again? Called? Messaged?*

Pippa shook her head. She'd filled her sister in on her interlude with Mason, and now Sophia wouldn't shut up about it.

Pippa: *No. Not to say I wouldn't mind another mind-blowing orgasm, but this is just casual. He's busy. This is not a relationship. So stop pestering me.*

Sophia: *Are you trying to tell me you aren't the slightest bit nervous that he hasn't reached out in a week?*

Yes. Okay, just a little. But he was a busy man, and his daughter came first; he'd made that clear.

Pippa: *I shouldn't have told you anything.*

She grabbed Lady's vest and harness, then secured them to her dog as the phone rang. *Sophia just can't take a hint.*

Pippa answered. "I swear, *nena, que si no te callas,* I'm going to tell Papi the truth about your trip to Canada."

A low chuckle filled the other end of the phone and Pippa froze. Her eyes widened. That wasn't Sophia. "Mason? I thought you were . . ." That was a close call. She thanked her lucky stars she hadn't said anything about him.

"Nena is an endearment for sister, so I'm guessing you thought I was her?" The smile was evident in his voice.

"*Si. Hablas Español?*"

"Just a little from my time in South America. Not enough to really carry on a conversation," Mason answered.

"I guess I'll stick to English, then."

"Actually, it's pretty sexy when you speak Spanish." His voice sounded rough, like he'd just woken up.

"Oh really?" A thrill shot through her as a wide smile broke out on her face. She deepened her voice so her words came out breathless and husky. "So if I told you *no mezcle los blancos y colores en la lavadora,* you'd get hot for me?"

He groaned on the other end. "Yes. What did you say?"

She giggled. "I told you not to mix whites and colors in the washing machine."

He barked out his laughter before it dissolved into a low chuckle. "Well, if talking about the laundry gets me this hard, I can't wait to hear about your grocery list."

"Mmm, I think I could use some more *juga.*"

"Sugar?" He questioned as the rustling sound of blankets filled the background. She pictured him, lying naked in his bed. His big, calloused hands roving down his abs to the fine line of hair leading lower.

"Pip?"

"Hmm? Oh, no, *juga* is juice."

A moment of silence passed before she cleared her throat.

"I was calling because I wondered if you wanted to join Aspen and me this weekend? We're going to the seafood fest in town. Maybe you were already going, but I thought we could, you know, go together—with Aspen," he clarified.

She bit back her smile. He was including her? Butterflies danced in her belly. "Absolutely."

"Okay. We'll be by to walk with you around one if that works?"

"See you then," she agreed and opened the door.

"Bye, Pippa."

"*Nos vemos*, Mason." She held on a beat longer before he exhaled and ended the call.

Pippa slipped the phone in her back pocket and locked her apartment door. Lady snorted beside her. Pippa turned to her animal as the dog eyed her. "Not you too. I get enough of a hard time from Sophia." She walked down the steps, her chest light and free. Sure, this was casual, but it didn't mean she couldn't look forward to an afternoon with the coolest young woman and her sexy Adonis father. Since when did the big girl get the chiseled Navy SEAL? Yes, it happened, occasionally. But never to her. She would make sure to enjoy every minute of their arrangement.

Lady barked, drawing her attention to the store. Pippa looked up and froze. Ice slid in her veins before it was replaced with hot anger.

Red slashes of spray paint scarred her once sparkling glass windows with the words, *All fags will burn.*

Lady whined next to her, pressing her soft coat against Pippa's bare legs, snapping her out of her shock. Pippa's eyes darted around the street. Several people across the road stared, holding up their camera phones.

"Pippa? Oh my God." Remy rushed to her side. "A few

customers were talking about this. I thought they meant some-where else."

"I need . . . I need to . . ." What did she need to do? Call the police? Families with their kids would be arriving later that day, and the last thing they needed to see was this shit on her store.

"I already called Bently. He's on his way."

The sheriff? Right, he was Remy's brother-in-law.

"Are you okay?" Remy placed her hand on Pippa's arm.

Pippa nodded numbly, tears blurring her vision. Seeing her safe place violated in such a disgusting manner made her stomach churn with bile. "I need to get this off before too many people see it."

"I wouldn't touch it until Bently arrives. Oh, look." She waved to the truck marked *Sheriff* pulling into an empty parking space. "He's here."

Bently got out of his vehicle before tucking a pair of avia-tors into the front pocket of his tan uniform. A dark-haired woman got out of the passenger side, her eyes glued to the storefront. She frowned and shook her head.

"I got here at five, and not that I really looked, but I didn't see anything amiss when I unlocked the café. Of course, I came in the back," Remy said to Bently.

He reached out his hand to shake Pippa's. "Ma'am, we didn't quite get introduced at the pharmacy. I'm Sheriff Evans. You can call me Bently like almost everyone else here does. Haven't quite made it in, but I believe my wife, Belle, has, and my foster son, Gage. They say it's quite the bookstore."

Pippa nodded. Gage's face flashed in her mind. He enjoyed the thrillers and a lot of non-fiction if she remem-bered correctly. "Yes. Thanks. I'm Pippa Davis."

"Did you happen to hear any disturbances, Miss Davis?" Bently asked.

"Please call me Pippa. No. Nothing out of the ordinary. I came outside earlier to let Lady out, but this wasn't here then."

"About what time was that?" He pulled out a pen as the woman next to him handed over a clipboard.

"Um, about seven thirty I think."

"Do you have security cameras installed that point towards the front of the store?" his partner asked.

"No." She shook her head. "I don't have any cameras at all."

"Okay, I'll take a look around. See if I can find any evidence as to who did this. You might want to hold off on opening just yet."

"Can I wash this off?" she asked.

"I'll grab what you need at the hardware store, and I'll help you get it cleaned up before the kids start showing up for story time." The woman beside Bently stepped forward, motioning to the window. "I know I don't want my son having to see this, even though he isn't reading yet."

Pippa cut her a questioning glance. The woman smiled and extended her hand. "Elena Vargas. My wife is bringing our son, Jay."

Recognition flared. "Oh, you're Millie's wife."

Vargas smiled. "Yes, ma'am."

"Vargas, see if any of the surrounding shops have cameras of Main Street that they're willing to share," Bently said.

Vargas nodded. "Will do." She turned back to Pippa. "I'll be back with the cleaning supplies. You might want to call Marsha and let her know."

Vargas disappeared down the street as Bently pulled out a

camera and took photos of her storefront, his shrewd gaze inspecting the area for evidence, Pippa assumed.

Remy placed a hand on her back. "Do you need me to stay with you? You're welcome to come hang out in the café if you need."

Pippa shook her head. "No, thank you. I think I'll just wait here."

Remy nodded and turned back to cross the street. Pippa pulled out her phone and dialed Marsha Divine's number.

"Hello?"

"Hi, Marsha. It's Pippa from the bookstore."

"How are you, dear?"

"Well, that's why I'm calling. The store was vandalized this morning," Pippa explained.

Marsha gasped. "Oh, I'm so sorry. Are you okay?"

"Yes. Whoever it was just spray-painted the front window. But it was some homophobic stuff. I wanted to let you know in case you didn't feel safe coming today."

After a beat of silence, Marsha cleared her throat. "Do you know why I chose the stage name Marsha Divine for when I perform in drag?"

"No."

"Marsha P. Johnson was a prominent figure in the Stonewall Uprising in nineteen sixty-nine. Johnson was also a founding member of the Gay Liberation Front as well as many other resources for my community. Not to mention a proud Boricua. Johnson was a voice for gay rights during some of the hardest times for the LGBT community."

"Wow. I had no idea," Pippa admitted.

"Marsha faced police raids and fought for the rights of people like me. I didn't choose this name lightly. Love always trumps hate. A little spray paint won't scare me away." Marsha Divine chuckled. "Besides, there's a group of children waiting to ask me questions and learn that I'm just as human as they are. I have feelings and emotions, thoughts and ideas, just like them. And they need to know that it is okay not only for *me*, but for *them* to express themselves in any way that feels authentic to them. Except by spray-painting someone else's property."

"You are one amazing person." Pippa smiled.

"So are you. Don't discount the work you're doing for our community. Have your moment, then brush your fabulous self off and get back to work. We can't let the bigots win."

"No, we can't," she agreed.

"I'll see you this afternoon," Marsha said before she ended the call.

Pippa tucked her phone back in her pocket and let out a big breath. Marsha was right. She wouldn't let this asshole steal any more of her energy. She wouldn't let this hiccup stop her; that was what the vandal wanted. No, she'd fight back. If someone wanted to spread hatred, she'd show them she wasn't afraid. She didn't cower to bullies anymore.

19

MASON

Mason's gaze slid over the barroom of The Shipwreck. It wasn't that busy, like other Tuesday nights. A handful of people played pool in the corner; the table was a new addition Finn and Charli had installed last month. A few couples enjoyed the upbeat rhythm that bled through the speakers from their position on the dance floor. Laughter and excited voices rose every now and then.

Mason leaned against the bar next to Link. His friend hadn't been in for a while. The woman he loved was away at some sort of rehabilitation center, and they had no idea when she'd be back, or *if*.

"Heard anything from Emma?" Mason asked.

Link shook his head, his shoulders sinking a little lower. "Nope."

Mason clapped a hand on his friend's back. "I'm sure you will soon."

Link nodded, but the tension weighing him down didn't ease from his expression.

"Fancy seeing you here," his brother, Sebastian, joked from Mason's other side.

Mason turned and teased, "I work here, asshole."

Sebastian shrugged and ran a hand through his dirty-blond hair. There was no mistaking they were twins: they had the same build and similar features, but where Mason was jagged and rough, Sebastian was soft and much more approachable.

Sebastian wrapped his arm around his boyfriend who approached from behind. "You remember Perry."

Perry, a freckled redhead a foot shorter than Sebastian, smiled and offered his hand.

Mason shook it. "Nice to see you again. How's things in the hospital administration office?"

Perry's blue eyes flashed in surprise. "Good, thanks."

Sebastian caught Finn's attention and ordered a couple drinks as Mason scanned the room again.

"Well, look what the cat dragged in." Sebastian slapped hands with Bently before pulling him into a hug.

Bently ruffled his hair and chuckled. "Hey, Seb."

"Bastard!" Sebastian shoved his hand away and elbowed Bently in the gut.

"You were too pretty. Had to bring you down to our level," Bently said. "Besides, I'm sure your boyfriend would agree. You look better when everything isn't always put together. Am I right?" Bently nudged Perry, who blushed almost as red as his hair.

"Ignore these assholes. They just like to give me a hard time." Sebastian handed his boyfriend one of Sand Dune's finest India pale ales.

"I heard about the incident at the bookstore. Any idea who did it?" Link asked as Bently took the empty barstool beside him.

Mason's ears perked up as he straightened. "What happened at the bookstore?"

Bently sipped on his beer. "Someone spray-painted some homophobic stuff on the windows. Vargas and I were gonna help her clean it off, but we got called off for an emergency. Waiting to hear back to see if any of the local shops had video footage around that time. She didn't have any."

Mason's shoulders rose as his stomach churned. Why hadn't Pippa told him? She could have messaged him. She must be shaken up.

"Is Pippa okay?"

Bently cut a look his way. "As good as can be expected. I didn't realize you and her were close?"

Mason shrugged. "Aspen basically lives at her store."

Sebastian nudged him. "Are you finally seeing someone?"

Mason wished he had a beer in his hands, but there was no drinking on the job. "No. We're just . . . friends." *That might enjoy some benefits in the near future.*

Pippa's moans and screams echoed in his head, making his cock hard. He forced his thoughts to what Bently had told him and anger quickly replaced desire. Who the fuck would mess with Pippa? His fists clenched. He wanted to head over there right now and check on her.

Sebastian's low chuckle interrupted his thoughts. "If you say so. You know you can have it all, right?"

Mason shook his head. "Not getting into this with you. She's just a friend."

Sebastian's laugh seemed almost in pity as Mason walked away.

Just after midnight, Mason drove past Main Street, taking the long way home. A light was on in Pippa's bedroom. It took everything inside him not to pull the car over and knock on her door. But he couldn't. Amara, Bently's foster daughter, was babysitting until Mason got home, and she needed to go.

Mason steered his way through Shattered Cove, until the streetlights disappeared and the houses became more and more spaced out. He pulled into his driveway. Lyric's car was already here to pick Amara up and take her home. Normally, he would be against leaving three teenagers alone in his house, but Amara was a responsible young woman, and Aspen adored her. Lyric was as shy as they came, and gave his babysitter a ride home, which made it easier on Mason. Mason hoped the kid got the nerves to tell Amara how he felt before it was too late.

Mason walked in the door. Amara and Lyric were playing cards on the living room floor.

She looked up when he closed the door. "Hey, Mr. Wright."

"Hey, guys. Aspen sleeping?"

Lyric picked up the cards while Amara got to her feet. "Yes. She went up at nine thirty."

"Perfect." He dug in his wallet and handed over the cash for her service.

She tucked the money into her back pocket as Lyric came up behind her and handed her his sweatshirt. "It's c-c-cold."

She smiled and wrapped the material around herself. The boy didn't say much, Mason guessed on account of his stutter. But when he did speak, it was mostly to Amara.

"Drive safe, you two." Mason nodded to Lyric.

"W-w-will do," the young man said, opening the door for Amara.

Mason locked the door behind them, waiting until the headlights left his driveway before he pulled his cell out of his pocket and texted Pippa.

Mason: *Are you awake?*

He jogged up the stairs and opened Aspen's bedroom door to check on her. She'd flung her covers off the bed and was sprawled out like a starfish. He stifled a laugh. Didn't matter if she was three or thirteen—she always slept the same. Pain flitted through his chest. His baby was growing up so fast. He picked up the covers and slid them over her before leaning down to kiss her forehead.

His phone dinged in his pocket, alerting him to a text. Aspen didn't even stir; she was dead to the world. He crept back to the hallway and pulled his cell out as he walked to his room.

Pippa: *Is this a booty call?*

Is that all she thinks I want?

Was it, though?

No, he wanted her friendship too.

Mason didn't bother responding. He dialed her number.

She picked up on the third ring. "Hello?" Her voice was husky, like she'd just woken up.

"Did I wake you?"

"No. I-I couldn't sleep." Her voice shook.

Concern twisted inside him. "I ran into Bently and he told me what happened with the shop. Why didn't you call me?"

She was silent a beat and then sighed. "Because I'm not your responsibility, Mason."

His own words came back to haunt him. "But we're friends, right? And friends tell each other when shit like this happens."

"I didn't think you'd care."

His chest squeezed tight. He shouldn't care. But he did. *Just like I would if Remy's café was vandalized.* "Don't know what kind of friendships you're used to, baby, but part of friendship is caring about each other's safety."

She sniffed. "I've never actually had really close friends before."

His brows drew together as he sat on his bed and untied his boots, slipping them off. "Why not?"

"My, uh, condition got really bad in middle school and then we had to move a few times. Between that and . . . well, the stuff that happened, I ended up kind of isolated. It was just me and my sister when I was sixteen for a while. I ended up doing homeschooling for the last few years of high school. I think it was just easier to keep casual acquaintances with people, and that sort of stuck with me, I guess. I have friends here, but not the type that come and check on me. I wouldn't want to add that strain on someone."

Mason pushed the speaker button and tore off his shirt. There was a lot in those few sentences she wasn't saying. "That sounds rough."

"Mmm, it was my life, so I didn't have a choice. It made me who I am today, and I kinda like the woman I turned out to be."

He smiled. "I kinda like her too."

She giggled. "Did you just get home from work?"

His belt clanked as he undid it before dropping his pants to the floor. "Yeah. Saw your light on when I drove by."

"It's already after one. Shouldn't you get some sleep before you have to be up with Aspen?" The rustle of fabric sounded in the background. He pulled the covers down and settled into his bed in only his boxers. Closing his eyes, he imagined her, sprawled out next to him, naked. If she were here, he'd take his time mapping every curve with his tongue. Only this time, he wouldn't come in his pants like a damn teenager.

"Mason?"

"Uh, it's fine. I'm trained to go on little to no sleep for long periods of time." *And talking to you would be worth it.*

"I keep forgetting you were a SEAL." She laughed.

"How can you forget when the evidence is all over my face?" His voice came out rougher than he'd intended. In many ways, he was a beast, and she, a beauty. Only real life wasn't a fairy tale. There would be no happy ending for them —except in the case of a few orgasms, hopefully.

"Do your scars bother you? I think they're kinda hot. They add to your whole bad-boy, security-guy aura."

Hot? His scars were *hot*? He blinked a few times in rapid succession. "Honestly, for the most part, they remind me of something I'd like to forget." *When I failed my men because I was too distracted with my priorities at home.*

This was why he didn't do distractions. They cost lives.

"We all have things we'd like to forget." She sighed.

He wanted to ask her what, but that would leave the door open for the return question and he wasn't going there with anyone but his therapist. "So, why couldn't you sleep?"

A beat of silence passed. "Because I'm scared."

Her voice sounded so small. It took everything in him not to grab his keys and head over there and just hold her in his arms. But he had Aspen to think about. Ugh! He was being torn in two!

"Put the phone on speaker and lie down in your bed."

"Okay . . . Done."

"I'm gonna stay on the phone with you, okay?" He turned off his light and moved to his side. Facing the empty bed beside him, he imagined her sweet face staring back at him.

"You'd do that for me?" Emotion seemed to choke her words.

Something foreign twisted in his chest, tightening his rib cage, making it impossible to draw a full breath. "Sure thing, baby. This is one of the advantages of our friendship."

She laughed, light and free, releasing some of the tension in his chest. "I thought it only came with sexy benefits."

He groaned. "Those will come. Now, close your eyes and listen to my bedtime story. I apologize in advance for any snoring you hear on my end tonight."

She sucked in a sharp breath. "You'll stay on till morning?"

"Promise." He plugged his phone into the charger and left it on the opposite side of the bed that had only ever had Aspen in it, and even then only on nights when she'd had a bad dream or was sick. But those days had ended.

"Thank you, Mason."

"Anytime, Beauty. Ready?"

"Mm-hmm."

"Once upon a time . . ."

20

PIPPA

Pippa put the stack of books on the shelf and stepped around Lady. Her phone rang from the front desk with a text message. *Probably Sophia.* She'd forgotten to charge it last night, and true to his word, Mason had stayed on the other end of the line all night. Who knew there were men out there who would tell stories?

It wasn't the classic prince-saves-the-princess tale either. His story had the woman saving herself, and even got pretty sexy at times. She'd drifted off to sleep dreaming of slain dragons and happily ever afters with a prince that looked a lot like Mason. Too bad it would only ever be a dream.

Around seven, his rumbly voice had come through wishing her a good morning with the clinking of dishes in the background. She'd never forget his kindness.

Buzzing and cranking sounds came from the front of the store. Pippa's heart raced. *Is someone vandalizing my shop in broad daylight?* She ran to the front, heading for her phone to call the police when a familiar figure caught her eye through the glass panes of her storefront. Pippa slowed her steps, and diverted to open the front door, her dog at her heels.

Mason stood on a ladder, equipped with a tool belt that brought a lot of dirty fantasies to mind. He had a drill in one hand and a circular device in the other. His muscles bunched under his thin T-shirt as he worked. Specks of wood landed on his veiny forearms. Her mouth went dry. Her gaze wandered down to his tight ass that his camouflage shorts hugged to perfection. Why hadn't she dug her nails into that when she'd had the chance?

I was too busy getting my pussy ate out by his expert mouth while trying to not scream loud enough for the whole town to hear.

A throat clearing had her gaze snapping back up to his amused deep blue eyes. Half his face turned up in a broken smile like he knew exactly what she was thinking about. He climbed down, his biceps flexing on the side of the ladder with each rung.

His eyes took their time roving over her before landing on her face with that half smile still firmly in place. "You look rested."

She bit her bottom lip. "I have a friend to thank for that."

"Here." He picked up a paper bag and cardboard coffee container from the ground and handed it to her.

She accepted it. "What's this?"

"Late afternoon snack?"

She eyed him curiously. "Another friendly benefit?"

He chuckled, sending a spark of arousal through her.

"I don't think you understand what *benefits* means in this little arrangement. Not that I'm complaining," she teased.

He leaned in, brushing his thumb over her lips. She shivered at the contact and his eyes darkened. "Oh, we'll get there too. Thought I'd give you the whole friendship experience first."

"What's all this?" She motioned to the ladder.

"Security cameras."

Her brows drew together. "But how much does something like this cost?"

He waved a hand. "I had these sitting in my truck just collecting dust. Thought they could be put to use finally." His gaze dipped to the ground before returning to her.

Liar. "Just sitting in your truck, huh?"

"Yup." He bent down and picked up another camera box, pocketing a small receipt discreetly, but not discreetly enough.

"There are some guys coming in about an hour to install a security system to your apartment."

Pippa's mouth dropped open. She couldn't afford that.

He held up his hands. "It's also a gift."

She crossed her arms over her chest. "There's no way a whole security system was just sitting in your truck collecting dust."

He scratched the back of his neck and smirked. "A friend owes me a favor."

"Seems like a pretty big favor." She raised a brow.

He leaned in again, his mouth only an inch from hers. "You see how well I treat my friends?"

Her heart stuttered. "Must have been one hell of an orgasm you gave him."

He barked out a laugh, backing away and shaking his head. His eyes were lit with humor, and he winked. "Nah, Beauty, I save those benefits for only you."

Butterflies danced in her belly and fluttered in her chest. "Why would you do this for me? I get that we're friends, but this is above and beyond . . ." Did he feel responsible for her? Was she becoming a burden on him?

"I just want to know you're safe." His voice was rough.

Something cracked inside her chest. So this would set his

mind at ease? She could do that for him. After all, the man told a pretty epic bedtime story.

"Alright. Thank you. For last night, and for this."

He set the drill and the box on the ladder before pulling her into his arms and kissing her forehead. She squeezed him closer, breathing in his clean, masculine scent. Safety and peace enveloped her.

"Pippa!"

Mason jerked his arms away, standing a few feet from her as Aspen bounded down the sidewalk towards them. A man in blue scrubs, who looked strikingly similar to Mason, followed her.

"Hey, sweet pea. You have fun with Uncle Sebastian?" Mason asked.

So this guy was Mason's brother?

Sebastian's gaze cut towards her, assessing her, before he smiled. "You must be Pippa. Mason's told me a lot about you."

A low growl came from beside her. Pippa's eyes widened as she glanced at Mason before focusing on his brother. "Oh, has he?"

"Pippa, this is my asshole brother, Sebastian," Mason grumbled the introduction.

Sebastian's grin widened as his eyes flashed with mischief. "Older brother."

"By five minutes," Mason corrected.

Pippa flicked her gaze between the two men. "You're twins?"

"Yes. And I learned a lot about life in those five minutes, brother. Don't discount them." Sebastian turned his attention to Aspen. "Be good, and don't tell your dad I let you get ice cream for lunch with cake for dessert."

"Seb." Mason sighed, wiping his hand over his face as if

frustrated.

"The girl needs to be spoiled every now and then. That's what her uncle is for. Okay, I'm off to work." Sebastian opened his arms to hug Pippa, and she returned the gesture.

He's a friendly guy.

He whispered in her ear, "Be patient with him."

Sebastian pulled back and gave his niece a hug before waving goodbye. Pippa swallowed. Her mind reeled from his comment and from the news Mason was a twin.

"Is the new episode of *Selfie* in?" Aspen asked, taking her hand and leading her inside the shop. Pippa shot Mason a quick glance, but he'd refocused on his work.

"Yeah, it's in the comic books section."

Aspen walked over to the correct location and pulled the comic off the shelf as her eyes greedily roamed over the cover. She squealed. "I can't wait to read it. Can you save me a copy for the week I go to summer camp?"

"Absolutely. What kind of summer camp is it?"

"Soccer." Aspen dropped Pippa's hand and flipped open the cover.

"Is Rachel going to be there?"

Aspen's eyes dimmed as she shrugged. "I guess so."

"Are things better between you two?" Pippa pressed.

"Not really. Hey, Dad said you're coming to the seafood festival with us this weekend." Aspen changed the subject.

"Yes. Do you like seafood?"

Aspen made a sour face, her nose scrunching up. "Only some. Not lobster."

Pippa laughed. "I thought everyone in New England liked lobster?"

"Yuck." Aspen shivered.

Pippa shook her head and bit back a smile.

"I'm glad you're coming with us this year." The young

woman gave her a hug. Pippa wrapped her arms around her, squeezing her back. Some of that peace and calm enveloped her with Aspen's embrace, but it was nothing like being in her father's arms.

Pippa's gaze wandered out the front again. Mason's large frame balanced on the ladder as his arms flexed, holding the drill. It had stung when he'd pulled away from her. But she got it. He didn't want Aspen to read more into this. A part of her heart ached, but this was what she'd signed up for.

Be patient with him.

But don't fall in love.

21

MASON

Mason's gaze darted to the gorgeous woman on the other side of Aspen as they walked towards the canvas *Seafood Fest* sign in the center of Green Park.

Pippa's eyes locked with his and she smiled. Something clamored loose in his chest, darting around and knocking his rib cage like a drunken moth.

Pippa licked her lips as they passed the first couple tables, her hand on Lady's leash. Vendors lined either side of the gravel walking path. Local farmers offered their produce and products. Artists had tables to sell their wares. But the big draw was the seafood. Fishermen were everywhere, and offered fresh, sustainable, wild-caught fish and seafood. Beyond them were a few food trucks off to the side by the shade of the trees. Music bled from a bluegrass band on the pop-up stage to their left.

"What kind of seafood do you like?" Mason asked.

"I love it all, except raw oysters." Pippa stuck her tongue out and grimaced.

He chuckled. She was adorable. "Really? No oysters?"

Pippa's nose scrunched up, and she shook her head. "They're like a ball of snot. No, thanks."

"Please tell me you aren't getting a lobster, Dad," Aspen piped up.

"Of course I'm getting a couple."

"Daaaad. They're so freaky-looking," Aspen whined.

Pippa's gaze darted to the first artist's table, Poseidon's Treasure. Her eyes roamed over the fine gems and natural stones wrapped in silver or gold, lingering on the pearl jewelry.

"Do you want to stop and look?"

Pippa turned towards him and shook her head, tucking her arms under her breasts, inadvertently pushing them up. "No. That's okay."

His eyes dropped to her lush cleavage before he cleared his throat and searched the vendors for the one man he was looking for. Mason nodded. "There's Nash's table."

"Nash?" Pippa asked.

"Yeah. Nash Emerson. Do you . . ." Of course. Pippa might not know the fisherman, but she knew his brother, Ricky. A fresh bout of jealousy burned in his gut. *I made it clear she was the only woman I was . . . "friends" with. But is she still seeing other men?*

"Oh, he's the oldest Emerson brother, right?" Pippa's eyes lit up with recognition.

"Yep," Mason grumbled.

"Can we get some scallops?" Aspen asked.

"Sure, sweet pea."

"Is that crawfish?" Pippa pointed to a table off to the right and clapped her hands together excitedly. "This is so cool. I've always wanted to have a big seafood bake-slash-crawfish boil."

"Why don't you do it?" he asked.

She shrugged, some of her earlier joy dimming from her eyes. "I don't really have the space. And I don't know who I'd invite."

"What about Charli?"

"Charli is great. And so is Tammy, who used to work at the bookstore, but she just had a baby."

"You should do it at our house! Dad has a lot of friends," Aspen commented, wrapping her arm around Pippa's.

Pippa smiled down at her. "That's sweet, but I couldn't do that."

"Why not?" Mason asked.

Pippa's mouth opened and closed as her eyes widened. "Because, well, I don't want to impose."

"You, cooking in my kitchen, is the farthest thing from imposition." If only she'd wear some kind of sexy apron and nothing underneath, it'd be a fucking fantasy come to life.

She held his gaze as if trying to see if he were genuine.

"Besides, I could use some more of your cooking." He winked.

"Yeah, I liked those plantain things you made for the dance," Aspen added as they approached Nash's table. *Emerson Fishing Co.* was written in blue lettering on the white sign hanging from the top of the canopy over his setup.

"Nash." Mason nodded.

Nash tipped his head. It was the most welcome anyone would get with the surly man. Nash came eye to eye with Mason, something few men could do in town at his six-foot-six height.

"What's good?"

"All of it," he deadpanned and then turned to Pippa. "And we use safe and responsible fishing practices, making our seafood ethical too."

Mason chuckled and wrapped a hand around Aspen's shoulder.

"That sounds so cool," Pippa chirped.

Nash's gaze bore into her, emotionless.

Pippa blinked and shifted on her feet awkwardly.

"Well, I think we're gonna take a dozen soft-shelled lobsters, a few pounds of scallops, and some of that salmon. Might as well add some tuna steaks." Mason pulled out his wallet. "Do we need anything else, Pippa?"

Nash got to work collecting his order.

"Else? Who are you feeding? An army?" she asked.

He smirked. "Just an ex-SEAL and a few friends. But I was hoping you'd help me do the feeding. What else do we need for the dinner party?"

"Dinner . . ." She blinked as if realizing he was serious. "Are you sure?"

"Unless you don't want to?"

Her eyes softened, growing glassy before she cleared her throat and blinked rapidly. "Sounds like fun." She turned to Nash. "Do you have any shrimp?"

He grumbled something unintelligible as Anthony, Bently and Belle's foster son, jogged over and scooted behind Nash's table, grabbing an apron from a box in the corner. "Sorry I'm late."

Nash handed him a couple bags with lobsters. "Here, ring them up."

Anthony smiled at Mason, his grin widening when his eyes landed on Mason's daughter. He straightened his spine and puffed out his chest. "Hey, Aspen."

Mason's brain temporarily derailed. *Oh, no. I'm not ready for this yet.*

"Hey." Aspen tucked a lock of hair behind her ear.

"Saw your soccer game last weekend. You did really good." Anthony's voice cracked.

Aspen blushed. "I missed the goal."

Anthony shrugged. "Happens to all of us."

Maybe Mason did like the kid after all.

Nash set another bag of seafood on the table, interrupting the teens' moment. Pippa was biting back a smile as she flicked her gaze to the kids and back to Mason as if to say, *Aren't they cute?*

He narrowed his gaze and shook his head. *No. I just tackled her period. I'm not ready for boys yet.*

Pippa giggled and returned her focus to the teens.

She's growing up whether I want her to or not.

"Can I get you anything else, sir?" Anthony asked him, and Mason gave him extra points for his manners. "Or ladies?"

Lady, by Pippa's side, perked up and whined. Pippa patted her head. "Not you, sweet girl."

"Nope," Aspen answered.

"Are we getting shrimp?" Pippa asked.

"No. We don't catch Atlantic Northern shrimp because of their dwindling supply. But some of the other vendors get it shipped in fresh from other locations," Anthony explained.

"Oh, I had no idea. Thank you." Pippa pulled her wallet from her purse.

Mason held up his hand. "I got this."

"But—"

"I insist. You're going to do the cooking, and they're mostly my friends we're feeding after all," he argued, handing over the cash to the young man.

Pippa sighed. "If you insist."

"I do." He winked and she smiled.

"Thank you for your business." Anthony lifted their bags of seafood, offering them up.

"You're welcome. Thank you too." Mason grabbed all the bags but one he left for Pippa. She grabbed it and tugged Lady's leash.

"Bye, Aspen," Anthony called after them.

"Bye." She waved.

Pippa nudged her playfully with a smile. Aspen shook her head as her cheeks bloomed bright red.

"I thought you were the grumpiest man in Shattered Cove but you've got nothing on Nash," Pippa teased Mason as they weaved their way through the crowd.

"Losing the woman you love will do that to a man." At least with Mason's wife, Amanda, he'd gotten closure. Nash didn't get that after his fiancée disappeared without a trace.

Pippa's eyes flashed with something he couldn't recognize before they darted to the gravel path.

"I'll run these back to the truck. You get whatever else you need from the farmers, and I can take a run to the grocery store after." Mason grabbed the last bag from Pippa.

"When are you thinking of doing this dinner?" she asked, still not looking at him, her gaze fixed on the stall on the left.

"Does tomorrow night work?"

"Sure. You guys are gonna get sick of me, you see me so much." She laughed.

"No way!" Aspen shook her head, reaching out for Pippa's hand once more.

"Impossible," Mason added.

Pippa's smile slipped as their eyes met. Something heated and vulnerable flashed in her gaze.

His chest squeezed tight. He cleared his throat. "I'll be back. We'll get lunch from the food truck if you girls want."

"We want," Pippa agreed with a grin.

"And shaved ice for dessert," Aspen added.

"Deal." Mason brought the seafood to his truck, where he'd brought a cooler for just this purpose already filled with ice so they could take their time this afternoon.

When he returned, Pippa and Aspen each carried a bag with some green vegetables sticking out as they meandered towards one of the food trucks. The hot air grew sweet and floral as he passed Lily's Flower Shop stall. Mason was thrusting his cash to the owner and holding two bouquets of wildflowers before he thought better of it.

As he approached Pippa and Aspen, they got into the line. His daughter spoke. "Do you want to come watch one of my soccer games sometime?"

"Hmm, I don't like to take the bus, so I would have to ask your dad to drive me and I don't want to impose."

"Why don't you use the bus to get around?"

Pippa's shoulders tensed and she dipped her head before turning back to Aspen. "I had a bad experience, and I don't really want to relive that."

"Did you have a seizure on the bus?" Aspen pressed.

He wanted to tell her not to push, but he wanted to know the answer too.

Pippa sighed. "Yeah, and let's just say, not all men are as helpful as your dad."

Anger heated his skin. Had someone hurt her? His fists clenched around the bouquets as a growl rumbled in his chest.

Pippa spun around, her eyes wide. Her hand pressed over her heart. Her eyes dropped to the flowers in his grip before flicking back to his face. Aspen turned.

Mason thrust the bouquets out to them. "Here you go. Saw these and thought you ladies might like them."

A sudden flash of nervousness twisted in his gut. Were the flowers too much? Friends gave friends flowers, right? And it wasn't like he could just get Aspen some and not Pippa. *Or did I grab them with Pippa in mind?*

Pippa's face split in a wide grin. "Thank you." She sniffed the floral arrangement.

"Yeah, thanks, Dad," Aspen added.

The warm summer breeze rustled through the park, giving them a brief break from the humidity. Families milled about, some of them picnicking under the tall oak trees. Conversation and laughter became background noise, mixing with the jazz music from the stage set up across the park.

"Our turn," Pippa said as they stepped forward to the counter.

The ladies moved closer to the food truck. Mason moved between them as they ordered what they wanted. His hand brushed Pippa's. He interlocked his pinky with hers. She tipped her head to the side, giving him a smile—a promise of secrets and tomorrows and more of those kisses. His heart thudded in his chest. She was stunning. A warm feeling seeped into his body, making him glow from the inside out with something that felt a lot like contentment.

He needed more. More of this feeling. And more of Pippa.

22

PIPPA

Pippa stirred the seared shrimp into the pan of creamy garlic sauce and checked over her shoulder. Aspen was busy cutting avocados and taking the pits out. Her tongue darted to the side of her mouth in concentration. Pippa giggled. Mason looked up from the cutting board, catching her gaze.

His mouth quirked into a half grin, and something that looked a lot like happiness shone back in his eyes. "How we doing, chef?"

"*Excelente.* How are those jalapeños coming along?"

He picked up his wooden cutting board and brought them over to her for inspection. "You tell me."

She eyed the diced green pepper. "Perfect. We'll just put one on each of the avocados once we've stuffed them with these shrimp."

"Smells good in here." He set the wooden board on the counter before peeking into the several pots of simmering seafood deliciousness.

Pippa's chest puffed out, filled with pride. If she closed her eyes, she could imagine her mother here with her, telling her just how much of the spices to add, or teaching her how to make rice.

"Okay. These are all done. I'm gonna grab the bags of stuff we got and set up the picnic tables in the back. David texted that they are on their way." Aspen wiped her hands on a towel before she headed to the back door.

"Put the radio on out there," Mason said before Aspen disappeared out of the kitchen.

The moment she left, the tension in the room thickened.

Mason stepped closer and smirked. "What's this called again?"

Pippa's body hummed with his nearness. She bit back a smile. "Aguacate relleno. Stuffed avocado. This is just one way to do it."

"If they're anything like that rice dish you made, I may have to keep them in here and not share." He chuckled.

She swatted his abs. *Good lord, those are hard.* No doubt from making ample use of the gym in his garage. The image of him shirtless, muscles flexing as sweat trickled down his torso, played in her mind. A flash of heat crept up her neck. It was getting hot in the kitchen. "I promise it will be the best thing you've ever tasted. Here, try some."

Pippa lifted the wooden spoon to her mouth and blew on the sauce before offering it to Mason. He kept his gaze locked on hers as he opened his mouth and brought it to the spoon. She swallowed and set the utensil aside before turning off the gas stove. The dish wasn't the only thing done in here.

He leaned in, a rough whisper tickling the sensitive skin on her neck. "It's the second-best thing I've ever tasted."

She shivered, heady with his closeness. Her mouth dropped open before her brows drew together. "What's better than this?"

She gasped as he moved behind her, wrapping his arms around her waist, and tugging her against him. Her back was to his front as his face dipped to her neck. He inhaled, breathing in her scent before he groaned. His arousal poked the top of her ass.

"You are, Beauty."

Oh. OH! Her heart raced. Tingles shot through her limbs as her knees wobbled.

"Tell me the ingredients in Spanish." His voice deepened as he spun her around to face him.

Pippa's gaze flicked up to his. Two fiery blue orbs focused on her mouth. She cleared her throat.

"Trying to learn a new language?" she teased, attempting to grasp a thread of self-control and not jump this sexy wet dream come to life in his own kitchen while his daughter was right outside the house.

He shook his head. "Just trying to learn you."

The panties she just so happened to be wearing under her dress were now ruined. Her chest squeezed as another piece of her heart disappeared. How was she not supposed to fall for a man like this?

She should end this now. He wanted friends with benefits, and usually she could do that. But this . . . this was . . . more. She should pull out while she still had most of her heart intact.

"Beauty?"

God, she loved the sweet name he called her. "Hmm?"

"Ingredients," he ordered, his voice strained as if he, too, was holding back.

"Haces que sea demasiado fácil enamorarte de ti. No me rompas el corazón." You make it too easy to fall for you. Don't break my heart.

She scanned his eyes for any inclination of understanding.

Mason's gaze grew darker than she'd ever seen as he

leaned in, his exhale teasing across her lips, blistering her with overwhelming desire.

Ding-dong!

Mason jerked back. He blinked as if trying to clear his sapphire gaze. "I . . . uh . . ."

Pippa panted, her blood pumping furiously in her veins as she tried to get a hold of herself.

Mason shook his head before a mask of indifference slipped into place. "I'll get the door."

Disappointment flooded over her as she turned back to the stove. Voices came from the other room. The timer beeped. She shut it off and then did the same with the stove. The food was ready, but she still needed a few minutes to get the swirling mix of emotions thrumming in her body under control.

"Something smells good in here." Aaron's voice carried through the room before he peeked his head into the kitchen, Mason trailing beside him.

"Hello," Aaron greeted her, holding up a plate of brownies.

She forced a bright smile and waved, afraid her voice would betray her.

Mason motioned to the back door and led his friend outside after placing the brownies on the counter. "The party is out here. Can I get you a drink?"

Pippa pressed her palms to her hot cheeks, trying to cool them.

She sucked in a startled breath when two large hands grabbed her from behind. She spun around as Mason's mouth crashed down on hers. She gripped his arm, holding on for dear life while he kissed her stupid. His tongue thrust into her mouth, hungry and sure. She opened for him, pliant and willing. Desire and excitement whirled inside her like a tornado leaving nothing but devastating lust in its path.

Mason pulled back, and the bluest eyes she'd ever seen stared back at her. His chest heaved as if he were as affected by the explosion of the kiss as she was. "I couldn't go through the rest of the night without tasting you."

She licked her kiss-swollen lips. "No complaints here."

The corner of his mouth turned up. "Ready?"

For you? No. Not even close.

He motioned to the large stock pot behind her. "Oh! The food. Of course. Uh, yeah—yes. Just needs to be strained and then you can take it out. Should we wait for the others?"

"They're already out there. They didn't bother coming through the house." Mason picked up two pot holders and lifted the pan.

His arms flexed as he drained the water. Pippa forced her gaze away. She scanned the white kitchen, devoid of color except for the muted grey walls, stainless steel appliances, and a few aged pictures taped to the fridge that Aspen must have drawn for him.

She got to work stuffing the avocados and pretended she wasn't picturing herself fitting into his world where they cooked more meals together, and this turned into the two of them becoming more than just friends. She risked a glance over her shoulder. His strong, muscled back flexed under his taut T-shirt.

Could he ever want more with her?

I can't handle any distractions. His words pierced her heart. If there was one thing Pippa brought to someone's life, it was more responsibility. No, she wouldn't do that to him. She had to keep her feelings in check. But she couldn't end this. At least not yet. She wasn't ready to give Mason up.

23

MASON

Mason's gaze scanned the scene in front of him. They'd pushed two picnic tables end to end to make one long banquet table. The crawfish and lobster boil had been dumped onto the waterproof tablecloth in the center, mixed with corn on the cob and potatoes. Dishes of salted butter were scattered across the table along with bowls full of delicious food he and Aspen had spent all morning helping Pippa create.

Aspen sat on the other side of Pippa, going to town on her pasta salad. David sat on her opposite side. Finn and Charli had joined them, as well as Brynn and Aaron.

Mason's thigh pressed against Pippa's, her soft, bare skin turning his cock into a steel rod in his pants. He shifted, trying to get comfortable. It didn't help that her cotton dress flapped in the breeze, rustling against his sensitive flesh and reminding him how easy it would be to slide his hand up her silky smooth thigh and under her hem. Even with all their friends around the picnic table, no one would know.

He peeked over his shoulder. Lady dutifully lay on the grass behind Pippa. Pippa laughed at something Charli said. The sound was like the sweetest birdsong playing the right chords to make his damaged heart skip a beat. Touching her had been an act of desperation. He'd thought for sure it would help him get the beast of his attraction under control. Kissing her had backfired. *What the fuck was I thinking?* Now the monster lust had been given the keys to its prison, free to poison his every cell with desire.

"Mmmm, this is so good. Pippa is the best cook." Aspen licked her finger.

Pippa smiled. "That's because I had the best helpers."

"I need this recipe." Sebastian held up his second stuffed avocado.

"I agree," Perry covered his mouth with his napkin as he commented.

"No problem." Pippa lifted a piece of lobster tail to her mouth. A drop of butter dripped onto her chin before the meat disappeared into her mouth.

Mason swiped his thumb across it before he thought better. Her eyes widened as she turned towards him. He licked the buttery remnants from his finger and her eyes grew heated.

"You had a little something there." He'd rather be laying her out on this table and feasting on her without the audience. It was good they had guests here. It would help stop him from crossing a line he shouldn't cross . . . again. Touching her was just so natural and easy.

Sebastian smirked knowingly. "Sure there was." He chuckled.

Pippa's laugh sounded nervous. "Oh, thanks."

His palm connected with her thigh as he gave in to his overwhelming need to touch her, give her some of the calm she brought to his day. Pippa placed her hand over his, resting it there as if they'd done it a hundred times before.

"Pippa, will you come see my tree house?" Aspen asked.

"Oh, you haven't seen it yet?" Charli asked, handing over her baby boy, Jamison, to Finn.

Finn held the sleepy baby over his shoulder before he stood, patting his back and swaying back and forth. *I can't believe Aspen used to be that little.*

Pippa shook her head. "I've heard all about it though."

"I think I'll get the dessert ready while you go do that." Charli stood.

"I'll help you." Brynn, who'd been more of a quiet observer up until this point, followed her inside.

Aaron's gaze followed Brynn before flicking back to David sitting across from him.

Pippa wiped her hands on a napkin and slipped off the bench of the picnic table. "Alright, show me this tree house." Lady got to her feet and followed after Pippa.

"Want to come, David?" Aspen asked her friend.

He shook his head. "No, thanks."

Mason grabbed a scallop and plopped it into his mouth before chewing. Someone kicked him under the table.

"What the fuck?" Mason asked.

Sebastian smirked and stood. "I don't think all the food here could quench the kind of hunger you have, bro."

"Stop antagonizing your brother." Perry got to his feet. "Come on, let's go get another drink."

"Listen to your boyfriend," Mason grumbled.

Aaron patted David on the shoulder before the boy wandered over towards Finn, who was holding the now sleeping Jamison. Aaron slid closer so that he was across from Mason.

Mason's eyes darted to the tree house. Aspen was waving

her arms and laughing with Pippa before she started climbing the ladder he'd built himself.

"Can't keep your eyes off her," Aaron commented before taking a drink of his beer. Aaron's head swiveled around to the back door of Mason's house as Brynn walked out, carrying a glass of lemonade.

Mason snorted. "I could say the same for you."

Aaron turned back, shaking his head. "Something tells me I'd have a snowball's chance in hell with that one."

Mason didn't doubt it. Brynn had become a part of their circle because of David's friendship with Aspen. And she flinched away from any man who got too close to her. She clearly had demons that put his to shame.

His gaze wandered back to the tree house, seeking Pippa out for the hit of calm her existence always brought him. She'd fit right in with his friends. But Aspen was the one who'd benefitted most from her presence. He swallowed as a flicker of hope he hadn't been ready to consider lit in his chest. *What if I could have both? What if this could be more?*

The real question was, would he take the chance?

"Dad!" Aspen screamed.

Mason shot to his feet. He raced towards the tree house, his heart sprinting.

"Daddy, help!" Fear bled from her sweet voice.

Terror gripped him like a vise as he moved as fast as humanly possible up the ladder. His little girl needed him. Was she hurt? Had she been stung by a wasp? Maybe a window had broken and sliced her arm open? A million scenarios raced through his mind.

As he peered over the top rung, Aspen's chalk-white face came into view. She was scared—yet she was fine. But her gaze was locked on a writhing woman on the floor.

Oh, God, no. Pippa.

24

PIPPA

Pippa glanced up the steps. She wasn't supposed to climb ladders, but this was a short distance. She turned to Lady. "Check me." Lady sniffed her obediently before licking her hand and sitting.

"Good girl." Pippa slipped out one of the small treats she kept on her and held it for Lady who gobbled it happily.

Pippa followed Aspen up to the tree house she'd heard so much about. It was a pretty good size. Big enough for her, Aspen, and maybe another full-grown adult. Aspen walked past the first screened-in window and past a built-in bookshelf packed full of *Selfie* comics and various fantasy and paranormal books. She sat on a thin blue cushion on a wooden seat built into the only other window.

The walls were painted, it seemed, by her own hand. Dragons and fantasy creatures like mermaids adorned them. "Did you do these?"

"Yeah." Aspen tucked a lock of the hair that had escaped her ponytail behind her ear self-consciously.

"They're great. You're quite the artist."

Aspen bit back a smile as her cheeks bloomed pink. She opened her arms wide. "So what do you think of the tree house?"

Pippa sat, leaning against the windowless wall. "I think it's awesome. You are very lucky to have this. You think I could get your dad to help me build a small tree house for the bookstore?"

Aspen's eyes widened, sparking with excitement as she smiled. "That would be so cool. Finn helped him build it, so you might need him too."

Pippa nodded, ideas forming in her mind. "You know what would make it even more cozy in here?"

"What?" Aspen leaned in.

"Maybe some throw pillows. And how do you feel about beads hanging from the windows? Maybe some curtains?"

"Oh my God, yes! Ooh, rainbow curtains. Do they make those?"

"I'm sure they . . ."

Aspen's brows drew together in confusion.

What is that word? Ringing filled her ears as Pippa opened her mouth to speak again. "Um . . ."

"Pippa?" Aspen's voice sounded far away, drowned out by a rushing noise.

Oh no. A seizure.

Pippa inhaled, trying to relax her body and hope it would pass quickly.

Her vision blurred. Aspen yelled. The hard wood on the tree house floor met her back. Anxiety twisted in her belly as she waited for the inevitable seizure symptoms to worsen. Everything went black.

. . .

A deep voice spoke around above her, muffled and quiet, like she was underwater. She blinked her eyes open, her stomach roiling with nausea. A pine wood ceiling was painted with a sun and moon above her. *Where am I?*

"I got you, Beauty. Just relax." Mason's voice pierced through her fog. She tipped her head. His face came into view above her. His eyes crinkled at the edges in concern. A rock sank in her stomach. She'd put that there. Because of her, he had one more responsibility.

"I'm sorry."

He rubbed across the crown of her head with his warm, soothing palm. "Shhhh. Just take a minute to get your bearings. What's your name?"

She swallowed at his gentle show of kindness. "Pippa."

"Do you know where you are?"

She blinked, searching the fog in her mind for answers. "Aspen's tree house."

"Do you want to get up?"

She nodded, noticing for the first time that her head was cradled in his other hand, as if he'd been protecting her from the hard floor while she had a seizure. It was too much. He was so thoughtful.

Run. He doesn't need a burden.

He kept his hand on the back of her head as she slowly rose. She winced at the new aches and pains lighting up her body. The room spun, and her stomach tipped. *Please don't throw up.* Her eyes darted to the floor between her thighs before she breathed a sigh of relief. *At least I didn't wet myself this time.*

"That's it, baby. Now, follow my finger." He walked her through some hand-eye coordination exercises before a smile returned to his face.

"I'm sorry for ruining the party," she said, looking at the wooden floor.

His brows drew together as if confused. "You didn't. Everyone is down there eating dessert or tossing a volleyball around."

Aspen poked her worried face through the door, her eyes scanning Pippa before she offered a relieved smile. "Are you okay?"

Mason's large palm pressed against Pippa's back, rubbing in slow circles. Emotion clogged Pippa's throat. These two amazing people didn't need this. Pippa nodded, forcing a smile. "Of course, sweetheart. I'm sorry I scared you. You did perfect getting help."

Aspen shrugged. "It's not your fault your brain short-circuits."

The little girl's words hit her full force. Pippa struggled to take a shaky breath. No, it wasn't her fault. But that didn't mean it wasn't her burden. One that she swore she'd never make anyone else take on again. She wouldn't ruin another life like she had her father's.

What was she doing here with Mason, playing house? *I won't do this to him.* Her heart thrummed, raw and aching from her decision.

Mason didn't deserve someone who would only cause him more responsibility.

"I'd like to go home," Pippa said, evenly.

"You sure you don't want to take the guest room and rest a while?" Mason offered.

She swallowed the burning emotion that launched up the back of her throat. "No, thank you. I just want my own bed." *Where I can fall apart in private.*

"Whatever you need." His gentle voice promised, tearing the hole in her heart even bigger.

Mason kept his hand on her lower back as she climbed down the ladder to get Lady. She said her goodbyes and apologized as tears burned the back of her eyes. She forced her smile even bigger.

The car ride was quiet with just Mason and her inside the cab. Aspen had stayed with her uncle at the party.

At the bookstore, Mason slipped out of the truck and opened her door, then carefully guided her up the steps. Her body ached, her muscles screaming at her to stop moving. Mason's hand on her lower back never wavered.

Finally, at the top, she plucked her keys from her purse to unlock the door but her hand was trembling so badly, she dropped them. "Sorry."

"No need to apologize." He bent down to grab them before sliding them into the lock and opening the door for her.

Lady went inside, Pippa following. She turned to close the door, but Mason's huge frame took up the space. His eyes locked on to her as if she were under a microscope.

"Thank you." She grabbed on to the handle for support as her knees wobbled.

He reached out, taking her face in his rough hands. The man was a contradiction of gentle and rough. A hard shell and a soft heart. It just made this moment that much harder.

"You're shaking."

She closed her eyes, summoning her last vestiges of strength as she straightened her spine. "I just need sleep. I'll be fine."

He waited a beat, his observant gaze not wavering from hers. "Need me to tuck you in?"

A desperate, raw sound escaped her. She dipped her head and forced a laugh to cover her moment of weakness. "I'm fine. I promise. I'm a big girl, remember?"

His thumb traced her jaw. "You keep saying that word,

'fine,' and as a father to a teenage daughter, I know that word means anything but *fine.*"

Why did he have to be that observant? She leaned in, kissing his lips one last time both to distract him and to savor this last taste of what it felt to be cared for by a man like Mason Wright. If things were different . . .

It didn't matter, because they weren't.

He gripped the back of her neck but she pulled away, fighting the tears with all her might. "Goodbye, Mason." She couldn't even look him in the eye for fear he'd see right through her.

"I'll call you later to check up on you." He pressed his mouth to her forehead and then slowly backed out into the stairwell. Pippa shut the door and waited until the creak of the stairs signaled his leave before she collapsed to the floor. Tears were wrenched from her soul.

She wanted him.

But he'd made it clear he couldn't afford distractions. And she wouldn't be someone else's responsibility.

It was best this ended now before she fell any more in love with the man.

She gasped. Yes, she did love Mason. It was impossible not to.

If only love could be enough.

25

MASON

Mason shifted the car into park, glancing at the yellow school bus. "You sure you got everything you need? Toothbrush—"

"Yes, Dad. First-aid kit, emergency numbers, and an extra kidney." Aspen listed off the items on her fingers.

Mason turned to her and smiled. "You're such a smart-ass."

She shrugged with a grin. "Wonder who I get that from?"

He sighed, unbuckling before he wrapped his arm around her. "I'm gonna miss you, sweet pea. You call me if you need anything."

"Soccer camp is one week. I think you can handle it. After all, only five more years and then I'm off to college." Aspen teased as she hugged him back.

"Don't remind me," he grumbled before kissing her cheek.

"Okay, stay here. I'll get my bag." Aspen reached for the door handle.

"Not gonna happen."

"Daaaad. Please? Don't embarrass me. Look, none of the other parents are babying their kids." She pointed towards the group of teens filing onto the bus.

Mason's chest grew tight. He hated this growing-up thing. "Fine."

Her eyes sparkled with excitement. "Really? Oh! Thank you." She threw her arms around his neck and hugged him.

He squeezed her tight, not ready to let go. She'd have to be the one to make that move.

Aspen released him, kissing his scarred cheek. "See you in a week. Oh, can you check in on Pippa for me?"

He frowned. Pippa had been avoiding him since the dinner two weeks ago. "Check in on her?"

Aspen slid out of the truck. "I think she gets lonely sometimes. Promise me you'll stop in at least once this week?"

"Are you that worried about her?" Concern bubbled in his gut.

Aspen shrugged, her eyes darting to the dwindling line for the bus. "I love her, Dad. She doesn't have anybody to look after her."

Aspen loved Pippa? He cleared his throat, mind reeling. "Sure thing, sweet pea. Love you."

"Love you too, Daddy." Aspen shut the door before jogging to the back and retrieving her duffle bag.

Mason waited until she was seated on the bus before he pulled out his phone to check the string of texts he'd exchanged with Pippa over the last two weeks.

Mason: *You feeling okay?*

Pippa: *Yes.*

Mason: *I have a ton of food left over. I should bring you some.*

Pippa: *I think I ate enough seafood to last me a lifetime.*

Mason: *I want to see you again.*

Pippa: *Tell Aspen I'll hold a copy of* Selfie *for her for when she returns from camp.*

Mason: *Okay. Is that a no?*

Pippa: *I'm really busy this week.*

He'd texted her a few more times. Her delayed responses had been short and clipped, as if she were trying to use as few words as possible. She was pulling away. He should be happy about that, right? He was the one who'd said no distractions. Then why was he so disappointed?

An hour later, Mason entered his therapist's office. The dark-haired woman motioned him to the seat across from her. He scanned the room as he always did. There were the same light walls with neutral cool-colored paintings adorning them. The only thing new was a bouquet of wildflowers in the vase on the coffee table between them. *Just like the ones I got for Pippa.*

"Mason, how are you?" Rebecca Cole, his therapist, asked.

He sat back on the couch, adjusting the pillow behind his spine before he crossed one leg over the other in a figure four. "Pretty good."

Rebecca smiled and pulled a notepad and paper onto her lap. "Did you want to continue with our EMDR therapy today?"

Mason swallowed. The only way to get through this was to rip the Band-Aid off. This woman had helped him when he was at his lowest. She knew the darkest parts of him. She was the perfect one to ask for advice. "Actually, I'd rather talk about the fact that I kinda met someone."

Her eyebrows rose. "Oh?"

He nodded. "She, uh, well, she's pretty great."

Rebecca smiled. "How did you two meet?"

Mason explained the whole debacle with Aspen getting her first period and the pharmacy robbery.

"Wow, that's quite the story."

He grinned. "We've been hanging out some. She and Aspen really clicked. And then Pippa and I . . ." He cleared his throat.

"Were intimate?"

"Sort of. And I was clear from the beginning that I couldn't give her more than that. That friendship was all I could offer. She's the one who suggested a friends-with-bene-fits situation."

Dr. Cole nodded. "And you're still happy with this arrangement?"

He sighed. "Honestly? I don't know. I mean, we've been hanging out with Aspen, and we haven't really had any more . . . benefits. But after she had a seizure at the dinner party a couple weeks ago, she's been . . . distant."

"Is she okay?" Rebecca's brows drew together in concern.

He waved his hand. "Oh, yes. With her epilepsy, it happens pretty often, from what I gathered."

Rebecca leaned forward. "So, let me get this straight. You met Pippa, had a connection, started spending time with her and Aspen, and then decided to entertain the idea of a phys-ical relationship with her without romantic entanglements. Now she's pulling away, and you don't like it?"

"Pretty much."

"Why are you so hesitant to enter into a romantic relation-ship with her? Is it because of her medical condition?" Rebecca asked.

"What? No." He shook his head.

"Then what is it?"

He shifted in his seat. "Aspen is my priority."

"I think a lot of women would be able to understand that, as a single father, your child comes first. What is it that you're really afraid of?" His therapist knew which buttons to push.

Mason leaned forward, his elbows on his thighs. "I let Amanda down when she needed me most because the SEALs were my priority. I let my men down because I was so distracted with getting back to my little girl after Amanda died. And Charli got attacked at the bar because I had to rush home to my sick daughter. Every time I have more than one priority to juggle, I fail. And it always has devastating consequences."

Rebecca set her pad of paper and pen on the coffee table between them before they locked eyes. "That's a lot of responsibility to carry on your shoulders."

He shrugged.

"You must think pretty highly of yourself if you believe you could have saved so many people's lives."

Mason's jaw tensed as he sat up straighter. It was the opposite. He was a failure, not a hero. "That isn't what I meant."

"Isn't it, though? You were in a contract with the SEALs. You couldn't just quit and go home to take care of your wife. Yes, maybe you could have been more supportive and found some help for her, but in the end, she made her own choices. You can't take the blame for her issues."

"I could've—" His eyes raced back and forth over the room, alternate scenarios he'd played a million times flashing in his mind. "What if I—"

"You can't go back. You can't save her. But you can still save yourself." Rebecca's voice was calm and even, unlike his racing heart.

"She was killed because I left her vulnerable. If I had been there, she'd never have crossed paths with that man."

"Do you think Amanda would want you to blame yourself?" Rebecca asked.

He sighed. It wasn't about what Amanda wanted. She was dead. And it took everything in him not to look up her killer again and find out where he was. Aspen was the only thing holding him back from revenge.

"If she was sitting here next to you, what do you think she would say to you?" Rebecca pushed.

"She'd tell me to pull my head out of my ass and take care of our girl. That's what I'm trying to do."

"But Pippa makes you want to change things?"

He drew in a shaky breath. "It's just so easy with her. She just . . . fits. Aspen . . . my daughter told me she loves Pippa. I don't want to fuck up their relationship, but . . ."

"But?"

"Even if she hadn't pulled away, I wouldn't be able to keep my distance. She brings me . . . peace. I haven't felt that in a while." He scrubbed his hand over his face and leaned back on the couch.

"I'm going to shoot straight with you, Mason. You've always responded better to that approach." Rebecca tucked a strand of hair behind her ear.

"Don't hold back on me now, Doc." He forced a chuckle.

"Your wife died over a decade ago. You've done a lot of growing, gained a lot of experience, and worked on yourself all that time. You are not the same young and naive man who once thought himself invincible. You are a dedicated father, and a wonderful man. You can let someone else in, and I promise you, the world will not end."

He sighed, something loosening in his chest with her permission.

"Don't beat yourself up for being human. You're not the only one who will suffer."

Were his choices affecting Aspen? Would she be better off if he started a relationship with Pippa?

"What if things don't work out between me and Pippa? Then Aspen would be hurt."

Rebecca leaned back in her chair. "What if they do work out? What would she gain? And is Pippa the type of person to ignore Aspen just because you and her fizzled out?"

No. Pippa had started a friendship with Aspen before he'd even met her. She didn't seem like that type of woman. Could he do this? He wanted to, especially after all these months they'd spent together, growing closer. She fit right into his life. Not to mention the fact that the chemistry between them was nuclear.

"The question to ask yourself is, will Pippa take away from or add to your life?"

"Add."

"Then the only thing holding you back is *you.*"

Mason walked out of the office and pulled out his phone, dialing Pippa.

She answered on the third ring. "Mason? Is everything okay with Aspen?"

His heart leapt. Her first concerns were for his little girl. "Yeah, she's fine. Off to soccer camp. Listen, I wanted to know if you would have dinner with me tonight?"

She paused. "I'm still training Brynn. And I already ate."

Disappointment flipped in his gut. "That's fine. How about tomorrow? I really want to talk to you."

A long exhale sounded on her end. "Okay. What time?"

"I'll pick you up at six?"

"I'll be ready."

Was he? Could he really do more? *Guess I'll have to find out.*

"Goodnight, Beauty."

"Night, Mase."

Something a lot like hope rattled in his chest at the nickname, banging on his rib cage. Maybe he could have it all this time.

26

PIPPA

Pippa swished another coat of mascara on her lashes and blinked before checking her appearance. Her belly flipped with anxiety. She took a deep breath and let it out as Lady whined and nudged her.

"I'm okay, girl. Just nervous for my date. Or, well, non-date—whatever this is." Her eyes flicked to the mirror and she turned sideways. Was the emerald-green dress too much? He was probably going to take her out and feed her before telling her this couldn't continue and that what had happened between them couldn't happen again. That would be fine. She'd been the one to pull away first. *So why does this make me feel so disappointed?*

Pippa shook her head as if it would help relieve some of her jitters. She walked over to the box on her coffee table, filled with battery-powered fairy lights, rainbow curtains she'd sewn, hanging beads, and even a book sculpture she'd made especially for Aspen to have in her tree house. A few colorful pillows stuck out from the top of the container.

A knock at the door had her stomach leaping to her throat. Lady walked over, sniffing before she sat.

"Here we go." Pippa took another fortifying breath as she opened the door with a trembling hand.

Her eyes ran from the shiny dress shoes up his black ironed slacks with the impressive bulge below the belt. The scent of fresh rainwater filled her senses as her gaze roamed farther, up the matching black button-up shirt that stretched across Mason's massive torso. Folded sleeves near his elbows revealed veined forearms that had once held her.

He cleared his throat, and her eyes darted to his. A smirk played on his lips, but his eyes were dark with his own lust. *Good to know I'm not alone in this.*

"Beauty, you look . . ." Those orbs dropped down the length of her before returning to her face, singeing every inch of her with desire. ". . . breathtaking."

Heat rose to her cheeks. Arousal bloomed in her core.

"These are for you." He thrust a bouquet of peach-colored roses already in a vase towards her.

She accepted them and inhaled their sweet fragrance. "Beautiful. Thank you."

"Ready for dinner?" he asked.

"Let me just put these somewhere." She darted to the kitchen and set them down on the small island before slipping on a pair of gold ballet flats and grabbing Lady's leash. "Oh, could you grab that box?"

Mason stepped inside, picking up her surprise for Aspen as his forehead wrinkled in confusion.

"It's for the tree house."

His large hand landed on her shoulder, halting her steps. "Thank you."

She shrugged like it wasn't a big deal, though her heart

skipped a beat and a thousand tiny fireworks exploded in her belly.

Mason waited patiently while she set the alarm and then locked her door. His hand pressed to the small of her back as he led her to his truck and opened the door for her and Lady to climb in. He set the box in the back of the vehicle before he got in his seat and started the car. Soft, slow music played on the radio.

"You look really good tonight too." *Did he get his hair and beard trimmed?* The top of his head was combed to one side, but the edges were neatly shaved. The man looked like Tom Hardy, but even sexier, if that were possible.

He smiled and reached out to take her hand in his as he navigated through the town. She should pull her hand away, put some more distance between them. His thumb stroked the soft flesh between her thumb and forefinger. Arousal swirled in her belly, unfurling and sending tingles through her. *Fuck, I knew I should have worn underwear.*

"So, what's in the box?"

"A few things to decorate Aspen's tree house. We talked about it at the dinner party and I wanted to surprise her." Pippa tugged down her dress self-consciously with her free hand.

Mason laughed softly. "You spoil her."

She shrugged. "Every girl deserves to be spoiled every now and then."

He squeezed her hand and glanced over before he turned down another road. "Well, tonight is my night to indulge you."

So maybe he wasn't going to tell her this had to end? Her sigh of relief was short-lived. Sure. She'd pulled away, but every time she saw him, her resolve wavered. *But then that would mean—was this a date?*

Mason parked the truck at Atlantis. She had no complaints about the return visit—the food was amazing, and she'd been craving that cheesecake since their last trip here. Mason helped her and Lady out of the car. His hot palm against the small of her back was doing her lady bits no favors. The man barely touched her and she was wet. He guided her through the restaurant.

Mason pulled out a chair for her at the small table they were seated at on the back deck overlooking the bay and the setting sun. She got settled as he took the seat across from her. A candle flickered in the mason jar between them, reflecting in his gaze.

He started with small talk after they put in their drink and meal orders. By the time the food came, Pippa was on pins and needles. Was this a date? It felt like one. But he'd made it clear he only wanted a friend with benefits. This wasn't how that scenario usually went.

The server came back, depositing their meals in front of them—seafood Alfredo for her and crab-stuffed ravioli for him.

"Aspen wanted to make sure I checked on you this week," Mason said before taking a sip of his scotch.

Is that was this is? A pity date? "Oh? I'm sorry if I scared her in the tree house." Pippa filled a fork with pasta but hesitated to take a bite.

Mason reached out, placing his hand over her arm. "It was scary, and I have some medical training. But I answered her questions and gave her a better understanding of your condition. At least, as much as I know. I'm just glad you're okay."

Pippa smiled and took a bite, buying her time to reply. "I'm fine. You never really get used to it, but you just learn to deal with it."

A soft, warm breeze blew over them, bringing the brine of the sea. This was her favorite thing about living on the seacoast—the ocean. She turned back to find him watching her. The burnt-orange sunset made him glow. Flecks of gold were highlighted in his hair and beard. Those gemstone orbs remained on her, giving nothing away.

"I know it's a lot. I would never ask you to . . . I get why you don't want this to go any further." She took another bite and looked away.

Mason set down his fork and rested his elbows on the table, rubbing his palms together. "That's actually what I wanted to talk to you about tonight."

Pippa took a sip of her iced tea, her dinner plate becoming that much more interesting. *Hold it together. You knew this was coming.*

"My wife was a few years older than me. When we met, it was a whirlwind ordeal." He blew out a breath. "I thought I'd met the love of my life while on leave. Amanda was in the military too. She understood the lifestyle. She got pregnant with Aspen really quick. She was already on her way out of the service. Didn't re-up her contract. We were married as soon as I could get back to the States. She moved to where I was stationed, in Washington."

A pang of jealousy lit in the pit of Pippa's stomach, which she immediately shoved aside with guilt. This was Aspen's mother. Without Amanda, that sweet little girl wouldn't exist. What had happened to her?

"It all happened so fast. I was a SEAL, which is what I'd always wanted. She was home taking care of Aspen, but . . . she struggled. She needed help and I missed the signs." He shrugged and sat back, crossing his arms over his chest. "Or maybe I was just too selfish to see what was right in front of me. Either way, I wasn't there for her and she was killed."

"I'm so sorry." Pippa reached out, her palm open on the table, offering it to him. After all, he was being vulnerable with her.

Mason slipped his hand in hers. "Drunk driver . . ." His mouth opened and closed as if he wanted to say more but couldn't.

"How old was Aspen?"

"Three. And I still had a couple years left of my contract. My dad and brother took care of her when I had to go on missions."

Wow. That was a lot for a young man to deal with. Good thing he had family to help. "She's lucky to have you."

He cleared his throat and took his hand back before taking a bite of his food. "Aspen is my priority now, with no exceptions."

"I understand there isn't room for . . ." *Me.*

The clang of his fork against his bowl made her look up. Mason's gaze locked on her, soft and hopeful as he reached out his hand once more to her. The pad of his calloused thumb softly stroked her wrist. "But I want there to be room . . . for you."

Pippa's mouth parted in a gasp. Of all the things she'd expected him to say tonight, that wasn't it. She hadn't dared to hope.

"Mason, I need you to be clear right now. Are you saying what I think you're saying? You want for us to be more than . . . friends with benefits?"

He leaned in, reached out his hand to stroke her jaw. "That's exactly what I'm saying."

Her heart raced. Chills skated up her arms. Lady moved, settling on her feet below the table.

"Not saying I won't fuck this up. I've never . . . this is all relatively new to me. I'm saying that I'd like to see where this goes. What do you think?"

Her ears rang as she swallowed, trying to gather some semblance of control. Joy burst like a million tiny water balloons in her chest, saturating her in hope. Could she do this? Would it be fair to him and Aspen? She didn't want to burden anyone, but how could she not take this risk?

"I'd like to try too."

He grinned, only half his mouth quirking up because of his scars, and it was one of the most beautiful things she'd ever seen.

"I was hoping you'd say that." He stood and came around the table to plant a light kiss on her mouth. She parted her lips to deepen the kiss but he pulled away, teasing her.

Mason took his seat once more, his dark eyes focused on her. "Eat your dinner before it gets cold. You're gonna need the energy."

She giggled. "I hope dessert is included in this evening you have planned for us?"

His gaze darkened with lust. "I've already ordered it to go. Atlas made a whole peanut butter chocolate cheesecake just for us."

Her eyes widened. "To go?"

"I was thinking we'd take it back to my place and I can feed it to you. Then I'll take my turn and eat it off your body."

Pippa's jaw slackened. *Oh, fuck me sideways.* Images of Mason doing exactly what he'd suggested flit through her mind.

Pippa's hand shot up. "Ch-check, please."

27

PIPPA

Pippa opened her mouth, her gaze locked on Mason's. His eyes flashed with arousal as she closed her lips over the fork.

"Mmm." The creamy peanut butter and rich chocolate cheesecake melted on her tongue.

Mason's throat bobbed as his gaze dipped to her mouth. His eyes drooped half closed, as if he were drunk. Spirals of lust spun up her body. She swallowed and licked her lips, her chest puffing out at the power of having such an effect on this man.

He leaned against the bedframe. Both of them knew where this was going. There was no need to pretend otherwise. They'd gone into his house, and like the gentleman he was, he'd gotten Lady situated with a bowl of water. Then he'd asked her if she wanted to eat in the kitchen, or the living room, or . . . Pippa had taken his hand and led him up the stairs. But he was the one who'd opened his bedroom door and led her over to the mattress where they sat, side by side.

He cut off another bite of the dessert and offered it to her.

Pippa took her time, slowly parting her lips, hoping she looked seductive as she slipped it into her mouth again.

"Don't you want some?" she asked.

He leaned in, capturing her mouth in a kiss, his tongue sliding in to duel with hers. She sucked, reaching out to cradle his head in her hands.

"Mmm." He groaned before pulling back. "Tastes almost as delicious as you."

Her eyebrows rose. "Almost, huh?"

"I like it better off your body." His finger traced over the swells of her breasts above the emerald dress.

"So what are you waiting for?" Her voice came out so quiet. Something about this moment required whispered reverence.

"What's the rush?" He set the cake on the bedside table. Besides his actual bed, there wasn't much in the dark blue room. It was clean, with military precision. A dresser with a box on top was the only other piece of furniture in the sparse space. A few pictures of Aspen adorned the walls, but that was it.

"I've been waiting a long time for this . . . for you." She met his gaze, lifting the hem of his shirt.

He helped her get it off his body and threw it onto the floor while getting to his feet. "Which is why we should savor every moment."

He reached out a hand to her. She took it and stood. She didn't say a word as he spun her around, locating the zipper on the back of her dress. The sound of the teeth parting as he slowly undressed her was the only noise in the otherwise quiet room.

"Should we put some music on?" Pippa asked as cool air rushed over her bare back. Nerves swirled in her belly, tying her belly into knots. He'd never seen her fully naked. He hadn't yet laid eyes on her rolls and cellulite. "Maybe dim the lights?"

Her dress dropped, and she closed her eyes. The silence was deafening. *Is he turned off by my naked body?*

"No. I don't want music to drown out your whimpers and sighs when I taste every inch of this gorgeous body." He rested his hands on her shoulders, spinning her around to face him. The blue in his eyes formed a thin ring around the black lust eclipsing his gaze.

Her chest rose and fell, her sensitive nipples grazing his hard abs. Whatever nerves she'd had were replaced with the burning desire to fulfill every single one of this man's fantasies.

"I want to hear each sexy sound that drips from these lips." Mason pressed his finger to her mouth. Pippa's tongue darted out, needing to taste some part of him, drive him half as crazy as he was making her.

A deep grunt came from his chest. "I don't want the low lights to dim the look in your eyes as I bring you to orgasm with my mouth." He kissed the corner of her lips. "Or with these hands." His palm slid down her back, squeezing her ass and pulling her tighter to him. "And finally, with this cock." He thrust against her, his erection teasing her.

Pippa gasped.

"Now, it's my turn to enjoy dessert. Why don't you spread that fucking sexy body on my bed for me?"

Yes! Anything you want, the answer is yes. Pippa backed up, crawling backwards onto the mattress just like he'd instructed. She'd expected demands from a military man, but Mason was . . . different. In so many ways. He treated her like she was precious.

He picked up the plate with the cheesecake, slicing pieces. Mason took some of the cold dessert and pressed it to her nipple. He swirled it around her hard bud before he sucked her tight peak into his mouth. She gasped at the conflicting temperatures and sensations.

"Your tits are perfect." He groaned. Mason laved and licked, raking his teeth over the sensitive peaks.

Hot need and hazy want throbbed in her core. She moaned, clutching his head to her breast. His calloused hands swept over her stomach before he released her nipple with a pop. He added another piece of cheesecake to the other breast and repeated the explicit act.

"Mason! Oh my God. Yes."

"Mmmmm," he hummed around her aching peak.

"Please. I need . . ."

Mason kissed down her stomach, trailing to her hips. "What do you need, Beauty? Tell me. Say it so I can give it to you."

"You. I need *you*. I need more."

Teeth raked over the stretch marks on her thigh before his tongue swirled to soothe the bite. "I'm gonna get there, baby. Promise."

Hot, wet kisses peppered the inside of her thighs before he hooked her legs over his shoulders. Something cold touched her clit. Pippa gasped and sat up on her elbows.

Mason smirked between her thighs. "Need one more bite of my favorite dessert."

"Oh my God, Mason, my cli—ohhhh. Don't stop."

His beard scratched her sensitive thighs as his head bobbed between them. His hot tongue contradicted the cool dessert on her clit. He licked and sucked, and pressure built deep in her core. Her hands clenched the sheets as her head fell back to the bed. Her thighs squeezed together the closer she got. Mason's tongue licked up her slit, lapping at her as he groaned his approval.

"Ooooh, fuuuuuck. Mason, I'm going to—" Her body

locked up, tensing as a hot surge of pleasure spun through her. She arched her back, crying out.

Mason's large hand dug into her hips, pressing her to the bed, forcing her to submit to the waves of her orgasm as they crashed over her again and again. His tongue lashed her clit as he slipped two fingers inside her, curving them so they reached *that* spot.

"Mason!"

"That's it, Beauty. Come for me." He looked up from her thighs, dragging his beard, soaked with her essence, over her pussy.

Had she ever been this worshipped by a man? *Never.*

"Please, Mason. I need to taste you."

He licked his lips and pulled off his pants and boxers, adding them to the growing pile of clothing on the floor. His gorgeous thick cock stood to attention, curving up slightly. He couldn't get any more perfect.

He crawled on the bed next to her. "Sit on my face."

Guess I was wrong. "I'll smother you," she protested.

He smiled. "What a way to go."

She giggled as he slapped her ass. Pippa climbed on top of him, keeping most of her weight on her knees as she leaned forward, taking his hard cock in her hand. Her fingers only just reached around the whole thing. She dipped her head and licked the pre-cum off the tip. His cock jerked in her hand as he dove into her pussy. Hands clasped her hips, forcing her sex against his face. He sucked her clit and hummed. Her eyes rolled to the back of her head. How was she supposed to focus on sucking him off when he was doing *that?*

Her mouth enveloped him as his tongue glided between her folds. She reached for his balls, rolling them gently in her hand as they tensed.

Fingers dug into her skin, hard enough to leave bruises. She sucked him down, running her tongue along his shaft.

She gasped as he lifted her, rolling her to the side. Mason turned around, climbing on top of her before his mouth captured hers, melding their arousal with the sinful kiss.

"Can't get enough." His chest heaved against hers. "Need you."

"I'm all yours." She kissed him back, reaching for his cock. "Do you have a condom?"

His hand clasped her wrist. "Fuck. No. I don't. Shit. It's been so long. I haven't . . . You're the first since . . ."

She blinked. Was he saying what she thought he was saying? "How long exactly?"

"Ten years, give or take." He looked down at the pillow under her. "We can stop. Or, I can run out—"

She kissed him, silencing his panic. "I'm clean, and I'm on the pill. We don't have to use one if you don't want."

His gaze shifted back to her and softened. "Really?"

"I trust you."

He stared at her, the air thick between them, charged with so much more than lust. Mason was the first man she truly wanted to let inside. She wanted enough of these nights to fill a lifetime. The thought should have scared her, but with those ocean eyes focused on her like she was the most beautiful person he'd ever seen, there was nothing but need.

Mason lined up his cock at her entrance, sliding just the tip in. "Are you ready?"

"Give it to me. Give me everything," she pled.

He thrust inside her. Their bodies collided like two halves of the same soul. Inevitable. Beautiful, yet devastating. Nothing would ever be the same after this.

Mason's forehead bunched as he pulled out and drove into her again and again. Bated breaths were shared between them. Limp and boneless, she could do nothing but brace herself against his thick biceps. His muscles clenched under her touch as he drove her closer to oblivion.

"So fucking sexy. So tight." His deep voice panted in between his grunts.

Pippa's ears rang, pleasure wrapping her in a warm embrace. Flames of lust unfurled from her core, seeping into every cell. Drunk on ecstasy, high on desire, Pippa cried out. His cock hit the most perfect, sensitive spot inside her. She lifted her legs, spreading them wider, inviting him deeper.

Mason bent and captured her mouth in his as he lifted her against the headboard. She wrapped her legs around him, holding on to his scarred shoulder as he kept her suspended, pinned to the wood behind her. He thrust inside her from his knees, burying himself so deep she wasn't sure where he ended and she began.

"Mason!" She closed her eyes, fighting the surging, prickling pleasure.

"You're mine. Say it."

"Yours. All yours." She was fully and completely at this man's mercy.

"You ready, baby?"

"Yes."

"Look at me. You're so fucking gorgeous when you come. Like heaven on earth."

Her eyes snapped open, locking onto his. He drove into her, hard. "Mine."

"Yours."

Higher and higher, he spun her. His grip tightened on her hips as her orgasm ripped through her, decimating anything she'd ever experienced before. She flew off the cliff, willingly diving into the abyss of all-encompassing pleasure.

"Mason!" Her eyes widened as she fought the urge to close them.

He roared her name as he came inside her, hot spurts of his cum filling her up. His body jerked. Mason's pupils widened, showing the flash of his soul for that one perfect moment in time where nothing else mattered but their shared vulnerable bliss.

Leaning in, his mouth slanted over hers. Emotion welled in her chest. The man kissed her like he loved her too.

"You're all mine, Beauty. I'm never letting you go now." He buried his head in her neck.

"I don't want you to," she admitted. How had she gotten this deep so fast?

"And I'm yours." His hot breath tickled her skin, sending a shiver through her.

She clamped her eyes shut. Hope and love burst in her chest, exploding like fireworks, lighting her up from the inside out. Was it really this easy?

She smiled, holding on to him just a little tighter. Was Mason the one man who would be there for her through it all? The one man who wouldn't leave her when she needed him most?

I hope so, because he already has my heart.

This huge risk was scary—but she had to do it. Loving Mason might be the bravest thing she'd ever done in her life.

28

MASON

Mason's eyes flickered open, dropping to the beauty in his arms. Pippa's naked flesh was still pressed against him, his cock nudging the opening of her bitable ass cheeks. *How long has it been since I've woken up to a woman in my bed?*

More than a decade. At first it had been deployment, and then grief. His whole life had revolved around diapers and baby dolls. Somewhere amongst those sleepless nights, Aspen had grown into a teenager, and he was still . . . waking up alone. He might have been an anomaly, but no one had ever tempted him to change the way he lived his life until Pippa.

A small snore came from her parted lips. He smiled, leaning down to inhale the juncture of her neck and collarbone before placing a kiss on her cheek. He pulled his arm out from under her, careful not to wake her. Pippa stirred, rolling to her belly and hiking her knee up so that it slipped out of the slate-blue sheets. *We'll have to try that position later.*

He shook his head and tugged on a pair of grey NAVY sweatpants—the same ones he'd let Pippa borrow.

Mason slipped into the en suite bathroom, brushed his teeth and relieved himself before he motioned to the dog and opened the bedroom door.

"Come on, girl. Let's let your mama rest."

Lady perked her ears up from her spot at the bottom of the bed. Mason had let her in after Pippa had fallen asleep. Lady sniffed her owner and then, seemingly satisfied, jumped off the bed. The dog stretched and then followed Mason downstairs to the back door. Mason let her out to the backyard to do her business while he made coffee and breakfast.

Birds chirping filtered in from the open door as the smell of coffee permeated the kitchen. Mason called Lady in, replenishing her bowl of water and putting out some leftover chicken cutlets he had sitting in the fridge. *I'll have to ask what kind of dog food Pippa uses for next time.* And there would be a next time. Nervous excitement burst in his chest.

"Come on, girl. Let's go bring your mommy some breakfast." Mason lifted the makeshift tray, which was really a cookie sheet filled with their mugs of coffee, a bowl of fruit he'd just cut up, and some bagels with cream cheese.

He padded up the steps, his stomach flipping, excited to get back to the sleeping goddess in his bed.

He smiled. Pippa was now sprawled across the bed like a starfish. The sheet had lowered, showing off the soft dip of her spine. Carefully, he set the tray on the bedside table before running his finger down her spine. He wanted to explore all her curves in the light of day. Pippa's shoulder twitched.

"Good morning, Sleeping Beauty." Mason sat on the edge of the bed.

Pippa turned her head towards him, flashing her eyes open for a moment before shutting them again. A pleased and lazy smile was painted across her face.

"Do you always sleep like a starfish?" he teased.

She frowned, her bottom lip pouting as she pulled her arms and legs back towards her body. "I'm not used to having to share my space."

He chuckled. "Me either."

Pippa sat, rubbing her eyes as she turned over. The sheet fell to her waist, but she made no move to cover herself. Mason drank in the view of her tits on display and swallowed. His cock shot to attention.

"Do I smell coffee?" She gave him a sleepy smile.

"I brought breakfast too." He scooted next to her and pulled the tray onto his lap.

Pippa's eyes widened. "Wow. I'm getting the royal treatment, huh?"

"I'd hardly call a couple bagels and a bowl of fruit the royal treatment."

She placed her hand on his naked chest. "No one's ever brought me breakfast in bed before. Thank you."

How could no one treat this woman like the queen she was? Every other man's loss was his gain.

"I should take Lady out first," Pippa said.

"Already done. And I fed her."

Pippa's eyes widened before she reached for one of the mugs of coffee. "You make it too easy."

His brows drew together. "Make what easy?"

Her eyes searched his, as if studying his reaction. "Falling for you."

Those words should have scared him. He never would have allowed things to go this far if he didn't see the possibility of a future with Pippa. He was falling for her too.

"Last night, you said you were all mine."

A light rosy hue tinted her cheeks. "If you want that. I mean, I know it was the heat of the moment—"

"Doesn't matter. I always say what I mean."

Her eyes widened. "Always?"

Mason's thumb trailed over her jaw. He leaned in, pressing a chaste kiss on her lips. "Always."

Relief flashed in her gaze. "Good to know."

"If you like this"—he motioned to the tray and smirked—"just wait until you see what I have planned for after breakfast."

"Oh, yeah? And what is on the agenda?"

Mason took a sip of his own coffee. "I'm thinking brunch, but you're on the menu this time."

Pippa coughed and set down the mug while she tried to catch her breath. "It's a good thing I have the bookstore covered today, then." She bit her lip. "I thought for sure you'd had enough of me last night."

Mason set the tray back on the table before he wrapped his arms around her. "I'm not sure that's possible, Beauty."

This kiss was slow and sensual. He took his time, coaxing her tongue with his. She tasted like coffee and new beginnings. Rolling over on top of her, he braced himself on his elbows, staring directly in her eyes.

Her nipples hardened against his chest as desire bloomed in her dilated pupils.

"Are you sore?" he asked.

She shook her head, her fingers threading through the longer hair at the top of his scalp.

"You're so goddamned sexy." Mason pressed a kiss to her mouth, and then her jaw, peppering more of them down her body as he trailed his hands to her breasts. Every part of her was soft and feminine. He couldn't get enough. Each touch was like a hit of the most potent drug. Arousal flooded through him as he situated himself between her thighs. Her mouth parted as she looked down at him.

Mason breathed in the sweet musk of her sex and groaned. "You smell so fucking good."

"Mason."

"I got you, baby. Just lie back and relax. Let me make you feel good." His cock pressed against the mattress painfully. He thrust his hips over the bed as he licked up her slick heat. She gasped, her thighs squeezing around his head. Going down on a woman had always been one of his favorite activities, but this —with Pippa—was so much better than he ever remembered.

"Play with your tits," he ordered before diving back into her pussy, finding her clit.

Pippa arched her back. "Oh my God!" she whined. "*Please*, Mason."

"Don't worry, Beauty. I'm gonna give you what you need." He was going to take her to the highest of heights. Maybe then she'd understand the free fall he was experiencing because of her.

Pippa had knocked him off his axis. *I only hope I don't fail her too.*

An hour and a half and one shower later, Mason's gaze was glued to Pippa's round ass as she climbed the ladder to the tree house ahead of him.

"You sure this is a good idea?" he asked, entering the structure behind her.

She plucked the pillows out of the box she'd brought and set them on the window seat for Aspen. "Yes. I have you to keep me safe. And I want to get all this set up so she has a surprise when she comes home from camp."

Another piece of his heart fell for the woman before him. The way she genuinely cared for Aspen, going above and beyond, was just one of the things he liked about her. "What can I do to help?"

She pointed to the window. "There's beads to hang on those with rainbow curtains."

He got to work, untangling strings of plastic sparkly beads before hooking them over the curtain rods between the colorful curtains. By the time he was done, Pippa had everything else set up. Sparkly lights hung around the ceiling, like blinking stars. A flameless candle with fake drippy wax adorned the small bookshelf. And a sculpture of a girl fighting a dragon, like the ones in the bookstore, sat on the shelf.

He was speechless. Pippa had taken the bones of the tree house and, with a few personal touches, turned it into a fairy land of infinite possibilities for a young girl's imagination. And wasn't that true for him too? Hadn't she swept into his life, leaving pieces of herself until she was imbedded in his DNA as well? Before Pippa, he was content with his life. Aspen was all he needed. But now . . . Pippa made him want more, and for the first time in his life, he believed it was possible.

"What do you think?" Pippa asked.

Mason sat against the wall, pulling Pippa against his chest. He kissed her forehead, rubbing his hand up and down her arm. His chest squeezed tight and his eyes burned. "I think . . . Beauty, I just might keep you forever."

29

PIPPA

Pippa eyed the woman setting a pile of books on the counter in front of her. "It's Mia, right?"

Mia smiled. "*Si.*"

Pippa yawned for the third time in five minutes as she scanned Mia's books and placed them in a bag. "Excuse me. I think I need some more coffee."

Mia studied her a moment before her mouth quirked up in a knowing smile. "Does a certain SEAL have anything to do with your lack of sleep, perchance?"

Pippa snapped her attention back to the computer screen. That was *exactly* why she was so tired. She'd spent the last few days with Mason. In between their work schedules, they'd spent every waking minute together, learning each other's bodies. Laughing with one another. The man even went as far as reading one of her romance novels to her. He was as close to perfection as one could get. "Why would you think that?"

Mia leaned in. "I knew it! The girls said something was going on between Mr. Serious All The Time and our lovely bookstore owner."

Pippa's face burned red hot. *How did anyone know?*

"*No te preocupes.* Your secret is safe with us."

Pippa peeked around the bookstore, making sure everyone else was out of earshot. "How did you know? And who are the girls? We barely started this."

Mia grinned. "My yoga studio is full of chatty Cathys who have been trying to catch that man's eye for years. The women of Shattered Cove notice when a man like that is seen around town with someone who isn't them."

"Really?"

Mia shrugged. "Small towns. Everybody wants to know everyone else's business. It can be both good and not so good if you intend to keep secrets—trust me. I know from experience."

"Look, Mason and I . . . we just . . ."

Mia waved her hand. "Don't worry about it. You don't owe me an explanation. I'm just glad to see someone put a smile on that grump's face for once besides his daughter."

Pippa bit back her own smile and accepted Mia's credit card before taking payment. "Would you like to come to our next romance book club meeting? We're finishing up the last book and picking a new one."

"*Sí.* I'm thinking I may vote for a military romance, maybe one starring a SEAL as the hero." Mia winked.

Pippa shook her head. "Have a great day."

"You too, *chica.*"

Mia left as Pippa's phone chimed. Pippa picked it up and read the message that flashed on her phone.

Mason: *I'll be by in ten minutes to pick you up. Want to eat in tonight?*

Pippa: *You know what happened last time we "ate in." I wouldn't want you to be late for work again.*

Mason: *I have tonight off. You know what that means?*

Pippa bit her lip, a myriad of dirty fantasies coming to mind.

Pippa: *No. Please tell me. In detail.*

Mason: *It means I'm cooking for you. You'll need your energy for the night I have planned.*

She was definitely looking forward to their evening together. But she couldn't help but wonder how this would work when Aspen got back. He hadn't as much as held her hand when his daughter was around before. Would it be different now?

Pippa: *And what exactly is on the agenda?*

"What's that smile for?" Troy's voice made her jump like she'd been caught with her hand in the cookie jar.

"Nothing," she squeaked, pocketing her phone as it dinged.

Troy set his water bottle on the desk with a sly smile. "I see."

A moment of awkward silence passed between them before Troy spoke again. "Anything I need to know before you go?"

She cleared her throat. "No. Same as usual. The new episodes of *Selfie* just got delivered. They're in the back room. Just save a copy at the front desk for me, please."

He nodded. "Got it."

"Alright, I'll be back at six to lock up."

"See you then."

Crash!

Pippa jumped and Lady barked, standing alert at her side. Troy darted in front of Pippa as they ran to the back of the store to the source of the noise. Her heart raced as she took in the scene. Broken glass littered the floor from her giant bay window. Jagged shards of glass framed the pane that over-looked the square of green grass and woods beyond the shop, almost like a ferocious set of teeth. A large brick sat in the center of the mess with black letters scrawled across it.

Depart from me, you cursed, into the eternal fire prepared for the devil and his angels.

Come to the Lord before it's too late, or you will burn.

"Are you okay?" Troy asked, holding out his arms to her.

Pippa fell into them, shaken and numb.

"I'm calling the police." Troy grabbed his phone, his voice fading into background noise as a memory ripped Pippa back into the past.

Pippa was nauseous and cold. Her body shook with chills as she struggled against the ropes.

"Be still, girl. Can't you see we are trying to save your soul?" Her foster mother's eyes were filled with tears and determination.

"Devil, you must leave this child of God alone. In the name of Jesus, I command you to leave her!" her foster father shouted, rolling pungent oil on her forehead in the shape of a cross as his wife started speaking in some unintelligible language.

"Please let me go," Pippa begged.

"Demons, I command you to leave this child. Be gone!"

"I don't have demons. Please! Just let me go."

Pippa cried, wishing her dad hadn't gone to prison when she needed him most. Praying to her mother's god that her sister's guardianship would be put through soon so that she could leave this hell.

"Please help me. Let me go!"

"Pippa? Pippa, you're shaking. Are you okay?" Troy's voice ripped her from the flashback.

Lady pressed her nose against her thigh, then licked her hand and whined, concern flashing in her big brown eyes. If only she'd had Lady in the past. She'd been with that foster family a day before they'd stopped her anti-seizure medication. The couple didn't believe in epilepsy; they'd been convinced some evil spirit inhabited her body.

"Pippa?" Troy pressed.

"Sorry. I—I just . . ."

"Are you two okay? Is anybody hurt?" Bently asked, his hand on his weapon.

"We're okay. Someone threw that through the window." Troy motioned to the brick.

Bently leaned closer and frowned, his expression growing hard. "Did you see who did it?"

"No." Troy looked to her.

Pippa shook her head.

"You've got cameras this time. Let's see what we can get from them." Bently walked closer.

Pippa pulled out her phone, swiping open the app for her security that Mason had installed. She pulled up the footage and handed it over to Bently. "There aren't any cameras in the back, just the front and the side where my steps lead up to my apartment."

"I'd still like to see the last couple hours, if you're willing?"

Pippa tapped the screen before handing it back to him. "Just enter your number or email here and it will send you a copy."

Bently typed it before he returned the phone to her.

"Do you have any idea who would do this?" Bently asked.

"No. I mean, I recognize the first part of the message. It's a Bible verse. I don't know who would be targeting me or the store." *Who would have—oh!* "I had a run-in with Cara's dad. I don't know his name."

Troy extended his arms to her for a second time, and she hugged him back.

"Lester Marby," Bently supplied.

She nodded. "He's the only one I've had a confrontation with . . . But maybe you should talk to Pastor Calvin too."

"What the fuck happened?" Mason's steely voice made

her jump. His gaze flicked between Troy's arms around her and Pippa.

She walked from one man to the other.

Mason's voice softened as he enveloped her in a hug. "Are you okay?"

She breathed a sigh of relief. Just being in his arms brought her peace in the chaos. *I am now.* She nodded.

"Why didn't you call me?" Hurt bled from his voice, ragged and raw.

She pulled back to look at him. *It only happened a second ago. And I don't want to be a burden.* "This isn't your problem."

"Someone is targeting you. I'd say that is my concern."

Her heart squeezed. Having this amazing man so protective of her brought a rush of warmth to her chest as she fell even more in love with him. But his worry also brought up the ugly dark truth: she was becoming a burden on him, a distraction, which he'd been explicitly clear he didn't want.

"Maybe you should stay with me for now. Until Bently can catch this fucker." Mason growled and held her tighter before kissing her forehead.

She shook her head. She wouldn't add to his stress. "No. I won't let fear win. I'll be fine."

He sighed. "Then I'll stay with you."

She closed her eyes. Could this guy get any more perfect? Where she expected him to go full alpha and take control of a situation, he swerved left. Instead, he listened to what she needed and gave it to her. Surely, he had faults, right? A tiny voice inside her told her to enjoy it while it lasted. But she shoved that annoying warning away, because right there and then, Mason Wright was holding her tight and offering her the world. She'd be a fool to turn him down.

30

MASON

Mason stepped down off the ladder and wiped some of the sawdust off his arm.

"Is that the last one?" Pippa asked, a handful of books pressed against her chest.

"Yes, ma'am. Every angle of this bookstore, inside and out, is now under video surveillance." He wrapped his arm around her and kissed her forehead.

She sighed, leaning into him. He hadn't let her out of his sight since everything had happened yesterday. He'd even called in someone to cover for him at the bar tonight so he could be there for her. Regardless of her stiff spine, and her fierce independence, the woman was shaken by the vandalism. This was a problem he could fix, so he did. He'd put up more security measures, and stayed with her in the comfort of her own home. But maybe tonight he could convince her to come back to his.

"Pippa?" Bently's voice came from behind them.

Mason released her, slipping his arm to her lower back as he set the drill on the ladder step.

"Did you find anything?" Pippa asked, hopeful.

Bently's eyes flicked to Mason's before returning to Pippa's. "No, I'm sorry. Nothing out of the ordinary. We couldn't lift a good set of prints off the brick. It's too porous. But we sent it off to a forensic lab to see if they would have any luck. And I spoke to Pastor Calvin. He had alibies for both times your shop was targeted."

Pippa's shoulders drooped as she nodded. "Thanks for the update."

Bently scanned the bookstore and the few gazes of interested onlookers they'd drawn the attention of. "You added more cameras?"

Mason nodded. "Every square inch is covered now."

"Just be on alert. I let the rest of my team know what's going on and they will all keep a lookout. I'll have someone close by unless we get a bigger callout. I would consider taking some self-defense classes. We offer them for free through the department at Tidal gym every week." Bently handed Pippa a card with the information.

"Thank you."

"Alright, you two have a great rest of your afternoon. My direct line is on the other side of that card. Feel free to call me if anything else happens, night or day. If you feel something is off, let me know." Bently's focus zoned in on Pippa.

"I will."

Bently gave him a nod and then turned and left.

"You know I happen to volunteer at those classes as an instructor," Mason supplied.

Pippa turned to face him, one eyebrow quirked up. "Oh, really?"

He shrugged. "I might be able to get you some private lessons if you want."

A small smile played on her lips. "Are these naked lessons, perchance?"

He chuckled and leaned in. "Not saying we won't end up that way, baby." Mason kissed her jaw, and then her neck. She shivered and leaned into him. *So responsive.* He pulled away, planting his hands on her shoulders. "But I think it's a great idea. Every person should know how to defend themselves. Who better to train you than your boyfriend, who just so happens to be a former SEAL?"

Pippa's eyes widened.

Yes. He'd said it out loud for the first time. But there was no way he was going to let this woman slip through his fingers. The more he had of her, the more his hunger grew. It went far beyond the physical. He loved who she was, so kind and empathetic and . . . and . . . wow. *I love her.*

"Boyfriend, huh?"

"That's what *more* means, doesn't it?"

She nervously moved her bottom lip into her mouth. Mason pressed his thumb to it, pulling it out of her teeth. "That okay with you?"

"I . . . you just . . . you keep surprising me."

"Is that a good thing?"

She nodded. "The best." She stood on tiptoes and melded her mouth against his in a chaste kiss.

He wrapped his arm around her and tugged her closer before she swatted his chest and turned her head to the old lady in the corner, reading a book in a rocking chair. "I'm at work."

"Fair enough." He pulled out his phone, checking the tide schedule quickly. "What do you say to an afternoon of paddle-boarding and watching the sunset at the beach?" She needed to get her mind off everything here and spend the day relaxing. He'd make sure she got that. He set his phone on the top shelf of his tool box.

"I'd say that sounds perfect."

"When does your replacement get in?"

"Brynn should be here in an hour, but Troy can lock up the—"

"Did I hear my name?" The man himself walked over to them.

Mason straightened and tugged Pippa closer to his side. Finding her in this man's arms yesterday had set him off.

"Yes, Mason was asking when you got in so we could take off," Pippa explained.

Troy's gaze cut to Mason's, his eyebrows rising. "Well, don't let me keep you. Will you be back at six to lock up as usual?"

"Actually . . ." Pippa dug a key from her pocket and handed it to him. "I made a copy so you can close up tonight, and leave it in my mailbox before you leave."

He tucked it against his chest and smiled. "I will guard it with my life, my lady."

Pippa giggled and Mason's fist clenched.

"Have a good afternoon." Troy waved them away.

"Oh, Brynn will be here in an hour. If you could show her where to shelve the new delivery of books, that would be appreciated," Pippa reminded her employee as Mason packed up the ladder and closed his toolbox.

Troy nodded and gave her a friendly smile.

"Come on, go grab what you need from your apartment and meet me at the truck." Mason guided her and Lady out the front door, and kept an eye on her ass swaying from side to side as she made her way up the steps to her apartment. He deposited his supplies into the bed of the truck and stashed his toolbox in the back. They'd need to stop at the general store for some sandwiches. They wouldn't last long on the coffee and treats from Stardust Café they'd had hours ago. He'd give her an afternoon to remember.

Ten minutes later, Pippa walked down the stairs, and he almost swallowed his tongue. Every tanned inch of her glowed bronze in the summer sun as she walked down in a red high-waisted bikini and a white flowing wrap. His cock jumped to attention. How was he supposed to keep his hands off her when Aspen got back this weekend? How was he supposed to go back to sleeping in his bed alone? He had to take this slow, for Aspen's sake. Mason was so fucked.

Hours later, and after a couple dips in the cold ocean, Mason had managed to keep his hands to himself—mostly. Being on two separate paddleboards helped.

The fuchsia and orange sunset lit the waves on fire. Flames danced along the blue-green waters. Mason turned towards Pippa. She was sitting on her board, holding his hand as they witnessed a one-of-a-kind display in front of them. They'd spent the afternoon walking down the beach with Lady, enjoying a picnic, and talking about everything and anything. It was so easy with her. She fit right into his life, like the other half of a puzzle piece he hadn't realized was missing until he'd found her.

"It's breathtaking."

His gaze locked on her sun-kissed face as their bodies swayed with the waves. "Sure is."

She inhaled, long and deep, a smile coasting on her sweet mouth. "Thank you for today. I really needed it."

"Anything for you, Beauty."

She scrunched her nose. "Every time you call me that, it makes me think of *Beauty and the Beast.*"

"Is that a bad thing?"

"No. It's one of my favorite Disney movies, but not fairy tales, because the actual story is much more tragic."

"Yeah, most of them are pretty fucked up," he agreed.

"Almost as bad as Greek myths." She giggled. "Troy tried to convince me we should get some mythology books for the store."

Mason clenched his jaw. "He seemed awfully flirty with you today."

Pippa turned towards him, her head tipped to the side. "What?"

"You're jealous."

"Damn right. The man had his arms around you yesterday," he admitted.

Surprise flashed in her brown eyes. "You're so honest."

"Is that a bad thing?"

A beat of silence passed. There was no sound but the watery clap of waves lapping at their boards and the few seagulls cawing and screeching.

She finally shook her head. "No, it's just . . . It makes it so much easier to trust you."

"Shouldn't you?"

Her gaze darted to the water as she sighed. Hesitation bled from her. Mason squeezed her hand in his. "Hey, baby, tell me what's on your mind."

"Everyone in my life leaves. My own dad, whom I love with all my heart—he was taken away when I was sixteen, when I needed him most. Every boyfriend I've had didn't stick around for the long haul. I . . . I really care about you. I've fallen for you and Aspen. I'm just . . . scared."

He wanted to pull her off her board and onto his lap, but that wasn't possible. They'd both end up getting soaked. "Look at me."

She focused her dark brown eyes on his.

"I'm here. Whatever you need. I know I told you I couldn't handle a relationship in the beginning, but I know I can now. The truth is, I can't imagine my life without you in it anymore." He inhaled a weighty breath before letting it go. He wrapped his hand around hers. "I need to slow this down once Aspen gets home. I'll talk to her and tell her I'm dating you. But I'm in this. We'll find a way to make this work."

Her eyes grew watery, the pink haze of the fathomless sky reflected in them. "Okay. I trust you."

And I love you. He lifted her hand to his mouth, pressing a kiss above her knuckles. "Should I tell Troy you're taken, or do you want to do the honors?"

She giggled. "He really bothered you, huh?"

Mason frowned.

Her expression softened. "He's harmless really. I would never date an employee. And he really isn't my type. I much prefer the Beast than the prince."

He shook his head. "This is the one time I hope I'm the monster in this analogy."

"Not a monster. A big, handsome, protective grump with a heart of gold behind the thorns."

His chest squeezed. Was that how she saw him? "I need to be inside you right now."

She picked up her paddle. "We better get back to the truck, then."

They paddled towards the shore, now empty of beach-goers as the sun finally set. Mason hurriedly carried their gear to the truck. He poured a water bottle into a bowl for Lady, who eagerly lapped it up.

Mason grabbed Pippa's waist and pressed her against the truck, capturing her mouth in a kiss. She moaned, her hands clutching his biceps, leaving half-moons of want tattooed on his flesh.

"Need you," he rasped.

"Where?"

He peeked around the empty parking lot before opening the passenger-side door. "Will she stay here or should we attach her leash to the back?"

Pippa reached inside her bag under the front seat, pulling out a longer leash. She attached it to the dog and hooked the other end to the tailgate of his truck before returning.

Mason set a towel down before he climbed in the seat and patted the spot next to him. Pippa got in and shut the door as he started the car, rolling down the windows to let cool, salty ocean air into the cab. Slow, sensual music quietly filtered in through the radio.

The indigo sky darkened by the minute, casting her in shadow. The glow of the dials was the only light in the car, coating her tanned skin in a neon green haze. The sound of their bated breaths was amplified in the tight space. Mason reached out for her, cradling her face in his hands as he drew her in for another kiss. He didn't normally rush, preferring to take his time and savor every sigh and moan she made as he committed her body to memory. But tonight, urgency roared. He needed to connect with this woman like the fate of the world depended on their union.

Pippa's eager hands tugged at his board shorts. He broke the kiss long enough to help her pull them off.

Pippa climbed on his lap, hovering over him on her knees.

Mason swiped her bikini bottoms aside before pressing two fingers into her tight heat. "Fuck. You're already wet."

"You have that effect on me." She smiled and swiped her tongue into his mouth. His cock jerked against her core, the head leaking with desire for her.

Mason worked his fingers inside her as she trembled and moaned into his mouth. She was so slick and hot. So ready for him.

"Mason, I'm gonna come."

"So, come, sexy. Let me hear you."

She shook her head, squeezing her thighs together as she lowered herself onto his aching cock. "Want to come with you."

He pulled out his fingers, swirling her juices to her clit before he lined his cock up at her entrance.

"It's all yours, baby." *All of me.* He gripped her hips, guiding her down over him, inch by slow, torturous inch.

She gasped as he filled her, root to tip. "So perfect. I love the way you fill me up."

"You were made for my cock." He clenched his abs as pleasure rolled through him. The scent of her arousal permeated the car, sending spirals of lust scorching through his veins. White-hot yearning melded with something deeper, something spiritual as he thrust his hips, driving her towards the peak they were both so desperate to reach.

"Mason," she pleaded, her voice bleeding with desperation.

"That's it, baby, let go. I've got you. Won't let you fall." He slipped a breast from her bathing suit, swirling his tongue over her hard nipple. She clutched the back of his head, her fingernails raking against his scalp as she rode him closer to oblivion. He shuddered and raked his teeth over her salty skin.

Her moans melded with his groans. She let out a keening cry as he whipped his head up, his cock pulsing past the edge of return. "Look at me, Beauty."

She obeyed. He thrust underneath her and pinched her pert bud with one hand, gripping her ass with the other, directing her movements. She fucked him, their eyes locked while he met her thrust for thrust, driving himself further, trying to reach the deepest parts of her. Sweat beaded on his forehead as pleasure gathered in his spine.

"Come with me now, baby. Come!"

Pippa's mouth opened, her eyes widening as his soul left his body to merge with hers for one perfect moment in time. He came with a roar, every muscle taut as he clenched around her, holding her down on him. Her body trembled with aftershocks as he slanted his mouth over hers and he slowly kissed her. She relaxed in his arms. She was putty in his hands now.

And he was irrevocably and inexplicably in love.

MASON

Mason turned down his street, a grin on his face he still couldn't get rid of. Pippa's hand was wound tightly around his. Once he got to his house, he was gonna run her a bath and wash every inch of her before he laid her out for round two and put her to bed.

"Whose car is that?" Pippa asked.

Mason's gaze jumped to his driveway. A black Jeep was parked there. His brows drew together. "My dad's."

He parked the car before walking around the other side to help Pippa out. Lady followed beside her owner. Pippa reached down to pet her. "I hope we didn't traumatize her with that little escapade back there." She giggled.

The front door slammed open, drawing Mason's attention to his father's distraught expression. The blood drained out of Mason's face. Panic lanced through him. "What's wrong? What happened?"

His father stomped down the steps, cutting a quick glance to Pippa before returning to Mason. "Aspen was hurt at camp—"

"What? Is she okay? Why didn't they call me?" Mason reached for the phone in his back pocket but it wasn't there. He rushed to the car, pulling it from the toolbox where he'd left it when they were in the bookstore before he got distracted by Troy flirting with Pippa. The battery was dead. *How could I be so careless?*

Mason stumbled towards his dad.

"They called you, I called you, Sebastian called you. Hell, no one could get a hold of you for hours!" His dad turned his attention back towards Pippa.

"Is Aspen okay?" Pippa repeated his question.

His father sighed and pointed his thumb over his shoulder. "She's inside. Got a pretty nice shiner."

"Aspen?" Mason ran to the front door, tore it open and ran inside.

"In here, Daddy." Aspen was curled up on the couch, holding an ice pack to her face.

Mason fell to his knees, a million possibilities of what could have happened running through his mind. *I was so stupid. Aspen needed me and I wasn't there. I failed.* He'd let himself get distracted again. How the fuck could he possibly think he could have the best of both worlds?

A gasp fell behind him as Pippa entered the room.

Aspen's eyes widened before they cut to Mason's. "You guys were together?"

Would Aspen forgive him for not being there when she needed him? Was she hurt because he'd been with Pippa? Mason straightened, brushing his thumb over his daughter's cheek before he kissed her forehead.

His dad leaned against the wall, arms crossed.

Pippa walked closer, Lady at her side as usual, and Aspen opened her arms for her. Pippa hugged his daughter, worry evident on her beautiful face. The sight tore a hole in his chest.

"What happened, sweet pea?" Mason asked.

Aspen clung tighter to Pippa, burying her head against her chest.

"Was it the bullies again?" he asked.

Aspen nodded.

"They escalated from name-calling to assault? Tell me what happened so I can fix this, Aspen." Mason clenched his fists. His baby girl had been hurt. Someone was going to pay.

"Did you tell him about Rachel?" Pippa asked.

Mason's gaze snapped to her. *What did Pippa know that he didn't?* "Tell me what?"

Aspen pulled away, wiping the tears from her cheeks. "Telling him only made it worse last time."

Mason's body grew cold. "Pippa, can I see you alone for a minute?" Mason walked towards the front door, passing his father's watchful gaze on his way out.

The warm summer air was much stickier here than it had been at the beach. How did that seem like a lifetime ago when, in reality, it was less than an hour?

A soft hand rested against his arm. "Mason—"

"I asked you one thing—to tell me if my daughter shared anything with you that put her in danger."

"I told her to tell you they were pushing her around. I should have made sure she did it. I'm sorry."

"She's *my* kid." He whipped around, pointing towards the closed door.

"I know that." Pippa's voice was soft as she hugged her arms around her middle.

"I don't think you get it. She's my little girl. My responsibility. My *priority*. Everything I do is for her. It's my job to protect her. No one else. *Me!*"

Pippa flinched. "I'm sorry, Mason. I had no idea it would

turn into this. When she told me what was going on, it was just—"

"I don't want to hear your excuses. My daughter was in danger. You knew and you did nothing after you promised me you would tell me."

"Mason—"

"My dad will take you home." He pushed past her, his heart tearing to shreds as he opened the front door.

"Wait. *Please.*" Her voice sounded so broken, like she'd swallowed shards of glass.

He froze, taking one long inhale before letting it out along with any hope that this was all just one bad dream. He'd been so concerned with Pippa in that red bathing suit, he'd never even thought about checking his phone in the car. Then to find out all this could have been prevented if he'd known the depths of the problem was the cherry on this fucked-up sundae.

He turned towards her once more. "I can't afford any more distractions. Certainly not ones that lie to me."

Her eyes glittered with unshed tears, hurt and anger pouring from her gaze. Her back stiffened. Lifting her chin, she nodded. "For what it's worth, I'm sorry. I never would have intentionally put her at risk. But you have no right to put this all on me."

Mason couldn't look away as the woman who'd managed to jump-start his heart and make him fall in love with her in a couple of short months walked away.

He was doing the right thing for Aspen. So why did it feel like his chest was being eviscerated from the inside out?

32

———

PIPPA

Pippa closed the door to her apartment before the first tear escaped. She clutched the newest episode of *Selfie* that had come in. *This makes four.* Four episodes of the comic that Aspen hadn't come in for. Pippa had been watching out for the little girl who hadn't shown in three weeks. *Not one word from Mason either.* Pippa wasn't sure what hurt the most—the fact that after everything they'd shared, Mason had ghosted her, or that he'd kept his daughter away, too, as if she wasn't fit to be around the young girl.

Pippa walked over to the couch and slumped on her belly across the cushions. Lady came over and licked her cheek. Pippa gave her a watery smile, hoping to ease her pet's concerns. She hadn't been herself since that awkward car ride with Mason's father. Since Mason had torn her heart out and shredded it into a million little pieces.

Everything ached, and for once it wasn't from a seizure, though they'd been coming more frequently too. *I'm probably due for my period soon.*

Ring! Ring!

Pippa's stomach flipped. Every time her cell went off, she couldn't help but hold out just an ember of hope. *I always say what I mean.* Mason's words used to be the biggest comfort; now, they were his sharpest weapon.

She took a deep breath and pulled the phone from her pocket. Her sister's name was displayed on the phone. Pippa sighed and sat up, carefully wiping the wetness from her eyes before she accepted the FaceTime.

She forced a smile. "Hey, *chica.*"

"What's wrong?" Sophia's brows drew together.

Pippa chuckled. There was no hiding anything from her sister. "Why do you think something is wrong?"

Sophia tsked. "You haven't taken a FaceTime call from me in three weeks. Only texts. I'm surprised this one went through. And don't bother to tell me you've been busy with the bookstore. You have employees and you're only open nine to six. There are plenty of evening times for you to call . . . unless . . ."

"Unless what?"

Sophia smiled. "Unless a certain marine is keeping your nights busy."

Tears burned the back of Pippa's eyes as she swallowed a lump of emotion. She shook her head. "He's a SEAL actually. But no, that's . . . over."

"You broke up with him?" Sophia asked. That was how it usually went. Pippa had almost always been the one to pull away.

"Tell me everything, *cariño.*" Her sister's voice softened with sympathy.

Pippa filled her sister in as the tears fell freely. *When would it stop hurting?*

"Oh, Pip, I wish I could be there to hug you. You should have told me weeks ago. That's it; we're coming this weekend. Vivian and I will drive up Friday after I get off work."

"No, Soph. Please. You guys have enough going on with the wedding planning. Don't even try to tell me you wouldn't have to cancel a dress fitting or something. I'll be fine. I'm a big girl, and this isn't my first broken heart." *But it's the only one that's been this painful, like a piece of my soul is missing.*

Sophia sighed and tucked a strand of her dark hair behind her ear. She looked so much like their mother, it was bittersweet. *I wish Mama was here.*

"If you're sure. But, *nena*, you can let someone in. You don't have to deal with everything on your own."

I did, and look what happened. "I know."

"Promise you'll call me if you need me?" Sophia leaned in toward the screen.

Pippa nodded. "I promise, you'll be my first call."

"How are the seizures? Are they worse with the stress?"

"Nope," Pippa lied. "Same as usual."

"Have you eaten dinner?"

"Actually, I was just on my way out to meet a friend. I better go so I won't be late."

Sophia's eyes lit up. "Oh, then don't let me keep you. Call you this weekend. *Te quiro.*"

"I love you too." Pippa ended the call and turned to Lady, scratching behind her furry ears. The dog's brown eyes met hers skeptically.

"Hey, I didn't lie. Brynn is a friend, and she's covering for someone at the diner tonight. Let's go get Mama a shake."

Lady's ears perked up. Pippa smiled and tucked her phone in her pocket as she got to her feet. A wave of dizziness swam through her. She reached out to steady herself on the arm of the couch as Lady barked.

"Check me, girl."

Lady sniffed and licked her hand. All clear. *Must have got up too quick.* And she hadn't eaten much lately either. But that would stop now. She was going to take better care of herself.

Pippa grabbed Lady's leash and set her alarm before locking up behind them. She walked down the steps towards the street, sweat beading on her brow. It was still so hot and muggy. *Perfect evening for a swim at the beach.*

Dark clouds moved to cover the sun, mirroring her emotional state. *Spoke too soon.*

She inhaled, the air wet and charged with energy. *Looks like a storm.* She hurried down the street, not wanting to risk getting caught in a downpour.

She slipped into the diner, the bell above the door ringing. Brynn looked up and offered her a friendly, yet reserved smile. Pippa took one of the blue seats at the counter, and Lady settled in beside her.

"What can I get you?" Brynn asked, taking out her pad of paper and pen.

"A peanut butter chocolate milkshake, a burger for Lady—just the meat, and an order of fries."

"Coming right up." Brynn ripped the paper off and walked back to the window leading to the kitchen where she slipped Pippa's order to the cook. She got to work making the milkshake while Pippa tapped the navy-blue Formica countertop.

"Here you go." Brynn slid the drink to her.

"Thank you." Pippa took the first sip and sighed. "This is just what I needed."

Brynn's brows drew together. "You okay?"

Pippa stirred her drink with the straw as she debated whether or not to share. But Brynn had begun opening up to her at work with small talk, which didn't seem like much, but Pippa got the feeling it was everything to someone like Brynn.

"I'm just missing Aspen." *And Mason.* "I wondered how she was doing after everything."

Brynn leaned in and nodded over Pippa's shoulder. "Why don't you ask her for yourself?"

Pippa turned around. A strawberry-blond head peeked out over the booth in the far right corner. David sat across from her.

Pippa got up, searching the room for the girl's father, but he was nowhere to be seen. Would he be mad at Pippa? She just wanted to see for herself that Aspen was well. *To say goodbye.*

Pippa's legs were moving towards the teens before she could second-guess herself. "Aspen?"

The young girl looked up, her eyes round before her mouth split in a grin. She jumped out of the booth and wrapped her arms around Pippa.

"Pippa! I missed you so much."

Pippa returned the hug, holding her close, one piece of her broken heart put back together. "I missed you too."

Aspen pulled away to look at her. "Dad won't let me go to your bookstore. I'm so mad at him." Her words were like daggers thrown at Pippa's chest.

Fighting tears, Pippa said, "Your dad only wants the best for you."

Aspen rolled her eyes. "He's overprotective."

Pippa chuckled. "Maybe so. But you looked pretty banged up last I saw you. I'm sure that scared him." Pippa searched Aspen's face for signs of injury. Her bruises had faded to a light yellow. "Your eye looks better."

Aspen ran her hand over the spot, only slightly discolored now. "Yeah. It's not bad. I broke Cara's nose though." Aspen smirked.

Pippa's eyes widened. "You what?"

"She hit me first and I did what you said and stood up for myself. I would have been fine if it wasn't four on one—well, three, technically. Rachel didn't hit me; she just tricked me to get me alone so they could ambush me. I thought she wanted to be my friend again."

"Holy shit! I mean, shoot." Pippa covered her mouth.

Aspen giggled. "I never got to thank you for my tree house. It's amazing, just like we talked about."

"You're welcome . . . Has David been bringing you the *Selfie* comics?" Pippa motioned to the young man intently focused on his sketchpad.

"Yeah, all but the latest one."

"I actually kept it aside for you. I'll go grab it and be right back." Pippa walked away, taking Lady with her. She retrieved the copy of the comic from her apartment and walked quickly back to the diner.

"Here you go." She handed the comic to Aspen.

Aspen took the book and set it on the table behind her before turning back to Pippa, her blue eyes watery. "Did my dad do something?"

"Why do you think that?"

"Because he's been so grumpy, and every time I ask to invite you over or come here he gets this really sad look and then he gets angry," Aspen explained.

Pippa sighed and pulled her into a hug, fighting her own tears. "I promise that no matter what, I'll always be here for you, okay? No matter how much time passes. I love you so much."

Aspen sniffed and squeezed her tighter as she nodded. "I love you too."

"I better get going." *Wouldn't want to run into Mason like this. I'm too vulnerable and raw.*

"Bye, Pippa."

"See you later." *Hopefully.* She winked and forced a smile that didn't betray the violent way her heart twisted as she walked away from the young girl she'd come to care about so much.

Her fries and Lady's burger were sitting on the counter. She wasn't hungry anymore. Pippa motioned to Brynn. "Can I get this wrapped up to go? I'm sorry."

Brynn took the food back without a word and produced a to-go bag and cup with her meal.

"Thank you." She grabbed Lady's leash, not because the dog would stray, but because Pippa needed something to tether her before the grief swallowed her up.

She walked outside. The first drops of rain fell, melding with the tears that streamed down her cheeks. She didn't bother swiping them away. Like the rain, they seemed endless. How was she supposed to go on with life without the other half of her heart?

That's what I get for trusting a man again. When would she learn?

33

MASON

Mason stood in the rain, not caring that he was getting soaked. Not when the one woman he'd avoided the last three weeks was hugging his daughter, hiding her pain with a smile so his little girl didn't see how much it was probably tearing her apart to be reminded of how Mason had failed them both in a single afternoon. Protecting Aspen like she'd done at gunpoint. *And how did I thank her?* He'd been shocked at finding his daughter battered and bruised, and was berating himself for missing those ten calls. When he heard the actual story from Aspen, Mason regretted his harsh words to Pippa. He'd panicked, seeing his little girl in pain.

"I was surrounded by them and Cara pushed me and called me names. I was so sick of it. Then I remembered what Pippa told me," Aspen explained.

"Pippa?"

Aspen nodded. *"She told me that it's best to stand up to them . . . so I finally put those self-defense moves you taught me to use . . . Pippa also told me to tell someone I trust to help me. Then she made me promise I would tell you, but I was scared. I'm sorry, Daddy."*

Mason's chest squeezed tight like a vise. "It's okay, sweet pea. I'm just glad you're safe. I'm sorry I wasn't there to get you."

She shrugged. "It's okay. Grandpa got me ice cream on the way home."

Mason had fucked up. And then he'd kept Aspen from Pippa.

A part of him had wondered if it would hurt Pippa more to see Aspen and be reminded of him.

I'm a coward. He'd been angry at himself and he'd blamed Pippa. He'd hurt her in the worst way. His father had ripped him a new one when he'd returned too.

"I don't know what you said to that woman, but she isn't the one who deserves your wrath. I know it was just an accident; I'm sorry if I made you feel like I blamed you. I was just so worried about it because it was so unlike you." His father took a step forward and set his hand on Mason's shoulder. "You missed a call; next time, you'll do better. Luckily you had me and Sebastian to pick up the slack when you needed it. And, son, I've never seen you with a woman since Amanda passed. If you were bringing her home, I imagine Pippa means something to you. But you're an idiot if you push her away because life happened."

Mason clenched his jaw. "I got distracted. I failed Aspen because I—"

"Your daughter got hurt, and she's okay. She defended herself like a champ. You want to take out that anger, call the camp, call the parents of those bullies. Grow the fuck up and stop feeling so sorry for yourself."

His father's words hit him back then like a ton of bricks. Was it true? Had he been filled with self-pity disguised as a drive to be the perfect parent?

Pippa had done what she'd thought was best in that situation. And she'd proven time and time again how much she cared for Aspen, going as far as risking her life for his little girl. *And still I doubted her . . . or was it me I doubted?*

Mason slipped his phone out, his thumb hovering over her contact for what seemed like the thousandth time in weeks. He owed her an apology at the very least. She deserved to know he didn't blame her and that he was wrong, even if she'd likely never forgive him.

The vision of her on that paddleboard flashed in his mind.

"I'm just . . . scared."

She'd bared her soul to him, and what had he promised her?

"I'm here. Whatever you need."

At the first test, not even an hour later, he'd turned himself into a liar.

"I trust you."

He'd fucked up. And his focus needed to be on Aspen. He couldn't fail his little girl again.

Mason pushed the phone back into his pocket and walked to the diner, rain trickling down his head, dripping onto his shoulders. He needed to make this right, to fix what he'd broken.

Aspen looked up as he approached her table. Her eyes rounded and she hid the comic behind her back and stood. "D-dad? I didn't think you'd be here for another hour."

"I see Pippa was here." Even saying her name aloud tore at his already mutilated heart.

She looked down guiltily before anger flared in her eyes. She straightened her spine and tipped her chin up, crossing her arms over her chest. "Yeah, she was. I miss her, and I love her, and I don't know why you are punishing me like this."

"I'm not punishing you."

"Yes, you are!"

He sighed and ran a hand through his wet hair. "When you get older, you'll understand."

She huffed. "Adults always say that. But really, it's simple. I like Pippa, and she likes to spend time with me, so we should do it. You care about her, and you should be with her."

"What?" He straightened, holding his breath. What had Pippa told her?

Aspen rolled her eyes. "You loooove Pippa . . . Oh my God, you didn't think I knew? You two are so obvious, Dad. Why do you think I set you up with her? I knew she would be perfect for you. Then you had to go and screw it all up."

Confusion swirled in his mind. "*You* set *us* up?"

She tapped the floor impatiently with her foot and gave another exaggerated sigh. "Remember I wanted to go to the beach, paddleboarding that day? Or why I begged you to let her come dress shopping with us?"

"You want me to date Pippa?"

"And here I thought SEALs were supposed to be some of the smartest people in the military," she deadpanned.

David grabbed his things and stuffed them into a backpack, his eyes glued to his bag. "I'm just gonna, uh, go." He slid from the booth and crossed the room to the counter.

Mason shook his head and focused on Aspen again, reeling. "*You* are my priority. You always come first in my life."

"I know that, Dad. But I won't be here living with you forever. I'm out when I'm eighteen; that's only five years from now. I don't want you to be lonely when I go. And I knew you'd want someone who could love me as much as you. Pippa literally saved my life from that robber," she reminded him.

He stared at his daughter, a calm acceptance settling into his chest. "You are diabolical."

She smiled and dropped her arms to her sides. "What can I say? I was raised by the best."

He grabbed the back of her neck and pulled her into a hug before he kissed the top of her head.

She squealed. "Ewww, Dad, you're all wet."

"I love you, kiddo."

"I'd love you more if you let me go and go fix whatever you fucked up with Pippa."

He held her away from him, his eyes narrowing. "Language, young lady."

"Too far?" She shrugged innocently.

"Yep. Don't go growing up on me too fast."

"You gonna apologize to Pippa?" she asked.

He turned his attention to the door, as if she would magically materialize. But instead of Pippa, Rachel and her mother walked in. Mason stiffened, stepping in front of his daughter.

Sandra locked eyes with him, her cheeks growing rosy before she bent down to whisper something in her daughter's ear. Rachel turned to him, her eyes dropping to Aspen, who hovered behind him.

Rachel walked towards them, head lowered, her mother by her side. They stopped a few feet in front of Mason. Sandra gave Rachel a little push forward.

Rachel fidgeted with her hands nervously as she spoke. "I wanted to apologize to you, Aspen, and to you, Mr. Wright." The young girl looked up at them, her eyes watery and red. "I'm sorry for going along with the plan to get you alone. I swear they said they only wanted to talk . . . not that that's an excuse for how I've treated you. I just wanted you to know how sorry I am, Aspen. And . . . and I miss hanging out."

Aspen moved to Mason's side. "Thanks for the apology."

It was more than the other parents and kids had done.

The bullies' parents had defended their kid's abhorrent actions—especially Lester Marby. He'd defended his daughter in front of the principal and their children and Mason had held his tongue—although he'd let the man know just what he was capable of when they were alone in the parking lot afterwards.

"Do you think we could be friends again?" Rachel asked.

Aspen tipped her head to the side. "I don't know."

Rachel nodded, her shoulders sinking.

Sandra wrapped her arm around her daughter. "I hope you both have a lovely dinner."

They turned and left, getting a booth at the opposite end of the diner.

Mason turned towards Aspen. "You think you and Rachel can patch things up?"

Aspen looked up at him. "Pippa told me that the people who really love me will make an effort to stay in my life. If they don't, it's their loss. Because I'm special, and smart, and talented."

Mason's breath halted. "Pippa told you that, huh?"

"Yup."

"Well, she's right."

"Thanks, Daddy."

Mason wasn't perfect. Perfection was an illusion. It was time he started making an effort to show Pippa just how sorry he was. But would she give him another chance? Or had he destroyed any hope with his Beauty?

34

―――

PIPPA

Trees swayed in the breeze. White puffy clouds drifted by in the ever-darkening sky. Insects buzzed and a hot breeze blew over Pippa's sweat-slicked skin. Lady panted, her hot body pressing against Pippa's chest. *Where am I?*

"Down." Pippa pointed to the spot next to her, grass tickling her arm.

Lady obeyed, sniffing her and checking Pippa over before licking her cheek.

"Good girl." Pippa sat up slowly, sucking in a pained breath. Had she pulled a muscle? Everything ached.

Lady whimpered near her like she knew just how sore her mama was. Pippa reached out and petted her as she tried to get her bearings. Grass and woods were beyond her. She carefully turned her stiff neck. The back of the bookstore was behind her.

How did I get here? Maybe she had taken Lady out to do her business? The last thing she remembered was forcing down a few bites of dinner. Had she locked the bookstore? *Troy must have.*

Pippa rolled onto all fours, slowly making her way to stand. Another breeze blew, making goose bumps rise on her thighs. Why was she wet? *Oh. At least no one was here to witness me peeing on myself this time.* That must have been a big seizure.

Pippa hobbled to the street and up the flight of stairs, her muscles screaming in exhaustion. There were aches and pains in so many places. Her head swam. Her seizures were coming so frequently lately. *Is the tumor back? I need to make an appointment with the doctor.*

She unlocked her door before relocking it behind her. She got Lady a big bowl of fresh water; there was no telling how long she'd been out there. Lady eagerly lapped as Pippa entered the bathroom. She was too fatigued to risk taking a shower. The last thing she needed was to pass out and hit her head. It was too dangerous.

She stripped and put her clothing in the washer before using a wet wipe to clean herself up as best as possible. She made her way to her bedroom and slipped on an oversized T-shirt and sleep shorts. The air conditioner sent a chill over her damp skin. She picked up her phone, finding Brynn's number as she sat in her bed and pulled the covers up.

"Hello?"

"Hey, it's Pippa. Are you working at the diner tomorrow morning?"

"Just for a few hours to cover for Betty-Lou. I'll be done by nine. Did you need me at the store?" Brynn asked.

"I wondered if you would mind covering my shift and opening the bookstore?"

"I can do that. Is everything okay?"

Pippa closed her eyes. "Yeah. I'm just not feeling that well.

I always get clusters of seizures around my cycle. I just don't think I can make it in tomorrow." *It's not usually this bad though.*

"No problem. I'll be in. Oh, Troy just walked into the diner. Should I get the key from him?" Brynn asked.

"Yes, that would be perfect."

"I'll come by and check on you tomorrow, bring you a bowl of soup or something," Brynn offered.

Tears pricked Pippa's eyes. She'd fought for her independence, saving every penny until she could afford her twenty-thousand-dollar service dog, waiting years for Lady in the hope that she could live on her own. Then, she'd turned around and done it again to save for the down payment on her shop. She'd even taken out a loan to buy this place. She'd wanted to give her family a break from the burden of her seizures. As much as she tried to not need anyone, it was nice to know there were people who cared about her. "I appreciate it."

"You get some rest. I'll see you tomorrow."

"Thank you, Brynn." Pippa ended the call, setting the phone on her side table, too tired to even look at the screen. She snuggled against the pillow as Lady jumped on the bed, settling by her. Pippa wrapped her arm around Lady and fell fast asleep.

Knock. Knock.

Lady sat up and barked. Pippa stirred, running her hand over Lady's fur.

The knocking repeated and so did Lady's woofs.

Who? Oh, Brynn must be here.

Pippa sat, rubbing the sleep from her eyes. What time was it? She picked up her phone. Dead. *How did I forget to charge it?*

Figured. The clock on the side table read eleven thirty. *Whoa, we really slept in.*

"Poor girl. You probably need to go to the bathroom."

Lady barked and jumped off the bed, waiting by the door.

Pippa followed her, opening the door as the scent of crisp rain washed over her.

"Mason?" Swirling blue eyes locked with hers. Dark bruises had formed under each of his eyes. His beard needed a trim, and his hair was ruffled like he'd been running his hands through it.

Lady whimpered.

Pippa tore her eyes away from the man who had stolen her heart only to smash it to pieces.

"Does she need to go out?" he asked.

Pippa nodded. "Yeah."

"We'll be right back. Come on, girl."

Lady darted down the steps as Mason slowly followed. She was in too much shock to argue.

Mason was here? Pippa touched her cheek and then her hair. *Oh, God. I must look a mess.* She ran back in the house to the bathroom, wincing with her movements. Her hair stuck out oddly. She grabbed a brush and ran it through it, pulling a leaf from her short locks. *Dios mio. I look a mess.* Quickly, she twisted her hair up into a messy bun. Next, she splashed some cold water on her face.

"Pippa?" Mason's voice made her chest cinch tight. *Why is he here? To tell me to stay away from Aspen?*

"I'll be right there." Her voice trembled. She dried her face, taking one last deep breath before she walked into the fray.

Mason stood by her door, his hands in his pockets. Lady was busy lapping up water from her bowl.

Pippa crossed her arms, keeping her distance from the man she loved but could never have. "Why are you here?"

Mason nervously ran his hand through his hair, causing it to stand up even worse than before. "I wanted to apologize."

She searched his face. Of all the things she'd expected from him, that wasn't one of them.

"The way I reacted . . . I was scared for Aspen . . . and that came out as anger towards you. I'm sorry for what I said and how I've treated you."

She swallowed and nodded. Love and loss, hope and grief swirled in her chest. "I'm sorry too. I should have told you. I believed her when she . . . It doesn't matter. I apologize as well."

"I've missed you." He stepped closer, his hands resting at his sides.

Pippa's focus darted from him to the ground. "I don't know what you want me to say."

He walked closer until he was in her space. His finger reached out and lifted her chin so that she had to look at him. His brows creased, his eyes darting back and forth between hers. She shivered. He was so close. All those feelings she'd tried to rid herself of this past month spun her up, twisting and pulling chaos from the wreckage of her heart.

"Tell me you feel this too," he said.

She nodded. There was no use lying. Just because they shared this connection didn't mean they got a happily ever after.

His hand cupped the side of her face. She closed her eyes and leaned into his touch. It was impossible to resist the temptation. She greedily accepted the peace and comfort connection with him offered.

"I fucked up, and I honestly don't know what I have to offer you. But staying away from you feels wrong . . ."

Pippa met his gaze. What was he saying? She couldn't go through this again. This would never work. "You had no problem ghosting me again."

He flinched, his shoulders sagging. "What I feel for you I've never felt for another woman, and it terrifies me." Mason's voice was rough and raw.

"Don't." She shook her head.

"Don't what? Don't love you? Too late. Somehow you made this heart surrounded by thorns beat again, just for you."

Tears leaked from her eyes, but he swiped them before they could fall down her cheeks.

"I love you, Pippa . . . damn, I don't even know your last name. It doesn't matter. I love you. And I want to make this right. Tell me what to do, Beauty."

She shook her head. "You completely disappeared after . . . after what we shared. I trusted you—"

"I know, baby. I wish I could take it back. I was terrified of not being enough for Aspen and you. I thought you were better off without me. I didn't want you to get hurt. But I guess I was the one doing the hurting."

She sniffed.

"Tell me, do I have a chance? Can I earn back your trust? Can we be together again?"

"I don't want to just be another responsibility for you to take on."

"You won't be—"

"But I am!" She pushed him away. Her chest heaved up and down. Emotions bled out from her eyes and her voice. She trembled. Pain lanced her chest. "I watched how much my condition drained my family of their energy, their finances, destroyed lives and relationships. I won't do that to you and Aspen. You both deserve the world."

Mason's jaw ticced. He stepped closer, stealing all the air in the room with his closeness once again. Two strong hands cupped her face, gentle yet forceful. His blue eyes clouded over as they bore into her. "What if I told you, *you* are the world to us?"

She shook her head. *No, there was no way.* "What do you want from me?"

"Probably more than I deserve," he grumbled before dropping his mouth to hers.

Pippa gasped. Tingles raced down her spine. Ropes of arousal unfurled from her center, winding through her body. Desire and lust, love and hope crashed through her in a tidal wave from the sensation of his lips on hers.

"You're not a responsibility; you're a privilege." He kissed her, winding her up only to pull away again. "You're not a burden, but a fucking benefit, Beauty."

Something loosened inside her rib cage. Tears poured from her eyes as sobs tore from her throat. Mason pulled her against his hard chest, holding her while she fell apart. *No. It's too good to be true.*

A memory flashed in her mind once more. *I don't say things I don't mean.*

She cried harder.

"Shhhh. I'm so sorry, baby. I let you slip through my fingers before, and I regretted it the moment you walked away. I thought you'd be better off without me. Won't do it this time."

She sniffed and pulled back to wipe her eyes.

"A wise woman once said that the people who really love you will make an effort to stay in your life. I'm gonna show you I can be what you need and be there for Aspen."

Pippa offered him a watery smile. "A wise woman, huh?"

"The wisest." He grinned.

"Mason, I don't . . ."

"I know I hurt you. I know words don't just make it better. So, I'm gonna show you how much you mean to me. I do learn from my mistakes, believe it or not. I won't let you go so easily this time."

His mouth slanted against hers, sealing his promise.

Pippa wanted him. Wanted what they'd shared that week Aspen was gone, and more. But was it safe to trust again? Could she survive him pulling away a second time? There was only one way to find out. But was she ready to jump and believe he would catch her?

35

MASON

Music blared from the speakers as bodies writhed and moved to the beat on the dance floor of The Shipwreck. Mason carefully scanned the room lit in a blue haze from the circular fish tanks on the wall. His focus landed on a couple of usual troublemakers in a dimly lit corner. They smiled cheekily at him. If they knew he was watching, maybe they'd behave themselves tonight. They were good guys, but after four beers they could get a little rambunctious.

Charli passed by them, serving appetizers to a small group of ladies at one of the tables. She returned to the bar, giving Finn a smile. *Jamison must be with his grandparents tonight.*

His phone vibrated in his pocket. Mason pulled it out.

Pippa: *Thank you for the flowers and the chocolates. You do know Valentine's Day is in February, not August, right?*

He grinned.

Mason: *Every day with you is a day that should be celebrated.*

Pippa: *Wow. Where do you get these lines?*

He frowned.

Mason: *It wasn't a line. It's the truth.*

Pippa: *Do you have any flaws? No man is this perfect.*

Mason: *Pretty sure you saw those firsthand.*

A text bubble appeared and disappeared. He waited. His gaze flicked up to the pool table in the back. *Fuck.*

Mason tore across the room, sidestepping as many people as he could without knocking them over. Lester Marby swung his fist, but Mason grabbed his arm, forcing it behind him before twisting the other and leaning him over the pool table.

"Better calm down," Mason warned, tightening his grip.

Lester bucked and struggled. "Get off me!" The stench of his sweat mixed with alcohol was terrible.

"Not until you calm down. Then you and I are gonna walk out the door and get you a ride home."

"Oh, come on, Mase. We were enjoying the entertainment," one of the troublemakers commented.

"Everything okay here?" Charli asked beside him.

"Call Bobby Jo and tell her to come get her husband," Mason instructed.

Charli stepped away as the man Lester was about to punch came closer. "He owes me twenty bucks from that round."

"You fucking cheated!" Lester argued.

"Let's go." Mason tugged Lester to his feet, keeping Lester's hands locked behind his back as he forced him through the crowd towards the entrance.

"Bobby Jo is already outside. Said she's been waiting an hour for him." Charli appeared by the door.

Mason nodded and pushed Lester out, past the bouncer. "Why didn't she come in?"

"That bitch knows not to interrupt me," Lester snapped.

Mason shoved him onto the ground. "You better get yourself under control if you want to come back to this establishment."

Lester scurried to his feet as his wife exited the beat-up truck in the lot and ran over to her husband.

"Are you okay?" Bobby Jo reached out for Lester.

He jerked away from her and slapped her across the face. "I told you to wait in the fucking car!"

Mason's hands squeezed around the man's throat, pinning him to the ground.

"No! Stop!" Bobby Jo hollered.

The bouncer outside the door said, "The police are on the way."

Lester turned red under the floodlights as he struggled for breath and Mason reluctantly eased his hold. Lester coughed and sucked in air. "You fucking monster! You're gonna pay for this." He got to his feet, his chest puffed out, his face darkening to cranberry as he snarled. "Just like that fucking bitch daughter of yours. You'll get what's coming to you."

A red haze covered Mason's vision. "You want me to tackle you back down to the ground again? You like the feeling of another man on top of you that much?"

Lester's eyes widened before he snarled and swung. Mason didn't move; he knew the rules of the game. The slimy fuck's punch clipped the edge of his jaw.

Mason grinned darkly. Lester's eyes widened, fear flashing in them as he stumbled back. Mason's fist met with the man's jaw. No one threatened Aspen and got away with it.

Bobby Jo's screams faded into the background as Mason let that dark part of himself surface. He hit Lester again and again. Every punch was for Aspen, for Pippa, for goddamned Bobby Jo who stayed with a loser like Lester.

"Boss." The bouncer grabbed his arm.

Mason jerked away and stood up straight. Red and blue lights flashed as the police truck entered the parking lot.

Mason turned to Bobby Jo. "When you're ready to leave this piece of shit, give me a call and I'll arrange your security to move out. You don't have to put up with this treatment."

"You monster!" she raged at Mason, her glare turning to concern as she knelt beside her bleeding husband who lay there, dazed. "You okay, baby?"

"Okay, pack it up, folks. Go back inside or leave. Show's over." Mason shooed the small crowd that had formed around them.

The crunch of approaching footsteps on gravel had Mason turning.

"What happened here?" Bently asked.

Bobby Jo pointed to Mason accusingly. "He attacked my husband for no reason."

Bently looked to Mason as another cop car pulled in.

"He was about to assault a patron. So I walked him out here where he assaulted his wife instead. He took a swing at me." Mason rubbed his jaw; there would be a small bruise there tomorrow. "And I responded."

Vargas exited the second vehicle and jogged over to them.

"Would you take care of Mrs. Marby?" Bently turned to Vargas.

"He's the one that belongs in jail." Bobby Jo pointed towards Mason as Vargas escorted the woman out of earshot.

Mason sighed and walked to the bar steps. He sat down as Bently and Vargas sorted out the details with the couple.

He turned to the bouncer. "You go inside. I'll stay out here."

"Yes, sir." The man turned and ushered a few straggling patrons back into the bar with him.

After loading Lester into an ambulance, Bently approached Mason.

"Didn't think he was hurt that bad," Mason commented.

Bently shook his head and sighed. "Just his pride. You broke his nose though."

Mason shrugged. *Like daughter, like father.* "I was just defending myself."

Bently gave him a knowing look. "I wish Bobby Jo would leave him. I've offered to help."

"Me too."

Bently nodded. "This have anything to do with the letter Pippa found today?"

Mason's shoulders tensed as he got to his feet. "What letter?"

Bently looked away. "I thought you knew. I figured you two . . . talked."

"What letter?" Mason growled.

"You know I can't share that with you. I shouldn't have said anything to begin with. I was under the impression you two were seeing each other."

Why didn't she tell me? "It's complicated."

His friend chuckled. "Isn't it always? You should get some ice on that hand." Bently turned and walked towards his truck.

Mason slipped out his phone, scrolling over their conversation again. As much as he hated it, Pippa was guarded again. *Because of me.* But how could he prove to her that he would be there for her if she didn't let him in?

She doesn't believe me.

Pippa owned him, body and soul. He wouldn't have it any other way. It was time he showed her exactly what that meant to him.

36

PIPPA

Pippa leaned against the couch and ran her fingers through Lady's soft fur. The dog's brown eyes closed as she nuzzled into Pippa's lap.

"You're such a good girl."

Lady's ears perked up a moment before she lifted her head and looked towards the door.

"What is it, girl?"

Knock. Knock.

Pippa glanced at the late hour on the clock. *Who could that be?* She got to her feet and padded over, glancing out the peephole. A small gasp escaped her. She'd endured so many weeks of not seeing or hearing from Mason, and now, all of a sudden, he'd visited twice in two days. She inhaled a steadying breath and opened the door.

Her eyebrows rose. "What are you doing here?"

His gaze darted over her cotton pajama dress that came to mid-thigh, but it wasn't sexual. It was as if he was checking her over for injury.

"Are you okay?" he asked, placing his big hands on her

shoulders and studying her face as he stepped inside, causing her to back up.

"Of course. Why wouldn't I be?" She pulled away from him to shut the door.

"Bently came into the bar tonight and told me something happened."

Oh. That. "Is nothing private in this small town?"

"Was it another brick with a message?"

"No, it was an actual handwritten note—more quotes from the Bible."

"Pippa! I need to do something about this. I'll change my shifts. I'll—"

She sighed. "This is exactly what I didn't want—to be a burden on you."

"I hate when you say that." He growled.

"Well, it's true."

He grasped the back of her head and pulled her into a kiss. She gave in, her lips softening immediately at his slow, languid touch. He pulled back and she blinked a few times, trying to get her bearings. This man's very presence threw her off her axis.

"I can't help but care about you. I fucking love you. So yes, I'm concerned for your safety. That's the price you pay for being my woman."

Her heart lurched. His confession sucked the air from the room. Tears burned the back of her eyes. *He loves me.* But life wasn't that simple. She shook her head. "No. I was your girl-friend and that lasted only a few short days. Then you ghosted me for three weeks instead of communicating with me. You don't get to assume I'm yours just because you apologized."

He took a deep breath and nodded. "What if I want you to be? If I can prove to you I learned from my mistakes and am here for you, will you give me a chance to earn back your trust?"

Yes! Her stomach twisted into anxious knots. Her heart screamed at her to just kiss the man and take him to bed. But something held her back. Fear that this wouldn't last. She was terrified of opening herself up to that kind of destruction. *But I love him too.* Her chest tightened.

Mason's hand cupped the side of her face, tipping her chin up as he leaned in. "You are the most beautiful, amazing, strong woman I have ever known. You've burrowed into here." He pointed to his heart. "You brought me out of mere existence back to the land of the living again. You gave me hope. I can't imagine my life without you in it. All I'm asking for is a chance to show you what you really mean to me, Beauty."

His eyes dropped to her lips. She licked them instinctually. This was it—this was the moment when she got to decide the trajectory of her life. Would it include this amazing man or not? She sucked in rainwater-scented air. His scent intoxicated her, spinning her emotions up. Every part of her screamed, *say yes to this man.* Still, a piece of her held back, terrified of what giving in to him would mean.

Maybe she didn't have to choose tonight. "I need to take this slow, start at the beginning. *Friends.*"

Something dark and hungry flashed in Mason's blue eyes before he grasped her hand and led her to the bed. He lifted the comforter and Pippa climbed under the covers.

"I'm not sleeping with you," she clarified.

"That's not what this is." Mason lay down on his side, his head propped up on his elbow.

He brushed his thumb over her chin. "I don't just want your body. I want this too." He dragged his finger down her neck to her chest and tapped above her heart. "I need all of you, Beauty. And until you feel safe enough to give that to me, I'm gonna show you exactly what being my woman entails."

Mason leaned in and placed a quick peck on her nose.

She giggled. "What was that for?"

He smiled and her heart skipped a beat. *I love you.*

"You're so goddamned cute." He tapped her nose. "And sexy." He kissed her forehead before burying his nose in her hair, inhaling her. He groaned and pulled away, his chest heaving. "And so fucking tempting."

"Well, you're pretty handsome yourself." She pressed her hand to the side of his face.

"This doesn't bother you?" He pointed to the scar tissue on his cheek.

"Not in the slightest. It adds character. Makes you look like a man who gave everything for his country. It's actually kinda hot." She smiled.

"Oh, it was definitely hot when I got it." Mason chuckled.

Her grin faded. "How did it happen?"

Mason's gaze clouded over.

"You don't have to tell me—"

"My team and I went into a compound to rescue a target held hostage. I can't go into all the details because it's classified. But something went wrong after we secured the target." His sigh was heavy and tired. "I'm not sure if it was the torture, but he didn't trust us. His mind was broken." Mason was silent a beat before he took a deep breath, as if steeling himself. "He grabbed a grenade from my gear. Before I could stop him, he removed the pin. My commander yelled at all of us to get out . . . but that was *my* grenade." He looked away as if ashamed.

"I couldn't leave him behind. We wrestled the target, and in the end, both my leader and the target were killed, and I was left with this."

Wow. Oh my God. No wonder he feels responsible. He's carrying the weight of the world on his shoulders. How awful.

"I'm sorry."

"Me too. It fucked me up for a long time. Therapy has helped."

Her eyes widened. "You see a therapist?"

He nodded. "Every couple of weeks for the last eight years."

His confession softened something inside her.

"Why are you smiling?" he asked.

She shook her head. "You just keep surprising me."

"How so? Didn't think a manly military man like me would see a head doctor to talk about my feelings?"

She winced. "When you put it like that, I seem awfully judgmental."

"Nah. I get it. Most of us vets don't get the help we need either because we're too afraid to ask or because the resources are not there for us." He looked away, his gaze clouding over again.

"Thank you for sharing that with me. It means a lot." She placed her hand on his shoulder, needing to physically connect with him in some way.

His eyelashes fluttered. "You're the first person I've told, other than my therapist, what happened."

Her mouth dropped open. *Wow. He must really trust me.* "I'm honored."

He pulled her onto his arm and lay on his back. She snuggled against his hard chest, listening to the steady beat of his heart. His warm arms brought her a sense of comfort and safety. Pippa closed her eyes. Everything was right in the world for this one stolen moment.

How much longer could she keep up the lie that she wasn't already, wholeheartedly his?

37

PIPPA

Pippa stirred awake, snuggling into her soft pillow. Her eyes blinked open as Mason's scent filled her nostrils. She smiled and reached out, finding nothing but cool sheets. She turned over. He was gone. A folded piece of paper with her name scrawled on it in blocky masculine print sat by the clock on the side table. Pippa picked it up, opened it quickly.

Good morning, Sleeping Beauty,

Wish I could be here to bring you breakfast, but I had to get back to Aspen and relieve the babysitter. (Don't let Aspen know that's what I refer to Amara as—Aspen hates that I won't leave her home alone yet.) Anyways, I might have bribed a certain someone to deliver a coffee and a treat to your door from the bakery. So you better check before it gets too cold. Delivery should be there about eight.

Text me when you'll be available for me to pick you up after work. Today's a good day to spend at the beach. So be sure to put on that red bikini I like so much.

Love you,

M

Pippa scurried out of bed and to the door. Lady followed her, barking once as if to say, *What are you doing, crazy woman?* Pippa opened the door, and sure enough, there was her breakfast. She plucked up the offerings and let Lady out to do her business before returning to her bedroom to find her phone.

Pippa: *Thank you for breakfast. I'm gonna get fat with all these cookies and muffins you feed me.*

Mason: *More of you to love.*

"Oh my God. This guy." Pippa pointed her phone towards Lady who barked and licked her hand.

"So he has your approval, huh?" Pippa giggled. Maybe this could work.

Pippa: *I'll be ready by one.*

Mason: *I can't wait. Love you.*

Pippa's thumb hovered over the keyboard but she wasn't ready to say it back yet—not after everything.

Her phone rang, and her father's name flashed on her screen.

"Papi?"

"Hey, baby girl."

"Where are you now?" she asked, going to her dresser to pick out clothes for the few hours she'd be at the shop.

"I'm in Pennsylvania, so not too far. How you been feeling?"

"I'm great." *Mostly.*

"That's good to hear. How's the bookstore?"

"Pretty busy. Lots of tourists are in town and that's helpful. I hired another part-time worker."

A honking car sounded from the background on his end of the phone. "Mm-hmm, sounds like you're making your dreams come true, baby girl. I'm so proud of you."

Tears blurred Pippa's vision. She sat on the edge of her bed. "Papi? I know how you sacrificed everything for me. I'm so grateful. And I'm sorry that . . ." Her voice broke. *That because of me, you went to prison.*

"Everything I do is for you girls, and your mama when she was alive. You are my world. Someday, if you ever have a child, you'll understand. I'm just so happy to see you going after what you want even with everything going on with your health. You are an inspiration, *mija.*"

The tears fell freely down her cheeks. Oh, how she missed her dad. She wanted to be wrapped up in one of his hugs.

He cleared his throat. "I'll come visit soon. You can show me what you've done with the place."

"I'd love that. And there's someone here I'd like for you to meet."

"You have someone special in your life, *cariño?*"

Pippa bit her lip and nodded even though he couldn't see her. "Yes."

"I'd be honored. *Te quiero mucho,*" he said.

"I love you too, Papi."

She ended the call, a riot of emotions churning inside her. Love and guilt. Pride and shame. But, overall, gratitude for the man who had sacrificed everything so that she could be here today. He was the best dad—much like Mason in a lot of ways. Would Mason want to meet her father when he came? Was she ready for that?

Later that afternoon, Pippa walked down the beach with Mason by her side. Aspen was playing catch with Lady. It was nice to be able to see her hard-working service pet just be a dog for a little while. Mason was by her side in case she needed assistance.

Cold seawater lapped at her feet before the waves receded

back out to the ocean. The process repeated over and over. He slipped his hand in hers and squeezed. Pippa looked up at him before flicking her gaze to Aspen laughing and running with Lady towards the ball.

"What if Aspen sees?" Pippa asked.

Mason smiled and shrugged. "I've already talked to her."

"You have?" Her eyes widened.

He nodded.

"And?"

Mason chuckled. "And she said she was running out of ways to get us to spend time together."

Pippa blinked and then burst out laughing. Mason joined her.

"She knew I would be at the beach that day," Pippa mused.

"She did. When she told me, it explained her sudden urge to go paddleboarding after having no interest the previous year. Not to mention how quickly she disappeared right after we found you." He chuckled.

"She set us up."

"See? Even she knows how perfect you are for me." He winked.

Pippa couldn't hold back her smile. She wrapped her arm around his waist and his spread out over her shoulder.

"You have a good day at the bookstore?" Mason asked, stopping to pick up a piece of blue sea glass before handing it to her.

She studied the object as they continued their walk, arms around each other. It was as blue as his eyes. She tucked it into her pocket. "Yes. It was busy, but I still managed to get some of the secret library cleaned out."

"Secret library?" he asked.

"Well, I hope it will be someday. For now, it's just an extra room like an old office. There isn't much in there, but I have a Pinterest board dedicated to it. I want to add some built-in bookshelves that go all the way to the high ceiling and add a ladder on those bar things. Oh, and I want to somehow make the door a secret door with a hidden book lever or something." She waved her hands animatedly as her excitement grew.

"Like a *Beauty and the Beast* type of library but on a smaller scale?"

"What is it with your obsession over that cartoon? I think I'll start calling you Beast from now on," she teased.

"Aspen made me watch it on repeat for a full year. It's still one of her favorite movies, so I catch it here and there. Pretty sure I know every word by heart. But you have to admit, it was a cool library."

"Oh, no doubt about it. It's totally my fantasy."

A seagull cawed overhead before dropping to the shore to devour a crab. Aspen's laughter filtered towards them in the breeze as she and Lady splashed in the coastline.

"I'd really like to hear more about your fantasies." Mason's hand dropped to her ass.

She giggled and elbowed him lightly in the ribs. "I'm sure you would."

He leaned in to speak in her ear, his voice deep and low, making her belly tumble with butterflies. "I have a fantasy involving this red suit on the floor of my bedroom, and you naked and wet on my bed while I eat your pussy like cake."

She swallowed hard and squeezed her hand tighter around him. "You sound so sure of yourself that it's gonna happen."

"*When* I take you again, you're gonna be mine, and I won't let go. When you're ready for that kind of commitment, you let me know."

She shivered. "Will you be making up for all this lost time with orgasms?"

"Baby, not one second spent with you is lost." He kissed her temple. "But I promise, when you figure out you love me just as much as I love you, I'll give you all the orgasms you want."

Oh, God. How could she not love him back? It seemed wrong to withhold those three little words and let Mason continue to believe she didn't feel the same way about him.

"I already know I love you too," she confessed.

He smiled. "But you don't trust me not to hurt you again yet. You're still holding back. And rightfully so. I'm a patient man, Beauty. I'll wait until you're ready for forever, because that's what I need with you."

Forever? Here she was still debating if her heart could take dating this man again and he was talking about forever. What did that mean? Marriage? This was all so fast. But if she did open herself up to him again, there would be no turning back. She wanted forever too.

"I can hear those wheels spinning." He chuckled and stopped walking before turning to face her. "I love you, Beauty." He kissed her lightly and pulled back to look in her eyes.

"I love you too, Beast."

"You guys are so corny," Aspen whined next to them. Lady panted beside her.

Pippa looked to Mason before they both burst out laughing.

He picked up his daughter. She screamed. He threw her over his shoulder as he rushed into the water.

"Dad! It's cold! No! Help me, Pippa! Help—"

Both father and daughter disappeared into one of the large waves. Aspen surfaced, her hair hanging limply over her face. She swiped it aside as Mason emerged from the sea like

Poseidon himself, wiping his face, laughing. Seawater dripped down the hard planes of his defined chest, glistening in the sunlight. Pippa's mouth grew dry. He was hotter than the August sun beating down on them.

Aspen splashed her dad and he laughed. Pippa pulled out her phone and snapped a picture of the two of them playing together. She captured the moment with a wide grin on her face.

Aspen jumped onto his back, hanging on to his neck, choking him before he threw himself backwards into the next wave. She came sputtering out of the water first, held up by his capable hands. He was playful and protective. Her heart thudded, melting to goo in her chest. Could this really be her life? Could she be a part of this family?

"Pippa, come on. I need your help to take my dad down."

"Two against one sounds hardly fair," Mason argued with a knowing grin.

Pippa placed her phone in her bag on the dry sand. She bent over and filled her portable bowl with water for Lady and set it next to the bag. The dog lapped the water as Pippa walked into the sea.

"You know us girls have to stick together," Aspen answered.

Mason met her partway. Her eyes traveled down his naked torso, need building inside her. "You ready to be outnumbered, Mr. Wright?"

"Only if it's you, Miss . . ." His brows drew together. "I still don't even know your last name."

"Davis. Pippa Davis."

A dark cloud covered his vision as he frowned, looking a little closer at her. He shook his head and blinked.

"What's wrong?"

He opened his mouth and then closed it, peeking over at Aspen who was getting closer to them. "Nothing."

"Get him!" Aspen yelled as she splashed water towards them. Mason grabbed Pippa's shoulders and forced her in front of him like a human shield.

"Hey!" Pippa yelled.

Mason laughed behind her.

Aspen tried to dart past, but he spun them around each time. Pippa giggled and struggled to get out of his iron grip, but had no luck.

"Okay, I give up!" Pippa yelled.

He turned her to face him, his eyes locking on her mouth. "Oh yeah?"

Pippa wrapped her arms around his neck and pulled him down as if she was going to kiss him. At the last moment, she jumped into his arms throwing off his balance so that they both fell into the waves. He used his arm to hold them just above water. Aspen joined her, giving her dad the final push underwater. Pippa climbed off him and Aspen gave her a high five.

Mason broke the surface, shaking his head and sending water flying around him. "You traitor."

Pippa shrugged. "Hey, like the woman said—us girls have to stick together."

Aspen beamed back at her.

"Alright, a man knows when he's been beaten. How about some pizza for dinner?"

"Yes!" both ladies said at the same time before turning towards one another and bursting into giggles.

"And some peanut butter chocolate cheesecake for dessert?" Mason smirked.

The last time they'd eaten that he'd . . . oh, that bastard was just trying to rub in what she was missing.

"Actually, I'm in the mood for some ice cream. What about you, Aspen?" Pippa asked.

"Yes!"

Mason hooked an arm around each of them as they made their way back to shore and a waiting Lady.

I could get used to this.

38

PIPPA

Pippa handed Troy a stack of books. "These are for the author signing tomorrow. Can you get them set up on the table over there?" She nodded towards the other side of the room.

"Yes, ma'am, I can. Do you want me to lock up this evening, or will you be down to do it?" he asked, adjusting the books in his arms.

"You go ahead. I'm not sure I'll be home in time."

"Oh? Big afternoon ahead?" He smiled as hot air blew into the shop.

Mason walked in, his gaze flicking between Troy and her as his jaw clenched. He wrapped his arms around her and pulled her in for a kiss before she could react. She pushed his chest and jerked her head back.

Mason smiled. "Hey, baby, ready to go?"

"I guess I'll see you tomorrow." Troy walked away.

Pippa gave him a smile. "Goodbye." She turned her attention to Mason and whisper-hissed, "What was that?"

Mason shrugged, still not letting her go. "Just wanted to make it clear that you were taken."

"So you had to piss all over me? Even Lady has better manners than that."

Lady huffed by her side.

Mason smirked. "A kiss is hardly comparable to urination."

Pippa shook her head. "That was unprofessional. This is my place of work, my business, and that was my employee. I can't be making out with . . . with . . ."

"With your boyfriend," he finished for her.

She shook her head. "You're my friend. Not my boyfriend. We've been over this."

"Why don't you show me your secret library before we go?"

"You're just changing the subject," she argued.

He shrugged and leaned in. "Show me."

She sighed. "Fine."

Pippa led him to the door in the back marked Private. She opened it and stepped in. Heat pressed against her back from his closeness. His head turned, as if he was taking in the mostly empty room. A lone desk sat in the center; a few boxes filled with books were piled on top.

Mason waited for Lady to walk in and closed the door behind them.

"What are you doing?" Pippa asked.

He spun her around and brought her back to his front. Lowering his mouth to the shell of her ear, he pointed. "Built-in bookshelves on every wall, right?"

She nodded. The scruff of his beard scratched against her cheek, sending tingles racing through her.

His finger moved to the one long window that arched at the top. "And a window seat for that space?"

"Yes."

"Anything else?"

"Comfy overstuffed seats, maybe a hanging chair or two. And lights—lots of sparkling lights."

"That doesn't sound so complicated."

She closed her eyes, soaking in his touch and his voice. "I think the door is the most complicated part."

"You thinking a book lever, or a candle that you pull?"

"Mmmm, probably a book. Something classic."

"Makes sense." His cock nudged her lower back.

"Mason?"

"Hmm?"

"You're turned on, talking about bookshelves?" she teased.

He spun her around in his arms, his eyes turning to burning embers of coal. "I kinda have a thing for sexy librarians."

"I'm a bookstore owner."

"Tomato, tah-mah-tow."

Pippa licked her lips before her eyes darted to the desk in the center of the room. Flashes of Mason laying her out on it and feasting on her pussy before bending her back over it and pounding her from behind played vividly in her mind's eye.

"We can't." Pippa wasn't sure if she was telling Mason or herself. Troy was outside. This was her business. And she wasn't ready. If only her lady parts would get that memo.

"I know. But being around you gives me a constant hard-on. So just ignore it for now. That's what I do."

"Maybe we should get out of here."

"I have a surprise for you."

"Oh yeah? What is it?"

He grinned, a sparkle in his eyes. "You'll just have to wait and see."

. . .

An hour later, Pippa held Lady's leash as she nervously peeked over the ledge of the Black Cliffs. "I can't believe people actually jump from this high up."

Mason placed his hand protectively on the small of her back. "They don't jump from here, but over there." He pointed to the left. "Closer to the beach."

She peered down into the dark blue-green water with jagged rocks sticking out so far below and swallowed nervously. "Still."

He grabbed her hand and tugged her back to the green, plaid picnic blanket he'd laid out for them. "Hungry?"

"I could eat." She sat and crisscrossed her legs. Lady lay in the grass by her side as Mason settled next to her on the blanket and opened the picnic basket.

"I never would have guessed you owned one of these."

He shrugged. "Comes in handy with a daughter who loves tea parties and picnics at the beach . . . or, she used to."

Pippa laughed, imagining a big, strong Mason holding a plastic pink teacup while wearing a beaded necklace.

"What?"

"I'm just thinking of you having a tea party with Aspen. I think it's sweet."

"Did your dad do stuff like that with you when you were little?"

Pippa grabbed a cracker and layered it with some meat and cheese from the charcuterie board he'd brought. "He did when he could. Once the seizures started, we spent a lot of time in the hospitals, or he'd be at work trying to pay for what our limited insurance didn't cover. He would read to me while I was in the hospital bed, though." She smiled wistfully. "His voice has a soothing quality, and he did all the different characters' voices."

"He sounds like a great dad."

"The best." She took a bite of the food and chewed.

Mason handed her a bottle of apple juice. She finished the rest of her cracker and opened the juice, then washed down her meal.

"Do you get to visit him often?"

"No. He's a truck driver, so he keeps pretty busy. He might come see me in a few weeks."

Mason nodded, loading up his own cracker before shoving the whole thing in his mouth.

"Are you and your dad close?" Pippa asked.

Mason nodded. "He and my brother have been a huge help with Aspen. I don't know what I would have done without them."

"He seemed like he cared for her a lot." She rubbed a hand over Lady's fur, handing her a piece of deli ham.

"I'm sorry I didn't properly introduce you."

"Aspen was hurt. I get it."

He reached over and squeezed her thigh. "Still, I should have handled everything better. I'll make it up to you."

"Is that where she is today? At your father's place?"

He nodded and grabbed another cracker. "Yeah, she wanted to have a campout with him before school starts next week. It's their tradition."

So he'd be all alone tonight?

"Are you close with your sister?" Mason asked.

She smiled and picked a grape from the board before popping it between her lips. She crunched down, a pop of sweet liquid filling her mouth. "Yes. My dad had to . . . well, he couldn't take care of me when I turned sixteen. And I went to live with my sister. She's older by ten years."

He whistled. "That's quite the age gap. I can't imagine having to start all over with a newborn after that long." His brows drew together. "Do you want kids of your own?"

Pippa looked away, her stomach flipping. "I-I don't think I can. I mean, my mother struggled with infertility; that's why I came along so late. They said I was their miracle baby." *Some miracle I turned out to be.* "I know a lot of people with epilepsy have babies, but I'm not sure I can." *How could I care for another life when I'm struggling to take care of me?* She turned towards him. "Do you want more kids?"

"I never really thought about it. Aspen is my world. I'm more than content with just her."

Pippa nodded. That was good. "My sister, Sophia, is getting married next summer to her fiancée, Vivian. She's *una chulería.*"

"*Una chulería?*" Mason asked.

"It basically means sweetheart."

"Is your sister why you have a lot of LGBTQ books and events in your store?" Mason grabbed a bottle of water from the basket and unscrewed the cap.

"She's part of it. Living with her and her partner, I saw how much discrimination they faced. Sometimes they can't even hold hands because they are afraid someone will target them. I just wanted to create a space that was safe and accepting for my customers, whoever they may be."

"Yeah, I get that."

"Because of Sebastian?" she asked.

"I mean, that makes it more personal. But I think any decent human being with any amount of empathy should be able to recognize that two people loving each other is one of the most beautiful things about life. Who cares if it's a woman and a man, two men, or two women. Hell, who cares if it's a throuple, as long as everyone is happy and getting their needs met."

"I just don't understand why people can be so hateful towards people who love each other."

He shrugged, staring off at the blue sky above them. The sun hung low, sparkling on the lapping waves below. A warm salty breeze blew over them.

"I think people fear what they don't understand. And having empathy takes vulnerability and emotional intelligence. A lot of people want to remain in their ignorance because it's comfortable. It's what they know, and they don't have to put in any work to change or try to see the world through someone else's lens." He took a deep breath and let it out. "At the end of the day, we're all just human beings doing the best we can to find love, acceptance, and connection. If my brother finds that with another man, who can say that's wrong? Their love is just as pure as a heterosexual couple's."

Respect and pride bloomed in her chest as another piece of her fell more in love with this man. But risking it all with him again was like contemplating jumping off the Black Cliffs. Scary and final. There would be no turning back after her feet left the ledge.

Mason's blue eyes met hers. "Whatcha thinking about, love?"

Pippa's heart skipped a beat at the endearment. Who was she kidding? She was already free-falling over the peak.

"I'm thinking how lucky I am to be here right now, sharing this moment with you."

He leaned in, hesitating an inch from her lips. "I wouldn't want to be here with anyone else."

Pippa met him the rest of the way, slanting her mouth over his. Mason's lips were hot and sweet. He kissed her like he savored her. She raked her teeth over his bottom lip, teasing him. His palm skated along the side of her face before he pulled back to press his forehead against hers. Their breath mingled between them.

"I'm letting you in. I'll share everything. Anything you want to know. It's all yours, Beauty."

Something much more powerful than lust hammered in her chest. All-encompassing love cinched her ribs tight. She sucked in a breath tainted with his scent. Her lips still tingled from his kiss. How could she hold back from him? This over-powering need spun her up in chaos, threads of his promises tangling inside her like webs of golden sunshine.

Soon, she'd have to make a decision. Would she hold back, or would she risk it all?

39

MASON

Mason laughed for what seemed like the hundredth time that evening as he cleared Pippa's plate away from in front of her.

"I can get that," she protested.

"Dad always says the cook doesn't clean." Aspen smiled, shuffling the deck of cards before she placed them in the worn box. "Okay, winners get to choose the movie."

"I don't think it counts if you cheat." Mason chuckled, wiping his hands on a dish towel.

"We didn't cheat." Pippa smiled innocently.

He narrowed his gaze, flicking it between her and Aspen. "I don't know how you did it, but you did. There's no way I could have lost so bad at six-hand rummy."

Pippa shrugged. "I guess Aspen gets to pick."

"*Twilight!*" Aspen jumped up from the table.

Mason groaned. "Not again."

"You promised." Aspen crossed her arms over her chest.

"Fine. Get it set up," Mason conceded.

Pippa laughed as the young woman skipped into the living

room. Mason walked over to Pippa and grabbed her hand. She stood before he wrapped his arms around her, pulling her into a hug.

He leaned in and inhaled her sweet scent. "I'll take the dog out while you guys get the movie started. There's popcorn on the counter to microwave."

"Okay," she replied.

He kissed her forehead and called Lady towards the rear door. He walked out to his backyard, taking a long drag of the late summer air. It was much cooler after the sun went down now. The beginning of fall was right around the corner.

He turned towards the brightly lit house. Pippa snuggled up on the couch next to Aspen, offering her the bowl of popcorn. She was talking about something animatedly, waving one hand in front of her. Aspen's eyes held on the woman in rapt attention as if she'd hung the moon. This was his life now. Pippa had been giving him more and more of herself. He'd be damned if he let anything tear their relationship apart again. He wouldn't get in his own way this time.

Lady walked past him to wait by the door. She was well trained. Mason opened it and followed her inside, then took his spot next to Pippa. He wrapped his arm around her shoulders, and she leaned against him.

The first movie wasn't as painful with the constant commentary from Pippa. Usually he and Aspen watched in silence. Anyone else and he might have been annoyed. But Pippa's voice was soothing and spellbinding. By the second movie, he closed his eyes, just listening to her and Aspen going back and forth on who Bella should pick, the werewolf or the vampire. Aspen was team Edward all the way. But Pippa made a strong case for the wolf.

"All clear. Move in." The command crackled through the radio. Mason's vision was green, his night-vision goggles on.

"First room, clear."

His gut clenched. Something didn't feel right. Hadn't felt right since he'd left his baby girl with his father back in the States.

Mason aimed his weapon ahead and held up a fist. He signaled the man to his side before he let his gun hang loosely from the strap. He pulled his FUBAR knife from his gear and snuck up behind one of the guards who were keeping their target hostage.

He drew in a breath, his body humming with adrenaline. He had his orders. With one slick movement, he cupped his hand over the man's mouth and dragged the knife across his throat, cutting off his attempted scream. The man gurgled on his own blood, as an iron tang filled the air. The stench of death overpowered Mason's nostrils as he listened carefully to the guard's radio to see if he'd been overheard. He laid the man on the ground as silently as possible as his fellow SEAL moved to the next room.

"Target located." A low voice came through the radio in his ear.

Mason wiped his knife on his pants leg and sheathed it before grabbing his gun again and headed into the next room.

The man was barely clothed—nothing but skin and bones with dark bruises and lesions all over his sickly pale skin. He was struggling with his commander.

"No, I don't know anything else. I swear! Please! Leave me alone," John Sebring, their target, begged.

"We're here to rescue you. Come on, we'll get you to safety, but you have to be quiet."

But John wasn't listening. He stumbled forward and Mason grabbed him, to steady him. "Shhh. We're here to help—"

John pulled the pin to the grenade in his palm, his eyes glassy and gleaming like a man possessed as he waved his weapon.

"Grenade!" someone else yelled.

"Clear the room!" his commander shouted, grabbing on to the target's hand with the explosive device gripped in it.

Mason joined the struggle as something hard hit the ground.

"Get the fuck out, Wright!" Those were the last words his commander spoke before he jumped onto the grenade.

The explosion rocked the room, and everything went black.

Mason sat up, sucking in a gasp of oxygen. *Fuck!* His heart hammered. The acrid smell of smoke filled his nostrils.

It's not real. It's just a flashback. He took a few slow, deep breaths, opening his eyes. The TV was off, and the only light came from above the stove. Aspen was nowhere to be found, but Pippa lay curled up against his lap, her dark hair falling over her face. A blanket from the back of the couch was spread from her lap to his. *Aspen.*

Mason carefully got up, trying not to wake Pippa. He lifted her, sliding her into his arms as she stirred.

"Shhhh. I've got you."

She snuggled into his chest as he carried her upstairs to his bed. Lady yawned and followed them. She jumped onto the foot of the mattress, curling into a ball at Pippa's feet. Mason covered Pippa and slipped in beside her. She turned towards him, reaching out for him in her sleep. He pulled her against his chest and stroked her back, wishing to dream of her sweet kisses and tinkling laughter instead of dark memories this time.

Mason's eyes blinked open. Lady barked. His body shook. *Earthquake?*

Lady barked again. Mason reached over and tapped the touch light by the side of his bed before turning back to Pippa. Her body jerked and trembled.

Shit.

Lady placed her front paws on Pippa's thrashing body. Pippa's eyes rolled to the back of her head.

"Oh, baby. It's okay. I'm here, sweetheart." Mason pressed

his hand to her forehead, swiping the hair out of her face as he checked the clock. *Five thirty.*

His gaze landed back on the woman in his bed. His heart broke for her. *I wish I could take this away for you.*

"It's okay, Beauty. I'm here. You'll get through this."

Her back arched off the bed. Lady whined.

Didn't matter how much he knew about epilepsy, or the fact that he'd done more intensive research these past few weeks. It was so hard to watch someone you loved going through something that was so scary. He couldn't imagine having his own body do something that he couldn't control.

"You're safe, baby. I'm here. You're not alone." He hoped his voice brought her some comfort.

This was one problem he couldn't fix for her, and it killed him.

40

PIPPA

Pippa rolled over and groaned. *Why am I so sore?* She blinked her eyes open. A ceiling fan drifted lazily above her, creating a soft breeze. She sat, the soft sheets falling to her lap. Navy-blue walls. *How did I get here?* And where was Lady? The last thing she remembered was watching a movie with Aspen and Mason. Then . . . warmth and feeling weightless.

She looked down at herself. Her fingers pinched the worn, soft cotton material. This wasn't her shirt. She lifted the covers. Heat flushed her cheeks. Her pants were gone, and she was completely commando underneath the T-shirt. *Why did he change my clothes? And where is my underwear?*

The padding of footsteps brought her attention to the door. Mason walked in, wearing a pair of black sweatpants that hung low showing off his V intersected by a line of brown hair. Her mouth went dry. How could the grumpy man she'd met a few months ago be one and the same as this one?

He offered her the beverages in his hands. "Wasn't sure if you felt like coffee or juice this morning?"

Pippa reached for the coffee. "Caffeine is always welcome."

"Cream and sugar, just how you like."

She took a sip and smiled. "Mmm. You know me so well."

His brows drew together, and concern marred his expression. "How are you feeling?"

She took another sip of her drink and studied him. Why was he asking the dreaded question? "I'm fine."

"Do you remember having a seizure last night?"

Pippa's mouth dropped open. "No." She set her coffee on the bedside table. So that was why she was so achy today . . . and half-naked.

"It was a tonic-clonic. I almost called an ambulance it went on so long." He sat beside her, setting the juice on his nightstand. Mason reached out and brushed the hair out of her face, then tucked it behind her ear.

"I'm sorry. They've been happening a lot more frequently lately. Maybe I need to adjust my meds." Had she peed on herself? Was that why she was changed? *I've put off calling the doctor too long. It's time to make an appointment.*

"You have nothing to be sorry about. But I would feel better if you called your doctor and made an appointment." He leaned against the headboard, echoing her thoughts. "I had to change you; don't know if you remember that part. Your clothes should be dry by now.

Humiliation rose to her cheeks once again, and she covered her eyes. *How mortifying.*

Mason pulled her palms away. "It's nothing to be embarrassed about."

Easy for him to say. He's not the adult who wet himself. "Is Lady with Aspen—oh, God!" Pippa covered her mouth. "I should go before she sees me in here."

Mason smiled, placing his hand on her thigh. "Aspen

already knows you spent the night here. She's gone with my brother for the day. She's gonna stay with them while I go on a job. I got a call for a last-minute security gig for a celebrity staying in Hampton. I'll be gone for a week. But I'll be home in time for her first day back at school."

She knows?

Mason's rough hand grasped the side of her face, turning her so she had nowhere to look but him. "I won't hide a healthy adult relationship from her. Aspen needs to understand how they work."

Pippa's eyebrows drew up as a teasing smile curved the corners of her mouth. "Who said we were together? I said we were friends, taking this slow."

He smirked and gently kissed her lips. His tongue caressed the seam of her mouth, gently prodding until she parted her lips to give him entrance. His kiss coaxed her alive, stirring need and igniting a fire of arousal inside her. She relaxed into his touch, her hand coming to rest on his chest, right above his beating heart which raced just as fast as hers.

He pulled away, locking his lust-soaked eyes with hers. "I like having you in my bed."

"I could get used to it." Her voice was all breath.

"I hope you do. I plan to keep you here as long as you'll stay. Maybe forever."

She swallowed. "You keep saying that word—*forever.*"

"Pippa, I thought I knew what love was. I thought I had it before. But now, I'm sure. I love you. Every piece of me is yours—body, heart, and soul. I belong to you."

She sucked in a breath of air, thick with anticipation. "I think I love you like that too."

Hope danced in his gemstone eyes. "Think? Well, I better make you sure."

Mason leaned in, trailing kisses over her neck. His beard scratched her sensitive skin as he ran his fingers under the hem of her shirt. His eyes met hers, seemingly asking permission. She lifted the top over her head and threw it onto the ground.

"When do you have to leave?" She panted, threading her fingers into the top of his hair as he moved to kiss between her breasts.

He ran his tongue over the soft swell of her chest held back by a thin layer of her red lace bra. "I've got a couple hours."

"Better make the most of it, then." She reached for his hard cock and squeezed it through the soft fabric.

Mason groaned, his chest heaving and his shoulders pulled taut. "Anything you want, Beauty."

"And what if I want you?"

He smiled like a kid set free at a candy store. "Then you'll have me."

He slid his pants off. His erect cock sprung free, thick veins protruding and the tip glistening with pre-cum.

She licked her lips as he climbed on top of her to lave at her breasts. She closed her eyes and hissed at the sensations spiraling through her body from his eager touch. Her nipples pebbled under his hot tongue as he kneaded the other peak. He licked and sucked down her belly as his finger dipped into her slick entrance.

"Oh, God."

"That's it, baby. Let me hear you scream." He sucked on the tender flesh of her hip.

"Mason!"

"Yes, baby?"

"Please, I just want you. I want your cock."

"I need a taste of this pussy, then I'm all yours." He

dipped in between her thighs, his flat tongue licking her from the core that ached to be filled by him up to her clit.

She pulled his hair, holding on as pressure built, compounding into illicit vibrations that hummed through her limbs as she curled her toes. He swirled the sensitive bundle of nerves winding her into a frenzy of need.

"Please," she begged, clenching the inner walls of her pussy in an attempt to satisfy the hollow ache that only he could fill.

He sat up, licking his lips as if savoring every last drop of her arousal that glistened from his beard. He crawled over her. "You sure, Beauty? Because there is no turning back after this. You're mine and I'm yours."

Her arms circled around his neck, every cell reaching out for the pleasure this man had to offer. She kissed him, tasting her essence on his lips. "Please. Give it to me. Give me everything."

He lined his cock up with her entrance, and she sucked in a breath. He flicked the head of her clit, and her back bowed in exquisite torture.

"Say it." He pushed inside the first inch, stretching her tight walls.

She clenched her muscles, clinging on to him as her body trembled. "Please."

"No." His voice was ragged with need and rough with barely held control. "Say you're mine."

She locked eyes with him, inhaling as he breathed in. They exhaled as one. She stared into the eyes of her future. Of her *forever.* "I'm yours."

He thrust his cock inside her from root to tip. A million sensations erupted inside her. It was a rebirth of hopes and dreams and a lifetime. *Forever.*

"Mine," he grated, the force of his hips driving into her sending her soaring.

Her ears rang. Time stopped. Everything else ceased to exist as he drove her higher and higher into new planes of ecstasy.

"Yours," she mouthed the word, but didn't know if she actually spoke it. Desperate, keening cries fell from her lips as her orgasm shattered into a million waves, each one hitting her like a tsunami. She wasn't sure she'd survive the onslaught of pleasure. He kissed her, spinning her up and setting her aflame. Mason turned her onto her side, sliding her leg over his shoulder before he kissed and nipped the soft flesh of her calf. His large hands gripped her upper hip, digging into the flesh as he pounded inside her. He hit a magical spot within her each time their bodies collided, sending erotic chaos exploding through her. Pippa's eyes widened as the room darkened. Hyper focused. Unable to do anything but feel. There was nothing but the sound of skin slapping against skin and his pleased groans.

His biceps bulged, veins popping in his sinewy forearms. His expression became strained. "I'm coming."

"Yes!" She squeezed her inner walls around him, choking his cock.

His hips bucked. Hands gripped her harder. Mason shouted something unintelligible as his abs clenched and he bowed over her.

"Mine," Mason roared as hot jets of cum spurted inside her, filling her with his release.

Their panting breaths filled the room as he relaxed over her. His sapphire eyes stared into hers.

"Yours," she confessed, her body boneless. Her soul was irrevocably tied to his.

His kiss was gentle and sweet as he pulled out of her. She immediately missed the connection. "I'm gonna miss you."

He tucked her against his chest. "I'll miss you too. But I'll be back in a week. You should stay here while I'm gone. I've got a security system, and it would make me feel better knowing you were somewhere safe. Whoever is harassing you is less likely to know where I live."

She played with the light sprinkling of hair on his chest around his nipple. "I can take care of myself."

His warm hand rubbed up and down on the side of her ribs. "I know you can. But those letters are getting more and more crazy."

He was right—they were getting more frequent. Almost every few days. But she couldn't live her life in fear. And besides… "That's why I have a security system at the apartment. Remember? This grumpy SEAL I know installed it."

He pinched her butt.

"Ow!"

"Don't be a smart-ass."

She giggled.

He sighed. "Alright. But promise me you'll call and let me know if you get another one, or if anything happens. Even if you just feel like something is off. I'm only a forty-minute ride away."

She traced a heart over his chest. "I promise."

Mason leaned down and kissed her. "Love you, Beauty."

"Love you, Beast."

41

______

PIPPA

Pippa rubbed the gel left on her forehead from the electrodes. She'd have to try and scrub it out with her shampoo later. She tugged her hat lower and sat in the doctor's office, glancing around at the framed certificates on the wall. Her eyes dropped to the pictures of the doctor with her happy family, smiling with life vests and helmets by a raft.

The door opened and in walked Dr. Krans. The fair-skinned, redheaded woman offered her a warm smile. "Sorry to keep you. I was just waiting on one last test to come through." She sat across from Pippa, shuffling a stack of paperwork in front of her before she slipped on a pair of reading glasses. Her pale green eyes narrowed on what Pippa assumed were her test results.

"Your EEG didn't really give me an explanation as to what is going on and why you are having more frequent episodes. But I'm glad we ran the battery of blood tests. I had a hunch, because the same thing happened to one of my other patients."

Pippa leaned in. "Do I need to up my medication dose?"

Dr. Krans folded her hands in front of her and looked at Pippa. "We will actually have to tweak your medication, depending on what you choose to do."

"What I choose? What are the options?"

"I believe the reason you're having more frequent tonic-clonics, as well as smaller events, is because of the hormone changes going on in your body."

Pippa nodded and pulled out her phone, then opened her period-tracking app. "Yeah, I usually get clusters around my period, but never this much." She brought her phone closer and narrowed her eyes. She was late . . . *really* late. Almost two weeks.

"I had them run a pregnancy test with your lab work."

Pippa's gaze snapped to the doctor's. The blood drained from her face. Her heart raced.

"You're pregnant, Pippa."

"But . . . how? I take birth control, and my mother struggled with infertility."

"Anti-seizure meds can lower the effectiveness of birth control. And just because your mother struggled conceiving doesn't mean you would necessarily."

Pippa's head spun. She was pregnant with Mason's child. "Is it safe? I mean . . . I've been taking my meds, and—"

"The medication shouldn't affect the fetus this early. We can adjust your meds to ones that are safer to carry a pregnancy to term if you want to go ahead with this."

Go ahead with the pregnancy? A baby? Ay puñeta. Why was the room spinning all of a sudden?

"Won't my epilepsy hurt the baby? What if I pass it on?"

Dr. Krans stood and walked over to Pippa, sitting in the chair next to her and placing her hand on her shoulder. "There are many people with uteruses and epilepsy who have perfectly healthy pregnancies. Yours was from the tumors as a child, so there is no reason to believe you will pass on anything like that."

Pippa's chest heaved up and down. She was going to have a baby. Did she want a baby? Hadn't she and Mason just talked about this? Oh, God. What if he didn't want to raise another child? Her chest tightened.

"Just breathe. I know it's a lot to take in. You do not have to make any rash decisions. I will adjust your meds, and you need to be aware that the hormones might increase events, and that you will also possibly experience the typical early pregnancy symptoms like fatigue, morning sickness, and so on."

Pippa placed her hand on her belly. *I'm going to be a mother.*

"I'll give you a few minutes and go get those prescriptions called in for you to pick up on your way home." Dr. Krans got to her feet and exited the room.

Pippa pulled out her phone and stared at it. *Can I do this?* Never in a million years had she envisioned herself responsible for a child when struggling to attain her own independence had always been the priority. *But I'm going to have a baby now.* What would Mason think?

I can't imagine starting all over. He'd said those exact words. Would he be mad at her? She was the one who'd insisted they didn't need condoms because she was on birth control.

As if thinking of him had conjured him up, her phone chirped. She jumped. His name flashed on the screen.

Mason: *Hey, baby. How did the doctor appointment go?*

She lifted her trembling hands and typed out a response.

Pippa: *She's gonna change my meds and hope that helps.*

She didn't want to tell him over text. No, something this big deserved a face-to-face conversation. She needed to read his reaction. She also needed time to process this herself. But she had to talk to someone.

Her phone beeped with a reply from Mason, but she ignored it and called the one man that always knew what to say. He answered on the second ring.

"Hey, baby girl."

"Papi—" Pippa broke down into a sob.

"What's wrong? . . . Pippa, you're scaring me."

"I'm p-p-pregnant." She inhaled a shaky breath, trying to regain her composure.

The silence on the other end was deafening.

"Papi?"

"You're sure?" Was he crying? Her heart lurched.

"Yes. The doctor just told me."

"Oh, Pippa, that's wonderful, sweetheart."

More tears fell down her cheeks. "I'm scared. What if something happens to the baby?"

"Your mother used to worry about that too. I've learned that it's impossible not to when you become a parent. Your mama would say to trust in God and have faith." He sighed. "The truth is, baby girl, we have no control over a lot in this life. You just have to be willing to take a risk and hope it all works out."

"That isn't very comforting."

"No, but that's the life of a parent. We do the best we can and hope our children have a better life than we had . . ." He cleared his throat. "I'm assuming the father of my grandchild is the special person you told me about? When do I get to meet him?"

She swallowed. "I haven't told him yet. He's away on a business trip."

"Is it serious between you two?"

She smiled. "Yes. I love him, Papi. And he loves me. He's already got a daughter; she's thirteen. I just . . ."

"Just what?"

"I'm worried this will be too much responsibility to ask him to take on. My epilepsy on top of a newborn. What if I'm too much of a burden?"

"You were never a burden, *mija*—only ever a gift. From the moment your mother found out she was pregnant with you, we cherished each day you grew in her womb. And when you were born, kicking and screaming, we knew you would be a fighter. You brought so much joy to our lives, and you still do."

A ball of emotion clogged her throat. "But because of me you went to prison."

He sucked in a breath, and she bit back tears. "Is that what you think?"

"If it wasn't for my hospital bills, you wouldn't have stolen that stuff."

He sighed. "Pippa, I want you to listen to me good. A parent will do anything to save their child from pain. Yes, we needed money desperately to figure out what was going on with you and get you on the right medications. But I made the choice to break the law in a desperate attempt to seize some of that illusive control. It was my own fault that I was arrested. Not yours. I deeply regret what I did, but never my motivation." He took a shaky breath. "I was still in the midst of grieving your mother. Even after all those years, I hadn't really taken the time. When you landed back in the hospital and I couldn't fix it . . . I just wanted to take the pain away. I lost what little insurance we had when I was fired for taking one too many sick days to be at the hospital with you. But that wasn't your fault. You didn't choose to have a brain tumor or develop epilepsy. Just like your mother didn't choose to get cancer. Stop blaming yourself for things out of your control."

Is that what I'm doing? Yes, her life was more challenging because of her epilepsy. And whoever was in her life would also have to deal with that. But if Mason was the one with epilepsy, she wouldn't care. She would love him and wish she could take it from him, but she'd stay by his side.

"I did something desperate because I wasn't going to lose you too. In the end, I ended up failing both my daughters."

"No, you didn't. We love you, Papi."

"I should have been there for you when you needed me. I should have figured something else out. Instead, you both suffered for my choices."

"You're wrong. Yes, it was hard with you gone. But you're here now when I needed you most. I called you because I needed to hear your voice, and I knew you'd make everything better."

He sniffed. "This will all work out, baby girl. And I'm gonna be there for you every step of the way."

"Thank you, Papi. I love you."

"I love you too."

42

PIPPA

Pippa checked her phone again.

Mason: *Are you up for a sleepover? I promise it's of the adult variety. Aspen is going to stay an extra day with my dad —her idea. I have a feeling we're being set up again. But I'm not complaining. I'm on my way. Can't wait to see you, love.*

Pippa inhaled a shaky breath and checked the time. He should be here any second.

Lady's head rose from her paws, staring at the door. *Dios mio. He's here and I have to tell him about the baby.*

Knock. Knock.

Lady stood, stretching before she turned to Pippa like she could sense the riot of anxiety churning in her gut. Pippa walked to the door, leaning her forehead against the cool metal.

I need your strength, Mama.

She twisted the knob and pulled it open. She gasped. "Sophia?"

Her sister's face lit with excitement. "I missed you." She squeezed her in an embrace. Lady wagged her tail excitedly before Sophia leaned down to pet her. "Hey, girl. You taking care of our Pip?"

Lady barked excitedly.

The girls giggled.

"It's so good to see you. How come you came to visit?" Pippa asked.

Sophia smirked. "You mean besides my only sister telling me I'm going to be an aunty? Let's just say a little birdy told me you needed a visit." Sophia nodded towards the open doorway as a man stepped inside.

"Papi?"

Her father's warm blue eyes locked on her, crinkling at the edges as he smiled and opened his arms for her.

He stepped inside, wrapping her up in a hug. The smell of sweet tobacco and pine wrapped her in a familiar embrace. Tears welled in her eyes. Her shoulders lightened for the first time since that doctor's visit a week ago.

"Everything will be okay, baby girl."

She pulled back, taking in her father's blond hair and his weathered skin. He seemed older than his fifty-five years. A lifetime of struggling and half a decade behind bars showed on every line and dark shadow on his skin. But his blue eyes glittered with nothing but love and happiness.

Lady barked in alarm. A flash of movement had Pippa glancing behind her father before he was ripped away from her.

Mason clutched her father's shirt, his face red with anger. Pippa's eyes widened. "Stop! Mason, stop!"

Sophia screamed. Everything happened so fast. Mason pulled back his fist, his eyes no longer blue but black with rage.

Pippa pushed in between her father and Mason. She reached out, shoving against his chest. "Mason! Stop!"

Sophia joined her side.

Something shifted in Mason's gaze, awareness creeping in. He wrapped his arms around her and pulled her behind him. "Stay back, Pippa. I'll protect you."

Her brows drew together. Did Mason think her dad was an intruder?

Sophia moved next to their dad, her expression fear-stricken.

"Mason, he's my dad. This is my father." Pippa pulled his arm away and stepped forward again.

Mason froze, his eyes dancing between her dad and Sophia, and back to Pippa. The blood drained from his face. His voice sounded as if he'd swallowed shards of glass. "Your father is Roy Davis?"

"How do you know his name?"

"I thought your last name was a coincidence." Mason's gaze hardened. "He's white and you're . . ."

"What does my race have to do with this?"

"You said you were Puerto Rican," he growled, staring down at her, anger bleeding from him.

Confusion spun inside her mind. None of this made sense. "I'm mixed; I told you. My mother was from Puerto Rico. What does that have to do with anything?"

Mason clenched his fists at his side. His jaw ticced.

Pippa looked towards her father, who kept his gaze pointed at the floor.

"Someone better tell me what the fuck is going on!" Pippa snapped.

"Your father killed my wife."

What? His accusation knocked the air from her lungs. Sophia gasped, protesting in a flurry of Spanish.

"No." Pippa shook her head. "You have to be mistaken. You said your wife was in a drunk-driving accident. My papi doesn't drink like that." She swallowed. Could it be true? *No.* "Tell him he has the wrong person, Papi. Tell him!"

Her father met her gaze, and what she found there made her knees buckle. She dropped to the floor. Pain erupted in her knees. Mason reached for her but pulled back as if he didn't even want to touch her.

No. Nononono. This isn't happening.

"Mason?" *Don't go.*

The man she fell in love with had been replaced by a hard, unreadable, stoic imposter. He turned and walked towards the door.

Pippa scrambled to her feet and touched his arm. He flinched, not looking at her. Instead, he stared towards the door. "Don't, Pippa . . . just don't."

Pippa. Not *Beauty.* Not *love.* Would she ever hear those endearments from him again?

"Don't shut me out," she pleaded. *I'm having your baby!*

His shoulders tensed. He turned back to her. Love had been replaced by anger with pain swirling in his gaze. "I can't . . . do this."

Pippa's jaw dropped open, hope leaving her body in a cascade of disbelief as he walked away. She was carrying his child, damn it. He'd promised her . . .

She raced out the door and down the stairs, yelling at him, not caring who was around to hear. "Mason Wright!"

He froze mid-step.

"If you need to leave to calm down, fine. But don't shut me out. Let's figure this out. *Please.* I need you," she choked out, confessing her worst fear.

He stayed silent. One minute turned into two. He turned around slowly, and her heart skipped a beat. An ember of hope glowed in her chest. Surely this wouldn't be the end. He'd promised.

His gaze softened, glittering with unshed tears. He still loved her. They would work through this. They had to.

Mason's mouth opened and closed. His chest puffed out like he was taking a deep breath. "I can't see a way through this. It's too much . . . I can't get over . . . Your father killed my wife . . . Aspen's mother."

Not once in their entire relationship had she felt like his wife's ghost was between them until now.

"I don't want this to be the end. But I need some space and time," Mason's voice was raw, as if he were holding back a torrent of emotions.

She shook her head. "We should figure this out together. I thought you loved me."

"I do. But I can't . . . Christ, Pippa. How can I be with you when there's so much getting between us?"

She shook her head. Something in her chest snapped. Anger quickly blended with the pain. "But it was just words. Because whenever something hard happens, you disappear. You're a coward."

He flinched as if her words were a physical blow.

"It was all just pretty promises from you. I was wrong. I don't need you." *We don't need you.*

Pippa turned and walked up the steps without looking back. How could she have believed this time would be any different? So much for the Disney ending of their fairy tale. So much for forever.

43

PIPPA

Pippa shut the door and walked numbly to the couch. Sophia wrapped her arms around her.

"Was that the father?" she whispered.

Pippa nodded. Hot tears streamed down her face. Her heart was destroyed, hacked into a million pieces. A sob broke free. One hand rested against her unborn child and the other, her concerned pet. Lady whined and nuzzled her nose against Pippa's thigh. Pain like she'd never known sliced through her chest. Pressure rose in her rib cage, threatening to suffocate her. Was she having a heart attack?

"Oh, sweetheart, I'm so sorry." Her father wrapped his arms around her, getting to his knees in front of her.

"Papi, what was he talking about? Did you . . . ?" Pippa pulled away to look her father in his watery blue eyes.

He sighed, his shoulders drooping. He sat on the coffee table. "I was driving the things I'd stolen to a drop-off point. The light turned green at the intersection and I . . . I didn't double-check before I went through. His wife ran a red light, and we crashed. That's how I was caught."

Her mind reeled. "It's my fault. It's because of me his wife is dead. Why Aspen has to grow up without a mother."

"Are you seriously doing this again?" Sophia snapped.

Pippa turned to her, her eyes wide. Her sister never took this tone with her.

"Stop blaming yourself for everything. You're not fucking God. You have no control over other people's actions any more than you do your seizures." Sophia snapped.

"How can you say that? Because of me, your relationship with Annie ended. I heard you both fighting. She resented you for having to take care of me and so much of your finances being put towards my health bills." She turned to her father. "And maybe if Mom wasn't so stressed about my tumors, she wouldn't have gotten cancer again."

"Oh, *mija*." Her father wrapped his arms around her, holding her close.

"Pip, Annie was a bitch. She showed her true colors when put through hard times." Sophia stepped closer, her tone softening. "I'm so thankful for you being with me. You helped show me who she really was. Cutting her out of my life was one of the best decisions I ever made. If not for you, I would have ended up wasting years with her and missed out on finding Vivian."

"Your mother's cancer had nothing to do with you." Her father's voice shook. "I can't believe you'd think that."

Everyone was silent, staring at Pippa. She took a deep breath and let it out. Her shoulders lightened a fraction.

"You think you're so unlovable. Why?" he asked.

"I don't—"

"You leave every relationship before they can leave you, or you never let them fully in," Sophia argued.

Pippa's skin heated in anger. "The pain in my fucking chest would disagree with you. The man I love just walked out the door and left me for the second time over something I can't control."

"Well, he's definitely being an idiot. I don't really know him, but I can cut him a little slack for the bomb that was just dropped," Sophia added. "Are you going to fight for him?"

Pippa's eyes widened. "Didn't I just do that?"

Sophia held her hands up. "Give him a few days. He'll calm down and realize that his wife and Papi's accident is no one's fault and he messed up. Try to talk to him then."

Pippa shook her head. "I can't do that again. I gave everything to him, and he just . . . It hurts so bad." She pressed her palm to her chest.

Sophia squeezed her shoulder. "I know, *cariño*. And maybe it isn't meant to be. But if you love him, then wait until you both have some time to calm down and talk to him."

Pippa pressed her hand to her stomach. "I won't have a man in my child's life who leaves when things get hard."

"From what you told me, he seems pretty protective of his daughter. Do you think he won't want the baby after everything?"

No. I'm afraid he doesn't want me.

God, her family was right. When did she start believing she was so unlovable? He'd run—he'd done the wrong thing. But could she deny her child a chance at a father like she'd had? And could she deny her heart that fleeting glimpse of happiness?

He'd said he needed time. She could give him that.

She sniffed and wiped her eyes. "I'll give him a week."

Her father took her hands in his. She looked across at him. "I love you with every fiber of my being. And regardless of what happens with that man, I will be here for you. Even if that means walking away so you can be happy with him."

"How can you say that, Papi?" Sophia asked.

"Mason thought I was here to hurt Pippa. He was protecting her. The way he looked at you was the same way I looked at your mother. He loves you, sweetheart, but seeing me tore that old wound of grief open. I'm sorry."

Pippa shook her head. "You have nothing to be sorry about. I won't give you up, Papi." She wrapped her arms around her father and squeezed. Her dad had always put action to his love, no matter the cost. Maybe that was why Mason's betrayal hurt so much.

But losing her dad again? *No.*

"Pippa?" Her father's voice sounded far away, echoing in her head before blackness swallowed her whole.

44

MASON

The next night, Mason drained the last of his glass of scotch as the room tilted. He stumbled down the hall, a half-empty bottle in his other hand. He pressed Aspen's bedroom door open. The night-light by her bed made her fair skin glow, or maybe that was the copious amount of alcohol he'd consumed after he'd gotten home from work. He walked closer. Her reddish-blond hair was spread out over her pillow like wisps of fire. She looked so much like Amanda.

Pain lanced his chest. He staggered back out of the room, managing to close her door quietly before making his way to his bedroom. He set the glass on the side table and drank straight from the bottle this time. Tomorrow was Saturday. He didn't have to worry about being sober at seven to bring her to school.

Falling apart was a luxury parents didn't have, especially single ones. He leaned against the headboard, not bothering to turn on the light. He didn't need it to know he was alone, like he'd been for over a decade.

A wailing child screamed. Mason jerked up. Again, the child screamed. Setting the scotch on the side table, he wandered through the house. He opened Aspen's door again, but she was sleeping soundly.

Where was that coming from? He followed the screaming downstairs, senses alert.

Silence.

He peered out the front windows.

Nothing.

Again a scream, only this time it was behind him. He spun around, stumbling to the back door. He ripped it open, searching the backyard as the motion-sensor light flicked on. Cold grass and a crisp chill brushed against his heated skin.

Sweat beaded on his forehead. Where was she?

"Ahhhh!"

He jerked around. His wife sat on the porch holding a screaming baby Aspen. Tears dripped down Amanda's face. "I can't get her to stop crying. I tried everything."

Mason blinked. This wasn't real. It couldn't be. Aspen was a teenager. His wife was dead.

A man walked by. *No.* A younger version of him. And Mason was no longer in his backyard but a bedroom they'd once shared, states away.

"Let me have her," younger Mason said, grabbing Aspen from her mother. "See? She just needed her daddy. Why don't you take a break, go meet your friends for coffee or something? I'll take over here."

She nodded, getting up and going out.

That was the first of many times Amanda had left him with Aspen. Until it became an everyday occurrence. When he was home, she wasn't. They'd gotten into countless fights over it. She'd said taking care of Aspen was too much. And she always came home smelling like a brewery. His marriage was hanging on by a thread by the time Aspen was three. He hadn't had sex with his wife in more than a year. The only time she wanted him was when she was drunk. And he didn't want her like that.

"Mason, I need help," Amanda said, sitting beside his duffle bag.

Younger Mason set a three-year-old Aspen on the bed before handing her one of her toys to play with. He packed his things to leave for his mission. "So hire some help. Take a yoga class. Take a trip to New Hampshire and stay with my dad. He'd love to have Aspen."

Amanda's shoulders slumped. Mason had worried about leaving Aspen with her, but she was always sober when he got home from work. She'd never gotten drunk when she was caring for their daughter.

Mason's phone beeped with a reminder for his flight. His team needed him to be focused. He'd deal with this when he got back.

"I'll be back as soon as I can."

"Don't go," older Mason shouted. "Don't leave her. Get her help."

Younger Mason didn't make a move to acknowledge he'd heard him—he dissolved into the air, leaving only Amanda and little Aspen.

Amanda locked eyes with Mason. "Take care of our little girl. Because I can't anymore."

Blood dripped down the side of her head, staining her white shirt.

Mason reached for her, grasping nothing but the cool night air on the porch. "No, wait. Don't go. She needs you."

Amanda shook her head. "No. She has you."

"I'm sorry. Mandy, I'm so sorry."

Her gaze softened. "It was never your fault . . . and it wasn't *his* either."

He sucked in the chilly night air as once again, his wife disappeared.

Mason sunk to his knees, pulling the hair at the top of his head. Images of her broken body in that hospital bed flashed in his mind. He'd been three days too late coming home from his mission. Fear had strangled him as he raced into the hospital. No one would tell him if his wife and daughter were alive or dead. Aspen had survived with barely a bruise, but her mother had not. Machines had pumped air into her lungs and kept her heart beating, but the Amanda he'd fallen in love with was no longer with them. He'd been selfish. He hadn't listened. He'd not gotten her help when she'd needed it. And now it was too late.

He'd made the difficult decision to donate her organs. She'd have wanted that. To help someone else. Mason had vowed that day to do whatever it took to keep Aspen safe and never be so selfish again.

Mason had pored over the police report. Roy Davis had been the one to hit her car. He'd killed Amanda and left his little girl without the most important woman in her life—her mother. All his grief turned into anger for the one man who'd ruined any chance Mason had of fixing things. The only thing that tethered him to reality was that little girl with strawberry curls who looked just like her momma.

And then I fell in love with the daughter of her mother's killer. Why did he think for one second he would get a second chance at love when he'd blown it so epically the first time? How could he be with Pippa without betraying his daughter?

Pippa loved her dad, idolized him. *And I exposed him for the monster he is.* And hurt Pippa in the process. Pippa was a casualty like Aspen. And he wouldn't risk putting her through any more pain because of the sins of her father.

This was the moment he'd seen coming from the beginning. When he'd have to choose between his daughter and Pippa. Being with Pippa would be selfish and a betrayal to Aspen. His daughter always came first, which meant Mason would stay away from Pippa for good this time.

It was never your fault . . . and it wasn't his *either.*

His wife's words came back to haunt him, whispered in the air.

No. It was Roy's fault. He'd taken Amanda from Mason before Mason could get her the help she needed. If he couldn't blame Roy, that would mean it was all Mason's fault for not seeing the signs sooner, for not acknowledging her disease.

Emotions swirled in his chest. His mind spun, reeling with that statement. He wouldn't blame Amanda; she was the mother of his child—and she'd been sick. Should he blame her commander, who'd taken advantage of her in basic training and inflicted trauma? Or the war she'd seen and the people she'd killed, all in the name of patriotism, that had left her with lasting emotional scars? Where did the buck stop? Someone was to blame. And the only one who had actually taken her life was Roy.

Pippa shouldn't have to choose between him and her father any more than he should have to choose between the woman he loved and his daughter. He'd do the right thing and make the choice so she didn't have to. He'd let her go for good.

45

PIPPA

Pippa sat at the front desk of her bookstore and scanned the room. A group of preschoolers had gathered for book-related craft and story time. Pippa would be gone before the teens got out of school and arrived for the YA fantasy book club. Aspen would be there, and Pippa couldn't bear to learn if Mason was keeping her away now or not. And if she showed up, then what was Pippa supposed to say? *I love your dad, but he's a coward. My dad killed your mom because he needed money for my medical expenses. Oh, and I'm pregnant with your half-sibling, but your dad doesn't know because he won't even talk to me.*

She blew out a frustrated breath. Afternoons were harder for her anyways. Her seizures tended to hit more often then, and so did the nausea that had started the last few days.

Brynn was helping an older woman in the mystery section and a few other people milled about.

Lady yawned near her. Pippa petted her head and reached for her phone to reread the texts she and Mason had exchanged over the last two weeks.

Mason: *I don't think we should see each other again. I'm sorry, but I need to focus on what's best for Aspen.*

Pippa: *Can we talk?*

Mason: *I don't think that's a good idea.*

Pippa: *You don't think I deserve a face-to-face conversation after everything you promised?*

Mason: *I told you, Aspen always will come first. I can't do this anymore.*

Pippa: *I have something to tell you that I won't do over text. Please, Mason. You owe me at least this.*

Mason: *Nothing you can say will change my decision. We're done, Pippa. Being with you would be betraying my daughter.*

Mason: *You deserve to find someone who can give you everything. And that someone isn't me.*

Pippa: *You're right. I do deserve better than this.*

Pippa rubbed a hand over her face and rested her elbows on the desk in front of her, the weight of everything bearing down on her shoulders. She was exhausted. Between the hormones, the uptake in her seizures, and her broken heart, she was barely getting through the day. *Can I really do this alone?* She pressed her hand to her belly, tears blurring her vision. She swallowed down the ball of emotion. She couldn't cry here. And she couldn't imagine having a baby by herself. As scary and as unsure as her future was, one thing was for sure: she was going to have to make a choice about whether or not she would be a mother. Could she be enough?

A warm, soft hand rested on her shoulder. She sat up.

Brynn's sympathetic gaze met hers. "Do you want to go rest upstairs?"

Pippa wiped her eyes and cleared her throat. "No, I . . . I can do this."

Brynn set down a stack of books on the desk before she leaned against it. "He looks like crap, too, you know?"

Pippa's chest tightened. There was no use pretending with Brynn; the woman was insightful and observant. "It's his own fault. He won't even talk to me." A tinge of bitterness coated her tone.

Brynn nodded and sat on the stool next to her. "I've known Mason for a couple years now, and he seems like a really good man."

That's what I thought too.

"But . . ." Brynn met her gaze. "I've recently reevaluated my standards for men, and they're a lot higher now. If a man can't stand with you in the most difficult times, he isn't the one for you."

Tears welled in Pippa's eyes once again. She opened her arms to Brynn. "Can I hug you?"

Brynn's smile was small and brief, but she nodded and wrapped her arms around Pippa.

Pippa sniffled. "Thank you."

"I can't imagine what you're going through, but I do know Aspen has been asking for you every time she comes in."

"She's been here?" Pippa grabbed a tissue and wiped her eyes.

"Yes, after school a few times a week, and she always asks for you. Sorry I didn't tell you sooner."

Pippa's heart broke a little more. This was so complicated. She loved Aspen, but did Mason not want her around his daughter? *He still lets her come.* What did all this mean? Maybe if the man would talk to her, she'd have a better idea on how to move forward.

"I don't want to hurt them any more than . . . than my situation has."

Brynn just nodded.

A wave of dizziness washed over Pippa. She closed her eyes and reached to the desk to steady herself. "I think I better go lie down. Can you close up and slip the key into my mail-box?" Pippa handed over the shop key.

"Absolutely."

Pippa waited until she could stand and led Lady out of the shop and up to her apartment. She slipped off her shoes at the door and walked to her bedroom, then curled into a ball under the covers. Lady slid in next to her, laying her head on Pippa's arm before she licked Pippa's cheek.

"It's just you and me, girl. You think we can handle a baby too?"

Pippa barked and wagged her tail as if to say, *Absolutely!*

Pippa chuckled as melancholy settled over her. "I'm not so sure. But it's good to know I have your support." She sighed. "I've got to make a decision sooner than later."

Pippa picked up the half-heart necklace from Aspen and slipped it on her neck. She held the charm in between her fingers and closed her eyes, not bothering to fight the tears that came this time. She was grieving for the past, Mason's cold shoulder and abandonment, the truth about her dad's role in Mason's wife's death, and missing Aspen. Everything hit her like a tidal wave. A sob tore free. Lady whimpered and nuzzled against her, climbing on her chest to conduct deep pressure therapy as if Pippa were having a seizure. But she wasn't. No, this time, the only thing short-circuiting was the last bit of hope Pippa had for a life with Mason Wright.

She'd given him time. She'd gone after him and tried to resolve the mess. But no relationship would work when only one person was fighting for it.

She closed her eyes and let sleep take her for a temporary escape from her pain.

Ring! Ring!

Pippa jolted awake.

Ring! Ring!

She grabbed for the phone on her nightstand. Mason's name flashed on the screen. She gasped as her belly tumbled with anxious butterflies. *Why was he calling her? Was he finally willing to talk?* Even if they could never be, he deserved to know about the pregnancy. *Or maybe I should make a decision first.*

Ring! Ring!

Her hand trembled as she clicked answer. "H-hello?"

"I need you."

46

PIPPA

Pippa swallowed and pushed away the cautious flicker of hope that sparked at Mason's words.

"What—"

"Aspen is in pain and she won't calm down or tell me what's wrong. She's calling for you and I . . . I don't know what else I can do . . . I'm sorry. I shouldn't have called but . . ."

But he would do anything for that little girl.

"I'll be right over." She hung up the phone without waiting for his reply and pulled up her Uber app. Luckily, she only had to wait ten minutes. That was enough time to wash her face, fix her bed hair, and take Lady out to do her business before she was picked up.

Her leg shook up and down the whole ride. Lady rested her snout on Pippa's thigh. Her nerves were wreaking havoc with her guts as her stomach flipped.

"Can you pull over?" she asked.

The driver glanced at her in the rearview mirror, his brows drawn together. "We're only a mile from your destination."

"Unless you want me vomiting all over the car, please pull over." She gagged.

His eyes grew wide before he put his blinker on, steered the car to the side of the road, and slipped it into park.

Pippa didn't have time to utter her gratitude before her light breakfast was all over the side of the road. She spat and grabbed the bottle of water from her bag, swished and then spat out again. She pulled the travel-size bottle of mouthwash out and did the same before wiping her lips with a tissue.

Pippa climbed back in the car. "Thank you."

The driver nodded, his cheeks crimson as he rolled down his window.

"Don't worry. It's not contagious."

"Whatever," he grumbled and finished the drive to Mason's house.

Pippa helped Lady out of the car and tipped the driver handsomely. When she spun around, Mason was holding the front door open. His shoulders sagged in relief.

Aspen must be pretty bad if he's relieved to see me. Worry cinched her gut. She took one shaky step and then another, sucking in deliberate slow, deep breaths. Her heart raced like a drum in her chest.

Mason's hair was wild and unkempt, as if he hadn't showered in a couple days and he'd been constantly running his hands through it. The vibrancy in his bloodshot eyes had dulled, and the dark circles under them made it seem like he hadn't slept in weeks. *Guess that makes two of us.*

He reached out his hand and then dropped it to his side, his fist clenching.

"She's in her bedroom. She didn't go to school today. She was in pain with her period and now she's inconsolable." He led her through the entryway, up the stairs, and to Aspen's room.

As he passed, she caught a whiff of stale alcohol. Her nose wrinkled. His gaze dropped to it and his jaw clenched.

Whimpers and broken sobs sounded through the door. Pippa's heart lurched. She didn't say another word and knocked.

"I want Pippa!" Aspen cried.

Pippa pushed the door open and walked in. "It's a good thing I'm here, then."

Aspen's red, puffy eyes widened as she sat up in bed, one hand pressing the heating pad to her abdomen. "You're really here?"

"Lady too." Lady hopped up on the bed and curled in a ball at Aspen's feet as Pippa sat beside Aspen and opened up her arms in invitation. Aspen threw herself into Pippa's embrace and sobbed.

"What's going on?" Pippa asked as Mason disappeared from the doorway.

Aspen sniffed and petted Lady's head. "Everything is going wrong!"

"Shhhh. It's okay. I'm here." Pippa rubbed her back.

"But you weren't! Did I do something wrong? Is that why you're staying away from me?" Aspen's voice broke with another sob.

Pippa's heart broke. "No, of course not. You didn't do anything, sweetheart."

"Then why haven't I seen you in weeks? Did Dad do something again?"

Pippa sighed. Her mind swirled as she tried to figure out how to explain this appropriately. "The truth is, I haven't been at the bookstore in the afternoons because I haven't been feeling well."

"Are you okay?" Aspen sat up to look her in the eyes.

Pippa grabbed a tissue from her bag and wiped her tears.

"I will be. But you need to understand that I love you and that will never change. And even if your dad and I aren't . . . friends anymore, I'm still here for you. Always." She touched the charm on her necklace, drawing Aspen's gaze to it.

Aspen reached under her shirt, pulled out her own half of the heart, and squeezed it in her hand.

Pippa swallowed the ball of emotion welling in her throat and grabbed a pen and paper from her bag. She wrote her number before handing it to Aspen. "This is my cell. You can call me anytime you need, day or night, as long as your dad is okay with it."

"What happened between my dad and you?" Aspen probed.

Pippa sighed. "Your dad loves you and wants the best for you."

Aspen clung to her neck again. "I love you too. You're the closest thing I've ever had to a mom. I can't remember mine, but I'd like to think she was as cool as you. You'd be a great mother."

The girl's words were like a spear to Pippa's heart. Tears blurred her own eyes. "Are you in pain?"

Aspen pulled away and adjusted the heating pad. "Yeah, I was, but you being here made it better."

Pippa wiped her eyes with the back of her hand. "Sometimes that can happen. Lie down, and I'll read to you."

Aspen got comfortable as Pippa picked up the newest edition of *Selfie*. She read until Aspen's eyelashes fluttered closed and then she just stared at the girl. Her heart was bursting with love and breaking all in the same moment. *This is why he ended things with me.* Mason was willing to do anything to protect his child. Even if it meant giving up what he wanted. She couldn't fault him for that.

But now, he may have another child. If he would hear her

out, maybe he'd realize that there was a lot more to this choice than he realized.

312

47

MASON

Mason leaned against the wall in the hallway as Pippa soothed his daughter in a way he was incapable of.

"Did I do something wrong? Is that why you're staying away from me?" Aspen's voice broke with a sob.

His chest constricted and his eyes slammed shut, barring the emotion from the two most important women in his life. His little girl was blaming herself for this whole fucked-up situation. *What can I do to fix this?* He'd been trying for weeks. Fighting off the overwhelming urge to run back to Pippa and beg her forgiveness, and struggling to get through the day when he remembered that they could never be. He'd reread the texts they'd exchanged a hundred times. He'd even stopped going to Remy's Stardust Café just to avoid seeing Pippa. Aspen and he had been getting into arguments every single day. He'd run out of patience, and she'd blamed him for messing everything up. He was in way over his head. Hopefully, someday she'd understand he'd only been protecting her.

"I haven't been feeling well." Pippa's voice drew his attention back to the room. Was she sick? Or was she having more seizures? She needed someone to check on her and make sure she was taking care of herself. *I wish it could be me.* Or was the stress from all of this causing her health issues to worsen?

"What happened between my dad and you?" Aspen asked.

A beat of silence passed. He pressed his ear closer to the cracked door as he held his breath.

"Your dad loves you and wants the best for you."

"I love you too. You're the closest thing I've ever had to a mom. I can't remember mine, but I hope she was as cool as you. You'd be a great mother."

Mason stepped away. He'd heard enough. The two women he loved most in the world were hurting because of him. *Because of Roy.* But how could he make this right? Her father would always be the man who . . .

Doubt crept into his mind. Roy Davis drove through an intersection and hit the car with his wife and daughter in it, killing Amanda. If he hadn't been driving . . . it would have been someone else. Because the truth was . . . the *truth* was Amanda ran the red light.

He forced one foot in front of the other until he was in the kitchen. He grabbed a glass from the cupboard and his face soured. What was that awful smell? He leaned in towards his armpit and sniffed.

Mason grimaced as the stench hit his nose. Stale cigar smoke and scotch. He was a wreck. After filling the glass with tap water, he drank it down and headed back upstairs for a quick shower. He changed into a pair of sweatpants and a T-shirt. On his way by Aspen's door, Pippa's voice carried out to him. She was reading a story to his little girl. Mason returned to the kitchen, sitting at the bar with his head in his hands.

Am I doing the right thing? Everything was spinning out of control and now he didn't know which way was up or down, and what was right or wrong.

A throat cleared from the entry to the kitchen. His eyes snapped open, locking on the woman whose absence tormented him and presence slayed him.

She tucked a stand of dark hair behind her ear as her gaze shyly wavered from his. "I . . . uh . . . Aspen's asleep."

Duty and love warred inside him, creating utter chaos as he soaked her in, his voice held captive. Her beautiful amber eyes locked on his, pleading for the impossible. He wanted to reach out and take her in his arms and tell her everything would be okay, but that would be a lie.

The light in her eyes dimmed before her gaze dropped to the floor. Her shoulders slumped. She shook her head and turned away.

"Pippa?" His voice was raspy.

She froze, tipping her head to the side without looking at him. Her shoulders trembled in silent grief that rolled off her in waves big enough to drown him.

"Thank you."

Her head dipped. She spun around. Tears glistened in her eyes. "I'm sorry about everything, but I understand why you think this is the way to handle things. I don't agree, but she's your daughter."

He staggered back a step, awed by this powerful woman. Despite her obvious pain, she understood.

"I told Aspen I was here if she needed anything and gave her my number. I hope that's okay. I hope . . ." Her voice broke as she struggled to regain her composure. Tears tracked down her face. His hands fisted at his sides before he did something stupid like try and hold her. He couldn't touch her, because if he did, he'd never be able to let her go again.

But could he tell his daughter when she was older that her

mother was killed by Pippa's dad? It would only make it harder on both women he loved if they got even more attached before Aspen found out. And he didn't want her to blame Pippa.

Her chin lifted. "I need to tell you something."

His eyes slammed shut, a poor attempt at a wall between his heart and the all-encompassing love this woman emitted. "I don't think that's a good idea."

"But—"

"No." He snapped, his gaze locked on her once again.

She flinched before her jaw clenched. Steel laced her voice. "I won't bother you again." She picked up her phone, tapped on the screen and then slipped it back in her bag, hiking it higher on her shoulder.

"I guess this is goodbye." Her gaze flickered to him before she headed for the door.

"Pippa, wait!" He darted towards her, powerless to the tug of the thread tying her soul to his. She spun back to him, her wide eyes filled with tears that tore at his heart.

"I wish I knew how to fix this, Beauty," he admitted, defeated.

She blinked. Her chin lifted with resolution. "Sometimes you can't fix what's broken. Sometimes you have to let the shattered pieces go because they are doing more harm to you and everyone else around you."

His chest caved in with grief for the loss of the woman standing before him.

She opened the door and hesitated. "You should know that it wasn't my father's fault."

"Pip—"

"It was mine."

He sucked in a gasp. *What?*

"He wouldn't have been there if it wasn't for me and my health issues."

His anger rose. She blamed herself? "But—"

She held up her hand. "Please don't. I know I can't control how my brain works, but it doesn't change the fact that because of me, my father made a decision that put him in jail and that caused him to be in the wrong place at the wrong time. Because of that, a little girl has to grow up without a mother."

Nononono. She couldn't blame herself. It wasn't her fault. *It was mine.* He sucked in a lungful of air, his chest constricting with the realization.

She stepped forward and pressed her hand over his heart. A warm frisson erupted in his chest from her contact. "You deserve to find happiness, Mase."

No. She had it all wrong.

Pippa turned and walked out the door, not turning back again. His chest heaved as every cell in his body screamed at him to go after her, drawing him to her like a powerful magnet.

He fell to his knees. She blamed herself all because he'd been too scared to see the truth. It was absurd that she would take the blame for Amanda's death. The truth was, it was Mason's fault. If he had listened to his wife and gotten her help, they probably wouldn't still be married, but she might be alive.

What have I done?

48

PIPPA

Pippa adjusted the bags of groceries in her hands as she walked down the sidewalk towards her apartment. Lady followed obediently, her tail wagging. The warm breeze carried a hint of crispness to it as they neared fall.

Yesterday had been so emotionally draining with Aspen and Mason, Pippa had given herself the night to cry and grieve what would never be. He wasn't willing to fight for her. He wasn't even willing to hear her out. As much as she loved the man, she wouldn't settle for that. Right now, her focus was on the tiny bean growing in her belly. She needed to make a decision today, and then she'd let Mason know if she decided to keep it.

Can I really raise a baby by myself? What would that look like, along with running the bookstore? Can I afford to hire more help?

"Excuse me, miss?"

Pippa slowed her walk and turned as the young man who'd been with Pastor Calvin that day jogged over to her side.

She gave him a friendly smile and stopped. "Hey, Peter, right?"

He grinned, his eyes lighting up. "Yeah." His eyes darted down to her dog before he reached his hand out to her.

"Oh, don't—"

Lady eagerly lapped up whatever was in his hand. Too late. Pippa couldn't pull the dog away; her hands were full of groceries. "Lady, left."

Lady obeyed, going to stand on the other side of Pippa, away from the man. "Please don't feed her anything or interact with her. It isn't safe for me. She's a service pet." She nodded towards the vest Lady wore with patches clearly stating what she'd just told him.

His eyes widened. "Oh, I'm so sorry. I won't do it again. I had a piece of steak left over from my lunch and wanted to bring it for her."

Pippa's brows drew together. "Were you coming to the bookstore to find me?"

"Yeah. I really wanted to talk to you. Oh, I'm being rude. Let me help you carry these." He reached for the groceries.

Pippa let him take one of the bags. "Thanks."

"No problem."

"So, what did you want to talk about?" She continued down the sidewalk as the bookstore came into view.

"Oh, well, I've been studying and learning a lot with Pastor Calvin. And a few weeks ago, he gave his congregation a challenge to reach out to the community and seek out a soul to save. It's our duty to spread the word."

Pippa's smile faded. *Oh, God, he wants to convert me.* "Well, I'll be honest. I'm not really interested."

She started up the steps of her apartment.

He followed. "Can I ask why not?"

"I don't believe I have anything I need to be saved from." She slipped the key into the door and unlocked it, then quickly entered the code into the alarm system as a pang of longing ripped through her. *Mason had these installed.*

She turned to grab the bag from his hands but he stepped inside as Lady walked to her water bowl.

"You can hand it to me. I've got it from here. Thanks for the help. I'll see you around sometime." She reached for the bag, but he shook his head and walked in to set the groceries in her kitchen.

"I take my job of service very seriously. And I always see that the task is completed."

The tiny hairs on the back of her neck stood on end as her skin prickled with unease. Her gaze tracked over him once more. He was young, but taller than her and strong. He pulled a phone from his khaki pants and switched the light on so that it flashed.

Pippa backed up a step. "You need to go."

"Sure thing." His smile faded as he walked towards the door. Pippa held her breath as he walked by her and slammed it closed.

"What—"

Peter held the flashing light up to her face and she closed her eyes from the brightness. "I saw you at the pharmacy when it happened the first time, and again in the bookstore. You need help, Miss Davis, and it's my duty to save you."

"Peter, I will call the police if you don't leave." She reached for the door but his hand wrapped around hers.

"Stop!" Her eyes flew open. She shoved him, and he dropped the phone before he blocked the exit.

Lady growled and barked, but she fell to her side. She tried to get up, growling, but her eyes faded closed. *The meat he'd fed her.* "What did you do?"

"It's just something to help her sleep so we'll have time."

"Time for what?" Her eyes raced to the alarm by the door. If she could hit the button, the police would come.

"To rid you of the evil spirits inhabiting your body."

Her eyes widened. He thought she was possessed because of her seizures, just like her foster family had. *No!*

She shook her head and dove for the button. Her hand slapped against the alarm system right before he gripped her arms over her head and pushed her to the ground, settling his weight on her. Her head hit the wood floor. Her ears rang, and pain radiated in her skull. Terror gripped her. Not again. She wouldn't be trapped again.

"It was you. The spray paint and the brick and the letters."

He smiled, his face deceptively calm as she struggled against him. His legs locked around her waist and his hands pinned her to the floor. "I warned you. Gave you the chance to come on your own to be saved, and you didn't listen."

"Peter, let me go. I have epilepsy; it's a medical condition. I don't have evil spirits!" She shoved against him. She was strong, but he was stronger.

"I will call the demons out and set you free." He reached for the flashing phone. "This will get them to surface."

She took her opportunity and pulled one hand free, punching him as hard as she could in his throat. He choked and grabbed his neck as she shoved him off her and scrambled for the door. Lady lay on the ground. Pippa was torn. She should grab her pet, but she might not make it out if she did.

Adrenaline raced through her veins as she swung the door open. Sunlight blasted her sensitive eyes. She winced. Her head throbbed as she ran down the stairs as fast as she could. Her vision blurred. She stumbled, cradling her stomach with one hand and her head with the other as she fell the last few steps onto the concrete.

Everything went black.

49

PIPPA

Pippa blinked her eyes open and winced. Even in the dim light, her head hurt.

"She's waking up, Papi." Her sister's voice made Pippa flinch.

"*Mija*, here, have some water." Her father's gentle voice soothed her before a plastic straw met her lips.

Pippa drank the cold water down her parched throat. Her voice came out raspy. "Where am I?"

Lady's head rested on her thigh. Pippa reached down to pet her soft fur.

"The hospital in Shattered Cove," her sister answered.

"How are you here?"

A beat of silence passed before her father spoke. "We got a call from Mason that you were attacked."

Pippa's eyes opened. Her family's faces were still fuzzy, but they were clearing up. "I was attacked?" Was that why her body felt as if she'd been in a car crash?

"You hit your head. And by the time the paramedics got there, you were in the middle of a status epilepticus."

She closed her eyes. A prolonged seizure that lasted more than five minutes was considered one of the more dangerous types that, if not treated, could end in brain deficits or even death.

"Is the baby okay?" She pressed her hand to her belly. Tears burned her eyes. She wanted this little bean. She'd do whatever it took to be the best mother she could be. This baby deserved everything she had to give. She could be enough. She'd figure it out, even if that meant asking her family for help. *Even if it means leaving the bookstore for a little while.*

"The doctor said they'd do an ultrasound when you woke to check and make sure everything was okay." Sophia's hand slipped into hers and squeezed.

Pippa looked at her family. "How did Mason know I was attacked?"

"He said he'd been monitoring your security setup. He got notified that the alarm went off. He got there before the police did. They have the young man in custody who admitted to assaulting you."

Mason had the alerts sent to his phone all this time?

"Who was it?" And why couldn't she remember!

"A boy named Peter."

"Peter? From the church? But why?" None of this made sense.

"Glad to see she's awake." Bently's voice drifted in from the doorway. He walked inside her room. "How are you feeling, Pippa?"

"I've got the headache to rival all headaches." She forced a laugh and winced.

His eyes filled with sympathy. "I know a little something about concussions. I wanted to let you know we have the man who attacked you in custody. He's admitted to the vandalism and the threatening letters, as well as assaulting you. I'll wait until you feel a little better to get your statement."

"I'm not sure how much help I'll be. I only remember working in the store this morning."

"You mean yesterday morning," her sister said.

Pippa turned her head. "I've been out a whole day?"

"In and out. You've been sleeping a lot, but you needed the rest." Sophia rubbed her arm soothingly.

"I better go. I'll be back tomorrow for a full statement." Bently nodded goodbye and left the room.

Pippa's head swam with all the information, but one glaring question rose above all others. "I need to know if the baby is okay."

Sophia rose to her feet. "I'll let the nurse know you're ready. Papi, you should come with me to stretch your legs and get some coffee. You've been by her bed the whole time."

His gaze locked on Pippa, concern and unconditional love pouring from them. "Will you be okay, baby girl?"

"*Sí*, Papi. You go get something to eat. Or go back to my place and shower and rest. I'll be fine."

"We'll be in the waiting room. We want to know how everything with the baby goes." He kissed her temple.

"Okay."

Pippa waited until her family disappeared before she let her guard down. Tears dripped over her cheeks. She'd been attacked and couldn't even remember. She'd almost died and her baby might not be okay. She swiped her cheeks and took a deep breath. She would wait to fall apart until she was in the privacy of her own home—not in a hospital room where anyone could walk in.

"We meet again."

Pippa's head snapped up. Her heart stuttered for a moment until it was clear the lookalike was not Mason, but his brother, Sebastian, wheeling a portable ultrasound machine into the room.

"Wish it was under better circumstances. How are you feeling?" he asked, setting the machine up.

"I've been better," she croaked.

"Well, I'm sorry to hear. But a little birdy told me we have a baby to check on." He offered her a sympathetic smile.

"Does Mason know? Did you tell him?" she asked, terrified of his answer.

"No. That would break HIPPA laws. Would you rather have the ultrasound tech assist you?" His smile softened.

Her brows drew together. "Aren't you the tech?"

"I'm actually the pediatrician, but once I saw you were here, and my brother called me, I figured I'd offer my services. Of course, he knows I can't share anything with him. I think it makes him feel better to know I'm checking in on you. But if you would prefer someone else?"

Would she? "No, it's okay. I just . . . I tried to tell him, but he . . . I didn't get the chance. And I wasn't sure if I wanted to continue the pregnancy. But now I'm sure. I want this baby, even if it means doing it by myself."

Sebastian nodded. "He's been in the waiting room since you came in."

Her gaze locked with his. "He has?" *And I just sent my dad there.* Panic flared inside her chest.

Sebastian pulled up the wheely circular chair, the kind you found in every doctor's office. "You know, ever since Amanda passed, Mason has been a shell of himself. He's been different. Harder and closed off, except where Aspen is concerned. Seeing him with you was the first time I got a glimpse of the old Mase—or the new one, I guess."

"But—"

"It was an accident." He leveled his gaze on her. "Amanda was driving drunk and ran a red light with Aspen in the car."

She gasped and covered her mouth with her hand. Amanda had caused the accident? With her daughter in the car!

"I think, instead of facing the fact that he blames himself for not getting her help when she needed it, he chose your dad to force the weight of his guilt onto. I won't stand by and let this guilt ruin my brother any longer. I'll knock some sense into him, even if it means I have to bruise these precious hands to do it." He wiggled his fingers and offered her a playful smile. "Now, how about you lift your shirt and lie back so I can check on my niece or nephew?"

She nodded, still reeling from everything he'd shared as he lowered the bed. Pippa pulled up her hospital gown, and he squirted some cold jelly on her belly.

"Sorry, you'd think they'd come up with a better warmer for these things." He placed the ultrasound device on her stomach.

A whooshing sound filled the room. Pippa's eyes locked on the grainy screen. A tiny dark blob appeared on the screen.

"Is that . . . ?"

He grinned. "It sure is."

"The baby is okay?"

"That's a healthy heartbeat. And from these images, it looks like everything is great, development-wise."

Pippa breathed out a sigh of relief. A smile stretched her face despite the pounding in her head.

"But . . ."

"But what?" Her chest constricted in panic.

Sebastian squinted at the screen as he moved the ultrasound wand over her belly again, pressing into her skin. The whooshing sound amplified. He blinked and turned to her. "I don't know how to tell you this other than to just rip the Band-Aid off."

She held her breath. What could it be? It didn't matter—so long as her baby would be okay. It would just be the two of them, but she'd make it work. "Just say it."

50

MASON

Mason paced the waiting room, waiting for any news of Pippa. Of course, that would require him having to actually talk to her family. The nurses gave him looks of pity but wouldn't share any private patient information with him after he'd admitted he wasn't related to her.

Stupid move. I should have lied.

Pippa's sister and father walked into the room, their gazes catching on his. Roy looked away and took a seat on the side of the waiting area farthest away from him. Sophia's eyes burned with anger as she lifted her chin, reminding him of Pippa, before she joined her father.

Nerves swarmed him. He'd held on to this blame for so long. He'd fucked up big-time. The thought of losing her made everything else seem so insignificant. It put their situation into a whole new perspective.

And when her seizure didn't stop, and they loaded her into that ambulance, he thought he'd lost her for good. A million regrets crashed over him, each one like a heavy boulder. *How could I have been so stupid?* Instead of holding on to one of the best things that had ever happened to him, Mason had let his guilt keep her and himself from happiness. Pippa was right; he had been a coward, thrusting his guilt on Roy instead of facing it. That ended now.

Mason put one leaden foot in front of the other until he stood in front of Pippa's family. "Mr. Davis?"

Pippa's father looked up, his jaw setting tight. "You want to know about Pippa?"

Mason motioned to the chair beside him. "May I?"

Sophia stood, moving in front of her father. "No, you may not. You almost assaulted my father and then you broke my sister's heart and left her to deal with—"

"Sophia." Roy's voice cut in, halting his daughter's speech.

She turned to him, and he gave her a pointed look. A silent conversation passed between the two of them before she sighed and took her seat once more, crossing her arms and spewing a litany of Spanish. For once, he was glad he didn't know the language to understand the list of insults she was probably sending his way. But he deserved every single one.

"Thank you, sir." Mason sat, angling his body to face the man he'd once hated and blamed for ruining his family's life. "I wanted to apologize for how I acted towards you."

Roy's eyes widened, his mouth dropping open.

"It . . . wasn't your . . . it wasn't your fault." The words left Mason with a *whoosh*. The tightness in his chest eased somewhat, and his shoulders lightened with the confession.

Roy blinked as his eyes grew glassy. "I've gone over that day a million times in my head. If I had checked the intersection better before going through, she'd still be alive."

"My wife was drunk. She never should have been behind the wheel."

Roy reared back. He hadn't known. The only person hurt in the accident was his wife, and being a small town, the sheriff back then had agreed to keep that detail from public knowledge. It wasn't relevant as fault was deemed to Amanda for the accident anyway, and Roy had been arrested for theft, not vehicular manslaughter.

"I didn't know that."

"Not many people do."

Roy's shoulders straightened as if he, too, had been relieved of a burden. "So that was your daughter I held until the EMTs got there?"

Mason flinched from the pain in his chest at the reminder of just how close he'd come to losing everything that night. "You held her?"

Roy nodded. "Yeah. I mean, I left her in the car seat, like they tell you to do for safety, but I held her hand and removed her from the car. I kept her calm until the ambulance arrived."

Mason's eyes blurred with tears of gratitude. "Thank you for being there for her when I couldn't be."

Roy laid his hand gently on Mason's wrist. "I never got to say it before. I'm sorry for your loss."

"I appreciate it." Mason sniffed and cleared his throat.

"Pippa doesn't deserve to pay for our mistakes," Roy added, looking him in the eye.

Mason shook his head. "No, she doesn't. It was easier to blame you than take responsibility for my part in it. My wife needed help, and I didn't recognize it until it was too late."

Roy sighed. "I think it's about time we both stop shouldering the blame for things we can't change, don't you, son?"

Mason nodded solemnly. "She chose to drink. To get into a car with our three-year-old and drive drunk. Aspen could have been killed."

"She had a disease, by the sounds of it," Roy added.

"Yeah. I think it's going to take me a while to unpack this," Mason admitted. After a beat of silence, he asked, "How is Pippa?"

"Now he asks," Sophia grumbled from the other side her father.

Roy sat forward, his tired blue eyes locked on Mason. "My girl's a fighter, just like her mother was. She's going to make it through this."

Mason breathed a sigh of relief. "I love your daughter."

"You've got a funny way of showing that, *cabrón*," Sophia snapped.

"Sophia is right," Roy agreed.

"I fucked up. I promised her I'd be there for her, and then I wasn't when she needed me most."

"You did. But the question remains, what are you going to do about it?" Roy asked. "If you love my daughter, then prove it. And be warned—she's her mother's daughter in more ways than one. She's going to make you work for it."

Mason got to his feet. "I'm willing to do whatever it takes."

Roy gave him a nod. "She's in room three twenty."

Mason turned around and headed for Pippa's room. His heart raced as he walked towards the woman who had come into his life like an explosion, ripping his walls down and splitting the marrow of his body, decimating her way into his soul. Pippa Davis was his, and he wouldn't stop until he proved that to her.

He walked into the room and pulled the curtain back.

Sebastian sat with his back to him, his hand holding an ultrasound wand on Pippa's lower abdomen.

Pippa's gaze was locked on to the grainy screen as Sebastian announced, "It's two heartbeats. You're having twins."

All the blood drained from his face. *Pippa was pregnant?*
That was what she'd tried to tell him.
He staggered back a step.
Oh, God. What have I done?

51

PIPPA

"Twins?" Pippa gasped, shock blanketing her whole body. She was just getting her mind wrapped around the idea of one baby, but two? *Oh, God.* Her stomach rolled as movement from the corner of her eye had her turning towards the doorway.

Mason's wide eyes looked between her and the ultrasound machine. "You're pregnant."

Shock was the only emotion in his tone. The tears she'd tried to hold back welled in her eyes. She blinked, sending them streaming down her cheeks. Lady licked her hand as if trying to comfort her.

Sebastian wiped her belly off quickly and packed up his machine. "I'll, uh, give you two some privacy."

Mason stepped to her side as Sebastian handed over the black-and-white photos of her little beans to her. She gripped the paper, thankful to have something to look at besides Mason's stoic expression. *Does he hate me now?* Well, he shouldn't. *I didn't get pregnant by myself.*

"This is what you wanted to talk to me about." His voice cracked as he took the seat next to her bed.

She nodded, afraid her voice would betray her. Hot tears trickled down her face. She wiped them away, trying to hold on to a semblance of her pride.

"I'm so sorry I left you to deal with this alone."

She sniffed. "Running away from me is what you seem to do best."

After a beat of silence, he cleared his throat. "You're right."

She risked a glance at him. His eyes glistened as he locked them with hers.

"I'm keeping it—them. And I don't expect anything from you. I told you I wouldn't bother you again, and I meant that." She pulled her arms against her chest, a poor attempt at protecting herself from the rejection he was sure to deliver.

Twins. How was she supposed to do this on her own?

"I thought you were on birth control?" he said evenly.

She closed her eyes, fighting the onslaught of tears that wanted to erupt. Did he blame her?

"Shit, I didn't mean—"

"I was. The doctor said my seizure meds can make them less effective. I didn't know."

"Is it safe for you to be pregnant?" He leaned in, resting his hand on the side rail of the hospital bed.

Her lungs squeezed tight with his growing closeness. "Yes."

"And the, uh, babies? Will they be . . . okay?"

Her gaze moved to his. Concern marred his brow, and fear shone in his eyes.

"Yes."

He let out a large exhale, like he'd been holding his breath.

His shoulders sagged in what seemed like relief. "Oh, thank God."

Confusion swirled in her mind. Her belly flipped. "I'm sorry. I know this is the last thing you need. I was thinking about relocating to Boston before the babies are born. I'll need help, and I don't want to complicate things any further with you and Aspen and my father."

Panic flashed in his expression. He reached out, grasping her arm. "You're leaving?"

She pulled her arm away, resting it on Lady's head. "I-I don't see how else I can do this."

"Let me help."

She blinked twice. Maybe the attack had left her with brain damage and she was now hallucinating. "What?"

"They're my kids too. I'm the one who got you pregnant. I should be the one to help."

Her eyes narrowed. "Mason, this changes *nothing* between us. You wanted to stay away from me, remember?"

Pain etched into his expression. "Baby, I fucked up. I was wrong for leaving you like that. Wrong to blame your father."

"But you did. And now we're here. You think this pregnancy is going to erase all the problems we've had? That this fixes things?" She pulled her arm out of his grasp. Her heart pounded. She wanted him more than anything, but not like this.

"That's not . . . damn it. I was coming to find you and tell you . . ."

She crossed her arms over her chest. "What?"

"That I love you, Beauty."

She sucked in a sharp breath. His confession was bittersweet. *I've heard that before.* Pain burst in her chest at those three little words. But fear that these were just more promises with no action lacerated her heart.

He looked pleadingly towards her. "I love you and I was an asshole. I've been a coward, just like you said."

"And I'm supposed to believe you? Take your word that you meant this? You've made me pretty promises in the past, and then you broke them and treated me like I was nothing more than a fuck."

Lady sat up, alert with Pippa's change of tone.

He flinched and ran a hand through his hair. His gaze flicked wildly around the room before he got to his feet and paced. "I don't know how to fix this." He halted in front of her, his eyes lighting up. "You can ask your dad and your sister. I told them before I came in here that I loved you, that I'd do whatever it took to prove it to you."

"You spoke to my dad?" Nerves tied her belly into knots.

"Yeah." His palm slid up the back of his neck. "I needed to apologize."

"For what?"

Mason slumped into the chair beside her. "For a lot of things . . . It wasn't his fault. The accident, I mean."

"I know."

His eyes widened. "You do?"

"Sebastian told me your wife was driving drunk with Aspen in the car. *She* ran the red light. She could have killed my father and Aspen, and *you* blamed my papi?"

"Pippa—" He reached out to her but she drew her arm back and shook her head.

He sighed, his shoulders drooping. "It was easier to blame him than face my role in all of it. She told me she needed help, and I didn't take the time to listen. I thought she needed space with her friends, or to get out of the house. I had no idea she was dealing with postpartum depression after Aspen." He blew a long breath out before continuing. "Our marriage was more like a roommate situation after Aspen was born. I'd get home and she'd take off and disappear. She'd come home drunk, and I figured she just needed to let off some steam. But then it was every day. She was never intoxicated around Aspen, so I thought . . . at least she was a good mom."

Pippa leaned back in the bed. It was hard to hear this story, but she needed the details.

"Amanda was in the Army. One of her instructors . . . violated her in basic." His jaw clenched tight.

Pippa's mouth dropped open. "Oh my God."

"He got away with it. She had PTSD from her deployments. And she never got the help she needed. Her pregnancy and delivery with Aspen must have triggered something, because she spiraled after that. She was so good at hiding things. But I was also pretty good at looking past them. I didn't want to face that my marriage had fallen apart, nor that my wife was an alcoholic. And I blamed myself for not being there when she and Aspen needed. I put my job, my duty to the SEALs before my family, and Amanda paid with her life."

"And you think that's your fault?"

"I was her husband. I was the one person who should have noticed the signs and done something about it . . . but . . ." He sighed. "In the end, I know she had a disease and no one could have helped her until she was ready herself. She's the one who chose to drink and then get in the car with our three-year-old while drunk."

"You blamed my dad so you could relieve yourself of some of the guilt, because blaming your child's mother felt disloyal."

His bloodshot eyes met hers. "Yeah."

"I'm really sorry that you all went through that, Mason."

"Thank you."

She took a deep breath. *Dios*, this was hard. "That doesn't change where we are now. You're a grown man who made decisions that broke my trust."

He nodded. "I know. But I'm done blaming others for my mistakes . . . is there any chance I could earn back your trust?"

She took a deep breath. "Honestly, I don't know."

The hope dimmed in his gaze. He cleared his throat and leaned in. "I love you with my whole heart, Pippa Davis. And if my actions have fucked up any chance we had, I'll regret them for the rest of my life." His chest inflated before he let out a large exhale, like he needed a fortifying breath for whatever he was going to say next. "But I'll find a way to live with that and still be here for you and *our* children. If you just want to co-parent with me, I'll respect your wishes. It isn't anywhere close to what I want, but if it will bring you happiness . . . you deserve the world. I'll do everything in my power to make sure you are taken care of." His voice cracked. "And I'll never stop loving you."

He reached out, drawing his knuckles across her jaw. She shivered from his warm electric touch and closed her eyes.

Everything in her was screaming to fall into his arms.

But sometimes you could love someone with your whole heart and it wasn't enough. Her trust in him had been shattered. And it would take a long time for him to earn that back. Maybe forever.

52

PIPPA

Pippa groaned and held her sister's hand as Sophia led her into her apartment. Her balance still wasn't great from the concussion.

Lady walked inside ahead of her, going directly to her water dish.

"Sofa or bed?" Sophia asked.

"Couch." Pippa pointed as she shuffled her feet forward. She reached out for the armrest, steadying herself as she settled onto the cushion.

"I'll get you water." Sophia walked into the kitchen before opening the fridge.

"Where is Papi?"

Sophia grabbed what she needed and closed the door before handing the bottle to Pippa. "He's helping out in the bookstore today until Brynn gets done at the diner."

"Doesn't he have to get back to his actual job?"

Sophia sat next to her and shrugged. "He said he had some time off for a family emergency. But I believe he is going back at the end of the week."

"What about you? I don't want to get you in trouble with your boss or mess up anything with your wedding plans."

Her sister sighed. "Pip, we know you can take care of yourself. Okay? But with this injury, your pregnancy, and your seizures, you should not be alone right now. You need us. We're your family, and we love you—of course we're going to drop everything to come help you."

"That's exactly what I didn't want."

"Well, there is a certain marine who seemed more than willing to have you stay with him."

Pippa unscrewed the water as her chest tightened. "He's a SEAL, not a marine."

"Tomato, tah-mah-tow."

The memory of Mason using the same phrase in the bookstore pummeled through her mind. She shook her head. Pippa hated to be in this place. Yes, she did need help. She hated that fact. But, what was worse was that she was a drain on her family. Mason might give her a place to stay while she recovered, but would it only be out of guilt? She didn't want to be another person for him to take care of. But what choice did she have? If she kicked her family out and didn't reach out to Mason, then her babies' lives could be in jeopardy.

Pippa took a long sip of water before screwing the cap back on the bottle and setting it on her coffee table. She leaned back on the couch. "What am I going to do, Soph?"

Her sister wrapped her arm around her shoulder and pulled her closer. "That, my dear, is your choice. Dad and I are willing to help you. But Dad will lose his job. I can work from home for the most part, except when I have court. But I would like to see my fiancée more than on weekends when she could come to visit."

"I don't want you to have to uproot your whole life for me a second time. Or have Dad lose his job."

"What other option do you have, then?"

"I don't know if Mason would be willing. It's a lot to ask of him, especially since there is his daughter to consider." Anxiety snaked in her gut. He'd said he'd be there for her, but when it came down to the moments she'd needed him, he'd abandoned her. Why would this time be any different?

"Yeah, but you're his baby mama now." Sophia laughed before her tone turned serious. "And he knows I'll gut him like a fish and feed him to the sharks if he hurts you again."

Pippa giggled.

After a moment of silence, Sophia said, "I have to tell you, the look on that man's face as he paced the waiting room was pure anguish and regret. And when he left your hospital room, I'd never seen someone so defeated but also determined. But I'm worried about you with him. He doesn't have the best track record."

What other choice did Pippa have? Her father would lose his job if she relied on him. Her sister had a wedding to plan, and her happily ever after to pursue. That left Mason.

"I . . . I'll call him."

Sophia sighed and stood. "No need. I'll go get him."

Pippa's brows drew together. "What?"

Sophia's eyes sparkled with mischief. "Oh, did I forget to mention? He's been at the bookstore . . . helping out."

Knock. Knock.

Sophia walked to the door and opened it.

"Hello, I'm Pastor Calvin. I was wondering if I could speak to Pippa?"

Sophia turned towards her sister and raised a brow. The silent sister speak was clear. *Do you want to talk to this guy or should I send him away?*

A spark of anger lit inside her as nerves twisted in her belly. Pippa nodded. "You can let him in."

"Are you sure?"

"Yes."

Sophia moved out of the way so Calvin could enter.

Calvin walked in, standing on the other side of the coffee table. Lady sat to attention by Pippa's side.

Pippa turned towards her sister. "Weren't you going somewhere?"

"I can wait." Sophia looked towards the pastor.

"It's okay. You go." Pippa offered her a reassuring smile.

"I'll be right back." Sophia gave the pastor a warning look before she left, closing the door behind her.

Pippa motioned to the couch next to her. "I'd stand, but I might fall over at this point. Would you like to have a seat?"

Calvin gave her a friendly smile and took the spot beside her. "I'm sorry. I won't take up much of your time. I heard about Peter, and I wanted to come and express how sorry I am that I didn't see he needed help. I never would have imagined he'd become violent. I put you in harm's way by introducing you, and I feel partly responsible."

Pippa released a breath she'd been holding. "I appreciate that. And I hope he gets the help he needs."

Calvin nodded. "Yes. I've been reflecting on this whole situation and praying for answers. My belief is that we should love everyone as Christ loved us. That is what I teach my congregation."

"But you also teach that being gay is a sin."

"Yes, I do."

"Peter thought because I support the LGBTQ community, and host drag queen story hour, that my epilepsy was a demon possessing me . . . or so the sheriff informs me."

A blush rose to his cheeks. "Yes, I-I'm not sure where he got that from."

"Your words matter, Pastor. My sister's love for her soon-to-be wife is no less pure than your love for your wife. You believe your god doesn't make mistakes. Then he wouldn't make people attracted to the same sex."

Calvin nodded thoughtfully. "I see your point. I think we might just have to agree to disagree on this one." He stood as her front door opened.

Mason walked in, his gaze snapping to the pastor. His shoulders tensed.

"Mr. Wright, good to see you. I was just on my way out." The pastor gave her a wave before he left, closing the door behind him and leaving Pippa and Mason alone.

"Are you okay?" Mason asked, stepping closer. Bits of sawdust stuck to the hair on his muscular forearms.

"Yeah."

"Sophia said you wanted to speak to me."

"Did you mean what you said about me being able to rely on you?"

Mason nodded.

She took a fortifying breath. "Because I need your help."

53

MASON

Mason locked the door to the bar and turned around to help Finn as they closed The Shipwreck for the night.

Finn wiped down the counter. "You look like shit, man."

Mason grumbled, "Thanks."

Finn crossed his arms over his chest. "Everything okay at home?"

"Sure. Pippa and Aspen are getting along great. Aspen is excited to be a big sister. And things have been . . . really good with Pippa living in the guest room these last couple weeks."

Finn's brows rose. "So what's the problem?"

Mason picked up a chair and tipped it upside down on the bar. "It's temporary."

"So, make it permanent. Did you ask her to move in?" Finn moved around the bar with a mop.

"I can't do that. She told me she wanted space. I broke her trust, and I don't know if I can fix it."

Finn held the mop handle to his chest. "You know when I fucked up things with Charli, you're the one who told me not to waste my chance because life was short. If you love her, then show her by being what she needs. Show her what life can be like with you. And invest in a florist. It's probably gonna take a lot of groveling."

Mason chuckled with his friend. "Yeah . . . You're right. I just don't know what I can do to prove to her I mean it this time."

"If I learned anything from my marriage, it's that trust takes time and consistency to rebuild. You just gotta be willing to put in the work." Fin swished the mop across the floor.

"You're right." Mason walked to the front door. Ideas swirled in his mind. How could he prove to her he'd carved out a permanent place for her in his life? There was one thing he could do.

It was a risk—but it had to work.

And she was worth risking everything for.

"Where are you going?" Finn called after him.

"To win my girl back."

The next day, Mason wrapped his arm around Pippa as she walked into the bookstore for the first time in weeks. Lady entered, her tail wagging as she sniffed the empty bookstore.

"I'm okay; you don't have to hold me. I won't fall."

"Do you want me to let go?" he asked, turning towards her. There was so much more weight in that question than just a simple palm to her waist.

She blinked, her mouth opening and closing before her gaze softened.

He leaned in. "I'm never letting go again."

She inhaled a shaky breath and turned her attention to sweep the room. "Looks like in my absence, everyone has kept the store in order."

"Troy has been a great manager," he admitted begrudgingly.

Her eyes lit with amusement as she smiled. "Maybe I should give him a raise."

"Come on, let me show you why we're here." He took her hand and led her to the new bookshelf—with a twist. He'd worked with his friend and co-owner of Sea View construction company, Andre, to build Pippa the secret door she'd envisioned.

Pippa's eyes grew wide as her gaze swept over the space that now looked like a regular built-in bookshelf, matching the wall beside it.

Her hand covered her mouth as her gaze darted to him. "Did you do this?"

He reached out to brush a piece of stray hair from her face. Locking eyes with her, he said, "This is the first of many dreams of yours I hope to be by your side when you realize. I know you don't need me. You're a strong and independent woman who can take care of herself. But I'm the lucky bastard who's in love with you so much so that I'll be happy if I can just live in your shadow." He stepped closer, her scent infiltrating his senses. His fingers threaded through the hair at the back of her neck as he angled her chin towards him. Her eyes darkened with lust, lined in hesitancy.

Mason leaned in so that he was close enough to taste her sweet breath. "I'll wait as long as it takes until you realize I'm not going anywhere. My home is you. My heart is yours. And, for the rest of my life, I will spend every waking moment trying to be the man you deserve and doing everything in my power to have you never doubt my love and commitment for you again."

She closed her eyes, tears glistening, trapped in her lashes.

His chest tightened. He hated that he'd been the cause of so much of her pain. That stopped today.

He pressed his forehead to hers, his nose resting on the other side of hers before he gently kissed the corner of her mouth. She trembled in his arms, and his cock jerked. Tingles raced down his spine as he breathed her in and savored this moment. Having Pippa in his arms made his heart race. He needed a lifetime more of this, right here. He wanted to lift her against him and take her on the desk, show her how much pleasure her body was capable of. He needed to sink into her heat and connect with her, feel her quake around him.

But that wasn't what *she* needed. *Not yet.* She needed him to keep his promise. So he used his remaining strength to pull back from her.

"Why don't you try it out?" He nodded to the hidden door.

She shook her head as if dazed before focusing on the shelf. She tapped her finger to her lips as if thinking. "Which one could be the lever? . . . Oh." An amused smile curled her lips.

Pippa's amber eyes sparkled as she flicked her gaze to him. "Really? Of all the books you could have chosen to let me into my secret room. I should have guessed you'd pick this one."

He shrugged, with a grin. "Wanted you to think of me every time you did something that made you happy."

She reached up and pulled the top of the *Beauty and the Beast* novel from the shelf.

The lever clicked as it released, and Mason pulled the door open for her. "This is it. The moment of truth."

Pippa beamed as she pushed past him to peek inside. Her hands clasped over her mouth, and her eyes grew round. "Oh my God. You did all this?" She stepped inside, Lady following.

"Aspen got me screenshots from your Pinterest board and

Brynn helped me decorate. Andre supplied the building expertise, so it wasn't all me."

She walked in, her watery gaze roaming over the space. Twinkling lights lit up the punched tin ceiling. Every wall was covered with built-in bookshelves with a sliding ladder to allow easy access to those high shelves. Light fixtures, made to look like candle sconces, brightened the space. She walked over to the window seat, complete with plush cushions and pillows. The desk that used to be in the middle of the room was gone, replaced by a couple of swinging chairs.

Pippa spun around. "I can't believe you did all this. And in two weeks, no less."

"Do you like it?"

Joy radiated from her, beaming from her smile. "I love it. This is so special. Thank you, Mason."

He stepped closer, grabbing her hand before pressing it to his lips. "This is just the beginning, baby. I plan on putting that expression on your face as often as possible for the rest of my life."

Her eyes widened. "That's an awfully long time to commit to."

"I told you forever once. I've fucked it up since then, but I meant it. I mean what I say. It's not nearly enough with you."

A flicker of doubt clouded her gaze. He'd promised her a future before. Now all he had to do was convince her he was in this for good no matter what storms came their way.

54

PIPPA

Pippa tiptoed downstairs to get some water. Lady yawned and followed her to the kitchen.

Pippa had gotten used to living in Mason's home during these past three weeks. She was more at home than she'd thought she'd be. Her head was much better, but she couldn't stare at screens very long, and her balance was still affected every now and then. *It's almost time to go back to my loft.* Her gut sank at the thought.

She flicked the light on and opened the cupboard to grab a glass. She let the tap run for a moment before filling her cup. The cold water slid down her dry throat. After draining the liquid, she refilled it to bring back upstairs with her. She turned, her other hand resting on the light switch, when a snoring sound startled her.

She flinched, her gaze roaming the dim living room across from her in the open-plan home. Heart racing, she let out a relieved sigh as her eyes landed on the handsome figure on the couch. Light snores drifted from Mason. He was in the same clothes he'd worn to work at the bar—black jeans and a matching dark T-shirt. His head tilted back on the couch, mouth open as his Adam's apple bobbed with each breath.

He must have come home from work and fallen right to sleep. Pippa's chest expanded with warmth.

She sat on the coffee table in front of him and set her drink down beside her. She took him in, taking advantage of the moment to really look at him. Dark circles formed rings under his eyes. He'd been working his security job at The Shipwreck and then getting up early to open the bookstore on days Troy couldn't or when he needed the extra help. Mason had been taking care of her shop. He then came home to spend time with Aspen and her. The Wrights included her in almost everything. Everything except whatever they did in his office every night this week while she'd read in her room, or taken her tea out to the back patio by the gas fireplace on the deck.

She swallowed the lump of emotion that rose in her throat. Mason had said he wanted her and apologized. Since then, every action he'd taken had been proving his words true. But could she trust him again? How did she know this would continue?

Pippa leaned forward and gently rested a hand on his knee. "Mason?"

He jerked awake, his blue eyes wildly scanning her and the room around them before his shoulders drooped. He rubbed his eyes and blinked. "Whoops. Thought I'd sit down for a minute. Guess I fell asleep. What time is it?"

She checked the clock on the wall behind him. "Three in the morning."

"What are you doing up? Is everything okay?" He sat straighter and reached for her hands, engulfing them in his.

A thousand hot spikes of awareness prickled through her. Her breath caught. "Came down for a drink and found you like this. I figured your neck would thank me if I got you to bed."

"I know a few other parts that would thank you if you were in that bed." He smirked.

She chuckled. Butterflies stirred in her belly as her core heated with arousal. "I don't think that's a good idea. It will . . . complicate all of this."

Mason leaned closer, pulling one of her hands to his lips and then the other. "I just want to hold you. I miss having you beside me while we sleep." He reached out and dragged his knuckles over her cheek, sending a shiver through her. "Miss having your scent all over me. And the warmth of your body wrapped around mine."

She closed her eyes. Something pulled Pippa towards him like he was gravity and she had no choice but to fall. "I miss that too."

"I never wanted just your body. From the first time I saw you, walking from the café to your bookstore, you stole my fucking breath away."

Her eyes flashed to his. "What?"

"I thought I was having a heart attack, the way my pulse raced. But I turned around and ran because I was terrified of what letting you inside would do to the carefully controlled world I'd built around me." He gave her a sad smile. "And then when you ran into me in the café, it was easier to be angry at you than admit you'd fucking knocked me off my axis. Like that coffee you spilled—I was done for."

She chuckled, tears welling in her eyes.

His gaze softened. "You saved my little girl that day, protected her with your life, and helped her through one of the most pivotal times for a young woman. I'll never be able to thank you enough. But, baby, I plan on doing my best every day to show my gratitude. I don't plan on wasting a second."

He stood, drawing her hands up so she got to her feet. His front pressed against hers as he leaned down and kissed her forehead and then her cheeks. "I'll be as patient as you need. But I'm not going anywhere."

Pippa stared into his determined gemstone eyes. Nothing but pure honesty and vulnerability was reflected back at her. She should say something. Tell him she wanted that too. That they would get through this together and come out stronger.

"Come on. I want to show you something." He took her hand and led her to the stairs, not letting go as they climbed each step. Pippa's heart raced. Everything that had happened between them flashed through her mind. How he'd treated her with respect from the very beginning, how he'd taken care of her and her dog even when they were not on the best of terms. And when he'd pulled away, it was because he was protecting his daughter and doing what he believed was best for both Aspen and Pippa. The problem was that he'd shut down and made those decisions on his own, closing her out.

Finding out she was pregnant was a curveball neither of them had seen coming. *And he stayed this time. He's been fighting for me every day since.*

Mason stopped outside the office door. His hand rested on the handle as he turned to her. Lady sat by her feet.

A hint of nervousness crossed Mason's expression. "I—uh, wanted to show you that I'm in this, and I'm willing to do whatever it takes. Wanted you to feel more welcome here. And . . . well, I guess I'll tell you the rest after you've seen it." He blew out a breath and pushed open the door.

Pippa followed him inside the dark room. She winced as he flicked the light on and gasped. Gone was the desk and office equipment that used to be there. Instead, two matching cribs sat against one wall. A mobile hung above each one, featuring felt roses and tiny books. To the left were a changing table and double rocking chairs. A white dresser that matched the cribs sat on the opposite wall with a bookshelf hanging above it displaying a collection of Disney stories.

Wow.

"What do you think?" Mason's voice was raw.

She turned to him, her eyes wide. "It's beautiful."

His blue orbs flashed with relief.

"When did you do all this?"

"Aspen helped me put it together. I moved the furniture out with Finn's help while you and Charli took that trip to the store."

Oh. "Sneaky."

Half of his mouth turned up in a smile. "I figured you could decorate it how you want, but I wanted to get the basics done."

She nodded, taking in the room again. "Why two rocking chairs?"

"I figure we'll have some nights when we might both be up feeding and rocking a baby each." He shrugged.

He was envisioning midnight feedings with her? "Do you expect me to move in here after the babies are born?"

He stepped closer, wrapping his arms around her waist and pulling her close. "If I have my way, you won't ever leave."

What? "This was supposed to be temporary, until I was feeling better from my concussion."

"Do you want this to be temporary?"

No. "That isn't fair."

"Why?" His deep voice vibrated through her.

"Because . . . you can't just treat me like a queen and then do something like build me a secret library of my dreams and. . ." Her eyes moved wildly around the room. "Now you've gone ahead and given up your space for a nursery. How could

I stand a chance of not falling in love with you, or wanting this to be permanent?"

He smiled as tears tracked down her cheeks.

"It isn't funny." She sniffed. "Stupid hormones are turning me into a water fountain . . . and that's your fault too."

"If this is all good, what's the problem?"

Her belly flipped as her fears came tumbling out. "What if I give you everything and you walk away again?"

Mason's hold tightened on her as he wrapped his arms around her and pulled her against his hard chest. He stroked her back and held her for a few moments without saying a word.

Is he going to give up and walk away now?

Mason fell to his knees, holding her hands and gazing up at her. "Beauty, there isn't a thing I can do to change the past. But I'd really like to move forward into a future with you. My therapist told me that in order to make this work, I had to be willing to be vulnerable, to share my feelings with you, even when it scares me . . ." He took a deep breath and let it out. "So, here it goes . . . Pippa, I'm terrified that I won't be enough for you, or Aspen, or these babies." He placed a hand on her stomach. "I'm afraid that I won't be able to protect you from everything. Which I know is impossible, but the fear is there, just the same . . . I fucking love you with everything in me and that scares me too. But I'm done running. I'm done being a coward." Mason squeezed her hand. "I decided I'm gonna be brave for you, Beauty."

She didn't try to stop the flood of happy tears welling up from the incandescent happiness that bubbled inside her. She fell to her knees, grasping his hard jaw in her hands, one side of his face smooth, with rough stubble, the other swirled with old burn scars.

"You be brave, and I'll fight for us. Together, we'll figure this out. Because I don't want to lose you again. You hear me?" She shook his head slightly in her palms.

He nodded.

"Good, now kiss me and take me to bed—"

His lips collided with hers, hungry and wanting. His hand slipped to the back of her head, pulling her impossibly closer. Finally, she was home.

"I love you, Beauty."

"I love you too, Beast."

He growled and lifted her in his arms. "I'm gonna show you just how much I've missed your gorgeous body."

She giggled as he led her into his bedroom and shut the door, leaving Lady whining on the other side.

"It's okay, girl. I got your mama. And I'm gonna take real good care of her." Mason laid her on his bed and touched the dim lamp on the nightstand on.

"Are you ready for this, baby?" Mason asked, his warm gaze filled with a mixture of awe and fathomless affection.

Pippa's heart leapt as her body tingled with awareness and heat. "I'm sure of one thing."

"And what's that?"

"That I want a lifetime of tomorrows with you looking at me like that."

"Like what?" His brows drew together.

"Like I'm everything."

He leaned down and kissed her on the nose. "You are everything to me."

Pippa walked towards the entrance of Hope Facility as a gust of crisp fall air blew over them, ruffling her gown. "Do you think your dad and Sebastian can handle the twins on their own? Did you pack the extra milk?"

"Yes, and yes." Mason pressed his hand to her lower back as he opened the door for Aspen, Lady, and her.

Pippa lifted the gorgeous gown as she stepped into the building. She watched where she stepped on the blue rug in the small vestibule leading to the second set of doors that would take them into the main room of the facility.

"Come on, Pippa, we're gonna be late." Aspen hurried them along. Her own dress glittered under the lights.

"Is your phone ringer turned up in case they need us?" Pippa asked.

Mason pulled her hand away from the second set of doors leading into the main room as Aspen slipped through them, leaving Pippa and him alone.

He held her face in his hands, bringing an instant hit of calm to her. "Babe, the twins are going to be fine. It's just for a few hours. My phone is as loud as it goes, and so is yours. Let's go and enjoy this party as our first date night out since Camila and Andrew were born."

She sighed, her eyes tracing down the fitted black suit he wore with the white dress shirt underneath, the first two buttons undone. God, he was sexy. "I know you're right. Does it get any easier? Leaving them behind?"

He chuckled. "Yes and no."

Pippa rolled her eyes. "Well, that's comforting."

"They're six months old, not newborns. My dad and Uncle Seb got this. Can you try and enjoy tonight? You look fucking edible in that dress." His finger traced the sweetheart neckline of her sparkly sunshine-yellow strapless gown. "God, your tits look amazing in this."

She giggled. "The benefits of breastfeeding."

"One of them." He gave her a salacious wink.

She playfully smacked his shoulder. "Alright, Mr. Wright, let's go to this fundraiser."

He smiled and pressed his hand to the small of her back again, leading her into the giant room.

Gold, white, and black balloons floated above them. Bachata music thrummed from the speakers as a DJ's voice split through the crowd that had all turned towards the entrance.

"Ladies and gentlemen, these, theys, and gays, I present to you the star of the ball, our *princesa quinceañera*, Miss Pippa Davis."

The audience clapped.

Pippa turned to Mason. "What's going on?"

Aspen appeared at her side, handing over the crown she'd given her for the midsummer's dance over a year ago. "It's a do-over."

"What?"

Mason plucked the crown from his daughter's hands and slipped it onto Pippa's head. "Your sister told me that your own celebration wasn't possible when you were fifteen because of your health problems at the time. So, I talked to Aaron, and he loved the idea of putting on a *quinceañera* for all the girls at the center and turning it into a fundraiser, with you getting to participate."

Her gaze darted to the crowd, who had begun dancing to the music, while others disappeared to round tables covered in white linen with red rose centerpieces. They'd transformed the space into a decadent ballroom.

A pair of pale blue eyes locked with hers across the space. "Papi?"

Her father walked forward, opening his arms to her. "It wouldn't be a proper *quinceañera* without a father-daughter dance, would it?"

Pippa wrapped her arms around her father's neck and breathed him in. Thankfully, she had seen quite a bit of her father in between his work trips. Mason had called him every week while she recovered at his house, which was now their home. Her father had even come for an extended stay that Thanksgiving.

Pippa glanced at Mason as her father led her to the dance floor and mouthed, *"Thank you."* Mason just smiled and winked before he took Aspen's hand and joined them.

"Surprise," Sophia said, bumping into Pippa playfully before she spun her wife, Vivian, around.

"I can't believe you knew about this and didn't tell me." Pippa beamed at her father as Lady moved closer to her.

Her father led her through the steps of the dance as he spoke, "I have to say, I'm so proud of you, *mija*."

"Thank you, Papi."

"You have so much of your mama in you."

The compliment was bittersweet. "I wish she were here."

"Me too." He spun her around. "Camila would be delighted to meet her grandchildren."

Pippa chuckled.

"She'd be happy with who you chose, Pip. Mason is a good man."

Her attention turned to her boyfriend who was dancing with Aspen, both of them smiling and laughing as he added his own flair to the routine.

"He's the best," she replied. Mason had proven his word true. Every day, he'd been there for her. And when the difficult moments came, he turned towards her rather than away. He was brave, just like he'd promised.

David, who now went as Danielle, walked over to Aspen, tapping on her shoulder. Danielle's usually short hair was pulled back into a neat bun. She'd come out as trans to her mother just this week, from what Brynn had shared with Pippa.

Her father spun her closer to the teens and Mason as Rachel carried over two cups of punch to the friends. Rachel and Aspen had eased back into a friendship and were once again inseparable, along with Danielle.

"What?" Aspen's jaw dropped open and her eyes rounded.

"My mom and Aaron are getting married," Danielle said loudly and smiled.

Pippa gasped, pausing mid dance, and looked at Mason. His shoulders rose as if he were just as shocked by the revelation as she.

Brynn and Aaron weren't even dating. Over the past year, she and Brynn had gotten closer, and as far as she knew, Brynn had no plans of even dating a man, much less marrying one.

What is that about?

She'd have to find out next week at the shop.

"May I cut in?" Mason asked.

"Yes, sir. I'm gonna go get some punch." Her dad waved before he walked towards the buffet table.

Mason's arms enveloped her, tugging her close. His clean aftershave tingled her nose. Shivers raced down her limbs, leaving goose bumps in their wake. As long as they were together, this feeling would never get old. His touch made her body hum with electricity.

Mason brushed the scruff of his beard over the crook of her neck before whispering kisses over her sensitive flesh.

"Mmm, you better behave yourself, Mr. Wright."

His low chuckle reverberated against her chest. "You turn me into a beast, wanting you." His fingers gripped her hips as he pressed his arousal against her.

Pippa gasped.

"What do you say we get out of here?"

Heat pooled in her center. "But it's early, and Aspen won't want to leave yet."

His eyes lit with mischief as his hand trailed down over her ass. "Your dad can bring her home later."

She turned towards the crowd before making her decision. "Lead the way."

Thirty minutes later, they crashed into their bedroom. Her hands slipped under his suit jacket, slipping it over his broad shoulders and letting it fall to the floor.

Mason spun her around, his hot fingers probing behind the zipper on the back of her dress. Such a delicate touch made her quiver with building anticipation. Soon, those expert hands would be all over her, leaving no inch untouched.

The sound of the zipper heightened her desire. Her heart boomed as he slipped the silk from her body, leaving her naked.

"You naughty girl. You mean to tell me you weren't wearing anything under this dress?" His hand slapped her ass, hard.

She jumped, lust pooling in her center. The sting only added to the sexual tension in the air.

"Turn around," he ordered.

She spun on shaky legs, her eyes falling to him on his knees. Her thighs clenched. "I can't wait for you to taste me. I need your cock. Need to feel you inside me."

He smiled and reached into his pocket. "You'll get that, baby. But first . . ." He pulled out a small blue velvet box with a gold trident logo emblazoned on it. Did that belong to the artist from the seafood festival?

Her gaze snapped to his as he cleared his throat. "Pippa, *love*, every time I picture my future, you're in it, front and center."

She gasped. *Dios mio!*

"I've waited a year to give you this. Waited until I thought I'd proved to you just how far I'd go for you. We've had good days, and we've had difficult days. But I love you more every time the sun rises. And I'll be by your side for all the challenges to come. Because you're a part of me. My best friend. My lover. Mother of my children. Will you be my wife, Beauty?"

She stood before him, naked, with tears of joy leaking down her cheeks as he opened the box. A perfect, shiny pearl rose shimmered in the light. "Yes!"

He slipped the ring on her finger, and she reached for him. He stood and she kissed him with everything she had. She gripped his shirt, ripping it open, sending buttons scattering.

He growled. The metallic clink of his belt sounded before the whoosh of his pants, dropping to the ground. His sweet tongue delved between her lips as she climbed backwards on the bed. Mason followed her; he was bare and hard. His muscles flexed as he settled his weight over her.

Pippa wrapped her legs around him, opening herself to the man she loved with all her heart.

Mason didn't hesitate. He lined his steel cock at her entrance and sunk in, stealing the oxygen from her lungs as he drove deeper and deeper. His breath staggered as his lips caressed hers.

"Mason."

"I'm all yours, baby." He thrust hard, filling her as they collided together in a flash fire. Lust swarmed her blood, buzzing through every synapse. Love bloomed, hot and heady. He rocked into her, over and over, spinning her up, higher and higher. She gripped his shoulders, digging her nails against his skin, slick with sweat. His eyes locked with hers; his were black, lined in sky blue. This was the man she would spend the rest of her life with. The one she'd grow old with. They'd raise their children, and cry together as they sent Aspen off to college. She'd be there to hold his hand when his little girl walked down the aisle one day. And when the twins left their home. Through it all, they'd have each other.

Mason thrust, the veins straining in his neck, his face focused and intent on her. "Come, Beauty. Come for me. Let me see you fly." He pressed his finger to her clit and slid his palm over her neck, adding just the right amount of pressure.

Pippa's orgasm exploded, shattering her into a thousand tiny shimmers. Her eyes widened, locked with the love of her life's. Mason increased his pace, pumping once—twice—

He roared her name as he soared, meeting her somewhere between this world and the one that connected their souls.

This was true love. It was messy and terrifying. Honest and true. It wasn't perfect, but their love was constant. And, above all, their love was brave.

Thank you! We hope you enjoyed reading *Brave Love*.

Now, turn the page for a sneak peek of Chapter One in the next and last book in this series, ***Hope Between Us***, (Book 8, featuring Brynn and Aaron's story).

Or visit the website below to order Book 8 in the Shattered Cove series right now.

WWW.AMKUSI.COM/HOPEBETWEENUS

SNEAK PEEK OF HOPE BETWEEN US: CHAPTER 1

Aaron

Aaron Ridley scrubbed a hand over his face as he sat back in the chair behind his gleaming cherry desk. Heaviness descended onto his shoulders as it did every year on the same day—the anniversary of his brother's death.

Aaron closed his eyes, trying to conjure a memory of his brother laughing and smiling, but it was faded and warped. Much like a real photograph would be after overuse.

More than a decade had passed, but Aaron still felt the loss. *I wish I could have saved you, E.*

His gaze circled his office, skimming over the certificates of philanthropy and his two degrees to the rainbow accent wall opposite his desk. The hundreds of overlapping handprints brought a little relief to the tightness in his chest. Kids he'd been able to help. But for each one he'd taken into his center, there were ten more sleeping under a bridge or trading their bodies for food in their belly.

Emmanuel's face popped into his mind again, cold and

lifeless. No trace of the horror his brother had faced before he'd taken his last breath. Aaron let out a deep breath and shook his head as if he could rid himself of the tragic thoughts. Emmanuel was the reason he'd built the Hope Facility with his college and short-term pro-basketball savings. It was his way of holding on to his brother, and making up for not being able to save him.

Knock. Knock.

Aaron cleared his throat and sat straighter in his chair. "Come in."

A blond head shyly peeked in the door. David walked in, tucking his shaggy locks behind his ear. "H-hey, Mr. Ridley. I, um, I wondered if I could talk to you for a minute?"

Aaron motioned to the chair across from him. "For you, I have two."

David took the seat, crossing his legs neatly and staring at his hands.

Aaron waited a beat. He'd learned a lot in his years working with homeless LGBTQ youth. Sometimes the teens needed your silence, and other times they needed a push. David, much like the young teen's mother, had seemed scared of his own shadow when he'd arrived. But during the last several months, he had come out of his shell.

"I need . . . I need your help." David let out a breath and looked up at Aaron. His blue eyes shone with unshed tears and determination.

This was the part Aaron lived for—when he was presented with a problem and had the power to fix it, helping make these youths' lives just a little easier. "I'm listening."

"Where I come from, people like the youth here . . . people like me are punished." David's voice broke.

Aaron's body heated as his mind raced. He didn't have much on David in the kid's file. He kept one for each teen that passed through the doors. Something told him that Smith wasn't David's legal last name. His mother had signed a permission slip, and he wasn't a border like most of the others here. Legally, he didn't need much more from them. But wanting it was another story. Aaron leaned in, listening intently to any morsels of information David was willing to share. Were he and his mother, Brynn, in trouble?

"When my mom brought me here . . . it was the first time I'd felt like I could be me." David blinked as if trying to clear the tears.

"That's what we're here for. You should be able to be you and not worry about your safety."

David nodded. "This place is so different. Even Shattered Cove is different from where I grew up."

"Where was that?" Aaron tried to sound as casual as possible.

David's back straightened, his eyes darting around the room nervously. "Uh, well, out west."

Aaron nodded. "How can I help you? Are you in danger?"

David shook his head, his blond hair falling in his face. "Not anymore."

Aaron's chest tightened, his heart thundered as righteous anger lit his body on fire. The thought of anyone trying to hurt David or Brynn made his guts twist. Brynn's face flashed in his mind, tugging him into a whole other riot of emotions. The woman had barely spoken five words to him, but something about her had sucked Aaron in. But anytime he even approached the woman, she'd gotten fidgety and nervous, eyeing the door for an escape. *What had happened to her?*

"Tell me what you need." Aaron focused on the thirteen-year-old in front of him.

David smoothed his hair back, his chin lifting and shoulders squaring. "I thought there was something wrong with me for my whole life. After we got away…"

"What do you mean, got away?" Alerts blared in Aaron's mind at the words the young man used.

David opened and closed his mouth before he looked down. His shoulders carried a tightness that wasn't there before. He eyed the door.

Aaron lifted his hand. "It's okay if you don't want to talk about it, but I'm here to help you any way I can."

David nodded and relaxed back into the seat. "Anyways, my mom brought me here because we both thought I was gay. I didn't know there were so many people like me."

"Sometimes it can take a while to figure out your sexuality. You're still young; it may take some experimenting."

David shook his head. "This isn't about my sexuality. It's about my gender."

Aaron tipped his head to the side, waiting to hear how he could help. "Go on."

"After doing some research, and reading some of the books you have here in the library, and talking to some of the other kids, I realized . . . I'm transgender."

Aaron sat back in his chair, his face softening as he gave the young *girl* what he hoped was a comforting smile. "I'm sure that's a lot to grapple with. But I'm proud of you for telling me, and taking a step towards living your truest life. Do you need some resources? Is that why you stopped by?"

David shook his head. "Not exactly. I wondered if you'd help me tell my mom?"

It wasn't uncommon for teens here to ask Aaron to mediate conversations with family, and he was happy to lend them that support. "Sure, no problem. And I have a packet of information here about what it means to be transgender, resources, the names of doctors . . ." Aaron stood and opened one of the file cabinets on the back wall, then found a packet of what he was looking for. He set the manilla folder on the desk in front of David.

"What should we call you now? Or do you still want to go by David for the time being?"

She shifted in her chair, smiling. "I thought about Danielle."

Aaron nodded. "Alright, Danielle. You can have your mom stop by anytime and—"

A knock interrupted his speech.

Danielle jumped to her feet. "That should be her."

Aaron's gaze flicked to the door as Danielle opened it. Brynn, roughly the same height as Danielle, glanced up at him with those brilliant green eyes that were always searching her surroundings.

Aaron reached out. "Come on in and have a seat." He motioned towards the chairs across from his desk.

Brynn crossed her arms over her body, bowing her head as she walked in timidly.

Aaron sat, hoping that position would make him seem a little less threatening than his six-foot-eight stature allowed.

"Is something wrong?" Brynn asked, looking to Danielle instead of him, her short brown hair falling over the side of her face. Brynn made no move to fix it, as if she was most comfortable hiding behind the curtain. She reached out a slender hand to Danielle's knee, the oversized threadbare T-shirt, drooping low enough for Aaron to make out her slender and pronounced collarbone. The woman was tiny, with barely any meat on her bones. *Do they have enough to eat?*

"No, nothing is wrong," Aaron assured her.

Brynn's magnetic gaze flicked to his before dropping to his broad chest, pink coloring her cheeks.

"I wanted to tell you something, and I wanted Mr. Ridley here while I did it," Danielle supplied.

Brynn focused back on her child.

"Mom, I'm transgender." Danielle's eyes lit with hope as she stared back at her mother.

Brynn's eyebrows drew together, her green orbs growing watery. "That means you . . . you're not a boy, right? It means you are really my daughter?"

Danielle nodded.

Brynn stayed silent for a moment as if digesting the news. When in similar situations, some parents had suspicions. For others, it could be a total shock.

Brynn lifted her hand to Danielle's cheek, caressing her skin softly. "I love you."

Danielle jumped from her seat to wrap her arms around her mother. They stayed like that for a minute. Aaron breathed a sigh of relief.

"What does this mean for me? What do we need to do?" Brynn asked, turning to him.

Something loosened in his rib cage. The woman trusted him to have the answers—at least where this topic was concerned.

He pointed to the manilla folder. "In here are some pamphlets and resources. There are the names of some doctors in Boston who specialize in this; they will be able to talk you through your options of possible puberty blockers, hormone therapy, and everything like that."

Brynn's eyes widened as her face fell. Her shoulders turned in again before she grew so still he wasn't sure she was breathing. She was terrified.

"What's wrong?" Aaron asked.

Danielle turned to her mother and back to him. "We can't go to the doctor."

"Why?"

Brynn's attention focused on her daughter, brushing the blond hair from her face with a smile full of sorrow. "I don't have health insurance."

Aaron interjected, "Oh, there are a lot of programs available. Maybe the state—"

Brynn shook her head, tears swimming in her eyes.

Danielle spoke up quietly, "We can't have our names on record. They might find us."

"David," Brynn chastised.

Danielle faced her mother. "I trust Mr. Ridley, Mom. If anyone can help us, it's him."

So they were hiding from something—some*one*. Aaron's fists clenched. He hated to think of someone hurting either of them.

"Are you in danger?" he asked Brynn.

She shook her head, getting to her feet. "No, I, uh, I don't . . . We better go. Thank you for your time."

"Brynn."

She stopped, looking up to him.

He held out his hands at his sides placatingly. "I just want to help. Whatever you tell me doesn't leave this room. I promise."

"Just tell him, Mom," Danielle pressed.

Brynn searched his eyes as if struggling with the decision. "We are safe now. But if our names were put into any legal database, we might not be. I'll figure something out."

She picked up the manila folder and wrapped her arm around Danielle. "Thank you for your time, Mr. Ridley."

Aaron's heart raced. *Do something.* His gaze flicked to Danielle.

"Queer youth who don't get the support and resources they need are at higher risk for homelessness, drug abuse—"

Brynn shook her head and wrapped her arm around Danielle, ushering her out the door.

"And suicide," Aaron finished.

Brynn froze. Her shoulders ratcheted up to her ears.

Aaron seized his opportunity, stepping forward. "Your child needs help. Let me help you find a way. I can protect you." *Let me save her.* This was why he'd started Hope Facility—so other kids didn't have to end up like Aaron's brother.

Brynn turned, her chest rising and falling as her guarded gaze locked on him. "I appreciate everything you have done for my so—my daughter, Mr. Ridley. But I can't . . . It's just not possible."

"This is your daughter's future!"

"You don't think I want what's best for my child?"

"Of course you do. I just—"

"Just what?"

"I just don't want Danielle to get hurt," Aaron blurted, but Brynn turned away, leaving once more.

Emmanuel's face flashed in his mind. His bruised and broken body. Danielle couldn't end up like that. *Do something!*

"Marry me."

The words fell from his mouth before his brain could catch up. Brynn gasped, turning to him, eyes wide. Danielle's mouth dropped open.

"Marry me, and I can get you on my insurance. You can change your name, and we can help change Danielle's name from David. She can go to the best doctors, and I'll take care of everything."

Brynn opened her mouth as if she wanted to say something and then closed it. Fear flashed in her wide eyes before they darted to the door like she needed an escape.

"I know it sounds crazy. It wouldn't be real. Just for show, only so you can get Danielle the help she needs."

Brynn wrapped her thin arm around Danielle protectively and shook her head. She opened the door, then turned back to him. "No."

The finality of her word sucked the remaining air from the room.

"I'll find another way." Brynn disappeared, closing the door behind her and her daughter.

Aaron paced the office, raking his hand through his hair. "What the fuck? Did I really just propose?"

Why couldn't he think when that woman was around? Maybe because it had been so long since he'd been interested in a woman. Why did he want to insert himself into her life and fix all her problems? *Did I just ruin the one place her daughter had to feel welcome and safe?*

"What have I done?"

The marriage wouldn't have even been real. So why was he so disappointed?

To continue reading Brynn and Aaron's story, visit the website below to get your copy of *Hope Between Us* today.

WWW.AMKUSI.COM/HOPEBETWEENUS

ACKNOWLEDGMENTS

We want to extend a special thank you to the r/Epilepsy community and moderators on Reddit. That community was such a helpful resource in educating us about what it is like to experience epilepsy, as well as some of the stigmas those with seizures have to deal with.

To our beta readers, YOU ROCK! Ada and Dayanara, thank you for sharing your beautiful culture with us and helping us brush up on our Spanish phrases, and all your enriching tips. Holly and Emilie, we are so grateful for you sharing your knowledge on epilepsy and seizures. Kayla, we love how much you love this series, and all the helpful feedback you gave us.

Lauren, our editor and writing coach, I know you will deny it, but this book truly wouldn't be as good as it is without your insight. So, thank you for what you and your team at Creating Ink do for us. We will forever be grateful.

Of course, our diversity editors, Renita and Curtis, you know you have a special place in our hearts for all you do for us. You've been with us since the beginning, and your belief in our stories are just one more thing to keep us pushing to continue putting stories out there.

Lastly, but certainly not least, we want to thank our ARC readers and everyone who takes the time to read our books, leave reviews, and spread the word about our books and this series. We love reading how our books have touched each of your lives.

THANK YOU!

Thank you for reading *Brave Love*. We hope you are emotionally satisfied with Pippa and Mason's love story. If you enjoyed this novel, please consider leaving a review on your favorite retailer and sharing it with your friends and family.

If you haven't read Remy and Mikel's story yet, check out ***A Fallen Star*** (Book 1 in The Shattered Cove Series. The eBook is FREE on all retailers.)

For Andre and Mia's story, check out ***Glass Secrets*** (Book 2 in The Shattered Cove Series)

For Belle and Bently's story, check out ***Defying Gravity*** (Book 3 in The Shattered Cove Series)

For Jasmine and Atlas, check out ***The Lighthouse Inn*** (Book 4 in The Shattered Cove Series)

For Charli and Finn, check out ***His True North*** (Book 5 in The Shattered Cove Series)

For Emma and Link, check out ***In The Grey*** (Book 6 in The Shattered Cove Series)

Lastly, if you haven't read our debut series, ***The Orchard***

Inn Romance Series, make sure you get your copy so you don't miss out on three wonderful love stories.

Thank you again for reading *Brave Love!*

Cheers,

Ash & Marcus.

ABOUT A. M. KUSI

A. M. Kusi is the pen name of a wife-and-husband team, Ash and Marcus Kusi. We enjoy writing romance novels that are inspired by our experiences as an interracial/multicultural couple.

Our novels are about strong women and the sexy heroes they fall in love with, are emotionally satisfying, and always have a happy ending.

Discover more about us at:

WWW.AMKUSI.COM

To receive updates about new releases, preorders, giveaways, and more, visit the website below to join our newsletter today:

WWW.AMKUSI.COM/NEWSLETTER

After you join the newsletter, we will send you a FREE novella to read.

To contact us, use this email address: amkusinovels@gmail.com

Happy reading!

Ash and Marcus

ALSO BY A. M. KUSI

A Fallen Star (eBook FREE on all retailers)

(Book 1 in The Shattered Cove Series)

Glass Secrets

(Book 2 in The Shattered Cove Series)

Defying Gravity

(Book 3 in The Shattered Cove Series)

The Lighthouse Inn

(Book 4 in The Shattered Cove series)

His True North

(Book 5 in The Shattered Cove series)

In The Grey

(Book 6 in The Shattered Cove series)

The Orchard Inn (eBook FREE on all retailers)

(Book 1 in The Orchard Inn Romance Series)

Conflict of Interest

(Book 2 in The Orchard Inn Romance Series)

Her Perfect Storm

(Book 3 in The Orchard Inn Romance Series)

9 781949 781212